CHILDREN OF THE SERPENT SKY

THE SKYREND PROPHECY BOOK THREE

JOSHUA J. WHITE

BERSERKER BOOKS

Stay Connected with Joshua J. White

Before you begin...

If you're drawn to myth, mystery, and stories that echo long after the final page, I invite you to join me on the journey ahead.

This world — and the ones that follow — are part of something much larger. By joining my mailing list, you'll get early access to new books, hidden lore, exclusive behind-the-scenes notes, and the occasional dispatch from the quiet woods where I write.

Sign up here: www.JoshuaJWhiteBooks.com/TheSkyrendProphecy

No noise. No spam. Just stories worth sharing!

— Joshua J. White

Author & Founder, Berserker Books

CONTENTS

PROLOGUE

Istara Nightweaver's fingers trembled as she traced the void in her charts where stars should have been. Three cycles of Alfheim's twin moons had passed since she'd first noticed the anomaly—a faint cluster of twelve stars forming a serpentine curve where emptiness had dwelled for generations. Night after night, the pattern grew brighter, more insistent, as if the very sky mocked the careful records kept within the Star-Tower's crystalline archives.

The elderly astronomer pressed her palm against the cool silver-bark of her observation platform. Her joints ached from the night's labor, but dread, not fatigue, made her hands unsteady. The constellation shouldn't exist. Countless astronomers before her had erased it, meticulously excised it from every chart for reasons recorded only in texts she wasn't permitted to access.

And yet, there it gleamed.

"Mistress Nightweaver?" A voice from below shattered her concentration.

Istara twisted the carved ivory meridian wheel of her starscope, locking the instrument's position. "Come, Therin," she called, recognizing her apprentice's light footfalls on the silver-bark stairs.

The young elf emerged onto the platform, silver hair gleaming in the starlight. His narrow face looked drawn, mouth tight with worry. "The messenger to Councilor Eloreth returned," he said, hesitating. "She wouldn't... she refused to believe the message."

"Did she even look through the scope?" Istara asked, already knowing the answer.

Therin shook his head, eyes dropping to the complex charts scattered across their work table. "She says the Stellar Council won't convene for such a... a 'senile delusion.'" His voice dropped to a whisper on the final words, shame coloring his pale cheeks.

"I see." Istara ran her thumb across the edge of the nearest chart, the paper unexpectedly rough beneath her touch. A curious sensation pricked her awareness. The chart crumbled slightly under her fingers, fine dust piling along its edge.

She froze, then deliberately pressed her thumb harder. More of the parchment disintegrated, the star-marks and measurements collapsing into powder.

"Therin," she said, keeping her voice steady, "bring me the protected texts. Second vault, seventh shelf. The bound volume with the silver clasp."

His eyes widened. "But those are sealed by Council mandate—"

"Quickly, child."

The urgency in her tone propelled him back toward the stairs. Istara turned to another chart, this one documenting five centuries of observations. She pressed her finger to it. Again, the parchment surrendered to her touch, crumbling like ash.

She tried another, older still. The same result.

A sickening realization spread through her chest as she moved through the tower room, testing scroll after scroll, chart after chart. Any document containing the coordinates where the forbidden constellation was now reappearing turned to dust at her touch.

Her heart pounded as Therin's footsteps returned, faster now, breath coming in gasps as he burst back onto the platform.

"They're gone," he choked out. "The sealed texts—they've turned to dust!" He opened his hand, showing a pile of fine gray powder with glints of what had once been silver binding. "It happened as I touched the spine. And... and there's a smell..."

Istara inhaled deeply, catching it now—a sharp tang like lightning striking stone, undercut with the sticky sweetness of tree sap.

She returned to her starscope, adjusting it with hands steadier now that she knew what she faced. "It's moving faster than I feared."

"What's happening?" Therin asked, brushing the dust from his trembling hands.

Istara didn't answer immediately. Instead, she flung open the curved doors of the ancient wooden cabinet that housed the most precious of the tower's artifacts. Within it rested nine crystal spheres of varying sizes, each containing what appeared to be miniature star systems. She reached for the third sphere—the one representing Alfheim—her heart lurching when she saw it had developed a perfect hairline crack across its surface.

"The records are being erased," she finally said, closing her weathered hand around the sphere. "Not just our physical charts. The memory itself is being culled from the pattern."

"But why? And how?" Therin asked, moving instinctively to collect the scattered astronomical instruments from the table, preserving what could be saved.

Istara stared upward, beyond the open ceiling of the tower, to where the forbidden stars now gleamed with undeniable brilliance. "Because something wants to be remembered, child."

She crossed to the west side of the platform and pulled a silken bell-cord, setting off a cascade of crystalline notes that would awaken the tower's guardians. Moving with new urgency, she swept the remaining intact charts into a leather cylinder.

"Take these to Findel at the Monument of Waters," she instructed Therin, securing the cylinder with a silver clasp. "They document constellations unrelated to the forbidden pattern. Tell him what's happened here and that I've gone to the Stone of First Light."

Therin clutched the cylinder, his slender fingers white with tension. "The Stone? But that's a three-day journey into the Deep Groves."

"There's no time for fear," she said, grabbing her starstaff—a length of silver-white wood topped with a crystal that captured and magnified starlight. "The Stellar Council must be forced to acknowledge what's happening, even if I must invoke ancient rites to make them listen."

"What should I tell them about the forbidden stars?"

Istara hesitated, meeting her apprentice's frightened gaze. In the sixty-seven centuries she had walked the groves of Alfheim, she had never witnessed a portent so dire.

"Tell them..." She looked up once more at the newly-visible pattern. "Tell them the serpent constellation returns. The one called Jörmungandr's Coil is reappearing, and its awakening heralds the ending of an age."

A flicker of movement caught her eye—a star falling among thousands suddenly tumbling across the heavens. No, not falling. Flowing, as if the night itself were a dark river carrying luminous fish toward some cosmic sea.

"Go, Therin. Now."

Footsteps sounded below—the guardians responding to her summons. She gripped her starstaff tighter, the crystal at its tip flaring with stored light.

"What if the Council still won't convene?" Therin asked, backing toward the stairs.

"They will," Istara said grimly, "when they realize what's happening to all their precious records."

She raised her free hand, palm outward toward the reappearing constellation. For a brief moment, the stars aligned with the lines etched into her palm—markings she'd carried since the day of her initiation into the order of Stellar Archivists. The pattern burned against her skin, a white-hot reminder of oaths sworn before she understood their cost.

"The serpent stirs," she whispered, completing the ancient warning. "The anchors shift. The cycle begins anew."

As Therin disappeared down the spiral staircase, Istara gazed once more at the forbidden constellation. She understood now that the records hadn't been destroyed. They had been reclaimed by the pattern itself—by that which existed before charts and measurements, before the careful structures imposed by the Council, before the cultivated forgetting that had preserved their realm for nine cycles of peace.

Even as she watched, the ancient wooden cabinet containing the nine crystal spheres began to deteriorate, fine cracks spreading across its surface. The smell of lightning and sap grew stronger, filling the tower chamber with its sharp sweetness.

Istara grabbed the cracked crystal sphere representing Alfheim and tucked it into her robe. She would need it to convince those who'd spent centuries ensuring this knowledge remained buried. Time was short. The constellation wouldn't remain visible for long before forces greater than the Stellar Council moved to obscure it once more.

The question was whether she could reach the Stone of First Light before those same forces reached her.

***

Beyond the firmament, where matter dissolves into potential and light bends under its own weight, the void stretched infinitely dark. Here, in the space between spaces, existence thinned to mere suggestion. The laws governing mortal realms held no dominion in this most ancient of domains.

And here, coiled among galaxies, the serpent slept.

Its body stretched across vast celestial distances, scales forged from condensed starlight that had burned for eons. Each scale contained the light of a thousand suns, pulsing with rhythms older than time. For an age beyond counting, it had remained dormant, consciousness dispersed across the void like scattered stardust.

But now, something stirred within the cosmic leviathan.

A flicker of awareness sparked along its immense form. Consciousness returned—glacially slow, yet inexorable. Dreams of emptiness gave way to memory, each recollection unfolding with the ponderous weight of mountain ranges rising from primordial seas. The serpent's mind reassembled itself, thought by patient thought.

One massive eyelid, forged from the compressed darkness of collapsed stars, trembled. Muscles that spanned solar systems tensed. Then, with deliberate effort, the eye opened.

A pupil vaster than worlds dilated, adjusting to existence after eons of slumber. Its gaze sharpened, focusing through layers of reality until it found what it sought: a tiny mote of light suspended in the void. Alfheim.

The serpent's consciousness fully awakened then. Memory crystallized into thought, and thought into purpose. The creature known in the tongues of the Nine Realms as Jörmungandr—the World Serpent, the Star-Devourer, the Cosmos-Coil—turned its full attention to the distant elven realm.

The anchors move.

The thought rippled through its mind, a vibration that sent subtle tremors across its stellar body. The serpent perceived reality differently than mortal creatures. It saw connections, patterns, and roles within the cosmic weave. And the pattern was shifting. Anchors meant to remain fixed were changing position.

The cycle begins again.

This had happened before. Nine times before. Each time, the pattern re-formed itself, sometimes subtly, other times with violent disruption. Always incomplete, never fully restored or fully broken. Balance maintained through oscillation between states.

The serpent's tail twitched, disturbing the dust of dead stars. It remembered its purpose, dormant for so long yet ever-present. To watch. To wait. To intervene only when the balance threatened to tip beyond recovery.

That time approached once more.

With deliberate intent, Jörmungandr began to uncurl its vast form. The movement was almost imperceptible at first—a slight adjustment of its cosmic coils. Stars shifted in their ancient dance. Galaxies swayed like kelp in deep currents. Reality rippled in concentric waves, propagating outward from the serpent's motion.

As it moved, fragments of its scales flaked away, dislodged by the friction of its body against the fabric of the void. These motes of consolidated starlight—each no larger than a grain of sand yet containing the energy of a sun—scattered across the firmament like seeds cast by a celestial farmer.

They fell toward the Nine Realms, trailing behind them ribbons of pure potential.

In Midgard, villagers huddled in their homes as the night sky erupted with streaks of blue-white fire. In Jotunheim, frost giants paused in their eternal war-dances to watch the heavens fracture with light. In Muspelheim, the flame-lords gathered at the edges of their molten lakes, their burning eyes reflecting the celestial display.

And in Alfheim, Istara Nightweaver stood upon the Tower of Stars, witnessing the meteor shower with growing dread. The countless falling stars confirmed what she had already feared: the pattern was changing once more.

The serpent's gaze remained fixed upon the tiny realm as it continued to uncoil. Its eye did not blink; its focus did not waver. Within that realm dwelled those who would play crucial roles in the cycle to come. The serpent could sense them, their presences glowing like coals in darkness. The anchors were drawing them together, pulling at the threads of fate.

Particularly bright among these presences was one marked by both root and flame. The serpent's ancient memory stirred. This combination was unusual—those energies typically remained separated. Yet here they mingled within a single vessel. Interesting. Different from previous cycles.

A second presence caught the serpent's attention—a fragment of potential that existed simultaneously across multiple points in the pattern. The serpent recognized this anomaly as a symptom of the pattern's instability, a being born of the space between breaking and binding.

The third path opens. The way between restoration and destruction.

These thoughts crossed the serpent's mind with the slow certainty of continental drift. Time meant little to a being whose consciousness spanned eons. What mattered was the pattern, and the pattern was changing.

As Jörmungandr continued to uncoil, its movement generated greater disturbances across the cosmic web. The meteor shower intensified. Reality trembled. In places where the veil between worlds already wore thin, it tore completely. Boundaries blurred. Creatures from one realm stumbled inadvertently into another. Ancient wards activated then burned out, overwhelmed by the surge of cosmic energy.

The serpent felt these disruptions but remained unmoved. Such chaos always accompanied the beginning of a new cycle. Order would emerge once more, though perhaps in forms unrecognizable to those who clung to the old pattern.

At last, the cosmic leviathan stretched to its full length—a distance so vast that mortal minds could not comprehend it. From this position, it could observe all Nine Realms simultaneously, watching as events unfolded across them.

The serpent settled into its vigil. Its task now was to wait and watch. To intervene only if absolute necessity demanded it. This was the role it had assumed since before gods walked between worlds, before mortal races kindled their first fires, before the pattern had crystallized into rigid structure.

The anchors move. The cycle begins again. But this time...

For the first time in nine cycles, the serpent sensed something different—a variation in the cosmic melody, a new harmony emerging from familiar notes. The flame-and-root presence disturbed the pattern in ways unpredicted by previous iterations. The boundaries between what was, what is, and what could be were thinning.

The serpent's tail coiled slightly tighter. Its scales shifted, releasing another cascade of stellar fragments that rained down upon the Nine Realms. In Alfheim, the sky blazed with falling stars so numerous they outshone the twin moons. Shadows danced across silver forests as light and darkness alternated in rapid succession.

Deep beneath Alfheim's surface, something ancient stirred in response to the serpent's movement. A fragment of Root, dormant for eons, pulsed with renewed vigor. Golden sap oozed from its surface, carrying with it memories that had lain forgotten since the last cycle's end.

The serpent perceived this awakening and adjusted its coils once more. The Root fragments were responding more quickly than in previous cycles. The flame-marked one must be drawing them together with unusual speed. This would accelerate events across all realms.

Let it begin, then.

This thought—the serpent's final one before returning to its state of watchful semi-consciousness—rippled across the cosmos, causing subtle shifts in the weave of reality. The consequences would manifest in myriad ways, from the mundane to the miraculous, as the Nine Realms adjusted to the serpent's awakening.

In the Tower of Stars, Istara Nightweaver collapsed to her knees as knowledge poured into her mind through the markings on her palms. Visions of a crown formed of living wood, a blade forged from memory, a bridge between breaking and binding. She saw a man transformed by root and flame, a woman whose arm had become living wood, a child who existed between moments.

"The cycle truly begins," she whispered, the words both prophecy and recognition.

Above, the meteor shower reached its crescendo, turning night to day across all Nine Realms. Then, as suddenly as it had begun, it ended. The serpent had completed its awakening. Now events would unfold according to the new pattern it had sensed forming—a pattern influenced by choices yet to be made, by anchors yet to be bound, by paths yet to be walked.

The World Serpent settled into its cosmic vigil, its gaze never leaving the tiny point of light that was Alfheim. There, the first moves in this cycle's great game would soon be made.

The stones were set. The players approached the board. The wager: nothing less than the shape of reality itself.

CHAPTER 1

INTO THE
LIGHTROOT REALM

The wind howled through the fractured mountains of the borderlands, carrying the scent of burnt stone and lightning-struck earth. Asvarr braced himself against the gale, each breath painful in lungs still raw from the Verdant Gate's closing. Three weeks had passed since that terrible moment—when the memory realm collapsed behind them and the path to restoration narrowed yet again. Three weeks of drifting between fever dreams and waking nightmares as his body struggled to accommodate what he had become.

What he was becoming still.

He ran his fingers across his chest where the Grímmark burned beneath his tunic, tracing the patterns that now extended up his neck and across his shoulders. Patterns no longer confined to his skin. The small branches that had sprouted from his shoulder blades flexed unconsciously, scraping against the rough-spun fabric of his shirt. They'd grown another finger's width overnight. Soon he'd need to cut holes to accommodate them.

"There," Yrsa said, pointing toward a narrow ravine ahead. "The falling stars have left their mark."

Asvarr squinted against the pre-dawn gloom. The old woman's eyes had always been sharper than his, but now he saw it too—a faint silvery sheen coating the rock face, as if the stone had partially melted and reformed. Curved gouges scarred the canyon walls, extending upward in a pattern that reminded him of the Root's branching patterns beneath his skin.

"The Starfall Path," he said, tasting metal on his tongue. A perfect golden leaf drifted from his lips, spiraling down to land at his feet. Still not used to that.

Three nights ago, meteors had rained across the nine realms—thousands upon thousands of silver-blue lights streaking through the darkness. Where they struck, reality thinned. New passages opened between worlds. Yrsa had recognized the significance immediately, dragging Asvarr from his sickbed to witness the celestial storm.

"The serpent stirs," she'd whispered, her face ghostly in the meteoric light. "The anchors shift. The cycle begins anew."

Now they stood before one such passage—a bridge to Alfheim formed where falling stars had burned through the veil between worlds.

Yrsa adjusted the crystal pendant hanging at her throat, its dim blue light their only illumination in the shadowed canyon. "The way won't remain open long," she warned. "Days, perhaps. Hours if we're unlucky."

"Then we should hurry." Asvarr rolled his shoulders, trying to ease the constant ache where wood met flesh. His body felt foreign to him now—heavier in some places, lighter in others. The verdant crown that had formed around his head after binding the second anchor had grown permanent, small branches extending down his back and shoulders like a living helm.

Yrsa studied him with those ancient eyes. "Are you certain you're ready for this? The third anchor will demand more than the previous two."

"And give less in return," Asvarr finished for her. They'd had this conversation before. "I'm as ready as I'll ever be."

She nodded, seemingly satisfied, and they began their descent into the ravine.

The path narrowed as they walked, walls crowding closer on either side. The silver sheen intensified, coating every surface until they appeared to be walking through a tunnel of polished mirror. Asvarr caught fragmented reflections of himself—a man transformed by Root and flame. His eyes flickered between their natural brown and an unnatural sap-gold. Bark-like patterns spread across his jaw. The crown of twisted branches encircled his head like some wild forest lord from ancient tales.

Mortality and magic, entangled beyond separation.

"The anchors grow impatient," Yrsa said, breaking the silence. "They call more insistently than before."

"I feel them," Asvarr admitted. The first two anchors he'd bound—flame and memory—pulsed within him like additional heartbeats. But now a third rhythm joined them, a cold, measured cadence that pulled at him from across the void between worlds. The starlight anchor awaited in Alfheim, and it sang to him with a voice of crystal and ice.

The path descended more steeply, forcing them to brace against the mirrored walls for balance. Where Asvarr's palms touched the silver surface, tiny golden roots spread from his fingers, etching themselves into the rock before withering away seconds later.

"Your transformation accelerates," Yrsa observed, watching the phenomenon with clinical interest. "The third binding will push you further still."

"Will there be enough of me left afterward to continue?" Asvarr asked. It was the question that haunted his dreams—how much humanity he could surrender before losing himself entirely.

Yrsa's silence spoke volumes.

***

They reached a point where the ravine ended in a perfect circle of silvered stone. The meteor's impact had transformed the rock into something between glass and metal, with a surface that rippled like water despite being solid to the touch.

"Now comes the difficult part," Yrsa said, removing her crystal pendant. The blue stone blazed suddenly brighter, illuminating the entirety of the circular chamber. "The passage requires a key."

Asvarr frowned. "You didn't mention a key before."

"Not a physical key." Yrsa nodded toward his chest. "The anchors you carry. They've changed the fundamental nature of your blood. A few drops should be sufficient."

With a grimace, Asvarr drew his bronze sword—the weapon that had accompanied him since the beginning of his journey. Golden veins pulsed beneath the metal's surface, matching the rhythm of his Grímmark. He pressed the blade to his palm and drew it across the skin.

Blood welled up, but not blood alone. Golden sap mixed with the crimson, creating spiraling patterns across his palm.

"Place your hand against the center of the wall," Yrsa instructed.

Asvarr pressed his bleeding palm to the silvered surface. For a moment, nothing happened. Then the stone beneath his hand turned liquid, rippling outward in concentric circles. The pattern spread until the entire wall undulated like the surface of a disturbed pond.

"Quickly now," Yrsa said, shoving him forward. "Before it reseals!"

Asvarr plunged through the liquid stone, the sensation like diving through a waterfall of ice. His every nerve screamed in protest. The cold penetrated to his bones, to the Root essence threaded through his being. He felt the branches on his back curl inward protectively, pressing against his spine.

For one terrible moment, he existed nowhere—suspended between realities, neither in Midgard nor Alfheim. The void tugged at his consciousness, threatening to scatter his thoughts across the cosmos.

Then his feet struck solid ground, and air filled his lungs once more. He staggered forward, nearly falling, as Yrsa emerged beside him with a wheezing gasp.

"That was... unpleasant," she managed, bracing herself against a tree trunk.

Asvarr could only nod, fighting the wave of nausea that accompanied their crossing. When the dizziness subsided, he took stock of their surroundings.

They stood in a silver forest under an impossible sky. Trees with metallic bark rose around them, their leaves translucent slivers that caught and refracted light. Above, stars blazed with unnatural clarity though dawn approached. He recognized none of the constellations. These patterns belonged to Alfheim alone.

"We made it," he breathed, another golden leaf falling from his lips.

"To the outskirts, yes." Yrsa straightened, adjusting her travel-worn robes. "The starlight anchor lies at Alfheim's heart."

As if in response to her words, pain lanced through Asvarr's chest. The Grímmark flared beneath his tunic, its heat momentarily unbearable. He dropped to one knee, pressing his palm against the burning mark.

A vision flashed behind his eyes—a crystalline structure floating in darkness, surrounded by stars that moved with deliberate intention. He felt its pull, undeniable as gravity.

"It knows we're here," he gasped, the pain subsiding as quickly as it had come. "It's been waiting."

"Of course it has." Yrsa helped him back to his feet. "The anchors are connected across all Nine Realms. When you bound the first two, this one stirred in response."

Asvarr gazed at the alien forest surrounding them. "How far?"

"Several days' journey, if we avoid the elven settlements." Yrsa pointed toward a distant peak that gleamed like polished silver in the pre-dawn light. "There. Starfall Mountain. The anchor awaits at its summit."

They set off through the silver forest, each step taking them deeper into the realm of light and memory. Asvarr moved cautiously, aware of how out of place he must appear in this elegant world—a man half-transformed into something else, neither fully human nor fully Root. His boots crunched against crystal formations that sprouted between tree roots. Light rippled upward from the impact points, traveling through the metallic trees and causing their leaves to chime softly.

"The entire forest is connected," Yrsa explained, seeing his fascination. "A networ like your Root, but formed of light rather than growth. The elves cultivate these connections, strengthening some, severing others."

"They shape reality itself," Asvarr mused.

"As do you, in your way." Yrsa cast him a sidelong glance. "The difference is one of method, not kind."

They walked for hours as the sun rose over Alfheim, casting the silver forest in shades of rose-gold. The light here behaved strangely, bending around certain trees and intensifying near others. Shadows fell in geometric patterns that bore no relation to the objects casting them.

By midday, they reached a ridge overlooking a vast valley. Below, a city of crystal spires and living trees intertwined in impossible formations. Towers spiraled upward, defying gravity. Bridges of pure light connected structures seemingly at random. At the city's center stood a massive tree with silver bark and leaves that glowed with internal fire—a distant cousin to Yggdrasil itself.

"Ljósalvheim," Yrsa named it. "The elven capital. We must avoid it. The Stellar Council would take great interest in what you've become."

"And what exactly have I become?" Asvarr asked, the question that had gnawed at him since his first binding.

Yrsa's expression softened slightly. "Something the Nine Realms haven't seen in nine cycles, child. A Warden with two anchors bound, seeking a third. The pattern shifts around you with each step. The old laws bend in your presence."

"I never asked for this," he said, more golden leaves spilling from his mouth with the words. They drifted down the slope toward the distant city, carried on a wind that smelled of stardust and possibility.

"Few who change the world set out to do so." Yrsa turned away from the valley, pointing toward a narrow path that hugged the ridge's edge. "Come. We'll circle around to the east. There's an ancient shrine at the forest's edge where we can rest before tackling the mountain approaches."

As they walked, Asvarr felt the weight of many eyes upon them, the attention of the realm itself. The trees whispered as they passed. The crystal formations hummed with resonant frequencies that made his teeth ache. Even the stars, visible even in daylight here, seemed to track their progress.

"The realm remembers you," Yrsa said, noticing his discomfort. "Or rather, it remembers what you represent. The last Warden who walked here left quite an impression."

Asvarr thought of the Ashfather—that fragment of Odin's regret given form, who had bound anchors through nine cycles. "Did he follow this same path?"

"Similar, but not identical." Yrsa's voice took on the formal cadence she used when recounting ancient lore. "Each cycle differs slightly from the last. The pattern changes, adapts. A tree growing through stone, finding new paths when old ones are blocked."

By late afternoon, they reached the shrine Yrsa had mentioned—a circle of crystal pillars surrounding a pool of silver liquid that perfectly reflected the sky above. As Asvarr approached the pool's edge, the liquid rippled, though no wind disturbed its surface.

"It recognizes what you carry," Yrsa explained, settling onto a stone bench with a sigh of relief. "The last time Root and flame walked together in Alfheim was before the gods withdrew from mortal realms."

Asvarr knelt by the pool, studying his reflection. The changes in his appearance shocked him anew. Beyond the verdant crown and spreading bark patterns, his very essence had altered. Light shimmered beneath his skin alongside the golden sap of the Root. His eyes flared sap-gold as he watched, then faded back to brown.

"Who am I becoming?" he whispered, more to himself than to Yrsa.

The pool responded, its surface swirling into new patterns. For an instant, Asvarr saw a possible future self—crowned with branches intertwined with crystalline formations, eyes permanently transformed to orbs of golden light, chest opened to reveal the pulsing anchors nestled where his heart should be.

He recoiled from the vision, stomach churning with dread.

"The third anchor's influence grows stronger as we approach," Yrsa said, watching him closely. "It shows you possibilities, not certainties."

"Small comfort," Asvarr growled, rising to his feet. More leaves fell from his mouth, these tinged with frost around their edges—the starlight anchor's influence already reaching into him.

As night fell over Alfheim, they made camp among the crystal pillars. No fire was needed; the pillars themselves emitted a soft blue glow that provided both light and warmth. Asvarr sat with his back against one such pillar, feeling its resonance hum through his transformed flesh.

"Tomorrow we begin the ascent of Starfall Mountain," Yrsa said, arranging her travel-worn robes into a makeshift bedroll. "The path grows steeper from here, in every sense."

Asvarr nodded, gazing upward at the night sky. The stars of Alfheim wheeled in complex patterns, forming and dissolving constellations with deliberate purpose. He recognized one arrangement—the serpent constellation that had heralded the new cycle's beginning.

"What awaits us at the summit?" he asked.

Yrsa was silent for a long moment. "The starlight anchor," she finally said. "And a choice. Each anchor demands something different. The flame anchor required dominance. The memory anchor required recognition. This one..." She hesitated. "This one will demand transformation itself."

"I'm already transforming," Asvarr said, gesturing to the branches sprouting from his shoulders.

"Physical changes are merely the outward sign." Yrsa's voice dropped to little more than a whisper. "The starlight anchor will require you to surrender the very concept of fixed identity. To become mutable, fluid—like light itself, which exists as both particle and wave."

A chill ran down Asvarr's spine that had nothing to do with the mountain air. "And if I refuse?"

"Then the cycle continues as it has for nine iterations before," Yrsa said. "Partial restoration, partial collapse. Balance maintained through oscillation between extremes."

"And if I accept?"

Yrsa's ancient eyes reflected the starlight above. "Then you walk the third path of transformation. A path no Warden has successfully navigated in nine cycles of breaking and binding."

Asvarr stared up at the serpent constellation, its stellar coils wrapped around Alfheim's pole star. The third anchor awaited, and with it, a transformation that might cost him whatever humanity remained.

But the alternative was to surrender what they'd fought for—the possibility of something beyond the endless cycle of breaking and partial restoration. The chance to reshape the pattern itself.

"We continue at first light," he said, decision crystallizing within him alongside the spreading patterns of bark and sap and starlight. "The anchor has waited long enough."

***

Dawn broke over Alfheim, painting the silver forest in hues of molten copper and rose-gold. Asvarr and Yrsa crested a final ridge, their path winding through crystalline formations that chimed with every footstep. The morning air tasted of metal and possibility, filling Asvarr's lungs with unfamiliar potency. His verdant crown flexed unconsciously in response, small branches unfurling toward the strange light.

Before them stood the observatory—and Asvarr halted, momentarily stunned by the impossibility of what he witnessed.

The structure rose from the mountainside like no building he had ever seen. A tower of white stone spiraled upward, but stone wasn't the right word for the material. It flowed like solidified light, surfaces rippling subtly though no wind disturbed them. The tower's base encircled an enormous root that defied natural law—it grew upward rather than down, reaching toward the heavens instead of the earth's heart.

"The Observatory of Ages," Yrsa named it, her weathered voice holding rare reverence. "Built during the First Dawn, before elves distinguished themselves from gods."

Asvarr circled the structure, marveling at the root's unnatural trajectory. Thick as ten men standing shoulder to shoulder, its surface pulsed with visible energy—a measured rhythm unlike the quicksilver beat of the anchors he carried within. Golden sap flowed through translucent channels near its surface, but this sap carried silver motes that glittered like captive stars.

"It grows toward the void," Asvarr said, another frost-tinged leaf falling from his mouth.

"Because it seeks what lies beyond." Yrsa ran gnarled fingers along the root's surface, her touch reverent. "The Ljósalvir call it the Eye-Root. It watches the stars. Remembers them."

Asvarr pressed his palm to the massive root, expecting resonance with the anchors he carried. Instead, a profound alienness swept through him—a consciousness vaster and colder than any he had encountered. The root's rhythm remained steady, uninterested in his intrusion, focused on concerns beyond mortal comprehension.

Gasping, he pulled away, flexing his fingers to dispel the lingering chill. "It's nothing like the anchors I carry."

"The Eye-Root predates them," Yrsa explained. "Its purpose differs. The anchors bind and restore. This... observes and remembers."

They climbed the spiraling staircase that wound around the massive root. Each step glowed briefly beneath their feet, leaving trails of light that lingered for heartbeats before fading. The stairs led to a circular platform crowned with a dome of crystal so clear it appeared not to exist at all.

As they reached the platform, Asvarr looked up—and his breath caught in his throat.

The sky of Alfheim stretched above him, incomprehensible in its complexity. Stars blazed with unnatural clarity despite the morning light, some pulsing in synchronized patterns, others drifting in deliberate motion. Constellations shifted as he watched, rearranging themselves like living creatures adjusting their posture. Most extraordinary of all, visible threads of silver-blue light connected the celestial bodies, creating intricate webs that formed patterns within patterns.

"Memory-threads," Yrsa whispered, following his gaze. "The physical manifestation of association. Each connection represents a relationship—cause and effect, action and consequence, birth and death."

Asvarr's eyes struggled to track the complex matrices above. When he squinted, the threads seemed to shift in response, certain connections brightening while others dimmed. With a jolt, he realized the sky was reacting to his attention—the very stars adjusting their patterns to observe him in return.

"They're watching us," he said, unease prickling along his spine where wood met flesh.

"Of course they are." Yrsa moved to a complex apparatus at the platform's center—a series of nested crystal rings that rotated on multiple axes. "Everything watches everything else in Alfheim. Observation shapes reality here."

The apparatus hummed with energy, each ring adjusting its position with micrometric precision. As Yrsa manipulated controls fashioned from a material like frozen starlight, an image formed in the air above the device—a perfect miniature of the sky, showing movements and connections invisible to the naked eye.

"The observatory was built to track the stars," Yrsa explained, "but its true purpose has always been to map the patterns between them. The connections matter more than the bodies themselves."

Asvarr stared at the projected model, recognition flooding through him. "It resembles the verdant crown," he said, fingers instinctively rising to touch the living branches that encircled his head. "The same branching patterns."

"They share a source," Yrsa agreed. "As does everything that grows, whether upward toward stars or downward toward earth." She adjusted another control, and the model zoomed in on a particular constellation—a serpentine curve of twelve stars.

"Jörmungandr's Coil," she named it. "The forbidden constellation. It reappeared three weeks ago, the same night the Verdant Gate sealed behind us."

Asvarr felt the anchors within him pulse in response to the name. "Forbidden by whom?"

"By those who fear what it represents." Yrsa's expression tightened. "Change. Transformation. The endless cycle of breaking and renewal."

She pointed toward the westernmost edge of the observatory platform, where a long telescope of crystal and silver extended outward, perfectly balanced on a fulcrum of iridescent stone. "Look through that, and you'll see why we've come here."

Asvarr approached the instrument cautiously. Unlike the wooden and bronze devices he'd seen human astronomers use, this telescope incorporated living crystal that hummed with its own consciousness. He placed his eye to the viewing lens, unsure what to expect.

The world exploded into color and connection. The telescope didn't merely magnify his vision—it expanded it, allowing him to perceive spectra beyond mortal limits. Through its lens, he saw Starfall Mountain as never before. The silver peak glowed with internal fire, and at its summit, a structure of pure crystalline light hovered above the ground, neither solid nor liquid but something between states.

"The starlight anchor," he breathed, another leaf drifting from his lips.

"Yes." Yrsa stood at his shoulder. "And now you understand why the journey won't be simple. Look again. Look at what surrounds it."

Asvarr adjusted the telescope slightly. Around the mountain's base, he saw movement—beings with elongated bodies that flowed like liquid silver, their shapes constantly shifting. They encircled the mountain in concentric rings, maintaining a perfect formation.

"Guardians," he guessed.

"Ljósalvir call them the Stellar Sentinels," Yrsa corrected. "Created during the last breaking to prevent anyone from approaching the anchor. They're conscious enough to identify and eliminate threats."

Asvarr continued observing through the telescope, sweeping its gaze across the landscape between their position and Starfall Mountain. The forest grew denser there, trees clustered so tightly their metallic branches wove together into impenetrable walls. Crystal formations erupted from the earth in jagged spires that would tear flesh from bone. And flowing between these obstacles, rivers of light that burned with cold fire.

"It's a labyrinth," he said, pulling back from the telescope. "Designed to prevent approach."

"Designed to test worthiness," Yrsa countered. "Those unworthy perish. Those worthy merely suffer." A grim smile touched her weathered lips. "The anchors never give themselves easily."

Asvarr felt the Grímmark burn beneath his tunic, the patterns spread across his chest pulsing in time with his accelerated heartbeat. His transformation after the first two bindings had already pushed his body to its limits. What would a third do to him?

"The eye-root knows the way," Yrsa said. "It has watched every approach since the labyrinth's creation. Every victory, every failure."

"How do we ask it?" Asvarr glanced at the enormous root pulsing with its alien rhythm.

"We don't ask. We observe. As it does." Yrsa gestured toward a basin of silver liquid positioned where the root breached the observatory floor. "That contains sap from the eye-root, mixed with crushed starlight. Place your hand in it, and you'll see what it has seen."

Asvarr approached the basin warily. The liquid within didn't reflect the observatory around them but showed a field of stars unlike any in the sky above. He hesitated, remembering how the Root consciousness had nearly overwhelmed him during previous bindings.

"Will I retain myself?" he asked.

Yrsa's silence spoke volumes.

Drawing a steadying breath, Asvarr thrust his hand into the basin. Cold beyond imagining engulfed his flesh, so intense it burned. The liquid clung to his skin like living frost, seeping into his pores, following the channels where sap already flowed through his transformed body.

His vision fractured into countless perspectives. He saw the observatory's construction during the First Dawn, elves with starlight in their veins raising the tower stone by impossible stone. He witnessed the growth of the eye-root, reaching upward through millennia with infinitesimal persistence. He observed countless approach attempts on Starfall Mountain—some failing against the guardians, others broken by the labyrinth's crystalline teeth, a precious few reaching the summit only to be rejected by the anchor itself.

And then, cutting through these kaleidoscopic memories, a single clear path revealed itself. Not physical—no secret tunnel or hidden road—but temporal. A window of opportunity when the Stellar Sentinels' formation would briefly weaken, creating a gap just wide enough for two travelers to slip through.

"Tonight," Asvarr gasped, withdrawing his hand from the basin. Frost coated his fingers, spreading outward along the bark patterns on his skin, accelerating his transformation. "During the conjunction of Alfheim's twin moons. The guardians will shift their formation to accommodate the altered tides of light."

"The eye-root has shown you the way," Yrsa nodded. "But not without cost."

Asvarr examined his hand. The frost hadn't melted but had been absorbed, transforming the bark patterns into something crystalline and alien. The change was spreading up his arm, branch patterns now infused with fragments that caught and refracted light like living prisms.

"The starlight anchor begins its work already," Yrsa observed. "It reshapes you to receive it, as the flame and memory anchors did before."

A musical tone interrupted them—pure and resonant, emanating from the eye-root itself. The enormous structure pulsed more rapidly, its rhythm synchronizing momentarily with the twin beats of the anchors within Asvarr's chest. Golden sap surged through its translucent channels, carrying more of those silver motes that resembled captured stars.

"Something approaches," Yrsa said sharply, moving to the platform's edge.

Asvarr joined her, following her gaze to the forest below. Among the metallic trees, a procession advanced toward the observatory—tall figures in robes the color of twilight, their movements fluid and precise. Elves, carrying instruments of crystal and silver. Their leader wore a circlet that seemed formed of captured moonlight, and even from this distance, Asvarr could see that his eyes contained galaxies.

"Ljósalvir astronomers," Yrsa whispered. "Custodians of the observatory. They must have sensed our intrusion."

"Will they help us?" Asvarr asked, though he already suspected the answer.

"The Stellar Council forbids any interaction with the anchors." Yrsa's expression hardened. "The Ljósalvir work to maintain the current balance—imperfect as it is. Someone like you—a Warden with two anchors already bound—represents a threat to that balance."

"Then we should leave before they arrive."

"Too late. They've already surrounded the base." Yrsa pointed to additional figures emerging from different directions, converging on the tower. "We'll have to negotiate."

"Negotiate?" Asvarr fought back a bitter laugh, more frost-edged leaves spilling from his mouth. "Look at me, Yrsa. What could I possibly offer that would make them overlook this?" He gestured to his transformed body—the verdant crown, the bark-covered skin, the branches sprouting from his shoulders.

"Not what, but who." Yrsa's eyes held an unexpected gleam. "The Ljósalvir have spent millennia studying the stars, documenting their movements, interpreting their patterns. And now those patterns change faster than ever before. Constellations rewrite themselves overnight. Stars vanish and reappear in new positions. They're desperate to understand why."

"And we know," Asvarr realized. "The serpent. The cycle beginning anew."

"Knowledge is power in Alfheim," Yrsa confirmed. "Perhaps enough to buy us safe passage to Starfall Mountain."

Before Asvarr could respond, movement above caught his attention. The stars were shifting again, constellations realigning themselves into new configurations. The threads connecting them brightened, pulsing with energy. The entire sky seemed to lean closer, focusing its vast attention on the observatory platform where they stood.

"They've noticed you," Yrsa whispered, awe and fear mingling in her voice. "The stars themselves recognize what you carry."

The memory-threads connecting the celestial bodies brightened further, some extending downward toward the platform like probing fingers of light. One such thread brushed against Asvarr's verdant crown, sending a shock of awareness through his transformed flesh. For an instant, he perceived the consciousness behind the stars—vast and alien, its thoughts unfolding with the ponderous inevitability of cosmic evolution.

Then the thread withdrew, and the stars resumed their previous patterns, though they continued to watch with unmistakable attention.

"We've been marked," Yrsa said quietly. "For good or ill, the powers of this realm now know we're here."

Asvarr stared up at the living sky, then down at the approaching elves with their instruments of starlight and crystal. The way forward had never seemed more uncertain. Yet the third anchor called to him with increasing urgency, its rhythm merging with his pulse until he could no longer distinguish between them.

"Then let's give them something worth watching," he said, straightening his shoulders as the branches there flexed in response to his resolve. "Tonight, we make for Starfall Mountain, with or without their blessing."

Frost-rimmed leaves fell from his mouth as he spoke, drifting to the observatory floor where they took root instantly, sprouting into tiny crystalline trees that reached upward with the same determined purpose as the eye-root itself.

CHAPTER 2

WINGS OF THE SERPENTBORN

The Ljósalvir entered the observatory in perfect formation, their steps synchronized to a rhythm Asvarr couldn't hear. Morning light caught in their silver hair and shimmered across robes woven with patterns that shifted like ripples in still water. The elves moved with fluid precision, arranging themselves in concentric circles around the platform's center. None spoke. None needed to.

Asvarr tensed, the branches sprouting from his shoulders flexing defensively. His hand drifted toward his bronze sword, but Yrsa gripped his wrist, her fingers surprisingly strong for their apparent frailty.

"Let me speak first," she whispered, her breath visible in the suddenly chill air.

The elves completed their formation, leaving an opening where their leader stood. Taller than his companions by a head, he wore a circlet of what looked like captured starlight. His eyes contained galaxies, literal spirals of light that rotated slowly within his pupils. When he moved, afterimages trailed his movements like echoes of possibility.

"Boundary-walker." He inclined his head toward Yrsa, his voice resonating with harmonics that made the crystal dome above them vibrate subtly. "It has been eight cycles since last you graced our observatory."

"Istari Stellarum." Yrsa offered a formal bow. "The circumstances are... unusual."

The elf's galaxy-eyes shifted to Asvarr, widening slightly as they took in his transformed appearance—the verdant crown, the branches extending down his back, the bark patterns across his skin now threaded with crystalline elements.

"Indeed." The word dropped like a stone into still water. "The anchors walk among us once more."

Murmurs rippled through the assembled elves, musical and discordant at once. Several made warding gestures, tracing complex patterns in the air that briefly glowed with inner light before fading.

"Two bound," observed Istari, his gaze penetrating deeper than flesh. "Flame and memory. The third calls to you even now."

Asvarr met the elf's uncanny stare, fighting the urge to look away from those swirling galaxies. "We need passage to Starfall Mountain."

A sound like breaking crystal swept through the observatory as the elves reacted with collective shock. Istari raised a long-fingered hand, and silence fell immediately.

"The Stellar Council has forbidden all approach to the anchors for nine cycles," he stated. "Such is our law."

"Laws change when circumstances demand," Yrsa countered. "Look to your sky, Star-Sage. Tell us what you see."

Something flickered across Istari's face—frustration, perhaps, or fear. He gestured, and a younger elf brought forward an instrument resembling a hand-held astrolabe, its nested rings crafted from materials Asvarr couldn't identify.

"Since the Shattering of Yggdrasil, Alfheim's stars have exhibited unprecedented behavior," Istari admitted, manipulating the device with practiced precision. "Patterns shift nightly. Colors change. Trajectories alter without explanation."

The astrolabe projected an image into the air above them—a perfect miniature of Alfheim's sky. Asvarr watched constellations move with deliberate purpose, stars pulsing in synchronized patterns, memory-threads connecting and disconnecting in complex matrices.

"And most disturbing," Istari continued, adjusting the device to highlight a particular formation, "the return of the Forgotten Patterns."

The projection zoomed in on a serpentine curve of twelve stars—Jörmungandr's Coil, the same constellation Yrsa had shown Asvarr earlier. The stars pulsed with unnatural brightness, the threads connecting them thicker and more defined than those of other constellations.

"This formation was deliberately erased from our records," Istari explained, his voice tight with controlled tension. "Every chart, every observation, every mention—methodically excised across generations."

"Why?" Asvarr asked.

Istari's galaxy-eyes fixed on him, swirling faster. "Because it heralds the ending of an age. Its appearance precedes great upheaval—the breaking of established order, the transformation of what was fixed into what could be."

"And you fear change," Yrsa suggested.

"We fear chaos," Istari corrected sharply. "Alfheim has survived nine cycles of breaking and partial restoration by maintaining balance. The Stellar Council preserves what remains rather than risking further collapse."

A golden leaf spilled from Asvarr's mouth as he spoke. "The cycle continues precisely because of such half-measures. Partial restoration, partial breaking—oscillation without resolution."

The leaf drifted to the floor where it immediately took root, sprouting into a tiny sapling that reached upward with determined purpose. The elves nearest to it stepped back, expressions ranging from fascination to revulsion.

Istari watched the sapling with narrowed eyes. "You speak of the third path."

"I walk it," Asvarr confirmed.

"Many have claimed such," Istari said, his tone dismissive. "The Ashfather himself once stood where you stand, proclaiming similar intent. Yet here we remain, nine cycles later, still caught between breaking and binding."

Yrsa moved forward, positioning herself between Asvarr and the elf-lord. "What matters now is understanding what happens in your sky. The serpent constellation returns. The stars change their ancient courses. Memory-threads rewrite themselves overnight. You seek explanations—we can provide them."

Istari's posture shifted subtly. Interest overcame caution in those galaxy-eyes. "Speak, then."

"The serpent stirs," Yrsa said, echoing the words she'd spoken when the meteors rained across the realms. "Jörmungandr awakens from slumber, uncoiling among the stars. Its movement disturbs the cosmic web, sending ripples through reality itself."

"Metaphor," Istari dismissed, though uncertainty edged his voice.

"Literal truth," Yrsa countered. "The World Serpent is real, Old One. It exists beyond the firmament, where reality thins to mere suggestion. Its body stretches across galaxies, its thoughts slower than the birth and death of stars. And it has awakened."

Asvarr watched the elf-lord's face, noting the flicker of recognition—and fear—that passed across those elegant features. Istari knew she spoke truth. Whatever records the elves had expunged, whatever history they had deliberately forgotten, some memory remained.

"The Stellar Council disputes such... literal interpretations of ancient texts," Istari said carefully.

"The Stellar Council buries uncomfortable truths," Yrsa replied. "As you buried knowledge of the Forgotten Patterns."

Tension stretched between them like a physical presence. Then, surprisingly, Istari laughed—a sound like wind through crystal chimes.

"Uncomfortable truths indeed," he acknowledged, his galaxy-eyes swirling slower now. "Come. This conversation requires more privacy than an open platform allows."

He gestured toward a spiral staircase on the observatory's far side, leading up into the crystal dome itself. The other elves parted silently, creating a clear path.

"The Stellar Council need not know of our discussion," Istari added, clearly reading Asvarr's hesitation. "Not yet."

Asvarr exchanged glances with Yrsa, who nodded almost imperceptibly. Together they followed the elf-lord up the winding stairs, each step illuminating briefly beneath their feet before fading back to translucency.

The dome's interior was larger than it appeared from outside—a vast spherical chamber with walls of crystal so clear they were nearly invisible. Constellations had been etched into the surfaces, creating a three-dimensional map of Alfheim's sky that surrounded them completely. At the chamber's center floated a sphere of what looked like liquid starlight, suspended in midair without visible support.

"The Astral Archive," Istari named it, circling the floating sphere. "Nine thousand years of stellar observations, preserved in memory-crystal. The collective work of generations of Star Rememberers."

He placed his palm against the sphere's surface, and it responded immediately, rippling like disturbed water. Images formed within its depths—elves in ancient garb recording stellar movements, constructing complex instruments, debating in circular chambers.

"The Ljósalvir have devoted millennia to documenting the stars," Istari explained, his tone softening with pride. "Not merely their positions and movements, but their meanings. The stories they tell. The futures they portend."

His expression darkened. "Since Yggdrasil's fall, our work has been... disrupted."

"How?" Yrsa prompted.

Istari manipulated the sphere again, and new images appeared—star charts with constantly shifting patterns, constellations rearranging themselves between one observation and the next, memory-threads forming connections that contradicted established cosmic laws.

"Stars changing color overnight. Constellations vanishing completely only to reappear in new configurations. Memory-threads forming between celestial bodies that share no natural association." Frustration tinged his musical voice. "Our most fundamental principles no longer apply."

"The pattern changes," Asvarr said, another frost-rimmed leaf falling from his lips.

"Change is expected," Istari countered. "Evolution, gradual adjustment—these are natural. What we observe now is unprecedented. Chaotic. As if..."

"As if what?" Yrsa pressed.

"As if the stars themselves had awakened," Istari finished reluctantly. "As if they watch us with conscious intent."

Asvarr thought of how the constellations had shifted to observe him, the way memory-threads had reached toward him like probing fingers of light. "They do."

Istari's galaxy-eyes fixed on him with renewed intensity. "You speak with certainty."

"I've felt their attention," Asvarr confirmed, absently touching the bark patterns on his chest where the Grímmark burned beneath. "They recognize what I carry."

Istari circled him slowly, studying the verdant crown, the crystalline elements spreading through the bark on his skin, the branches extending from his shoulders.

"Two anchors bound," the elf-lord mused. "Flame and memory. The third calls to you from Starfall Mountain." He stopped, facing Asvarr directly. "Yet you hesitate. Why?"

The question caught Asvarr off-guard. "I don't hesitate."

"You've been in Alfheim nearly a full day," Istari observed. "Had you proceeded directly to the mountain, you would have reached its base by now. Instead, you sought the observatory. Knowledge before action. Wise, perhaps, but unlike previous Wardens who pursued the anchors with single-minded purpose."

"The third path requires understanding," Yrsa interjected.

Istari nodded slowly. "Perhaps." He returned to the floating sphere, placing both palms against its surface. "Let me show you why the Forgotten Patterns were deliberately erased from our records."

The sphere's contents shifted, darkening to the color of deep space. Within that darkness, points of light arranged themselves into the now-familiar serpentine curve—Jörmungandr's Coil. As Asvarr watched, the constellation writhed, its twelve stars flowing like liquid. The image expanded, zooming outward to show how this single constellation connected to others, forming a vast network that spanned Alfheim's entire sky.

"The Coil is merely one fragment of a larger pattern," Istari explained. "When complete, it forms..." He hesitated, then continued reluctantly, "It forms the World Serpent itself, stretched across the entire celestial sphere."

The image continued expanding until Asvarr could see the full pattern—a massive serpentine form composed of hundreds of interconnected constellations, its coils wrapping around Alfheim's sky in a cosmic embrace. The serpent's eye, formed by a spiral galaxy, seemed to stare directly at them through the projection.

"Nine cycles ago, when the first breaking occurred, this pattern appeared in our sky," Istari said quietly. "It remained visible for nine days and nine nights. Those who gazed upon it too long lost their minds, their consciousnesses stretched beyond mortal comprehension. When it faded, the Stellar Council ordered all records of it destroyed, all memory of it suppressed."

"Why?" Asvarr demanded.

"Because it nearly destroyed us," Istari answered bluntly. "The pattern is too vast, too complex for mortal minds to comprehend. It contains... everything. Past, present, future—all possibilities, all iterations, all cycles of breaking and binding. To perceive it in its entirety is to lose oneself in infinite potential."

The projection shifted again, showing elves writhing in apparent agony, their bodies contorting as they stared at the sky. Some appeared to dissolve into light, others collapsed into empty husks.

"Those who survived were... changed," Istari continued. "They spoke of the serpent's voice in their minds, of visions too profound to articulate. Many took their own lives rather than live with what they had glimpsed. Others wandered into the void between worlds, never to return."

He banished the troubling images with a gesture. "When the pattern began reappearing in fragments, the Stellar Council implemented systematic forgetting. It wasnt just the destruction of physical records, but ritual erasure of memory itself. For nine cycles, this strategy has preserved us from madness."

"And now it returns," Yrsa said.

"Yes." Istari's galaxy-eyes reflected the floating sphere's contents. "Each night, more stars join the Coil. More memory-threads connect to form the larger pattern. We estimate complete manifestation within nine days."

Asvarr felt the weight of the elf's revelation settle into his bones. "And when it fully appears?"

"Unknown," Istari admitted. "Perhaps nothing. Perhaps the end of Alfheim as we know it. The records that survived from the first breaking are... incomplete."

Silence fell over the dome chamber, broken only by the faint crystalline humming of the observatory itself. Asvarr processed what he'd learned, connecting it to what he already knew of the pattern, the anchors, the cycles of breaking and binding.

"The serpent's awakening coincides with the anchors' movement," he said finally. "They're connected—parts of the same cycle."

"Yes," Istari agreed. "The questions are: how, and why now?"

"I believe I can answer both," Yrsa said, stepping forward. "But our knowledge comes with a price."

Istari's expression hardened slightly. "Of course it does. What do you want?"

"Safe passage to Starfall Mountain," she stated firmly. "Tonight, during the conjunction of Alfheim's twin moons when the Stellar Sentinels shift their formation."

Surprise flickered across the elf-lord's face. "You've seen the path."

"In the eye-root's memory," Yrsa confirmed. "Grant us passage, and I'll tell you why the serpent stirs now, after nine cycles of slumber."

Istari considered for a long moment, galaxy-eyes swirling in contemplation. "The Stellar Council has forbidden all approach to the anchors," he repeated his earlier statement.

"And yet, your observatory stands upon the greatest anchor of all," Yrsa countered, gesturing toward the massive eye-root below. "You study the stars while standing on the very thing that connects them to the earth."

Asvarr watched tension ripple across Istari's elegant features. The elf-lord was caught between duty and curiosity, between preserving established order and seeking understanding of the chaos unfolding in his sky.

"If the full pattern manifests without our comprehending its purpose," Yrsa pressed, "how will you protect your people from what follows?"

The argument struck home. Istari's shoulders dropped slightly, his posture shifting from resistance to resignation.

"I will grant you passage," he decided. "Not official sanction—the Stellar Council would never approve— I will ensure the sentinels do not intercept you during the conjunction."

Relief washed through Asvarr, quickly followed by wariness. "In exchange for what, exactly?"

"Information," Istari said simply. "Everything you know about the serpent, the anchors, the cycles of breaking and binding. And..." he hesitated, then continued more firmly, "And your blood."

Asvarr's hand dropped to his sword hilt. "My blood?"

"A small sample only," Istari assured him. "Your transformation is unique—flame and root combined, with starlight now beginning its work as well. Such a combination has never been documented in nine cycles of breaking. If the pattern changes as you claim, your blood may help us understand how."

Asvarr glanced at Yrsa, who nodded almost imperceptibly. "Agreed," he said. "But the blood comes after your part is fulfilled—when we return from Starfall Mountain."

"If you return," Istari corrected, his galaxy-eyes solemn. "The anchor has rejected all previous supplicants for nine cycles. What makes you think you'll succeed where others failed?"

Asvarr met the elf's uncanny gaze steadily. "Because I don't seek to control it, as the Ashfather did. Nor to submit to it, as others attempted. I seek transformation—to change as it changes, to walk the third path."

Istari studied him for a long moment, those galaxy-eyes searching for deception or uncertainty. Finally, he nodded. "Perhaps you will succeed. For Alfheim's sake, I hope so. The current chaos cannot continue without consequences."

He placed his palms against the floating sphere one final time, and it darkened completely before dissolving into mist that settled around their shoulders like a cloak of stars.

***

"Return here after nightfall," Istari instructed. "I'll provide what you need for the approach. Until then, rest. The path to Starfall Mountain demands complete strength of both body and mind."

As they descended the spiral staircase, returning to the main observatory platform, Asvarr noticed the other elves had vanished. Only a few remained, tending to the various instruments with focused attention.

"They fear you," Yrsa murmured, noting his observation. "Or rather, what you represent. Change is rarely welcomed by those who've thrived under the current order."

"And have they thrived?" Asvarr countered quietly. "Nine cycles of partial breaking and restoration, never complete, never resolved. Is that truly prosperity?"

"For some," Yrsa replied cryptically. "The question is whether the third path will truly offer something better, or merely different."

Asvarr had no answer to that. The weight of his transformation pressed against his awareness—the verdant crown growing heavier, the crystalline elements spreading through the bark on his skin, the alien rhythm of the starlight anchor calling to him from Starfall Mountain's peak.

Tonight they would answer that call, pushing his transformation further still. The third binding might cost him whatever humanity remained—a price he'd accepted in theory but now faced in immediate reality.

What would emerge from Starfall Mountain: a Warden with three anchors bound, or something else entirely?

"Return here after nightfall," Istari's final instruction lingered in the air as he departed. The elven astronomers dispersed throughout the observatory, resuming their work with practiced precision, though many cast wary glances toward Asvarr when they thought he wouldn't notice.

Asvarr stood at the platform's edge, staring out over the silver forests of Alfheim. Nightfall seemed an eternity away. His fingers absently traced the crystalline patterns spreading through the bark on his skin, following their branching paths up his arm. The transformation accelerated with each passing hour, his body becoming less his own.

"You're brooding," Yrsa observed, joining him at the railing.

"Thinking," Asvarr corrected, another frost-rimmed leaf falling from his lips.

"About what remains after the third binding," she guessed.

He didn't answer. The question haunted him: how much of himself would survive? The flame anchor had taken his rage, transforming anger into purpose. The memory anchor had claimed fragments of his past, reshaping recollection into understanding. What would the starlight anchor demand?

***

A sudden hush fell over the observatory. The elven astronomers froze mid-motion, their attention captured by something above. Asvarr followed their gaze upward, through the crystal dome to the sky beyond.

The stars were moving.

Not the subtle shifts he'd witnessed before—this was deliberate, coordinated motion. Entire constellations flowed like liquid across the heavens, rearranging themselves into new patterns that pulsed with inner light. Memory-threads brightened, some breaking while others formed in complex, unfamiliar configurations.

Istari rushed back onto the platform, his galaxy-eyes swirling with agitation. "It happens faster than predicted," he announced, voice tight with controlled fear. "The pattern accelerates its formation."

Above, the stars continued their impossible dance. Jörmungandr's Coil undulated like a living thing, its twelve stars flowing in serpentine rhythm. Other constellations joined it, linking together to form larger segments of the cosmic serpent.

"How long until complete manifestation?" Yrsa asked.

"Hours, not days," Istari replied grimly. "The conjunction of the twin moons tonight will catalyze the process."

The same conjunction they needed to reach Starfall Mountain. Asvarr felt the weight of coincidence settling over him—or perhaps pattern.

"Look!" One of the astronomers pointed upward, her voice cracking with awe or terror.

Through the dome, Asvarr saw it—a disturbance in the fabric of the sky itself. Reality rippled like the surface of a disturbed pond, concentric circles spreading outward from a central point. The stars in that region dimmed momentarily, then flared with renewed brilliance.

Something was coming through.

The ripples intensified, reality thinning until Asvarr could see beyond the sky into the void beyond—a darkness so complete it hurt his eyes to look upon it. Within that darkness, shapes moved—vast and sinuous, their forms composed of consolidated starlight.

"Serpentborn," Istari whispered, his musical voice reduced to a harsh rasp. "Impossible."

The first one breached the boundary between void and sky, its massive body flowing through the rupture like water through a broken dam. Long and serpentine, it measured longer than the observatory tower was tall. Its scales gleamed with captured starlight, each one containing what looked like a miniature galaxy. Where its eyes should have been, spiral nebulae rotated in hypnotic patterns.

A second followed, then a third. Soon, half a dozen of the creatures glided through Alfheim's sky, their bodies undulating with fluid grace. They circled the observatory, movements synchronized in what could only be described as a dance.

The elven astronomers had scattered to various instruments, recording the phenomenon with frantic energy. Only Istari remained motionless, his galaxy-eyes tracking the serpents' movements with stunned recognition.

"They haven't manifested physically in nine cycles," he said quietly. "Not since the first breaking."

Asvarr watched the aerial dance with a mixture of awe and unease. Despite their alien nature, the serpents displayed unmistakable intelligence in their coordinated movements. They were no mindless beasts, but conscious entities with purpose.

"What are they?" he asked.

"Fragments of the greater whole," Yrsa answered, her voice hushed with rare reverence. "Scales shed from Jörmungandr itself, given independent life. They dwell in the void between stars, watching the cosmic pattern unfold across eons."

As if hearing her explanation, the serpents altered their flight pattern. One by one, they descended toward the observatory platform, their enormous bodies coiling in the air above. The elven astronomers retreated to the far side of the platform, instruments abandoned in their haste.

The largest serpent—its body the color of deep space flecked with points of light—lowered its head until it hovered just above the platform's edge. Its nebula-eyes fixed on Asvarr with unmistakable intent.

"They recognize what you carry," Istari murmured, maintaining his position despite visible terror. "The anchors draw them."

The serpent's mouth opened, revealing a swirling vortex of stars and void. No sound emerged, yet Asvarr heard a voice—not in his ears but directly within his mind. The sensation was utterly unlike telepathy he'd experienced before; this communication bypassed language entirely, conveying complex concepts in instantaneous bursts of understanding.

Splinter-self, the voice named him. *Fractured hatchling.*

The words made no sense, yet carried unmistakable recognition. The serpent saw him as kin—distant and malformed, but kin nonetheless.

"I don't understand," Asvarr said aloud, unsure if spoken words held meaning for the creature.

The serpent's nebula-eyes rotated faster. *You wear fragments of the pattern. Root and flame combined—a configuration unseen in nine cycles. Soon starlight as well. You become as we are: neither one thing nor another, but something between states.*

Again, that sense of recognition—the serpent saw something of itself in Asvarr's transformation. He glanced down at his arms, the bark patterns now threaded with crystalline elements that caught and refracted light. The verdant crown around his head felt suddenly heavier, more significant.

"What are you?" he asked.

We are memory given form. Thought made flesh. The void-between-stars granted consciousness.

The creature lowered its head further, bringing one nebula-eye level with Asvarr's face. Within that spiral of stars and dust, he glimpsed entire solar systems forming and dying in accelerated time.

Do you remember the first sky, before branches carved it into fragments?

The question resonated deep within Asvarr, stirring something beneath conscious thought—ancestral memory perhaps, or knowledge imparted by the anchors he carried. Images flashed behind his eyes: a cosmos unmarred by division, reality flowing seamlessly between states, the pattern whole and perfect in its complexity.

"I've never seen such a sky," he answered truthfully.

Yet you carry its echo. The serpent's mental voice carried what might have been sadness. *The anchors remember, though they too are fragmented.*

The other serpents had descended as well, arranging themselves in a loose circle around the platform. Their nebula-eyes focused on Asvarr with unnerving intensity, as if peering beneath his flesh to the anchors he carried within.

One serpent—smaller than the others, its scales shifting between silver and blue—drifted closer to Yrsa. The old woman stood her ground, showing none of the terror that had driven the elven astronomers back.

Boundary-walker, it named her. *Nine-times-passing.*

Yrsa inclined her head in acknowledgment. "I remember you, Starweaver. Though you were smaller when last we met."

The silver-blue serpent rippled with what might have been amusement. *Time flows differently in the void. What seems nine cycles to you has been both longer and shorter for us.*

Istari stepped forward hesitantly, his galaxy-eyes fixed on the largest serpent. "Great Ones," he addressed them formally, "why do you return now, after nine cycles of absence?"

The largest serpent turned its attention to the elf-lord, nebula-eyes spiraling slower. *The pattern nears completion. The cycle reaches its apex. Change comes to the nine realms—transformation or dissolution. Your Stellar Council sought to prevent this moment through systematic forgetting, but memory transcends conscious recall.*

"What pattern?" Asvarr pressed. "The World Serpent constellation?"

The constellation is merely reflection. The true pattern exists beyond stars, beyond realms, beyond branches. The serpent's mental voice intensified, the concepts it conveyed growing more complex. *Before Yggdrasil, before gods, before division into Nine Realms, all existence flowed as one. The breaking fragmented the whole. Anchors scattered. Cycles of partial restoration followed, never complete.*

Asvarr felt the weight of cosmic history pressing against his mind. "And now?"

Now comes the tenth cycle. Different from those before. The third path opens—neither restoration nor destruction but transformation. You walk this path, carrying fragments that seek reunion.

The verdant crown around Asvarr's head pulsed in response to the serpent's words, small branches extending further down his back. The Grímmark burned beneath his tunic, golden sap seeping through the bark on his chest. Even the crystalline elements spreading through his skin brightened, catching and amplifying the strange light emanating from the serpents above.

"The anchors," he realized. "They're fragments of something larger."

Yes. Scattered when the pattern broke. Each containing a piece of the whole. None complete alone.

Another serpent—its scales red-gold like a dying sun—drifted closer. *The flame anchor preserves. The memory anchor connects. The starlight anchor transforms. Two you carry already. The third awaits at mountain's peak.*

"And after the third?" Asvarr asked, dreading the answer yet needing to hear it.

Two more remain. Death in Helheim's heart. Creation in Muspel's forge. When all five unite, the choice comes: restore the old pattern, shatter it completely, or transform it into something new.

The largest serpent twisted its massive body, creating a living diagram in the air above the platform. Its coils formed a five-pointed star, each point glowing with different colored light—red for flame, gold for memory, silver for starlight, black for death, white for creation.

Five points. Five anchors. Five aspects of the whole. United, they form the sixth—the pattern itself.

Asvarr stared at the living diagram, understanding dawning. The anchors weren't merely fragments to be collected but aspects of a greater whole—pieces of a puzzle that, when assembled correctly, would reveal... what? Restoration? Transformation? Or something else entirely?

"Why show yourselves to us?" Yrsa asked the serpents. "After nine cycles of watching from the void?"

The silver-blue serpent twisted toward her. *Because this cycle differs. The flame-root vessel stands before us, two anchors bound, seeking a third. The third path opens—possibility where before stood only oscillation between extremes.*

"The third path," Asvarr echoed. The concept had guided him since binding the second anchor, yet remained frustratingly abstract. "What exactly is it?"

Neither domination nor submission. Neither preservation nor destruction. Balance found through continuous transformation. The largest serpent's nebula-eyes fixed on him with unnerving intensity. *It has never been walked successfully in nine cycles of breaking and binding. Many have tried. All failed, becoming either tyrants or vessels, controllers or controlled.*

"Why would I succeed where others failed?" Asvarr challenged.

Because you are already transformed. Root and flame combined—opposites that should destroy each other, yet in you, they find balance. The serpent's mental voice carried what might have been approval. *Your crown grows from the pattern itself, connecting you to what was and what could be simultaneously.*

The elven astronomers had cautiously returned to their instruments, recording the serpents' presence with reverent precision. Istari stood beside Asvarr now, his initial fear replaced by scientific fascination.

"The Stellar Council must be informed," the elf-lord murmured. "This changes everything."

"The Council already knows," Yrsa countered. "Why else enforce systematic forgetting? They recognize the pattern's return but choose ignorance over acceptance."

The largest serpent twisted its massive body again, nebula-eyes rotating faster. *Time grows short. The conjunction approaches. The gateway to Starfall Mountain will open briefly. If the third anchor is to be bound, you must prepare.*

"Will you help us?" Asvarr asked.

We cannot. Our manifestation in this realm is temporary—a reflection of the pattern's growing strength. When the conjunction peaks, we return to the void. The serpent's mental voice carried regret. *But know this: the third binding will demand more than the previous two. The starlight anchor transforms all it touches. What emerges from Starfall Mountain may no longer be what entered.*

The warning sent a chill through Asvarr's transformed flesh. "Will I remain myself?"

Self is illusion—a boundary drawn around aspects of the pattern, claiming them as separate. The serpent twisted closer, its nebula-eye filling Asvarr's vision. *You will remain, but changed. As all things change. The question is whether you direct the transformation or surrender to it.*

Before Asvarr could respond, the sky above darkened suddenly. The stars flared brighter, then dimmed as if something massive passed between them and Alfheim. The serpents reacted immediately, their bodies tensing into rigid lines.

It comes, the largest serpent announced, mental voice tightening with what could only be described as alarm. *The void-hunger stirs, sensing the pattern's movement.*

"Void-hunger?" Istari repeated, galaxy-eyes wide with fear. "I know no such entity."

Because your Council erased all record of it. The anti-pattern. The un-maker. That which exists between branches, feeding on possibility.

The sky continued darkening, stars winking out one by one as something vast and invisible moved across the heavens. The serpents began ascending rapidly, their bodies flowing like liquid starlight as they returned to the rift they had created.

Prepare yourselves, the largest serpent called back to them. *The void-hunger seeks what you carry. It hungers for the anchors, for the pattern they represent. When you bind the third, its attention will fix upon you fully.*

"Wait!" Asvarr called. "I still don't understand my connection to you. Why call me 'splinter-self' and 'fractured hatchling'?"

The serpent paused at the rift's edge, its nebula-eyes spiraling one final time. *Because we recognize our own. Before worlds, before breaking, before fragments scattered—we were one. Remember the first sky, when next we meet.*

With that cryptic statement, the serpent vanished through the rift. The others followed swiftly, their sinuous bodies flowing back into the void beyond stars. The rift sealed behind them, reality knitting itself back together until only the faintest ripple remained as evidence of their passage.

Silence fell over the observatory. The elven astronomers stood frozen, instruments still raised toward where the serpents had been. Istari's galaxy-eyes had dimmed to mere pinpricks of light, his face drained of color.

"Nine cycles," he whispered. "Nine cycles of careful study, and never once did we glimpse what truly moves beyond our sky."

"Because you weren't meant to," Yrsa said quietly. "Some knowledge is deliberately hidden to protect what they might discover."

Asvarr stared up at the sky, watching as stars reappeared, constellations reforming in their wake. The serpents' warnings echoed in his mind: the void-hunger stirring, the pattern accelerating, the third binding approaching. With each revelation, the stakes grew higher, the consequences more profound.

"What now?" he asked, his voice sounding strange to his own ears—deeper, resonant with harmonics like wind through branches.

"We prepare," Yrsa answered simply. "The conjunction approaches. Starfall Mountain awaits."

The crystalline elements in Asvarr's transformed flesh caught the starlight, refracting it in complex patterns across his skin. The third anchor called to him with increasing urgency, its rhythm merging with his heartbeat until he could no longer distinguish between them.

When night fell, they would answer that call. And whatever emerged from Starfall Mountain—whether still Asvarr or something else entirely—would face the consequences of binding a third fragment of the cosmic pattern to mortal flesh.

CHAPTER 3

BRYNJA'S RETURN

The words of the sky-serpent rang in Asvarr's head like a forgotten melody from childhood. *Do you remember the first sky, before branches carved it into fragments?* His throat tightened. The verdant crown upon his head shifted, branches rustling against his scalp as though stirred by an unfelt wind.

"I don't..." he managed, his voice scraping raw. The largest serpent—scales shimmering with nebula-light—coiled closer, its massive eye reflecting galaxies unknown to any mortal observer. Golden sap leaked from the corners of Asvarr's mouth, dripping onto the silver floor of the observatory platform.

Istari Stellarum backed away, his star-filled eyes wide with wonder and terror. The other astronomers had already retreated to the crystal dome's edge, leaving Asvarr and Yrsa alone with the celestial creatures.

Before Asvarr could speak again, darkness swept across the platform. It wasn't the gentle shadow of a cloud passing before moon, it was something deliberate and solid. The serpents twisted their luminous bodies upward, their attention captured by the intrusion.

A shadow darker than the spaces between stars fell across the observatory floor. The air cracked with tension, splitting like frozen lake-ice under spring sun.

"Warden of Root and Flame."

The voice struck like steel on stone, familiar and foreign at once. Asvarr turned, the crown of branches creaking with his movement.

She stood upon the edge of the platform, silhouetted against Alfheim's impossible sky. Her left arm—once flesh, now entirely wooden—gleamed with patterns that mimicked the constellations above. Spiraling galaxies and stellar formations were carved into the grain itself, glowing with amber light. Her face, half-covered in bark that had crept from neck to cheekbone, bore runes that pulsed in time with the starlight filtering through the crystal dome.

"Brynja." Her name tasted of both honey and bile on his tongue.

Her eyes—no longer entirely human—reflected the starlight in prismatic fractures. The right remained recognizably hers, though rimmed with gold. The left had transformed completely, its iris a swirling vortex of cosmic patterns that mirrored the night sky beyond the dome.

"You've traveled far, branch-crown." She stepped forward, the wooden fingers of her transformed arm clicking against the crystal floor. Each step left a momentary imprint of starlight that faded seconds later.

The sky-serpents undulated around her, neither retreating nor approaching. The largest one—the one that had addressed Asvarr as "splinter-self"—regarded her with a gaze that contained entire nebulae.

"Where is Leif?" Asvarr demanded, searching the shadows behind her for the boy's familiar form. The absence stung more sharply than he'd anticipated.

Brynja's mouth tightened. "Not with me."

"That wasn't my question." Asvarr's fists clenched, the bronze sword at his hip humming in response to his tension. Golden veins beneath the metal's surface pulsed in time with his accelerating heartbeat.

She crossed to the center of the observatory platform, ignoring the elven astronomers who pressed themselves against the wall to avoid her path. Her gait had changed—fluid yet mechanical, as though the wooden parts of her had forever altered how she moved through the world.

"You're different," she said, ignoring his question entirely. Her eyes scanned him, lingering on the crown of branches that had spread across his brow and down his shoulders. "The memory anchor changed you more than I anticipated."

Yrsa stepped between them, her crystal pendant blazing with cold blue light. "You bear the mark of the Verdant Five." Her voice carried accusation and wariness in equal measure. "What have they done to you, root-tender?"

Brynja's transformed eye swirled faster, constellations shifting within its depths. "They showed me truth." Her wooden fingers flexed, the joints creaking like ancient trees in winter wind. "But not all of it."

The oath-sigil on Asvarr's palm burned suddenly, sending shoots of pain up his arm. He turned his hand upward, examining the mark they had shared since their blood-oath in the Thorned Vale. The once-vibrant wooden spiral had darkened, its tiny leaves withered and blackened as though touched by frost.

Brynja held up her own palm in response. The matching sigil had transformed, becoming something wilder, less controlled. The wooden spiral remained, but it now sprouted thorns that pierced the bark around it, bleeding golden sap that traced alien constellations across her palm.

"The binding still holds," she said. "But it has... evolved."

"As have you." Asvarr kept his voice steady, though the crown of branches tightened around his temples, responding to emotions he fought to suppress. "Our paths diverged at the Verdant Gate. How did you find me?"

She laughed—a sound like winter branches shattering under the weight of ice. "Find you? The anchor you carry burns like a beacon across all Nine Realms. You might as well have lit a pyre on mountaintop and called my name into the void." She gestured toward the night sky beyond the crystal dome. "Besides, the pattern directed me. The stars remember, even when we forget."

The largest sky-serpent drifted closer, its enormous head lowering until it hovered beside Brynja. It regarded her with ancient curiosity, then turned toward Asvarr.

"She walks between patterns," it spoke directly into his mind. *"Like you, fractured-self. Unlike you, willingly."*

Brynja's transformed eye swirled faster. "You hear them too." Not a question.

"What happened to Leif?" Asvarr pressed again, unwilling to be diverted.

A shadow passed across Brynja's face—pain, guilt, or something less definable. She turned away, her wooden arm creaking as she clenched her fist.

"He chose a different path." Her voice dropped, nearly inaudible. "Or perhaps the path chose him."

"That tells me nothing." Asvarr stepped forward, branches from his crown rustling with the motion.

Brynja whirled back, unexpected fury flashing across her features. "Nothing? You speak of nothing when you stand with celestial guardians discussing the first sky? When your flesh transforms with every breath you take?" She stalked toward him, her wooden arm extending slightly beyond natural reach. "You've bound two anchors, Flame-Warden. Don't speak to me of nothing when you've barely begun to understand everything."

The sky-serpents writhed above them, their luminous bodies twisting into patterns that made Asvarr's eyes water. The air thickened with tension, tasting of metal and stardust.

"Enough." Yrsa's voice cut between them, her crystal pendant flaring brighter. "The twin moons approach conjunction. We waste precious time with old arguments when the starlight anchor awaits."

Istari Stellarum finally found his courage, stepping forward from the huddle of astronomers. "You speak of the anchor at Starfall Mountain?" His galaxy-eyes fixed on Brynja. "The Stellar Sentinels guard it. None approach without permission."

"Permission?" Brynja's laugh cracked the air again. "From whom? The Stellar Council that hides truth behind ritual and mandate? The same Council that ordered all records of the World Serpent destroyed?" She gestured toward the sky-serpents undulating above them. "How well did that erasure work, star-gazer?"

Istari's face tightened. "Our reasons were—"

"Fear," Brynja interrupted. "Always fear. Fear of what waits beyond the pattern. Fear of what sleeps beneath the roots." Her voice dropped to a whisper. "Fear of what happens when all five anchors converge."

The largest sky-serpent drifted between them, its massive eye reflecting Asvarr's own transformed face back at him—the crown of branches spreading further than he'd realized, the bark patterns creeping up his jaw, crystalline formations beginning to appear at his temples.

"*Time thins,*" it spoke into all their minds simultaneously. "*The convergence accelerates. What was nine cycles becomes one moment.*"

"We need to reach Starfall Mountain," Asvarr said, addressing both the serpent and Istari. "Before the twin moons align."

Brynja's transformed eye whirled. "The mountain, yes. But not for the reasons you believe." She turned her attention fully to Asvarr, her expression shifting to something almost gentle. "You still think this is about restoration, don't you? That binding the anchors will heal what was broken?"

"The third path," Asvarr said firmly. "Not restoration, nor destruction. Transformation."

"Transformation." She spoke the word like tasting unfamiliar food. "Perhaps. But into what?"

Before he could answer, the sky-serpents suddenly twisted upward, their luminous bodies stretching toward the dome's apex. A tremor passed through the crystal structure, sending vibrations through the floor beneath their feet.

"*She comes,*" the largest serpent projected, its thought-voice tinged with alarm. "*The blind one sees. The bound one breaks.*"

Istari rushed to the observation apparatus, spinning the nested crystal rings into new configurations. "There!" He pointed to a section of sky visible through the dome. "Something approaches from the void. Too fast, too... deliberate."

A streak of silver-blue light cut across the starscape, moving against the celestial patterns in defiance of natural law. Unlike a meteor's straight path, this light zigzagged purposefully, changing direction mid-flight several times.

"What is that?" Asvarr demanded, the crown of branches tightening painfully around his skull.

Brynja moved to his side, her wooden arm brushing against his. The contact sent jolts of recognition through him, the oath-sigils in their palms responding to proximity.

"A hunter," she murmured. "One of the Stellar Sentinels, broken from its pattern." Her transformed eye tracked the approaching light. "Someone has disturbed the binding that holds them in formation around the mountain."

The sky-serpents began to withdraw, their bodies coiling protectively around specific star-clusters. The largest one paused, its eye fixing on Asvarr one final time.

"Find us where starlight touches Root," it projected. *"We will speak again, fractured-self, when the third binding is complete—if you survive it."*

With those words, the serpents vanished upward, becoming indistinguishable from the stars they resembled.

*   *   *

Istari barked orders to his fellow astronomers, who scrambled to adjust instruments and secure scrolls. "We must alert the Stellar Council. If a Sentinel has broken formation—"

"It's too late for warnings," Brynja interrupted. Her wooden fingers gripped Asvarr's arm with unexpected strength. "The Sentinel comes for us—for what we carry." Her gaze shifted to Yrsa. "Boundary-walker, can you open a path from here to the mountain's base?"

Yrsa's face tightened. "Not directly. The boundaries around Starfall are too rigid, deliberately reinforced across nine cycles." She touched her crystal pendant, which had dimmed slightly. "But I can get us close—to the Silver Grove. From there, we'll need to find our own way."

The streak of light grew larger, its path clearly directed toward the observatory. The crystal dome groaned under some unseen pressure as the entity approached.

"Then do it now," Asvarr commanded, drawing his bronze sword. The golden veins beneath the metal's surface pulsed rapidly, responding to the threat.

Yrsa nodded, raising her crystal pendant before her. The blue light expanded, creating a doorway of shimmering energy that wavered like heated air.

"Quickly," she urged. "The boundary will only hold for moments."

Istari stepped forward, galaxy-eyes fixed on Asvarr. "Wait. The information you promised in exchange for safe passage—"

"Will have to wait," Asvarr cut him off. "Unless you'd prefer to explain to your Sentinel why you allowed anchor-bearers into your observatory."

The astronomer's face fell, but he nodded. "Go. I'll direct it elsewhere if I can."

Asvarr turned to Brynja, who stood watching the approaching light with strange fascination. "Are you coming?"

Her transformed eye swirled with cosmic patterns as she turned to him. "To witness what you become when starlight reshapes your flesh? When the third anchor burns its pattern into your soul?" A smile lifted one corner of her mouth—the side still fully human. "Wouldn't miss it for all nine worlds, flame-bearer."

The streak of light struck the crystal dome with devastating force. Cracks spiderwebbed across the transparent surface, sending spears of light refracting throughout the chamber.

"Now!" Yrsa shouted, stepping through her boundary-door.

Asvarr followed, pulling Brynja after him by her still-human arm. The doorway collapsed behind them with a sound like shattering glass, cutting off Istari's shout of alarm.

The world dissolved into blue light and spatial disorientation. Asvarr's last coherent thought was the memory of the sky-serpent's words: *Do you remember the first sky, before branches carved it into fragments?*

For a single, terrifying moment, he thought he did.

The boundary-door collapsed behind them, severing the pursuit of the rogue Sentinel. Asvarr stumbled forward, disoriented by the sudden shift in reality. The verdant crown on his head swayed, branches scraping against his scalp as though searching for purchase in this new environment.

***

They stood in a silver grove, trees rising around them like polished spears thrust into Alfheim's soil. The air tasted of metal and stardust. Above, through gaps in the canopy, twin moons hung low—one gold, one silver—their approach to conjunction accelerating visibly in the strange physics of this realm.

"We have less time than I thought," Yrsa muttered, her crystal pendant dimmed from the effort of creating the boundary-crossing. "The conjunction approaches faster than in previous cycles."

Brynja swayed on her feet, her wooden arm creaking as she steadied herself against a silver trunk. The constellation patterns inlaid in the wood pulsed with internal light, responding to the celestial energy saturating the grove.

"Brynja?" Asvarr stepped toward her, instinctively reaching out.

She jerked away, her movements suddenly erratic. "Don't—" The word fractured halfway through. Her transformed eye whirled faster, constellations blurring within its depths. "Remember when we hunted twilight-birds in the marshes? Before the clans warred?" Her voice shifted, becoming child-like, disconnected. "Mother said never to drink the water. Stars in the depths. Watching."

Asvarr exchanged a glance with Yrsa, whose face had tightened with concern.

"We never hunted together as children," he said carefully, keeping his distance now. "Your clan was north of the fjord. Mine south."

Brynja's head jerked up, her gaze clearing momentarily. "Of course." Her voice returned to its normal register. "That was... someone else's memory. The roots hold many stories." She pressed her human hand against her temple. "Hard to separate sometimes. Their voices. Mine. What was. What might be."

Yrsa approached, her crystal pendant extended. "Let me see." She studied Brynja with clinical precision. "The transformation progresses differently in you. The Severed Bloom fragment seeks dominance rather than partnership."

"Partnership." Brynja spat the word. "Is that what you think you have, Flame-Warden?" She turned her dual-natured gaze on Asvarr, one eye human, one cosmic. "Wait until the starlight anchor turns your bones to crystal, until memories that aren't yours crowd out what little humanity remains." She laughed—a brittle, fractured sound. "Then talk to me of partnership."

The branches of Asvarr's crown tightened, responding to the spike of anger her words provoked. "You chose this path. You walked willingly with the Verdant Five."

"Willingly?" Brynja's wooden fingers scraped against the silver bark. "What choice is there when truth burns away everything you believed? When you learn the roots don't nurture—they imprison."

Yrsa stepped between them. "We must move. The Silver Grove offers temporary shelter, but once the Sentinel re-orients, it will track us here." She pointed toward a barely visible path winding between the metallic trunks. "Starfall Mountain lies south. We can reach its base before the conjunction if we hurry."

Brynja ignored her, fixing Asvarr with her strange gaze. "Do you still think this is about restoration? Healing what was broken?" The constellation patterns in her wooden flesh pulsed brighter. "The Tree is not what we believed, Asvarr. The Verdant Five showed me its original purpose, and it was never about sustaining life."

The air around them chilled suddenly. Silver leaves shivered, though no wind moved through the grove. Asvarr felt the anchors he carried—flame and memory—pulse within him, resonating with something in her words.

"What are you saying?" he demanded, stepping closer despite Yrsa's warning gesture.

"The pattern beneath the pattern " Brynja's voice dropped to a whisper. "The prison beneath the Tree." Her human eye widened, the pupil contracting to a pinpoint. "They never told us what it holds."

Above them, through gaps in the canopy, stars shifted. The sky-serpents they'd encountered at the observatory now coiled in the void, their luminous bodies wrapping protectively around specific constellations. They moved with deliberate purpose, as though hiding celestial knowledge from view.

"We should go," Yrsa insisted, her pendant flickering with renewed blue light. "Something approaches."

Brynja gripped Asvarr's arm suddenly, her wooden fingers digging into his flesh with painful precision. "Listen carefully," she said, her voice clear and urgent, all fragmentation gone. "The anchors were never meant to be reunited. Each binding awakens it further. The Verdant Five know this—it's why they separated our bloodlines for nine cycles, why they ordered our clans destroyed when we began remembering across generations."

"Remembering what?" Asvarr asked, the crown of branches creaking with his mounting tension.

"What sleeps beneath the roots." Her fingers tightened further. "What dreams beneath the Tree."

A tremor passed through the silver grove. Trees groaned, metal against metal. The ground beneath their feet shifted, soil cracking to reveal glints of starlight buried beneath Alfheim's surface.

"Brynja, we need to move," Yrsa commanded, her voice sharper than Asvarr had ever heard. "Your words disturb the pattern. The Sentinels will converge."

Brynja released Asvarr's arm, leaving perfect indentations where her wooden fingers had pressed. She staggered backward, the coherence fading from her expression. Her transformed eye whirled chaotically, star-patterns shifting and reforming within its depths.

"The first branch," she muttered, voice slipping back into fragmented rhythm. "First root. First binding. First prison. They think—they call it sustenance. Connection. They lie. The Tree doesn't... doesn't grow. It restrains."

"Who?" Asvarr demanded, following as she backed away. "Who lies? The Verdant Five?"

"Everyone." Brynja's laugh cracked the air. "Gods. Five. Ashfather. Different means, same purpose. Control what must never awaken."

The silver trees around them began to hum, vibrating at a frequency that set Asvarr's teeth on edge. The sound built slowly, metallic and unnerving. Through the canopy, he glimpsed the sky-serpents coiling tighter around their protected constellations, their luminous bodies forming barriers of light.

"What happens when I bind the third anchor?" Asvarr pressed, ignoring Yrsa's increasing urgency. "What awakens?"

Brynja's coherence returned suddenly, her gaze snapping into sharp focus. "I don't know." Her voice steadied, gaining authority. "Neither do the Five, not fully. But they fear it enough to maintain the separation across nine cycles. They fear it enough to manipulate gods into withdrawal."

"Gods don't withdraw," Asvarr objected "They rule from Asgard. They walk the nine realms."

"When did you last see one?" Brynja countered. "Not the Ashfather—he's just a splinter, an echo. A true god, in their full power?"

The question struck Asvarr like a physical blow. The branches of his crown tightened painfully. He had no answer.

"Exactly," Brynja whispered. "They retreated when the first breaking occurred. Withdrew to 'spaces between branches' where they could maintain power without responsibility." Her wooden arm creaked as she gestured toward the sky. "They watch, but they no longer walk among us. Because they fear what might wake if the Tree fully restores."

The humming of the silver trees intensified. A subtle vibration passed through the ground beneath their feet, growing stronger by the moment.

"Sentinel approaches," Yrsa announced, her expression grim. "More than one. We've drawn their attention."

Asvarr turned to Brynja. "Come with us to Starfall Mountain. See what happens when I bind the third anchor."

"See what you become, you mean." Her mouth twisted. "I've already witnessed too many transformations, Flame-Warden." Her wooden fingers flexed. "Besides, I have my own path now."

"What path?" Asvarr demanded.

"The third way." She smiled—the expression uncanny on her half-transformed face "Not restoration, nor destruction. Something else."

Before he could respond, a flash of silver-blue light tore through the canopy above. The rogue Sentinel had found them, joined now by two others. They streaked through the sky like hunting falcons, their light cutting through the grove's metallic foliage.

"We must go!" Yrsa seized Asvarr's arm. "The mountain path—now!"

"Brynja?" Asvarr called, but she was already backing away, her form merging with the shadow cast by a massive silver trunk.

"Find me in Muspelheim when your bones are crystal and your blood runs with starlight," she called, her voice fading. "If you survive the third binding, if you still remember your name, I'll tell you the rest."

"I need to know now!" Asvarr lunged toward her, but Yrsa's grip was surprisingly strong.

"She can't tell you what she doesn't fully understand," Yrsa hissed. "The Severed Bloom fragment within her knows pieces, but not the whole."

The Sentinels spiraled downward, their light intensifying as they located their quarry. The silver trees began to bend inward, their branches curving to intercept the celestial hunters—offering momentary protection.

"How do I find you?" Asvarr called after Brynja's retreating form.

"The oath-sigil will guide you," her voice drifted back. "If anything of you remains after starlight remakes your flesh."

She vanished into the metallic shadows, leaving only the echo of her strange laughter. The withered oath-sigil on Asvarr's palm burned suddenly, a shooting pain that traveled up his arm and into his chest.

***

"Now!" Yrsa pulled him toward the southern path. "The trees buy us time, but not much."

Asvarr allowed himself to be dragged away, the bronze sword at his hip humming with tension. Above, the Sentinels fought against the silver canopy, their light fragmenting through the metallic leaves.

"Why would she come all this way just to leave again?" he demanded as they ran, the branches of his crown scraping against low-hanging boughs.

"To warn you," Yrsa replied, her breathing steady despite their pace. "And to see if you still follow the path she abandoned." She cast him a sidelong glance.

"She carries the Severed Bloom fragment—the first Root to rebel against control. It chose her bloodline for a reason."

They emerged from the densest part of the grove onto a path that wound between silver trunks toward a distant peak—Starfall Mountain, its crystal summit catching and fracturing the light of the approaching twin moons.

"She spoke of a prison," Asvarr said, his mind racing to process Brynja's fragmented warnings. "That the Tree restrains rather than sustains. What could the Tree possibly imprison that would frighten gods?"

Yrsa's expression closed. "We all carry pieces of truth, Flame-Warden. None holds the complete pattern." She touched her crystal pendant, which had begun to glow brighter as they neared the mountain. "The starlight anchor will show you more than I can tell. If you survive its binding."

The ground trembled beneath their feet. A resonance that came from beneath Allheim itself, as though something vast stirred in response to their discussion.

"Did you feel that?" Asvarr asked, slowing his pace.

"Don't stop," Yrsa urged. "We're being listened to."

"By what?"

"By what sleeps beneath the roots," she whispered, her gaze darting to the ground. "By what dreams beneath the Tree."

The tremor intensified momentarily, then subsided. Ahead, Starfall Mountain loomed larger, its crystal peak seeming to pulse in time with the approaching conjunction of the twin moons.

"Will the third binding wake it?" Asvarr asked, his voice barely audible.

"Not fully," Yrsa replied. "But it will notice you. All nine anchors must converge to break the restraints completely."

"Nine? You said five."

"Five we know of," Yrsa corrected. "The others lie hidden, waiting. Five anchors, nine fragments, one pattern."

The Sentinels' light flashed again, closer now. Their pursuit had broken through the silver canopy. Asvarr and Yrsa increased their pace, racing toward the mountain's looming presence.

As they ran, Asvarr felt the withered oath-sigil on his palm pulse once more. Through it came a final whispered warning from Brynja, carried across the bond they still shared:

"Remember who you are when starlight fills your veins. Remember your name when memory becomes stardust. The third binding will show you truth you never wanted to see, and you will never be human again."

The verdant crown upon his head tightened in response, branches digging into his scalp until golden sap ran down his temples. The anchors within him—flame and memory—resonated in disharmonious tension, preparing for the third to join their chorus.

Above, the twin moons drew closer to alignment, their combined light casting bizarre shadows that moved independent of their sources. The time of conjunction approached, and with it, the moment of binding.

Whatever waited at Starfall Mountain's peak, Asvarr knew with bone-deep certainty that Brynja was right about one thing: after the third anchor, nothing would ever be the same again.

CHAPTER 4

THE GARDEN OF MEMORY-STARS

Asvarr's lungs burned as he and Yrsa crested the final rise before Starfall Mountain's northern slope. Behind them, silver streaks cut through Alfheim's night sky—Sentinels still in pursuit, though more distant now. The twin moons hung suspended above, their convergence slowing as though time itself stretched to accommodate some cosmic purpose.

"Wait." Yrsa seized his arm, her grip firm. Her crystal pendant pulsed with renewed blue light. "Someone approaches."

Asvarr drew his bronze sword, the golden veins beneath its surface blazing to match his racing heartbeat. The branches of his crown shifted, scraping against his scalp as they contracted around his skull—a warning system more reliable than any scout.

A figure emerged from the shadows of a crystalline outcropping, silhouetted against the dual moonlight. Asvarr raised his blade, the flame anchor within him surging with defensive heat.

"Lower your weapon, Warden of Root and Flame." The voice belonged to Istari Stellarum. The astronomer stepped forward, his galaxy-eyes reflecting the cosmos above. "I've been waiting for you."

Asvarr kept his sword raised. "You sent the Sentinels after us."

"I redirected them." Istari gestured toward the distant silver lights, now circling a formation far to the east. "Temporarily. They'll return once they realize the deception."

Yrsa studied him, her weathered face tight with suspicion. "How did you reach this place before us?"

"There are paths known only to those who have studied Alfheim's night sky for millennia." His gaze shifted to Asvarr's verdant crown, now visibly spreading down his neck and across his shoulders. "The starlight anchor calls to you already. I can see its influence in your transformation."

The crystalline formations at Asvarr's temples had grown, catching moonlight and fracturing it into prismatic shards that danced across his vision. He felt the third anchor's pull—a cold, mathematical certainty unlike the fierce burn of flame or the resonate hum of memory.

"Why help us?" Asvarr demanded, lowering his blade slightly but maintaining his guard. The branches of his crown creaked with his movement.

"Because I wish to know what lies beyond the pattern." Istari's pupils expanded, galaxies swirling within their depths. "Nine cycles I've watched the stars shift and restore. Nine cycles of the same prison strengthening and weakening in turn." His voice dropped. "I want to see what happens when someone finally chooses the third path."

Yrsa's crystal pendant flared suddenly. "The conjunction pauses. We have more time than I anticipated."

"The pattern adjusts," Istari explained. "It seldom unfolds the same way twice. This cycle proceeds differently from those before." He extended a hand toward Asvarr. "Will you trust me enough to show you something? Something the Stellar Council would execute me for revealing?"

Asvarr glanced at Yrsa, who nodded almost imperceptibly. He sheathed his sword, the golden veins beneath the metal's surface pulsing with residual tension.

"Show me."

Istari led them along a hidden path that wound between crystal formations jutting from Starfall Mountain's lower slope. The stones hummed with subtle vibration, the sound intensifying as they progressed. Above, the twin moons hung motionless, their alignment paused in cosmic suspension.

"The Stellar Council believes they control all knowledge of what came before," Istari said as they walked. "They believe knowledge carefully curated is knowledge safely contained." His galaxy-eyes flicked toward the distant Sentinels. "Those entities you flee aren't guardians of the mountain. They're censors, erasing what must never be remembered."

They reached a narrow cleft in the mountainside, barely wide enough for a single person to pass. Beyond lay darkness absolute—a void cut into reality itself.

"This passage has existed since the First Dawn," Istari explained. "Before elves, before the Tree. It leads to one of the few places in Alfheim the Sentinels cannot enter."

"Why not?" Asvarr asked, eyeing the darkness with instinctive wariness.

"Because what grows there remembers them. And they fear being remembered." Istari stepped into the void.

***

Asvarr followed, his crown of branches scraping against the narrow walls. The darkness swallowed him completely, cutting off all sensory input for three jarring heartbeats. Then light returned—soft, silver, impossibly distant yet immediately present.

He stumbled forward into a hidden valley cradled between Starfall Mountain's crystal spires. The bowl-shaped depression stretched before him, illuminated by thousands of suspended lights that drifted like dandelion seeds caught in an unfelt breeze. Above, the sky appeared different—closer somehow, stars moving with more deliberate patterns than elsewhere in Alfheim.

And they were falling.

Every few moments, a star would detach from the firmament and descend, trailing silver fire. Instead of burning out or crashing destructively, each settled gently into the valley floor, where it nestled among plants unlike any Asvarr had ever seen.

"The Garden of Memory-Stars," Istari said, his voice hushed with reverence. "One of nine such gardens scattered across the realms."

Asvarr moved forward in stunned silence. The plants growing throughout the valley defied categorization—neither tree nor flower nor shrub, but something that combined aspects of all three. Their structures shifted subtly as he watched, branches unfurling and petals closing only to reopen in different configurations. Each bore glowing fruit that pulsed with internal light, colors shifting through spectrums both familiar and alien.

"What are they?" Asvarr asked, the verdant crown upon his head rustling in response to their proximity.

"Memory made manifest." Istari gestured toward a falling star, which drifted to earth near their position. Where it touched the soil, a new growth immediately sprouted—unfurling from seedling to mature plant in moments, its fruit already swelling with captured light. "Each star that falls contains fragments of cosmic memory. The gardens preserve what would otherwise be lost when stars burn out."

Movement caught Asvarr's eye. Figures glided between the strange plants—elves unlike any he'd seen before. Their skin gleamed like polished obsidian, reflecting starlight rather than absorbing it. They wore no clothing, their bodies covered instead in swirling patterns of luminescence that shifted with their movements. Most striking were their eyes—pupilless orbs of pure silver that seemed to look through reality rather than at it.

"The caretakers," Istari explained. "They've tended these gardens since before my people learned to build shelters. Before the Tree reached through reality. They harvest the star-fruit when it ripens, preserving the memories within."

One of the caretakers approached, moving with fluid grace that suggested joints different from those of any creature Asvarr had encountered. It carried a basket woven from what appeared to be solidified light, filled with fruits of various sizes and colors.

"They don't speak," Istari warned as the figure drew near. "At least, not with words."

The caretaker stopped before them, its silver eyes fixing on Asvarr's verdant crown. It tilted its head at an angle physically impossible for normal anatomy, then extended the basket toward him. Inside, the fruits pulsed with synchronized light—a deliberate pattern.

"It recognizes what you carry," Yrsa murmured, her expression caught between wonder and apprehension. "The anchors."

The caretaker's free hand rose to touch its own chest, then extended toward Asvarr in a fluid gesture. Its finger pointed directly at the withered oath-sigil on his palm.

"It asks if you seek knowledge," Istari translated. "The fruit offers memory, but always at a price. What is given cannot be unuttered."

Asvarr studied the basket's contents. The fruits varied in both form and illumination—some blazed with fierce white light, others pulsed with gentler radiance, still others spiraled through rainbow hues in complex sequences.

"What would it show me?" he asked.

"That depends on which you choose." Istari's galaxy-eyes reflected the fruit's glow. "Each star falls with its own story. Some contain memories of creation, others of destruction. Some hold knowledge of what came before the Tree."

The caretaker moved its hand in another impossible gesture, silver eyes never blinking.

"It says you already carry fragments," Istari continued. "The flame anchor preserves what was. The memory anchor connects what is. The star anchor—" He paused, searching for words. "It would translate what will be."

"And what about what must never be?" Asvarr asked, Brynja's warning echoing in his thoughts. "What about what sleeps beneath the roots?"

The effect was immediate and alarming. Every caretaker in the garden froze in place, their silver eyes suddenly blazing with furious light. The fruits in their baskets flared painfully bright, then dimmed to sullen ember-glow.

The caretaker before them lifted its hand, pointing directly at the sky. Asvarr followed its gesture to where the sky-serpents still coiled protectively around specific constellations, their luminous bodies forming barriers of light.

"They guard the memory," Istari whispered. "What you speak of... it's one of the Nine Great Forgettings."

"The what?" Asvarr demanded.

Yrsa's crystal pendant pulsed with warning light. "Cosmic events deliberately removed from memory. Wounds in reality stitched closed and left to heal." Her expression hardened. "Or to fester."

The caretaker lowered its arm, then reached into its basket and selected a fruit unlike the others. Where most glowed with starlight, this one absorbed it—a perfect sphere of deepest indigo that bent light around its surface. It extended the fruit toward Asvarr with a gesture that somehow conveyed both offering and warning.

"I wouldn't," Istari cautioned, his voice tight with sudden fear. "That's a void-memory. It shows what existed before stars."

"Before the Tree," Yrsa added. "Before pattern."

Asvarr studied the strange fruit, feeling the anchors within him respond to its proximity. The flame anchor burned with defensive heat, while the memory anchor hummed with recognition. Most surprising was his awareness of the star anchor not yet bound—a cold pressure at the base of his skull, drawing him toward the fruit with mathematical certainty.

The caretaker made another gesture, this one directed at Asvarr's verdant crown. The branches shifted in response, golden sap beading at their tips.

"It says the branching-one already knows but doesn't remember," Istari translated, his galaxy-eyes wide. "It asks if you wish to remember what you've always known."

"I don't understand," Asvarr said.

"None of us do," Yrsa interjected. "That's why the Wardens exist. To remember what must never be forgotten, even as it's erased from cosmic memory."

The caretaker placed the void-fruit back in its basket, then selected another—this one a spiraling structure that glowed with gentle amber light. It offered this instead, its gesture less urgent but equally deliberate.

"A safer beginning," Istari explained. "It will show how the gardens came to be, before revealing deeper truths."

Asvarr reached for the fruit, but Yrsa caught his wrist.

"Once taken, memory cannot be unlearned," she warned. "Each binding transforms you. Each truth reshapes what remains of your humanity."

Asvarr glanced around the garden, watching the caretakers move between their strange plants. The falling stars continued their gentle descent, each sprouting new growth where it touched the earth. Above, the twin moons remained frozen in near-conjunction, waiting.

"I need to understand what I'm binding myself to," he decided. "What the anchors truly represent."

He took the spiraling amber fruit from the caretaker's obsidian hand. The moment his fingers touched its surface, the fruit liquefied, flowing up his arm like living metal. It penetrated his flesh without pain, golden spirals spreading beneath his skin to merge with the patterns of his transformed body.

***

Knowledge flooded his mind as sensory impressions, emotions, and fragmented images. He saw the void before stars, felt the first light cutting through nothingness, tasted the birth of matter from energy. The experiences overwhelmed his senses, dropping him to his knees in the garden's soft soil.

Through the chaos of impressions, a pattern emerged. Nine gardens, nine anchors, nine cycles. The caretakers tending the memory-stars since before consciousness itself had formed. The careful cultivation of knowledge, harvested and preserved against forces that sought to consume all record of what came before.

And beneath it all, something vast stirring in twilight spaces between reality—dreaming of freedom, of consumption, of returning to the formlessness that preceded existence.

The vision receded gradually, leaving Asvarr gasping on the garden floor. The caretaker stood over him, its silver eyes reflecting his transformed face back at him.

The branches of his crown had extended further, now reaching past his shoulders and down his back. The crystalline formations at his temples had spread across his forehead, forming patterns like frozen lightning.

"What did you see?" Yrsa helped him to his feet, her expression tight with concern.

"The beginning," Asvarr managed, his voice raw. "Before the Tree. Before gods." He turned to Istari. "The gardens preserve what the Sentinels erase—truth the Stellar Council fears."

Istari nodded slowly. "The Council believes some knowledge is too dangerous to exist in accessible form. The caretakers disagree. Thus, the gardens."

The caretaker made another series of impossible gestures, its silver eyes fixed on Asvarr's.

"It asks if you would know more," Istari translated. "If you would taste the void-memory now that you understand the context."

Asvarr glanced at the basket, where the indigo sphere still bent light around its perfect surface. The anchors within him pulled toward it with undeniable force—recognition beyond conscious thought.

Before he could respond, a tremor passed through the garden. The plants swayed, their fruit flaring with sudden brilliance. Above, the twin moons shuddered in their suspended position, edging fractionally closer to conjunction.

"Someone approaches the mountain," Yrsa warned, her pendant blazing with blue warning light. "Something powerful enough to disrupt the pattern's pause."

The caretaker gestured urgently, pointing toward a path that wound deeper into the garden, where the strangest plants grew in structured geometric patterns.

"It offers shelter," Istari explained. "And knowledge we'll need before the conjunction completes."

Asvarr felt the star anchor's pull intensify, a cold certainty directing him toward the mountain's crystal peak. The caretaker offered its basket again, the void-memory now floating at its top.

"We don't have time," Yrsa insisted. "The conjunction resumes. We must reach the anchor before alignment completes."

The caretaker's silver eyes flashed with what Asvarr somehow recognized as frustrated urgency. It selected the void-memory and pressed it directly against his chest, where the Grímmark lay beneath his tunic. Though the fruit didn't break, Asvarr felt its essence seep into him—a cold knowledge that settled in his marrow, waiting.

Istari watched with wide galaxy-eyes. "It's given you the memory without showing it to you," he whispered. "It will unfold when you need it most."

Another tremor shook the garden, stronger than before. The falling stars paused in mid-descent, hanging suspended like frozen tears. The caretakers moved with sudden purpose, gathering their baskets and gliding toward the shelter of the deepest plants.

"We must go," Yrsa urged, pulling Asvarr toward a path that led back to the mountain slope. "Whatever approaches, the caretakers fear it enough to hide their harvest."

Asvarr nodded, the new knowledge settling into his transformed flesh. The void-memory pulsed within him, a cold weight waiting to be acknowledged. He followed Yrsa, glancing back once at the caretaker who had gifted him the fruit.

The obsidian figure stood watching, its silver eyes reflecting the suspended stars. It made one final gesture—touching its heart, then pointing to the sky where serpents coiled around hidden constellations, then pressing its hands together as though closing a book.

"What did it say?" Asvarr asked Istari, who hurried alongside them.

"That some truths reveal themselves only when they must," the astronomer replied. "And that what you carry will show you the war before the Tree when you're ready to remember it."

The verdant crown tightened around Asvarr's skull, branches digging into his flesh until golden sap trickled down his temples. The void-memory pulsed once more within him, then went dormant—a seed planted in fertile soil, waiting to bloom.

Above, the twin moons shuddered again, resuming their inexorable drift toward conjunction.

They ascended the mountain path, Istari leading them through passages only visible to those who understood Alfheim's celestial geometries. The twin moons inched closer to conjunction overhead, their combined light casting prismatic shadows that shifted and elongated with each step. The void-memory pulsed within Asvarr's chest like a second heartbeat, foreign yet increasingly familiar.

"We should move faster," Yrsa urged, her crystal pendant flaring with warning light. "Whatever approaches gains ground."

Asvarr paused, the branches of his crown scraping against an outcropping of crystal. The garden receded behind them, already half-hidden by the mountain's curve. Something tugged at his awareness—a pattern demanding recognition.

"Wait." He turned back, studying the arrangement of the memory-stars as they fell into the garden below. They weren't random. Their descent formed geometric shapes that repeated with mathematical precision. "There's a message in their fall."

Istari followed his gaze, galaxy-eyes widening. "You see it already? The star anchor influences you before binding."

"What do you see?" Yrsa asked, her weathered face tightening with concern.

Asvarr couldn't articulate the pattern precisely, but it resonated with the cold pressure at the base of his skull—the third anchor calling. "Something's missing from the garden. Something the caretakers want us to find."

Before either could respond, the void-memory flared within his chest, releasing a pulse of knowledge that dropped him to his knees. The world around him dissolved, replaced by visions that tore through his consciousness with brutal clarity.

Primordial darkness. Potential—unformed, unbound by law or structure. Through this void moved entities beyond comprehension: vast serpents of living starlight coiling through nothingness, their bodies stretching across dimensions, their thoughts slower than the birth and death of galaxies.

Asvarr gasped for breath, the verdant crown contracting painfully around his skull. Golden sap beaded at his temples, dripping onto the crystalline path.

The serpents weren't alone. Angular beings of pure geometry moved through reality by folding space itself—entities made of perfect mathematics, their consciousness a calculation extending to infinity. They observed the serpents' freedom with what might be called envy, if such beings could experience emotion.

"Asvarr?" Yrsa's voice came from impossibly far away. "The void-memory awakens. Fight through it, don't let it consume you."

War erupted for the fundamental nature of existence. The serpents fought for endless possibility, movement without constraint; the angular beings for perfect order, reality bound by immutable law. Their conflict tore holes in the fabric of potential, creating the first fixed points in what would become space-time.

The vision shifted, showing impossible geometries collapsing into more recognizable forms. Asvarr felt the knowledge pouring into him, filling spaces created by his previous bindings—flame and memory making room for star.

From this war, consciousness emerged—the first awareness separate from the combatants themselves. It watched, it learned, and it grew fearful. Neither infinite freedom nor perfect order could sustain what was becoming. A third option must exist.

Asvarr found himself floating in formless space, watching as a small light kindled between warring forces—a seed of potential different from anything that came before. It grew, extending threadlike connections in all directions.

The first root formed, then branched. Grown—a weapon fashioned from the stuff of both order and chaos. It spread through primordial darkness, reaching toward the serpents and geometric entities alike, offering connection rather than dominance.

The vision expanded, showing the root system expanding throughout nascent reality. Where it touched, structure formed—but flexible, evolving, alive. The angular beings recoiled, retreating to spaces between dimensions. The serpents responded differently, some fleeing beyond the root's reach, others allowing themselves to be touched, transformed, bound.

But one serpent, vaster than the others, fought with primordial fury. It coiled through nothingness, consuming everything in its path—including its own kind. As it fed, it grew, becoming something beyond even cosmic understanding. Its hunger threatened to unravel the fragile pattern being woven throughout existence.

Asvarr watched in horror as the entity devoured light, matter, potential itself—a void-hunger that could consume reality before it fully formed. The roots responded, growing with desperate speed, surrounding the entity from all directions.

Nine root-anchors formed, extending from what would become Yggdrasil—the World Tree connecting Nine Realms. They did not nurture. They did not sustain. They imprisoned, binding the void-hunger in layers of reality so complex it could never break free.

The vision zoomed outward, showing the completed structure—a cosmic tree with nine realms suspended among its branches, nine anchors driven deep through its roots. At its center, barely visible through layers of binding, slumbered the void-hunger—dreaming of freedom, of consumption, of returning everything to the primordial chaos from which it came.

The gods emerged later—beings born from the pattern itself, claiming credit for creation they merely inherited. They named the tree Yggdrasil, claimed the realms as their domain, and forgot—deliberately or otherwise—what slumbered at its heart.

With brutal suddenness, the vision collapsed. Asvarr found himself face-down on the crystal path, his body wracked with tremors. The verdant crown had tightened to the point of drawing blood, golden sap mixing with crimson as it trickled down his face. The crystalline formations at his temples had expanded, now covering the upper half of his face in patterns resembling frozen lightning.

"Asvarr?" Yrsa knelt beside him, her crystal pendant hovering inches from his transformed flesh. "Can you hear me?"

He pushed himself upright, struggling to process what he'd witnessed. The void-memory still pulsed within him, but the most critical knowledge had already been absorbed. "The Tree," he gasped, voice raw. "It wasn't created to sustain life."

"No," Istari confirmed, his galaxy-eyes reflecting the twin moons' approach to conjunction. "It was grown to imprison what came before."

Asvarr struggled to his feet, swaying as new awareness settled into his transformed body. "The void-hunger. The entity that devours. That's what sleeps beneath the roots. That's what the anchors restrain."

Yrsa helped steady him, her weathered hand surprisingly strong. "Now you understand the true purpose of the Wardens. To maintain the prison that holds what must never escape."

"And the starlight anchor? What role does it play?" Asvarr gestured toward the mountain's crystalline peak, now glowing with reflected moonlight.

"Transformation," Istari replied. "The flame anchor preserves, the memory anchor connects, the starlight anchor transforms." He pointed to the twin moons, now alarmingly close to conjunction. "It sits between worlds, between states—neither wholly of matter nor energy, but something that can shift between."

Another tremor shook the mountain beneath them, stronger than before. Cracks formed in the crystal path, golden light seeping through from somewhere deep below.

"We must hurry," Yrsa urged. "The conjunction approaches its zenith."

Asvarr nodded, forcing his leaden limbs to move. The vision had changed him fundamentally, altering his understanding of his own purpose. Each binding revealed more of the cosmic truth, even as it transformed him into something less human and more pattern.

As they climbed higher, the air thinned, taking on a metallic taste that coated Asvarr's tongue. The crystalline formations on his face spread further with each step, resonating with the mountain itself. He felt the starlight anchor's call intensify—a cold, mathematical certainty directing him upward with inexorable purpose.

"What happens when I bind all five anchors?" he asked, voicing the question that had haunted him since the Garden of Memory-Stars. "What do I become?"

Yrsa and Istari exchanged glances laden with unspoken meaning.

"No one has bound all five in nine cycles," Yrsa finally answered. "The transformation becomes too complete. The vessel loses what makes it individual, becoming merely an extension of the pattern."

"Even the Ashfather only bound three before his transformation overtook him," Istari added. "He sought the fourth in Helheim and lost himself in the attempt."

Asvarr absorbed this in silence, the branches of his crown shifting with his troubled thoughts. The void-memory pulsed again, offering another fragment of knowledge—a glimpse of nine previous cycles, nine previous attempts, nine failures to maintain the prison through full restoration or complete breaking.

"The third path," he murmured. "Transformation rather than restoration or destruction."

"Your path," Yrsa confirmed. "Neither to control the pattern as the Ashfather attempted, nor to surrender to it as the Five require."

"But to become something new," Istari finished. "Something that has never existed through nine cycles of breaking and binding."

***

They crested a ridge and found themselves staring across a vast plateau near Starfall Mountain's summit. The crystal surface reflected the twin moons' light, creating an illusion of standing among the stars themselves. At the plateau's center rested a structure unlike anything Asvarr had seen before—neither building nor growth, but something between states.

"The Cradle," Istari whispered, reverential awe filling his voice. "Where the starlight anchor waits."

Hovering several feet above the crystal surface, the structure appeared simultaneously solid and ephemeral. Its architecture defied conventional geometry, with doorways that led into themselves and staircases becoming möbius strips. It pulsed with internal light that matched the rhythm of the approaching conjunction, silver-blue radiance cycling through its impossible form.

"It's not in this realm," Asvarr realized, the crystalline formations on his face resonating with the structure's energy. "Not fully."

"It exists between Alfheim and the void beyond," Yrsa explained. "Built from celestial ore that negates gravity, it drifts in perpetual orbit around the silver moons."

As they watched, the structure shimmered, briefly showing its true nature—a temple floating in the void between worlds, tethered to reality by threads of pure starlight. Then it solidified again, its appearance conforming more closely to comprehensible architecture.

"How do we reach it?" Asvarr asked, noting the gap between the crystal plateau and the hovering structure.

Istari produced a silver vial from within his robes. "Distilled starlight. It temporarily transforms flesh into something closer to the stuff of constellations. It will allow you to bridge the gap between states."

Asvarr accepted the vial, its contents swirling with internal light. The anchors within him responded to its proximity—flame with defensive heat, memory with resonant recognition, and the unclaimed starlight anchor with mathematical certainty.

"What will happen when I bind the third anchor?" he asked, studying the vial's shifting contents.

"The starlight anchor will show you the path forward," Yrsa said. "But at greater cost than the previous bindings. The flame anchor took your rage, the memory anchor your identity. The starlight anchor requires transformation itself—neither fully human nor wholly pattern, but something between states."

"Like Leif," Asvarr realized suddenly. "That's why he exists across multiple points in the pattern. He's not bound by singular reality."

"Born in the space between breaking and binding," Istari confirmed. "A possibility that exists only because the pattern fractured. The anchors will reshape you similarly, if you survive the binding."

Another tremor shook the plateau, more violent than before. Cracks spread across the crystal surface, golden light bleeding through from deep below. The

Cradle shimmered in response, its form wavering between states as the twin moons inched closer to perfect conjunction.

"What pursues us?" Asvarr demanded, sensing the approaching presence growing stronger.

"The void-hunger stirs," Yrsa replied, her pendant flaring with warning light. "It senses the anchors moving, the pattern shifting. Each binding weakens its prison by altering the structure that contains it."

"Then why bind them at all?" Asvarr asked, frustration edging his voice. "If each binding risks releasing what the Tree imprisons?"

"Because the prison already fails," Istari said. "Nine cycles of partial restoration and breaking have weakened it beyond recovery. The tenth cycle must end differently, or the void-hunger escapes regardless."

The revelation settled into Asvarr with cold certainty. There was no path backward, no restoration that could return the Tree to its original strength. The only way forward lay through transformation—becoming something the pattern had never known, finding a third option neither the serpents nor the angular entities had imagined.

"The conjunction reaches its peak," Yrsa warned, pointing to the twin moons now almost perfectly aligned. "You must decide now."

Asvarr uncorked the vial, the distilled starlight within pulsing with hypnotic rhythm. The branches of his crown tightened around his skull, golden sap trickling down his face. The crystalline formations spread further, now covering most of his features in patterns resembling frozen lightning. He felt himself balancing between states—human and pattern, matter and energy, flesh and starlight.

The plateau shuddered beneath them, cracks widening to reveal glimpses of golden roots far below—the Tree's deep structure exposed by the cosmic disturbance. Through those glimpses, Asvarr sensed something vast stirring from eons of slumber, its awareness expanding outward with hunger beyond comprehension.

"It comes," Istari warned, his galaxy-eyes wide with fear. "The void-hunger wakes."

Asvarr lifted the vial to his lips, the contents shimmering with possibility. Brynja's warning echoed in his thoughts: *Remember who you are when starlight fills your veins. Remember your name when memory becomes stardust.*

"I am Asvarr, Flame-Warden, Memory-Keeper," he declared, his voice resonating with power drawn from the two anchors already bound. "I choose the third path."

He drank the distilled starlight in a single swallow, and the world dissolved around him into cosmic radiance.

CHAPTER 5
THE CRADLE ABOVE THE MOON

The distilled starlight burned through Asvarr's veins like liquid frost, transforming flesh into something neither solid nor ephemeral. His fingers rippled with cosmic light, skin becoming translucent then opaque in rhythmic pulses that matched the twin moons' approach to perfect alignment. The verdant crown upon his head shuddered, branches extending upward toward Alfheim's impossible sky as though yearning for home.

"It hurts." The words emerged as crystalline fragments that hung in the air before him, glittering with internal light before dissolving into prismatic dust.

"Transformation always does," Yrsa replied, her voice distorted as though traveling across vast distances. She had consumed only three drops of the distilled starlight, enough to witness but not fully transform. Her weathered form remained mostly solid, only the edges of her silhouette blurring into starlit mist.

Istari stood several paces away, galaxy-eyes fixed on the hovering Cradle. "The conjunction peaks in moments," he said. "When the moons align, the way will open."

Asvarr's transformed perception revealed new dimensions to the crystal plateau beneath his feet. What had appeared solid now showed itself as a lattice of energy—mathematical patterns extending downward through Starfall Mountain into Alfheim's core, where golden roots pulsed with restrained power. Through these patterns, he sensed the void-hunger stirring in its prison of interwoven reality.

"It knows I'm here," he said, the words fracturing into luminous shards. "It feels the anchors moving."

"Focus on the Cradle," Yrsa commanded. "The binding must complete before the hunger fully wakes."

Asvarr lifted his gaze to the floating temple. With his transformed sight, its true nature became apparent—a structure existing in multiple dimensions simultaneously, its architecture folding through spaces his mind struggled to comprehend. Doorways led into themselves, staircases curved into möbius strips, and the entire structure pulsed with silver-blue radiance that drew him upward with mathematical certainty.

The twin moons inched closer to perfect conjunction, their combined light intensifying until the crystal plateau blazed like a mirror reflecting distant suns. Asvarr felt his transformed body growing lighter, the gravity of Alfheim loosening its hold as the distilled starlight rewrote the fundamental rules binding him to singular reality.

"How do I reach it?" he asked, watching the gap between the plateau and the hovering temple.

"The same way stars cross the void." Istari gestured toward the aligned moons. "Through intention made manifest."

As the conjunction reached its apex, a bridge of pure light formed between the plateau and the Cradle—not solid but suggestive, a possibility rather than a physical structure. Asvarr understood instinctively that it would support him only if he accepted complete transformation, surrendering the last illusion of physicality.

"Will I come back?" he asked Yrsa, the branches of his crown now extending past his shoulders and down his back, forming patterns that pulsed with the bridge's rhythm.

"Not unchanged," she replied, her pendant flaring with blue warning light. "The star anchor demands transformation itself. You will return, but what returns may wear your name and face while being something more."

"Or less," Istari added, his galaxy-eyes reflecting the aligned moons. "The starlight anchor balances between states—preserving what must survive while transforming what cannot remain unchanged."

Another tremor shook the crystal plateau, more violent than before. Cracks spread through the lattice-structure Asvarr now perceived, golden light bleeding upward from deep below. The void-hunger stirred more forcefully, drawn by the anchors' proximity and the weakening prison of nine cycles.

"Time grows short," Yrsa warned. "The pattern unravels."

Asvarr took a step toward the light-bridge, his transformed flesh separating slightly from itself—molecules drifting apart like stars in an expanding galaxy, held together only by intention and the anchors' power. He felt the flame anchor burning within him, preserving what remained human. The memory anchor hummed with recognition of the starlight's mathematical patterns. And beyond it all, the third anchor called with inexorable certainty.

"The Cradle contains more than the anchor," Istari said, his voice threaded with urgency. "It holds knowledge the Stellar Council has hidden for nine cycles—truth about what came before the Tree, before the gods. About what sleeps beneath the roots."

"And what dwells beyond branches," Yrsa added. "Knowledge that bridges nine broken cycles into a tenth that might end differently."

Asvarr's gaze fixed on the hovering temple—its impossible geometry shifting and refolding as the moons reached perfect conjunction. At that moment, a section of the structure opened like an iris, revealing a chamber within that pulsed with silver-blue radiance.

"That's the anchor," he whispered, golden sap leaking from the corners of his mouth. "I can feel it."

"Not just the anchor," Istari corrected. "The Cradle itself was built by those who understood the pattern's true nature. The temple contains memories from before the breaking—from all nine cycles."

The information registered in Asvarr's transforming consciousness. He thought of Brynja's warning: *Remember who you are when starlight fills your veins. Remember your name when memory becomes stardust.* The verdant crown tightened around his skull, branches digging into flesh until blood mixed with golden sap. The crystalline formations on his face resonated with the Cradle's energy, patterns expanding across his features like frozen lightning.

"I'm ready," he declared, taking another step toward the light-bridge. His foot passed through the crystal plateau without resistance, flesh now sufficiently transformed to ignore conventional boundaries.

"Wait," Yrsa called, hurrying forward. From a pouch at her belt, she withdrew an object wrapped in cloth that glimmered with contained power. "Take this."

She placed it in Asvarr's semi-solid hand—a small crystal no larger than his thumbnail, clear as water yet containing swirling patterns resembling galaxies in miniature.

"What is it?" he asked, feeling the crystal pulse with recognition of his transformed state.

"A fragment from my pendant," Yrsa explained. "It will help you remember yourself when starlight fills your awareness. A boundary-stone between states."

Asvarr closed his fingers around the crystal, feeling it merge partially with his transformed flesh, integrating, becoming a fixed point in his increasingly fluid existence. The branches of his crown shifted in response, several curling protectively around his hand.

"The starlight anchor is guarded," Istari warned, glancing anxiously at the cracks spreading across the plateau. "Beings formed of living constellation patterns protect its chamber. They test all who approach, allowing passage only to those who demonstrate complete harmony between spoken intent and inner truth."

"What happens if I fail?" Asvarr asked, the question fragmenting into crystalline shards before his eyes.

"Those who fail remain in the Cradle," Yrsa replied. "Neither alive nor dead, but frozen between moments—between heartbeats. The guardians preserve them as warnings to those who follow."

Asvarr absorbed this information, feeling the anchors within him respond. The flame anchor burned defensively, preserving what remained of his humanity. The memory anchor hummed with recognition, preparing to connect him to the star anchor's transformative power.

"I sought restoration," he said, watching his words crystallize before dissolving into mist. "Then transformation. What do I seek now?"

"The third path," Yrsa answered. "Balance between what was and what must be. Preservation of pattern without imprisonment of potential."

The crystal plateau shuddered again, cracks widening to reveal glimpses of golden roots far below. Through his transformed perception, Asvarr sensed the void-hunger's growing awareness—ancient beyond comprehension, patient beyond measure, hungry beyond satiation. Nine cycles of partial restoration and breaking had weakened its prison to the breaking point. The tenth cycle would end differently, or it would end entirely.

"Go," Istari urged, his galaxy-eyes wide with fear and wonder. "The conjunction holds for moments only. The Cradle will drift beyond reach when the moons separate."

Asvarr nodded, feeling the branches of his crown bob with the movement. He stepped fully onto the light-bridge, his transformed body responding to its immaterial nature. Gravity released him completely, leaving only intention to direct his movement. He thought upward, and his form drifted toward the hovering temple with dreamlike grace.

The light-bridge responded to his passage, rippling with patterns that matched those spreading across his face and body. The crystalline formations resonated with the structure's energy, drawing him forward with mathematical certainty. Beneath him, the crystal plateau receded, Yrsa and Istari becoming distant figures on a surface now revealed as merely the exposed tip of a vast cosmic calculation.

As he approached the Cradle, its architecture grew more complex, more impossible. Doorways opened onto chambers that couldn't physically fit within the structure's dimensions. Staircases folded into themselves, creating endless loops that somehow arrived at different destinations each cycle. Walls became transparent then solid in rhythmic pulses that matched his heartbeat—or perhaps his heart had begun to match the Cradle's rhythm.

***

The iris-like opening expanded as he drew near, revealing a chamber of pure starlight contained within geometric constraints. At its center floated a crystalline structure resembling a tree, something more fundamental than Yggdrasil's massive form, more mathematical. Its branches extended in precise angles, forming patterns Asvarr recognized from both the sky-serpents' movements and the angular entities from his vision of cosmic war.

"The starlight anchor," he whispered, the words dissolving into mist before him.

The Cradle pulsed in response, recognizing his approach. From within the iris-opening, figures began to materialize—beings formed of living constellation patterns, their bodies composed of stars connected by precisely angled lines of force. They emerged from the anchor chamber, taking positions around the entrance like sentinels guarding a sacred threshold.

"Boundary-crosser," they spoke in unison, their voices bypassing his ears to resonate directly within his transformed awareness. "Flame-Warden. Memory-Keeper. You seek the Starlight Anchor."

"I do," Asvarr confirmed, hovering before them on the edge of the light-bridge.

"It is not yours by right of birth," they continued, their constellation-bodies shifting to form new patterns. "Nor by right of strength. Nor by right of knowledge."

"I know," Asvarr replied. "I come seeking transformation, not possession."

The guardians' star-patterns shifted again, forming configurations that reminded Asvarr of the runes carved into standing stones near his village—ancient symbols predating even the gods' ascension.

"The anchor tests intent," they said. "It reveals disharmony between spoken word and inner truth. Those found wanting remain here, preserved as warnings to those who follow."

They parted slightly, allowing Asvarr to see past them into the anchor chamber. Along its walls hung suspended figures—previous seekers frozen in various stages of transformation. Some appeared nearly human, others had progressed further toward starlight's mathematical certainty. All remained locked in perfect stasis, neither alive nor dead but preserved between moments.

"To proceed requires specialized preparation," the guardians intoned. "Distilled starlight allows approach, but binding demands more."

One of the guardians drifted forward, its constellation-form reconfiguring into a complex pattern resembling the crystalline formations spreading across Asvarr's face. It extended what might be called a hand—a concentration of starpoints connected by lines of force.

"Show us what you carry," it commanded.

Asvarr opened his palm, revealing Yrsa's crystal fragment now partially merged with his transformed flesh. The guardian's constellation-pattern shifted in what might have been surprise.

"Boundary-stone," it acknowledged. "Useful, but insufficient."

Another guardian approached, its form changing to mirror the branches of Asvarr's verdant crown. "You carry flame and memory," it observed. "Two anchors bound. Those who came before carried fewer, yet failed."

"The Ashfather carried three," Asvarr said, remembering Istari's words. "And failed at the fourth."

"The one you name Ashfather sought dominance," the guardians replied in unison. "Control rather than communion. His pattern remains incomplete."

The first guardian extended its star-hand again. "The Cradle demands specialized preparation. You must drink deep of cosmic memory to bind the starlight anchor."

It directed Asvarr's attention to the chamber's center, where vessels of impossible geometry floated around the crystalline tree. Each contained liquid starlight more concentrated than what Istari had provided—purer, older, drawn from sources beyond mortal understanding.

"Those who drink become vessels themselves," the guardians warned. "Neither fully human nor wholly pattern, but something between states. The transformation cannot be undone."

Asvarr thought of Brynja's wooden transformation, of Leif existing simultaneously across multiple points in reality, of the Ashfather's three-anchor binding that left him twisted between states. Each step along this path moved him further from humanity toward something both more and less than mortal.

"What happens when I bind all five?" he asked, voicing the question that had haunted him since witnessing the void-memory's vision of cosmic war.

The guardians' constellation patterns shifted uneasily. "None has bound all five in nine cycles," they answered. "The answer remains unknown."

"The void-hunger stirs," Asvarr pressed. "The prison weakens with each cycle. What happens if all five bind in the tenth?"

The guardians remained silent for several heartbeats, their star-patterns pulsing with internal communication. Finally, the one mirroring Asvarr's crown spoke alone:

"The pattern completes. The prison either strengthens beyond breaking or dissolves completely. The tenth cycle ends differently—through transformation, not restoration or destruction."

Below, Asvarr sensed the crystal plateau cracking further, golden light from Yggdrasil's deep roots bleeding upward as the void-hunger pushed against nine cycles of weakening restraints. He felt the twin moons beginning to shift from perfect conjunction, the window of opportunity closing with each passing moment.

"I'm ready," he declared, the words crystallizing before dissolving into prismatic dust. "I choose the third path."

The guardians parted, creating an opening into the anchor chamber. "Enter," they intoned in unison. "Drink deep of cosmic memory. Become the vessel that bridges what was with what must be."

Asvarr drifted forward through the opening, leaving the light-bridge behind. Within the chamber, gravity reasserted itself in strange ways, pulling inward, drawing everything toward the crystalline tree at its center. The vessels of concentrated starlight orbited the anchor in complex patterns that folded through multiple dimensions simultaneously.

The guardians followed him into the chamber, their constellation forms reconfiguring to match the chamber's internal geometry. "Choose," they commanded, gesturing toward the orbiting vessels.

Asvarr studied them, feeling the anchors within him respond differently to each. The flame anchor recoiled from vessels glowing with cold blue light, while the memory anchor resonated with those pulsing amber and gold. The unclaimed starlight anchor pulled him toward a vessel containing liquid silver-white radiance that seemed to exist partly in this reality and partly beyond it.

He reached for this vessel, his transformed fingers passing through its impossible geometry to touch the concentrated starlight within. The liquid responded to his presence, swirling upward to meet his touch as though drawn by inevitable attraction.

"This one," he said, lifting the vessel from its orbital path. Its contents shifted continuously, forming and dissolving patterns that matched the crystalline formations spreading across his face.

"The choice is made," the guardians intoned. "Drink deep of cosmic memory. Bridge what was with what must be. Become the vessel that completes the pattern."

Asvarr raised the vessel to his lips, the concentrated starlight within pulsing with anticipation. Before drinking, he looked back toward the opening where the crystal plateau was now barely visible, cracks spreading across its surface as the void-hunger strained against its prison far below.

He thought of Brynja's warning: *Remember who you are when starlight fills your veins. Remember your name when memory becomes stardust.*

He thought of the nine cycles before, each ending in either partial restoration or incomplete breaking, the pattern weakening with each iteration.

He thought of the vision from the void-memory—cosmic serpents coiling through primordial nothingness, angular entities imposing mathematical order, and the Tree grown as weapon rather than nurturer.

He thought of his human name, his human flesh, his human purpose—all about to transform into something neither mortal nor divine but something between states.

"I am Asvarr," he declared, watching his words crystallize into geometric patterns before dissolving into the chamber's atmosphere. "Flame-Warden. Memory-Keeper."

Then he drank the concentrated starlight, accepting transformation itself.

The concentrated starlight seared through Asvarr's veins, transforming him at a molecular level. His awareness expanded exponentially, perception splitting across multiple dimensions simultaneously. For one terrifying moment, he forgot his own name, identity dissolving into cosmic patterns that stretched toward infinity.

Then Yrsa's crystal fragment pulsed within his transformed flesh, anchoring him to a singular point in the pattern. *I am Asvarr*, he reminded himself. *Flame-Warden. Memory-Keeper.* The words formed geometric structures in the air around him, crystallizing his identity into something the starlight anchor could recognize.

The chamber around him shifted, geometry rearranging as the guardians moved to surround the crystalline tree at its center. Their constellation bodies shimmered with internal light, stars connected by precisely angled lines that formed patterns resembling the runes he'd seen on ancient standing stones.

"The vessel transforms," they spoke in unison, their voices resonating directly in his consciousness. "Approach the anchor."

Asvarr drifted toward the crystalline tree, his transformed body responding to intention rather than physical movement. The structure grew more complex as he approached—branches extending in mathematically perfect angles, forming patterns that encoded cosmic knowledge beyond mortal comprehension.

Before he could reach it, the chamber's entrance irised open again. Through the opening drifted a figure he hadn't expected to see—Brynja, her wooden body transformed by what could only be another form of the distilled starlight. Her left arm, entirely wooden before, now contained patterns that precisely matched the constellations in the guardians' bodies. Her transformed eye whirled with cosmic patterns, while the human one widened in shock at the sight of him.

"Asvarr?" His name fractured from her lips into crystalline shards. "You've already begun the binding."

Behind her floated Yrsa, her form less drastically altered but still partially translucent, edges blurring into stardust. Her crystal pendant blazed with blue-white light that formed protective geometries around her.

"How did you find me?" Asvarr asked, his words forming and dissolving in the space between them.

"The oath-sigil guided me." Brynja raised her palm, showing the wooden spiral now inlaid with stellar patterns that pulsed in time with Asvarr's heartbeat. "I felt you drinking the starlight. I knew I had to witness."

The guardians shifted position, constellation patterns rearranging to accommodate the newcomers. They circled Brynja with particular interest, their star-forms reflecting in the constellation patterns embedded in her wooden flesh.

"Root-vessel," they addressed her. "Carrier of the Severed Bloom. You have no claim to this anchor."

"I make no claim," Brynja replied, the transformed portion of her face catching starlight in intricate patterns. "I come as witness."

The guardians' constellation forms shifted in what might have been skepticism. One moved closer, its pattern reconfiguring to match the thorn-runes carved into Brynja's wooden flesh. "Truth compelled," it observed. "The runes bind you to honesty. Unexpected. Useful."

Asvarr studied Brynja with his transformed perception. Her wooden transformation had evolved since their parting in the silver grove. The constellation patterns embedded in her arm and face had grown more complex, shifting in response to the chamber's energies. Most striking were the thorn-runes carved into her flesh—they glowed with golden light that pulsed with the rhythm of truth itself.

"Why are you really here?" he asked, suspicion tightening the branches of his crown.

Brynja met his gaze without flinching. "To ensure you remember your name when starlight fills your veins." Golden light blazed from her thorn-runes, confirming the truth of her words. "To see what the third binding reveals about the fifth."

The guardians drifted closer, their constellation patterns intensifying. "The binding approaches," they announced. "The vessel must be tested."

They surrounded Asvarr in a perfect circle, their star-forms connecting to create a complex geometric cage of light. Within this structure, he felt his awareness splitting further—consciousness expanding across multiple planes simultaneously while his physical form remained anchored in the chamber.

"To bind the starlight anchor requires perfect harmony between spoken intent and inner truth," the guardians intoned. "Those found wanting remain here, preserved as warnings to those who follow."

They gestured toward the frozen figures lining the chamber walls—previous seekers caught between transformation and binding, locked in perfect stasis. Asvarr felt the concentrated starlight shifting within him, seeking disharmony it could exploit to trap him similarly.

"We will test your claim through riddles," the guardians continued. "You must answer with both voice and thought simultaneously. Any dissonance between spoken word and inner belief will be detected."

The first guardian approached, its constellation form reconfiguring into patterns resembling the crystalline formations spreading across Asvarr's face. "First riddle: What do you seek?"

The question struck Asvarr as deceptively simple. He opened his mouth to answer, then hesitated. The concentrated starlight within him resonated with the question, revealing layers of complexity he hadn't immediately perceived. What did he truly seek? Restoration? Transformation? Something else entirely?

"I seek the third path," he finally answered, watching his words crystallize before dissolving into the chamber's atmosphere. "Balance between what was and what must be. Transformation that preserves essential nature while allowing evolution."

The guardian's constellation pattern shifted, stars realigning to reflect his answer. "Voice and thought align," it declared. "The vessel speaks truth."

Asvarr felt the concentrated starlight within him respond, flowing more smoothly through his transformed veins. The first test had been passed, but he sensed more difficult questions to come.

The second guardian approached, its form matching the branches of his verdant crown. "Second riddle: Why do you seek?"

Again, the seemingly simple question contained dangerous complexity. Why had he begun this journey? Vengeance for his destroyed clan? Duty to restore what was broken? Desire to understand his own transformation? The answers had evolved with each binding, his motivations shifting as the anchors reshaped his perception.

"I began seeking vengeance," he answered truthfully, the words forming geometric structures that revealed each facet of his intent. "I continued seeking restoration. I now seek transformation for the pattern itself. The prison weakens with each cycle. The tenth must end differently."

The guardian's star-pattern shifted again, assessing the harmony between his spoken words and inner beliefs. "Voice and thought align," it confirmed. "The vessel speaks truth."

The concentrated starlight flowed faster through Asvarr's transformed body, resonating with the crystalline tree at the chamber's center. The anchor responded to his presence, branches shifting subtly to align with the patterns forming across his flesh.

The third guardian approached, its constellation form more complex than the others, containing patterns Asvarr recognized from both the cosmic serpents and the angular entities from his void-memory vision. "Final riddle: What will you sacrifice?"

This question struck deepest. The flame anchor had taken his rage, the memory anchor his identity. What would the starlight anchor demand? What was he willing to surrender? The concentrated starlight within him surged, demanding an answer that contained no evasion, no qualification, only absolute truth.

Brynja drifted closer, her thorn-runes blazing with golden light. "Remember," she whispered, the word fragmenting between them.

Asvarr looked deep within himself, past the transformations already wrought by two anchor bindings, to what remained essentially human. The answer came with crystalline clarity—terrifying yet undeniable.

"I sacrifice my singularity," he declared, the words forming complex geometric structures that encoded every nuance of his meaning. "The illusion of separate existence. The comfort of limited perception. I offer transformation itself—becoming neither entirely human nor wholly pattern, but something that can bridge between states."

The third guardian's constellation pattern reconfigured, stars shifting to reflect his answer in perfect symmetry. For several heartbeats, it remained silent, assessing the harmony between spoken word and inner belief.

"Voice and thought align," it finally announced. "The vessel speaks truth."

The three guardians moved in unison, their constellation forms merging to create a singular pattern of startling complexity. "The vessel passes all tests," they declared. "The binding may proceed."

***

Before they could continue, Brynja spoke, her thorn runes glowing with golden truth-light. "Ask him what he fears."

The guardians paused, their merged constellation pattern shifting in what might have been surprise. They turned toward Asvarr, star-forms reconfiguring to focus their collective attention on him.

"What do you fear, vessel?" they asked in unison.

Asvarr hadn't expected this question. The concentrated starlight within him surged, revealing fears he'd buried beneath determination and purpose. The branches of his crown tightened painfully as he confronted truths he'd avoided acknowledging.

"I fear losing myself completely," he admitted, watching the words form intricate patterns that encoded his deepest apprehensions. "I fear binding all five anchors and having nothing human remain. I fear becoming merely a vessel for the pattern with no will of my own."

The guardians' merged constellation shifted, assessing. "Voice and thought align," they confirmed. "The vessel speaks truth."

"Now ask him what he hopes," Brynja continued, her transformed eye whirling faster.

The guardians turned to Asvarr again. "What do you hope, vessel?"

This question struck even deeper. Hope had been scarce since his clan's destruction, since witnessing the void-memory's vision of cosmic war. Yet something remained—fragile but undeniable, growing stronger with each binding despite the cost.

"I hope to find a third option," he answered, the words forming luminous geometries that encoded his deepest aspirations. "Neither perfect order nor absolute chaos, but balance that allows both structure and freedom. I hope that what emerges from the tenth cycle creates a pattern that neither imprisons nor destroys, but transforms."

"Voice and thought align," the guardians declared. "The vessel speaks perfect truth."

They turned to Brynja, their constellation pattern reconfiguring to match the thorn-runes carved into her wooden flesh. "The Root-vessel speaks with purpose beyond witnessing. Why these questions?"

"Because intention shapes transformation," Brynja replied, golden light blazing from her thorn-runes. "The starlight anchor responds to what he fears and hopes as much as what he seeks and why."

The guardians studied her for several heartbeats, their star-patterns shifting in silent communication. Finally, they addressed her directly: "The thorn-runes reveal wisdom beyond your vessel's understanding. The Severed Bloom speaks through you."

"Not through me," Brynja corrected, the thorn-runes confirming her sincerity. "With me. Partnership, not possession."

This distinction seemed to interest the guardians greatly. Their constellation forms separated briefly, then reconnected in a new configuration that somehow encompassed aspects of both Asvarr and Brynja's transformations.

"The binding proceeds differently," they announced. "The vessel comes with witnesses. The anchors merge through observed transformation."

They gestured toward the crystalline tree at the chamber's center, which had begun pulsing with intensified light in rhythm with Asvarr's heartbeat. The branches reconfigured, forming patterns that matched both the crystalline formations on his face and the constellation patterns in Brynja's wooden flesh.

"Approach the anchor," the guardians commanded. "Complete the binding."

Asvarr drifted toward the crystalline tree, feeling the concentrated starlight within him resonate with the anchor's energy. As he drew closer, the branches extended toward him, recognizing, reaching for the transformed vessel prepared to receive them.

"Remember who you are," Brynja called, her thorn-runes blazing. "Remember your name when starlight fills your awareness."

The branches touched Asvarr's transformed flesh, connecting with the crystalline formations spreading across his face. The contact sent shocks of cosmic knowledge pouring into his consciousness—star-birth and death, void-spaces between realities, mathematical certainties underpinning existence itself. His awareness expanded exponentially, perception splitting across multiple planes simultaneously.

For one terrifying moment, he forgot his own name, identity dissolving into cosmic patterns that stretched toward infinity. Then Yrsa's crystal fragment pulsed within his flesh, anchoring him to a singular point. Brynja's voice reached him through their oath-sigil, reinforcing his sense of self as the starlight anchor merged with his transformed body.

I am Asvarr. Flame-Warden. Memory-Keeper. Starlight-Vessel.

The binding completed with explosive force, sending waves of silver-blue energy radiating outward through the chamber. The guardians' constellation forms shimmered with reflected power, while Brynja's wooden transformation responded with resonant patterns of its own. Yrsa's crystal pendant blazed with protective light, shielding her from the worst of the backlash.

Asvarr floated at the chamber's center, the crystalline tree now merged with his transformed flesh. New awareness filled him—cold, mathematical certainty balanced against the flame anchor's preservation and the memory anchor's connection. The starlight anchor granted him perception beyond normal boundaries, allowing him to see through layers of reality to the patterns underlying existence itself.

Most striking was his physical transformation. The crystalline formations had spread across his entire face and down his neck, forming patterns resembling frozen lightning or stellar cartography. His eyes had transformed completely, becoming pools of silver-blue light that contained galactic swirls. The verdant crown had evolved as well, branches extending around his head in a complex lattice that incorporated crystalline elements alongside living wood.

"The binding is complete," the guardians declared. "The vessel becomes Warden of Three. Flame-Keeper. Memory-Bearer. Starlight-Vessel."

Asvarr extended his hand, watching starlight ripple beneath his transformed skin. He could feel all three anchors resonating within him—flame burning with preservative heat, memory humming with connective recognition, and now starlight pulsing with transformative certainty. Together, they granted him awareness beyond anything he'd imagined possible.

Through this expanded perception, he sensed the void-hunger stirring far below—ancient beyond comprehension, patient beyond measure, hungry beyond satiation. It felt his binding, recognized the pattern's shift, and responded with increased pressure against its weakening prison. The tenth cycle progressed differently than the nine before, and the entity imprisoned beneath the roots took notice.

"What happens now?" he asked, his voice carrying harmonic overtones that matched the chamber's resonant frequency.

"Now the true pattern reveals itself," the guardians replied. "The fourth anchor awaits in Muspelheim's forge-heart. The fifth in Helheim's frozen depths. The path grows more perilous with each binding. None has completed all five in nine cycles."

"Because the vessel loses itself before completion," Brynja added, her thorn-runes pulsing with golden truth-light. "The transformation becomes too complete."

Asvarr turned toward her, seeing her clearly through his transformed perception. The Severed Bloom fragment within her wooden flesh was more evident now—a consciousness separate yet integrated, rebellious yet purposeful. It recognized him as Warden of Three, assessing his transformation with ancient intelligence.

"You knew this would happen," he said, realization dawning. "You knew the starlight anchor would transform me beyond humanity."

"Yes." The thorn-runes confirmed her honesty. "I knew. The Severed Bloom showed me visions of previous Wardens. None survived with identity intact after binding three."

"Yet here I stand," Asvarr replied, feeling the three anchors stabilize within him. "Transformed but remembering."

"Because you chose the third path," Yrsa explained, her pendant's light dimming as the chamber stabilized. "Not dominance over the anchors like the Ashfather, nor submission to them like previous Wardens. Partnership through transformation."

The guardians' constellation forms shifted, creating patterns of startling complexity. "The vessel must proceed to the chamber beyond," they announced. "Where those who witnessed before remain."

They gestured toward an opening that had appeared in the chamber's far wall—an archway formed of perfectly aligned starpoints connected by lines of force. Beyond lay darkness shot through with points of silver light, suggesting a vast space awaiting discovery.

"What awaits there?" Asvarr asked, the branches of his transformed crown shifting with his curiosity.

"Those created during Yggdrasil's first formation," the guardians replied. "Witnesses to events too important to trust to memory alone. They have waited for the Warden of Three since the first breaking."

Asvarr exchanged glances with Brynja and Yrsa. His transformed perception allowed him to see beyond their physical forms to the patterns of possibility surrounding them—threads of potential futures branching outward from this moment of decision. Most paths led to darkness, to failure, to the void-hunger's escape. But a few—tenuous and unlikely—led toward something new, something transformed.

The starlight anchor pulsed within him, urging exploration of these mathematical possibilities. The memory anchor hummed with recognition of cosmic patterns too vast for simple understanding. The flame anchor burned with protective heat, preserving what remained of his humanity against complete dissolution.

"I'll go," he decided, drifting toward the starpoint archway. "Whatever witnesses await will help chart the path forward."

Brynja moved to follow, her wooden transformation responding to his decision. "I witnessed your binding," she said, thorn-runes confirming her sincerity. "I'll witness what comes next."

Yrsa joined them, her crystal pendant pulsing with renewed light. "The boundary-walker accompanies the Warden," she declared. "As in nine cycles before."

***

The guardians made no move to stop them, their constellation forms shifting to create a path toward the archway. "Beyond lies the Silent Choir," they said in unison. "Children of the Serpent Sky, created to remember what gods and mortals forget. They have waited for the Warden of Three since the first shattering."

Asvarr drifted through the archway, Brynja and Yrsa following close behind. His transformed perception split across multiple planes as they entered a space that existed both within the Cradle and beyond normal reality—a chamber constructed to bridge dimensions otherwise separate.

The last thing he heard before crossing the threshold was the guardians' final pronouncement, echoing through layers of existence:

"The tenth cycle has begun. The pattern changes. The prison weakens. What emerges from the Warden of Three will determine whether all reality endures or returns to primordial void."

CHAPTER 6
THE SILENT CHOIR

The central chamber of the Cradle opened before them like the inside of a massive bell, impossibly vast despite the temple's outer dimensions. Asvarr's transformed senses struggled to process the contradictions—space folding back on itself, angles that should not exist, distances that stretched and compressed with each breath. The starlight flowing through his veins made his vision pulse with silver-blue clarity, illuminating details his human eyes would never have perceived.

He stepped onto the polished floor, smooth as frozen midnight yet warm beneath his feet. His transformed body felt lighter than breath, each movement leaving crystalline echoes that hung in the air before dissolving into prismatic dust.

"By the roots," he whispered, voice rippling with harmonics that weren't entirely his own.

The chamber formed a perfect circle, its ceiling lost in darkness or perhaps nonexistence. A raised dais occupied the center, simple and unadorned except for nine concentric rings etched into its surface. But it wasn't the architecture that stole Asvarr's breath—it was what surrounded the dais.

Children. Dozens of them, standing in a perfect circle around the central platform. Unnaturally still. Unblinking. Motionless as carved stone yet unmistakably alive.

Brynja moved beside him, her wooden arm creaking softly as she raised it toward the figures. "What manner of trap is this?" she asked, voice low.

The children were identical in their strange, ageless beauty. None appeared older than perhaps ten winters, yet their eyes held the weight of eons. Their skin gleamed with a soft luminescence, like starlight trapped beneath ice. Each wore a simple robe of shimmering fabric that moved without wind, colors shifting between midnight blue and silver white.

Most disturbing were their eyes—tracking Asvarr and his companions with perfect unison, pupils expanding and contracting in synchronized rhythm.

"Not trap," Yrsa said, her voice uncharacteristically gentle. "Witnesses."

She moved forward, surprisingly confident in this impossible space. Her crystal pendant—the twin to the fragment now embedded in Asvarr's transformed flesh—pulsed with steady blue-white illumination.

"The Children of the Serpent Sky," she continued, stopping at a respectful distance from the silent figures. "Created during the First Formation."

The words sparked recognition deep in Asvarr's mind, memories that weren't his own unfurling like frost patterns across glass. The void-memory pressed against his sternum, still dormant yet stirring with each heartbeat.

"They witnessed the Tree's growth," Asvarr said, the knowledge rising from somewhere beneath conscious thought. "The breaking too."

Yrsa nodded. "Some events are too important to trust to memory alone. They serve as living records—what they witness becomes true beyond question or manipulation."

Asvarr studied the children more carefully. Despite their unnerving stillness, they didn't appear hostile. Their faces held no expression at all—neither welcoming nor threatening, simply... present. Observing. Recording.

"What are they witnessing now?" he asked.

"Us," Brynja answered. Her cosmic eye swirled with amber light, constellation patterns shifting across her wooden features. "The binding. The choice. The third path."

Asvarr took another step forward. The moment his foot crossed some invisible threshold, every child's head turned in perfect unison, eyes fixing on him with sudden, terrifying intensity.

He froze. Remembered Brynja's earlier warning about the third anchor's danger. The crown of branches tightened around his skull, thorns digging into flesh that was no longer entirely solid.

"Do they... speak?" he asked Yrsa, voice strained.

"Rarely. And never without purpose." She moved carefully to stand beside him, voice dropping to a whisper. "They were here before gods walked between worlds, Asvarr. Before the Verdant Five shaped the first branches. What they know could shatter minds. What they've seen—"

"—could break reality," finished an unfamiliar voice.

Asvarr spun toward the sound. The children remained motionless, lips unmoving. But something had changed. The air above the central dais shimmered with accumulated starlight, coalescing into patterns that hurt his eyes.

"Who spoke?" he demanded, hand instinctively reaching for his bronze sword.

The starlight patterns shifted, forming shapes reminiscent of the Constellation Guardians they'd faced earlier, yet more fluid, more complex. And more familiar, somehow. Asvarr sensed patterns similar to those flowing through his own transformed flesh—the unmistakable signature of a bound anchor.

"I did," came the same voice, emanating from everywhere and nowhere. "Or we did. It matters little."

Brynja stepped forward, thorn-runes blazing golden across her wooden features. "Show yourself properly," she commanded. "No more riddles, no more games."

The light patterns swirled faster, concentrating into a more defined form—a figure tall and slender, formed of interwoven light and darkness, star-bright eyes fixed on Asvarr.

"Coilvoice," Yrsa breathed, recognition and something like fear crossing her face.

The name sparked another flash of not-his-memory in Asvarr's mind. "The Tree's final thought," he murmured. "As it shattered."

The figure inclined its head, a gesture almost human despite its cosmic substance. "An approximation close enough to serve. I have been called many names through nine cycles. Coilvoice. The Pattern-Keeper. The Rememberer."

As it spoke, the children's eyes tracked its movements with eerie precision, heads turning in unison to follow its path as it drifted around the chamber.

"Why are you here?" Asvarr asked, fingers still resting on his sword hilt.

"For the same reason as you, Warden." The figure's voice contained multitudes—man and woman, elder and child, unified into something both larger and stranger than any individual voice. "The binding. The third anchor. The choice that breaks nine cycles of repetition."

Brynja stepped closer to Asvarr, her wooden arm brushing against his. He felt her tension through the oath-sigil that connected them, her suspicion bleeding across the bond.

"What do you know of our purpose?" she demanded.

"Everything and nothing," replied Coilvoice. "I remember each previous binding—failed attempts, partial successes, patterns almost broken only to reform anew."

The figure gestured toward the silent children. "They remember too. But where I preserve purpose, they preserve fact. Uncolored by interpretation. Uncorrupted by desire."

The chamber seemed to contract around them, the distant walls drawing closer though neither had moved. Asvarr felt a strange pressure building in the space—anticipation or warning, he couldn't tell.

"The binding approaches," Coilvoice continued. "But first, you must understand what you seek. What you will become."

The figure drifted toward the central dais, raising both arms in a slow, deliberate motion. The children responded immediately, stepping forward in unison, forming tighter concentric circles around the platform.

"The Silent Choir speaks only in harmony, and only when beyond-memory must be shared," Coilvoice explained. "Listen carefully, Warden. What they show you now has not been witnessed in nine cycles."

The starlight embedded in the children's skin brightened until Asvarr had to shield his eyes. Even through his fingers, he saw their mouths opening in perfect unison, though no sound emerged. Instead, the chamber itself began to resonate, vibrating with a frequency that bypassed his ears entirely, resonating directly in his mind.

The floor beneath them shifted, transparency spreading outward from the dais like ice forming on a pond. Through it, Asvarr glimpsed impossible depths—space without end, galaxies spiraling beneath his feet.

"What's happening?" he gasped, the crown of branches tightening further, golden sap mingling with blood that ran down his temples.

"Memory," Yrsa answered, her voice tight with awe or fear. "Older than the Tree. Older than gods."

The vibration intensified. One of the children—smaller than the others, standing directly across from Asvarr—raised a hand toward him. The gesture carried unmistakable summons.

"They want you to join them," said Coilvoice. "To stand upon the dais. To witness what came before, and what must come after."

Brynja gripped Asvarr's arm with iron strength, her wooden fingers digging into his transformed flesh. "This wasn't in our bargain," she hissed. "We came for the anchor, not for—"

"The anchor is memory," interrupted Coilvoice. "The binding is understanding. You cannot have one without the other."

The summoning child took a single step forward, breaking the perfect circle. The motion was so unexpected, so contrary to their previous stillness, that Asvarr felt the shock of it like physical impact.

"You must choose, Warden," Coilvoice said. "The dais, or retreat. Memory, or ignorance. The third path, or repetition of failure."

Asvarr looked between the waiting child and his companions. Brynja's face was rigid with distrust, thorn-runes pulsing golden with truth-tension. Yrsa's expression was unreadable, her ancient eyes fixed on the children with something between reverence and dread.

The child took another step forward. Now Asvarr could see its features more clearly—neither boy nor girl, its face a perfect amalgamation of all possible human countenances. Its eyes reflected the cosmos itself, spiraling galaxies captured in miniature.

The summoning hand remained extended, patient and inexorable as gravity.

The decision crystallized in Asvarr's mind. He had come too far, sacrificed too much, to retreat now.

"I need to understand," he said to Brynja, gently removing her hand from his arm. "Whatever waits on that dais—knowledge, vision, trial—I must face it."

He turned to Yrsa. "Will they harm me?"

The boundary-walker's gaze remained fixed on the waiting child. "Not intentionally," she answered, choosing her words with obvious care. "But memory itself can wound. Truth can break minds unprepared to hold it."

Asvarr nodded, decision made. "I'll risk it."

He stepped away from his companions, moving toward the child and the waiting dais beyond. Each step felt heavier than the last, as though he walked against an invisible current. The starlight in his veins pulsed faster, resonating with the chamber's silent harmony.

The child's eyes met his, vast and ancient despite its youthful face. Up close, Asvarr saw what hadn't been visible from a distance—small crystalline formations at the child's temples, identical to those now growing from his own transformed flesh.

"You've been waiting for me," he said, not a question.

The child nodded once, a movement so precise it seemed mechanical. Its extended hand remained perfectly steady.

Asvarr reached out, his transformed fingers—partway between flesh and starlight—hovering inches from the child's.

"What will I see?"

The child's lips moved silently, forming words without sound. But somehow, Asvarr understood.

What was. What will be. What must never come again.

He took a deep breath, steadying himself against the crown's constriction and the resonance building in his bones. Then he closed the distance, pressing his palm against the child's.

Light exploded behind his eyes. The floor fell away. The chamber, Yrsa, Brynja, even Coilvoice—all vanished in an instant, replaced by endless, rushing stars.

Asvarr was falling—or flying—through pure cosmos, the child's hand still locked with his, guiding him through the void between worlds. Constellations blurred past, forming and dissolving too quickly to comprehend. Time stretched and compressed simultaneously.

Then everything stopped.

***

He stood on a vast plain beneath an impossibly starlit sky. Before him rose Yggdrasil—not as he had known it, broken and fractured, but whole. Perfect. Immense beyond comprehension, branches extending beyond sight, roots plunging into depths that made his mind recoil.

And standing before the Tree was a figure.

The First Warden.

Asvarr knew it immediately, recognition flooding through him with certainty that transcended conscious thought. The figure turned, and Asvarr saw his own face reflected back—but older, wearier, marked by transformations far beyond what Asvarr himself had undergone.

The vision opened its mouth to speak, and Asvarr braced himself for revelation.

Beneath his feet, the world shattered.

The vision shattered like ice beneath a hammer blow. Asvarr gasped, lungs burning as though he'd been drowning rather than flying through stars. His knees struck the chamber floor, sending jolts of pain through a body that felt suddenly, jarringly solid again.

The child still gripped his hand, its small fingers surprisingly strong. The perfect face remained expressionless, but something burned in those cosmic eyes—urgency, perhaps. Or warning.

"What—" Asvarr began, but his voice cracked. He tried again. "What was that?"

***

The child released his hand and took a single step back. Then, with deliberate slowness, it raised both arms. The motion rippled through the Silent Choir, each child mimicking the gesture in perfect unison until they formed a forest of upraised arms, fingers splayed toward the chamber's unseen ceiling.

For three heartbeats, silence stretched between them, absolute and expectant.

Then the child spoke.

Its voice wasn't human. The sound bypassed Asvarr's ears entirely, resonating directly in his bones like the toll of a distant bell across frozen lakes. Each word vibrated with harmonic undertones that made his teeth ache and the sap in his veins pulse golden-bright.

"We remember the first Warden."

The words hung in the air, crystallizing into visible symbols that hovered momentarily before dissolving into prismatic dust. The child took another step forward, bringing its face uncomfortably close to Asvarr's. He held his ground despite the unsettling proximity.

"It was not a role," continued the impossible voice, "but a prison sentence."

The child reached up and touched Asvarr's verdant crown. The moment its fingers brushed the living branches, Asvarr's vision doubled. He saw himself as though from outside his body—a man half-transformed, bark patterns spreading across his cheeks, crystalline formations gleaming at his temples, eyes swirling with starlight.

And superimposed over his image, he saw the child—features shifting, blurring, becoming a mirror of his own. For one disorienting moment, they shared the same appearance, as though the child were a reflection of what Asvarr might become.

"You carry three anchors now," said the child. "Soon four. Then five. The tree grows through you."

Behind him, Asvarr heard Brynja draw in a sharp breath. The child's eyes flicked toward her, then back to him.

"Show me," Asvarr demanded, voice steadier than he felt. "Show me the First Warden."

The child nodded, a single precise movement. Its fingers tightened on the verdant crown, and the world around them dissolved again.

This time, Asvarr remained aware of the chamber floor beneath his knees, the child before him. But layered over reality came visions of impossible clarity—memories preserved with perfect fidelity across nine cycles of breaking and binding.

A figure stood before the intact Tree, smaller than in Asvarr's previous glimpse yet more substantial somehow. Human, or once-human—a woman with skin dark as fertile soil and eyes that held the same cosmic awareness now growing in Asvarr's own. Branches grew from her shoulders, forming a crown more elaborate than his, with flowers that opened and closed in rhythm with her breathing.

"The First Warden," the child's voice explained, though its lips remained motionless. "She who bound the five anchors. She who remade herself to save what remained."

The vision shifted. The woman changed, her humanity receding with each binding. After the first, her skin hardened to bark along one arm. After the second, crystalline formations spread across her face, identical to those now growing from Asvarr's temples. After the third, starlight replaced the blood in her veins, shining through her skin in web-like patterns.

The fourth binding transformed her voice, removing it from human registers entirely. She spoke, and mountains trembled.

The fifth binding stole her name. She forgot who she had been before the anchors.

"The price of Wardenship," said the child. "Neither human nor tree, but cornerstone. Neither living nor dead, but pattern."

The vision expanded. Asvarr saw the First Warden's consciousness stretching thin across creation, fragments of her selfhood embedded in roots that spanned worlds. She became a foundation stone upon which reality rested, aware yet unable to act, present yet impossibly distant.

The Tree grew through her and from her and because of her.

"Nine cycles," the child continued. "Nine Wardens. Nine failures."

Fresh visions cascaded through Asvarr's mind—eight figures after the First, each bearing anchors, each surrendering pieces of themselves to the pattern. Some reached the fourth binding but faltered. Some achieved the fifth but could not complete the transformation.

The last face in the procession sent ice through Asvarr's veins.

The Ashfather. Younger, his face unmarked by the bitterness that now twisted his features. Three anchors bound to him, a fourth hovering just beyond his reach in Helheim's depths.

"He was meant to be the Ninth," the child said. "But he saw what waited at the end of the path and turned aside. Sought control rather than transformation. Dominance rather than surrender."

The vision faded, leaving Asvarr once again fully present in the chamber with the Silent Choir. The child's hand dropped from his crown, but the weight of what he'd seen remained, pressing against his chest from the inside.

"Why show me this?" he asked, voice raw. "If every Warden before me failed or surrendered to the pattern, what hope have I to find another way?"

The child tilted its head, an unsettlingly birdlike movement. "The choice remains yours. The third path exists. But it has never been walked."

"What third path?" Asvarr demanded. His hands closed into fists, golden sap oozing between his fingers as the pressure of transformation built behind his sternum. "Speak plainly!"

"We cannot," the child answered, something almost like regret touching its voice. "We witness. We remember. We preserve. But we do not guide."

From behind him came the sound of Yrsa's steady footsteps approaching across the chamber floor. "They can only show what was, Asvarr," she said, her voice gentle yet firm. "Not what could be. The future remains unwritten, even for them."

The child nodded at her words, then turned its gaze back to Asvarr. "The Tree remembers you," it said, the bell-voice growing stronger. "Flame-tender. Memory-keeper. Star-walker. It remembers what you were before this cycle, and what you might become after."

A cold certainty settled in Asvarr's gut. "I've done this before, haven't I? In previous cycles."

The child's expression didn't change, but something in those cosmic eyes shifted. "You have been many things across many cycles. As have we all."

It lifted a hand, extending one finger toward Asvarr's chest, stopping just short of touching the Grímmark that burned beneath his tunic. "The pattern remembers, even when the vessels forget."

Before Asvarr could demand further explanation, the child turned away, resuming its place in the circle. The Silent Choir lowered their arms in perfect unison, returning to their previous stillness. The moment had passed.

Asvarr rose unsteadily to his feet, his mind churning with fragmented visions and half-formed questions. The crown of branches tightened around his skull, responding to his agitation.

"Did you know?" he asked Yrsa, voice low. "About the First Warden. About the price."

Yrsa's ancient eyes met his without flinching. "I suspected. Fragments endure through memory, if one knows where to look."

"And you didn't think to tell me?"

"Would you have believed me?" she countered. "Would you have understood, truly understood, without seeing for yourself?"

Before he could answer, Brynja approached, her wooden arm creaking softly with each step. The constellation patterns embedded in her transformed flesh pulsed with internal light.

"So this is why the Verdant Five kept our bloodlines separated," she said. "Why they ensured no single Warden could bind all five anchors. They were preventing another First Warden from forming."

Yrsa nodded slowly. "The Tree requires foundation stones. But a conscious cornerstone—one that remembers itself—poses risk to those who would control the pattern."

Asvarr turned back toward the silent children, questions burning on his tongue. But the moment he moved, the child who had shown him the visions stepped forward again, its movements holding new urgency.

***

"Your time grows short," it said, bell-voice chiming with warning. "The binding awaits, and that which sleeps beneath grows restless."

"Binding? But I've already—" Asvarr began, then stopped as the child shook its head.

"Not past. Not complete. The third anchor shifts within you, not yet fully claimed. What you have taken into yourself must now take you."

The child lifted both hands, and the entire Choir moved in response, forming new patterns around the central dais. The chamber itself seemed to shift, angles changing, dimensions expanding. The floor beneath Asvarr's feet grew transparent, revealing stars wheeling beneath.

"I don't understand," Asvarr said. "What more must I do?"

"Surrender," answered the child. "Not to dominance, but to transformation."

It gestured toward the dais, which now glowed with accumulated starlight forming complex, shifting patterns. "Stand upon the threshold. Complete what was begun in the Cradle's heart."

Asvarr looked toward his companions. Brynja's face remained impassive, the truth-runes etched into her wooden features glowing softly golden. She nodded once.

"I've come this far," she said. "We've all paid prices. Finish what you started, Flame-Warden."

He turned to Yrsa, whose ancient eyes held knowledge and sorrow in equal measure. "The third binding changes more than flesh," she warned. "It alters perception itself. What you see, what you understand—it will never be human again."

"Was that not already true after the second?" Asvarr asked, touching the crystalline formations at his temples.

A ghost of a smile crossed Yrsa's weathered face. "Those were mere footprints in snow. This will be avalanche."

Asvarr took a deep breath, steadying himself. The starlight in his veins pulsed faster, resonating with the patterns forming on the dais. Whatever waited there called to him, tugging at the anchors already bound within his transformed flesh.

Decision crystallized. He stepped forward, crossing the circle of silent children, and climbed the three steps to the platform's surface.

The moment his foot touched the central dais, power surged through him—raw, unfiltered cosmic energy pouring through channels opened by the first two bindings. His body arched backward, mouth opening in a silent scream as starlight exploded behind his eyes.

He saw everything at once: past, present, future entwined in patterns too complex for human minds to comprehend. His consciousness expanded outward, touching distant stars, feeling their burning hearts as though they were extensions of his own body.

The verdant crown burst into new growth, branches extending down his back, forming a lattice of living wood that merged with the crystalline structures already present in his transformed flesh. His skin hardened further, bark patterns spreading across his chest and arms, while starlight condensed in his eyes until they became twin galaxies in miniature.

Through the agony of transformation, Asvarr fought to maintain some core of selfhood—some fragment that remembered the man he had been before the

Grimmark, before the anchors. His mother's face. His clan's hearth-fire. The weight of his bronze sword in his hand.

The child's words echoed in his mind: *It was a prison sentence.*

He could feel it happening—his consciousness stretching thin, spreading across patterns of connection that spanned realms. Pieces of his identity fraying, dissolving, becoming indistinguishable from the cosmic forces pouring through him.

Just as the First Warden had. Just as eight others after her.

No.

The refusal rose from somewhere deeper than thought—a core of stubborn humanity that refused extinction. Asvarr gathered the fragments of himself, clutching them close even as transformation tore through him.

I am Asvarr. I am flame-keeper and memory-bearer and star-walker, but I am also myself. I choose the third path. Neither domination nor surrender, but transformation on my terms.

The power faltered, patterns shifting in response to his resistance. The Silent Choir began to move, circling the dais with increasing speed, their identical faces turned upward in expectation or alarm.

Coilvoice reappeared, its form more substantial than before, writhing with complex patterns of light and darkness. "The binding must complete," it said, voice urgent. "The anchor must seat—"

"It will," Asvarr growled through teeth that were partly crystal, partly bark. "But I remain myself while it does."

The dais trembled beneath his feet. The chamber's walls blurred, reality thinning around them as cosmic forces pressed against the boundaries of the Cradle.

And then, with a sound like the breaking of chains that had never been forged, the third anchor found its place within him. Through partnership with it. The starlight in his veins settled into steady rhythm, no longer fighting his humanity but flowing alongside it.

The transformation stilled, neither complete nor rejected but balanced on knife's edge.

Asvarr sank to his knees, gasping as the pressure eased. The Silent Choir ceased their frantic circling, resuming their original positions with mechanical precision.

"Impossible," Coilvoice whispered, voice rippling with harmonics of disbelief. "Nine cycles, and never..."

The child who had shown Asvarr the visions approached the dais, looking up at him with those ancient, cosmic eyes. It studied him for a long moment, head tilted in that unsettling birdlike manner.

"The third path opens," it said finally, bell-voice resonating with something almost like hope. "Neither foundation stone nor broken vessel, but bridge."

It reached out, touching Asvarr's transformed hand with cool, small fingers. "The pattern remembers this moment," it continued. "As do we."

From beyond the chamber walls came a sound like splitting stone, followed by a concussive impact that shook the entire Cradle. The silent children turned as one, eyes fixing on the chamber's sealed entrance.

"What was that?" Brynja demanded, wooden arm extending into protective branches.

The child turned toward her, face expressionless yet somehow conveying alarm. "That which sleeps beneath stirs," it said. "The anchors' movement wakes it."

Another impact struck, harder than the first. The chamber walls rippled like water, structure straining against forces never meant to contain.

"Something comes," Coilvoice said, voice fading as its form began to dissolve. "Something that should not be..."

The child rejoined the circle, its movements precise despite the chamber's increasing instability. The Silent Choir began to hum—a discordant melody that tugged at reality, making the air flicker and distort around them.

Asvarr stumbled from the dais, finding his balance in a body transformed yet still his own. The starlight anchor thrummed within him, lending clarity to his expanded senses. Through the chamber's transparent floor, he saw something streaking toward Alfheim—a comet burning blue-white against the void, moving with deliberate purpose rather than cosmic accident.

It struck the planet's surface directly below the Cradle, burrowing into the crust with impossible precision. The impact sent shockwaves through reality itself, rocking the floating temple and sending fractures spiraling across its impossible architecture.

The Silent Choir's humming intensified, their discordant melody warping the chamber around them. Reality flickered, dimensions folding, unfurling, collapsing.

"What are they doing?" Asvarr demanded, seizing Yrsa's arm. "What's happening?"

Yrsa's ancient eyes reflected the cosmic distortions rippling through the chamber. "Warning song," she said, voice tight with fear unlike anything he'd heard from her before. "They sing only when the pattern itself faces threat."

"From a comet?"

"Not a comet," she answered, grabbing his transformed hand and pulling him toward the chamber's exit. "Something that should never have awakened. Something the anchors were meant to keep sleeping."

The Silent Choir's voices rose in unified dissonance, bending space until the chamber's exit and entrance became one. Pathways opened where none had existed before.

"We must go," Brynja shouted over the mounting chaos, her wooden features twisting with urgency. "Now!"

Reality buckled. The third anchor blazed within Asvarr, no longer fighting his identity but lending him strength to navigate the collapsing dimensions. He seized Brynja's wooden arm with one hand, Yrsa's weathered fingers with the other, and pulled them through the tear in existence the children's song had created.

As they fled, Asvarr glanced back once. The Silent Choir remained, unmoving despite the chamber's disintegration, their ageless faces turned downward toward whatever had crashed into Alfheim's surface below.

The child who had shown him visions raised a hand in what might have been farewell, or warning.

Then the Cradle folded around them, and everything fell away.

CHAPTER 7

THE GOD WITHIN THE COMET

A svarr crashed through fractured reality, clutching Brynja and Yrsa as dimensions collapsed around them. His newly transformed senses reeled with input—space folding upon itself, time stretching and compressing in nauseating waves. The Cradle's architecture twisted behind them, its impossible geometries breaking further as the Silent Choir's warning song grew distant.

They fell through nothing and everything at once. The crystalline formations at Asvarr's temples burned cold, resonating with the broken patterns surrounding them. His verdant crown tightened around his skull, branches digging deeper, sending roots of awareness through his mind that anchored him against the chaos.

"Hold fast!" he shouted, voice carrying harmonic undertones that carved pathways through the disintegrating space.

The starlight flowing through his veins pulsed in response to his command, carving a stable pocket within the collapsing boundaries. With desperate strength, he pulled his companions through this momentary haven toward what felt like solid ground below.

They struck a crystalline surface with jarring force. Asvarr's transformed body absorbed most of the impact, but Brynja grunted in pain as her human portions took the brunt of their landing. Yrsa rolled with surprising agility for her apparent age, coming to rest several paces away.

Asvarr rose first, orienting himself in this new space. They had emerged on a high outcropping of Starfall Mountain, a flat expanse of silver crystal that caught and fractured light from Alfheim's twin moons overhead. The Cradle floated above them, its structure visibly distorted, sections phasing in and out of existence as the Silent Choir's song continued to warp reality around it.

"What in Hel's nine halls was that?" Brynja demanded, her wooden arm creaking as she pushed herself upright. The constellation patterns embedded in her transformed flesh pulsed with agitated light.

Before Asvarr could answer, the mountain beneath them shuddered. The vibration traveled up through his feet, resonating with the starlight in his veins and the crystalline formations at his temples. Another impact followed, stronger than the first. Then another. Each strike precisely timed, deliberate.

Yrsa moved to the outcropping's edge, her weathered face illuminated by the glow of her crystal pendant. "There," she said, pointing toward the horizon.

Asvarr joined her, enhanced vision piercing the distance. Something streaked across Alfheim's star-washed sky—a burning comet, its trail blue-white against the void. Unlike natural celestial bodies, this one didn't follow a smooth arc but moved with jerking, purposeful shifts, changing direction mid-flight like a predator tracking scent.

"That's what struck below the Cradle," he said, recalling the impact they'd witnessed through the chamber's transparent floor.

"No," Yrsa countered, voice tight. "What struck below was merely herald. This comes after."

The comet grew larger, its trajectory now unmistakably aimed at the same impact site as its predecessor. Asvarr's enhanced vision caught details that would have been invisible to human eyes—patterns swirling across the comet's surface, geometric and precise, reminiscent of the constellations above but impossibly condensed.

"It's not natural," Brynja said, joining them at the edge. Her transformed eye swirled with amber light as she focused on the approaching object. "There's purpose in its movement."

Another tremor shook the mountain, stronger than those before. Fractures spread through the crystal beneath their feet, silver lines spiderwebbing outward from the point of impact.

"We need to move," Asvarr said, reaching for his companions.

Too late.

The comet struck with devastating force, boring into Alfheim's surface at precisely the same point as the first impact. The shockwave rippled outward, visible as a physical distortion of reality that warped the landscape below. Trees bent sideways, streams reversed course, and the very air shimmered with displaced energy.

When the wave reached Starfall Mountain, the crystal beneath them shattered.

Asvarr lunged for Brynja as the outcropping collapsed, seizing her wooden arm with desperate strength. His other hand found Yrsa's robes, fingers tangling in the fabric as they began to fall. With the third anchor's power flowing through him, he twisted in mid-air, pulling his companions against his chest as they plummeted toward the mountain's lower reaches.

His transformed body reacted instinctively. The verdant crown extended branches downward along his spine, spreading outward to form a protective cage around the three of them. Crystalline formations sprouted from his skin, hardening into faceted armor that gleamed with internal light. The starlight in his veins burned brighter, lending impossible lightness to his movements.

They struck another outcropping, bounced, and continued their descent in a controlled slide rather than a fatal plunge. Asvarr's transformed feet carved furrows in the crystal surface, shedding momentum as they careened downward. With each impact, the living armor of branches and crystal absorbed and redistributed the shock.

Finally, they came to rest on a broad plateau halfway down the mountain's face. Asvarr released his companions, breathing hard despite his enhanced strength. The branches retracted into his flesh, leaving his skin marked with whorls and spirals that pulsed with golden light.

"Are you hurt?" he asked, scanning them for injuries.

Yrsa brushed crystal fragments from her robes, remarkably unperturbed by their near-death experience. "I've survived worse falls across worse boundaries," she said, though her voice held a tremor that belied her calm exterior.

Brynja stood at the plateau's edge, her attention fixed on the impact site below. "Look," she said, pointing with her wooden arm.

The comet had left a perfectly circular crater, edges too precise to be natural. No debris surrounded it, no scattered fragments or ejected soil. The impact had somehow compressed rather than displaced the landscape, as though reality itself had been punched inward.

And at the center of this impossibility, something moved.

"We need a closer look," Asvarr said, straining his enhanced vision. Despite the clarity the third anchor had granted him, he couldn't discern details at this distance—only a sense of writhing movement and pulsing light.

Yrsa grabbed his arm, fingers digging into transformed flesh with surprising strength. "Listen first," she said, voice urgent. "Hear what warns."

Asvarr stilled, focusing his altered senses. At first, he heard only the wind whistling across the mountain's crystal face and the distant rumble of disturbed earth. Then, faint but growing stronger, came the discordant melody of the Silent Choir—their warning song carrying impossibly across the distance and through solid matter.

The sound changed as it reached them, no longer merely vibrating through air but resonating directly in Asvarr's transformed flesh. The branches of his verdant crown trembled in response, and the crystalline formations at his temples rang with sympathetic tones.

"What are they warning against?" he asked, the question directed more at himself than his companions.

Another tremor shook the mountain, stronger than any before. Fractures spread through the crystal plateau, forcing them to shift position to avoid falling again. Above them, the Cradle's architecture continued to distort, sections phasing in and out of existence as the Silent Choir's song warped reality around it.

"The seal is breaking," Yrsa said, eyes fixed on the impact site. "What was bound stirs again."

"What seal? What was bound?" Brynja demanded, wooden features twisting with frustration. "Speak plainly for once, boundary-walker!"

Before Yrsa could answer, movement caught Asvarr's eye. From the crater's precise center rose a column of light, a deep, pulsing crimson that seemed to absorb rather than emit illumination. It stretched skyward, perfectly straight, until it reached what appeared to be a fixed point in the void above Alfheim.

The moment the column connected with this point, every constellation visible in Alfheim's night sky shifted.

"Impossible," Brynja breathed, her cosmic eye swirling faster as she tracked the changes. "The stars don't move like that. They can't."

But move they did. Entire patterns rearranged themselves, ancient formations dissolving and reforming in configurations that stroked alarm down Asvarr's spine. Most disturbing was what replaced Jörmungandr's Coil—instead of the serpent pattern, a new constellation took shape, resembling a perfect circle bisected by nine precisely placed stars.

The Silent Choir's warning song grew louder, no longer distant but surrounding them completely. The air itself seemed to carry their voices, reality fluctuating with each discordant note.

"We need to get closer," Asvarr said, decision crystallizing. "Whatever's happening, it's connected to the anchors. I can feel it."

Yrsa shook her head, pendant blazing with blue-white light. "Too dangerous. The boundaries thin. What comes through—"

"Might destroy everything if we don't understand it," Asvarr interrupted. "I've bound three anchors. If this threatens the pattern, I need to see it clearly."

The crown of branches tightened around his skull, responding to his resolve. The starlight in his veins burned brighter, lending clarity to his transformed senses. Though part of him recoiled from approaching whatever had emerged from the impact, a deeper instinct—the Warden's instinct—pulled him toward it.

"There's a path," he said, pointing to a crystalline formation that resembled a natural staircase winding down the mountain's face. "We can follow it to the crater's edge."

Brynja studied him, her face half-wooden, half-human, truth-runes gleaming golden against her transformed features. "You're changed," she said. "The third binding has altered you more than you realize."

Asvarr met her gaze steadily. "I'm still myself. The third path, remember? Neither dominated nor consumed."

"For now," she replied, but nodded acceptance. "Lead on, Warden of Three."

They descended the crystal staircase in tense silence, each step carrying them closer to the disturbance below. As they moved, Asvarr became increasingly aware of pressure building against his senses, perceptual, as though reality itself grew thinner with their approach.

The impact site came into clearer view. What had appeared as a perfectly circular crater from above revealed new complexities up close. The edges weren't merely precise but inscribed with patterns similar to those Asvarr had seen in the Cradle—concentric rings marked with symbols that burned with internal light.

At the center, where the column of crimson light rose skyward, something pulsed within a cocoon of crystallized energy. Asvarr strained his enhanced vision but still couldn't discern its exact form—only impressions of movement, of potentiality rather than concrete existence.

They had descended perhaps halfway to the crater when another tremor shook the mountain, this one violent enough to dislodge massive crystal shards from above. Asvarr reacted instantly, verdant crown extending protective branches over all three of them as fragments rained down.

When the deluge passed, they found their path blocked by fallen debris. The staircase ahead had shattered, leaving a gap too wide to cross safely.

"Now what?" Brynja asked, wooden arm creaking as she kicked a crystal shard over the edge.

Asvarr studied the terrain, considering options. The crater lay perhaps a thousand paces below their current position, with treacherous crystal slopes between. Without the staircase, descent would be difficult even for his transformed body.

"I could perhaps find another boundary," Yrsa suggested, pendant pulsing with steady light. "Though with reality so thin here, crossing might lead us... elsewhere."

Before Asvarr could respond, the Silent Choir's warning song changed. No longer discordant, it shifted into perfect, terrible harmony—thousands of child-like voices synchronized into a single pure tone that cut through reality like a blade through flesh.

The effect was immediate. The air around them rippled visibly, thinning to transparency in places. Through these gaps, Asvarr glimpsed other realms overlaid on Alfheim—fragments of Midgard's forests, Muspelheim's volcanic plains, Niflheim's frozen wastes, all simultaneously present yet separate.

"The boundaries collapse," Yrsa whispered, face pale with fear unlike anything Asvarr had seen from her before. "They shouldn't be able to do this. Not without—"

Her words cut off as another change swept across the landscape. The column of crimson light pulsed once, twice, then expanded outward in a perfect circle that engulfed the crater and surrounding terrain. When it receded seconds later, what remained wasn't the impact site they had been observing, but something else entirely.

A structure stood where the crater had been—a temple or monument of impossible architecture, surfaces gleaming with the same material as the Cradle. Its design incorporated elements that hurt Asvarr's eyes to focus on—angles that shouldn't connect, curves that folded back on themselves, spires that extended into dimensions he could almost but not quite perceive.

"By the roots," Brynja breathed, wooden features contorting in shock. "It wasn't a comet at all."

"No," Yrsa agreed, voice hollow. "It was a key. And now the lock has opened."

As if responding to her words, the structure's central portion split vertically, panels sliding apart to reveal an entrance that pulsed with the same crimson light as the column. The light spread outward in waves, washing over the landscape and climbing the mountain toward them.

When the first wave reached their position, Asvarr felt it pass through his transformed body like fire through ice. The anchors bound within him resonated in response—flame, memory, and starlight singing in harmonies that both paralleled and opposed the Silent Choir's warning.

The second wave brought sound—a deep, persistent hum that vibrated at frequencies both above and below what human ears could detect. Asvarr's enhanced senses parsed it into patterns, into meaning that wasn't quite language but carried intent nonetheless.

Awakening. Release. Becoming.

The third wave carried images directly into his mind—fragmented visions of beings neither god nor mortal, existing in states of perpetual transformation. He saw cities built of thought and emotion rather than stone, civilizations that spanned conceptual space, histories written in dimensions his mind couldn't fully grasp.

"What is this?" he gasped, clutching his head as the verdant crown tightened painfully.

Yrsa seized his arm, eyes wide with recognition and horror. "God-seed," she said. "Divinity unformed, pure potential without chosen shape or purpose."

"Impossible," Brynja countered, though her truth-runes remained dark. "Gods can't just... arrive."

"Not gods as you understand them," Yrsa replied. "Something older. Something that existed before distinct realms, before fixed time. The anchors were meant to keep them bound, sleeping, forgotten."

Another tremor shook the mountain, stronger than any before. Crystal shattered beneath their feet, the path crumbling as the structure below pulsed with intensifying light. The Silent Choir's warning song reached fever pitch, their harmonized voices cracking reality further with each sustained note.

Asvarr seized Brynja's wooden arm with one hand, Yrsa's weathered fingers with the other. "We need to get down there," he shouted over the mounting chaos. "Now!"

"How?" Brynja demanded. "The path is gone!"

In answer, Asvarr pulled them both against his chest, verdant crown extending protective branches around them once more. The starlight flowing through his veins burned with terrible brightness as he channeled the third anchor's power.

"Hold tight," he commanded, voice resonating with harmonics that carved stability through the fracturing reality.

Then he leapt from the edge, plummeting toward the structure below.

***

They fell through space distorted by the Silent Choir's warning song, dimensions folding around them like cloth crushed in a fist. Asvarr's transformed senses tracked their descent, calculating angles and forces with inhuman precision. The branches extending from his crown hardened into a protective cage, crystalline formations spreading across his exposed skin to form living armor once more.

They struck the ground with tremendous force, crystal shattering beneath them on impact. Asvarr absorbed most of the shock through his transformed body, branches bending and reforming around his companions to shield them. When the debris settled, they found themselves mere hundred paces from the structure's entrance.

Up close, its true nature became apparent. What had appeared from a distance as a temple or monument revealed itself as something organic—living material shaped into architectural forms. Surfaces rippled with slow, deliberate movement, as though breathing. Patterns flowed across them like blood through veins, pulsing with rhythms that matched neither Alfheim's rotation nor any human heartbeat.

But most disturbing was what waited at its center, visible through the vertical split that served as entrance. Within a chamber of crimson light floated what Asvarr could only describe as an embryo—a being of pure potential, neither formed nor unformed but existing in a state of perpetual becoming.

It had no fixed shape, shifting between countless forms in the space between heartbeats. One moment it appeared humanoid, the next serpentine, then geometric, then something beyond description. Its surface rippled with patterns identical to those Asvarr had seen in the Cradle and on the approaching comet.

"What do we do?" Brynja asked, her voice hushed despite the chaos surrounding them. The truth-runes etched into her wooden features pulsed with golden light, responding to some unspoken reality.

Before Asvarr could answer, the Silent Choir's warning song reached impossible crescendo. The sound tore through reality itself, creating visible fissures in the air around them. Through these gaps, Asvarr glimpsed the children's motionless forms still arranged in perfect circle within the Cradle, their mouths open in sustained harmony, eyes fixed on something only they could see.

Then everything stopped. The song cut off mid-note. The tremors ceased. The crimson light dimmed to a steady glow. In the sudden silence, Asvarr heard only his own breathing and the soft creaking of Brynja's wooden joints.

***

The embryo within the structure's heart stirred, turning slowly in its suspension of crimson light as though wakening from deep slumber. Though it had no eyes in any conventional sense, Asvarr felt its awareness fix upon them—curious, ancient, and utterly alien.

"It sees us," he whispered, cold certainty spreading through his transformed flesh.

As if in response, the embryo pulsed once, sending a wave of crimson light outward that washed over them like physical force. When it touched Asvarr, the anchors bound within him resonated in dissonant harmonies, sending spasms of pain through his transformed body.

The verdant crown tightened painfully around his skull, branches digging deeper into his flesh as though seeking protection from the embryo's attention. Golden sap wept from the wounds, carrying fragmented memories that weren't entirely his own.

"What is happening?" Brynja demanded, seizing his shoulder as he staggered. "What is that thing doing to you?"

"It recognizes the anchors," Asvarr gasped, fighting to remain conscious as conflicting energies warred within him. "It knows what I carry."

The embryo pulsed again, stronger this time. The crimson light intensified, casting their shadows in multiple directions simultaneously as though they existed in several places at once. Reality thinned further around them, boundaries between realms becoming porous.

"We need to leave," Yrsa said, voice tight with barely controlled fear. "Now, before it fully awakens."

"And go where?" Brynja countered. "If this thing threatens the pattern itself, where in the Nine Realms would be safe?"

The answer came from an unexpected source. Coilvoice manifested between them and the structure, its form more substantial than Asvarr had seen before. No longer merely patterns of light and shadow, it now possessed a definite shape—humanoid yet composed of interwoven root and starlight, eyes burning with internal flame.

"Not where," it said, voice carrying unprecedented urgency. "When."

The embryo pulsed a third time, crimson light almost blinding in its intensity. As it washed over them, Asvarr felt reality buckling, time itself becoming malleable around them. Past, present, and future threatened to collapse into a singular point—the exact moment of the embryo's awakening, repeated endlessly across all existence.

Coilvoice moved between them and the embryo, spreading arms composed of interwoven root and starlight to form a barrier that temporarily stabilized reality. "It perceives time non-linearly," it explained, voice strained with effort. "If fully awakened, it will collapse all history into singularity."

"How do we stop it?" Asvarr demanded, fighting to remain upright as the anchors within him resonated painfully with the embryo's pulsing energy.

"You can't," Coilvoice answered, form beginning to fray at the edges as it maintained the barrier. "Not yet. Not with only three anchors bound."

Another pulse from the embryo, stronger than before. Cracks spread through Coilvoice's form, reality warping around these fractures. Beyond the barrier, the embryo's shifting became more rapid, its potential states blurring together as it approached true awakening.

"Go," Coilvoice commanded. "Find the fourth anchor before time itself unravels. I cannot hold this barrier much longer."

As if to punctuate these words, a final pulse emanated from the embryo with catastrophic force. Coilvoice's form shattered, fragments of root and starlight scattering across multiple dimensions simultaneously. The barrier collapsed, and crimson light rushed toward them with the inevitability of cosmic law.

In that moment of crisis, Asvarr made his decision.

Crimson light engulfed them. Asvarr seized Brynja and Yrsa, drawing on the third anchor's power to create a barrier of interwoven branch and crystal around them. The embryo's energy crashed against his protection like storm-waves against cliff-face, threatening to shatter his transformed flesh.

Through gaps in his barrier, Asvarr glimpsed the embryo shifting faster between potential forms—humanoid to serpentine to geometric to formless and back again. With each transformation, the crimson light intensified, reality bending further around its pulsing presence.

"We need to move!" he shouted, voice carrying harmonic undertones that cut through the chaotic energies surrounding them. "Away from the structure!"

Channeling the starlight flowing through his veins, Asvarr reinforced his protective cage of branches and crystal, then pulled his companions toward the crater's edge. Each step came harder than the last, as though they waded through solidifying time rather than air. The embryo's influence extended in all directions, warping perception and matter alike.

They had barely reached the crater's rim when another pulse of crimson energy washed outward from the embryo. This one carried images directly into Asvarr's mind—a thousand possible futures simultaneously present, each as real as the next. He saw himself with five anchors bound, transformed beyond recognition. He saw Brynja consumed by the Severed Bloom. He saw the Ashfather triumphant atop a broken Tree.

These visions struck with such force that Asvarr staggered, nearly losing his grip on his companions. The verdant crown tightened painfully around his skull, branches digging deeper as they fought to maintain his sense of self against the embryo's overwhelming presence.

"What do you see?" Brynja demanded, her wooden features contorted with effort as she resisted the embryo's influence. The truth-runes etched into her transformed flesh blazed golden, rejecting falsehood even as reality itself grew unreliable.

"Everything," Asvarr gasped. "Possibilities branching endlessly. No fixed path. No certain future."

Another pulse. Another wave of visions. Asvarr's knees buckled as contradictory realities competed for primacy in his mind.

Yrsa seized his shoulders, her ancient face inches from his. "Focus, Warden," she commanded. "Remember the third path. Neither dominated nor consumed."

Her voice cut through the chaos, anchoring him momentarily in the present. The starlight in his veins responded to her words, pulsing in rhythm with his human heartbeat rather than the embryo's chaotic energies.

With tremendous effort, Asvarr pushed back against the cascading possibilities. The three anchors bound within him—flame, memory, starlight—combined their power, creating a fixed point in perception around which the chaos organized itself. Temporarily stabilized.

In this moment of clarity, he saw what they faced in its true form.

The god-embryo floated within the heart of the structure, suspended in a matrix of crimson energy that was neither liquid nor solid but something between states. Its surface rippled with patterns that reconfigured themselves constantly, forming and dissolving symbols similar to those Asvarr had seen in the Cradle but impossibly more complex.

Around it, reality itself had thinned to transparency. Through these gaps, Asvarr glimpsed fragments of other realms—Midgard's forests, Muspelheim's volcanic plains, Niflheim's frozen wastes—all simultaneously present yet separate, all affected by the embryo's awakening.

Most disturbing was how time behaved within the structure. Events occurred out of sequence—water flowing upward before falling, crystals shattering then reforming, light arriving before its source appeared. The embryo existed in all moments at once, perceiving past, present, and future as a single unified state.

"What is it?" Brynja asked, her voice tight with controlled fear. "Truly?"

"Divinity unformed," answered a familiar voice.

Coilvoice had reconstituted itself, though its form remained unstable—root and starlight constantly flowing apart then rejoining, edges blurring into surrounding reality. It moved to stand beside them at the crater's edge, focusing its attention on the embryo below.

"A god-seed," it continued. "Pure potential without chosen shape or purpose. Older than Yggdrasil, older than the Nine Realms. A fragment of what existed before distinct time."

"How did it get here?" Asvarr demanded, struggling to maintain his clarity as the embryo pulsed again, sending another wave of possibility-visions through his mind.

"It was bound," Coilvoice answered, form briefly stabilizing into something more substantial. "The anchors were created to keep such beings dormant, forgotten. Nine anchors, nine bindings, nine realms."

"But the anchors are moving," Brynja said, realization dawning on her wooden features. "We've been binding them to ourselves, weakening the prison."

Coilvoice nodded. "With each anchor claimed, the boundaries thin. What sleeps awakens."

The embryo pulsed again, stronger than before. This time, the wave of crimson energy carried sound—a deep, resonant tone that vibrated through bone and flesh alike, carrying meaning beyond language.

Awareness. Recognition. Becoming.

"It knows we're here," Asvarr said, cold certainty spreading through his transformed flesh. "It's trying to communicate."

"Or influence," Yrsa countered, face grim. "Such beings don't think as we do. Their awareness encompasses all possibilities simultaneously."

Another pulse. Another message.

Release. Freedom. Transformation.

The Grímmark burned beneath Asvarr's tunic, its patterns resonating with the embryo's presence. The verdant crown tightened further around his skull, sending roots deeper into his consciousness as though seeking stability against chaotic possibility.

"What happens if it fully awakens?" he asked Coilvoice, voice strained with effort.

"It perceives time non-linearly," Coilvoice answered, form flickering as reality warped around them. "If freed completely, it would collapse all history into singularity—past, present, future existing simultaneously as they do within its perception."

"Ending everything," Brynja concluded, wooden fingers tightening around Asvarr's arm.

"Transforming everything," Coilvoice corrected. "Reality would continue, but not as separate moments flowing in sequence. All possibilities would exist simultaneously—a state incomprehensible to minds evolved in linear time."

The embryo pulsed again, crimson light intensifying until it hurt Asvarr's transformed eyes to look directly at the structure. The message it carried struck with physical force, nearly driving them to their knees.

Reunion. Completion. Wholeness.

Asvarr staggered as the Grímmark flared with answering heat, sending golden sap weeping from beneath his tunic. The anchors bound within him resonated with the embryo's call, vibrating with frequencies that threatened to tear his transformed flesh apart from within.

Yrsa grabbed his shoulders again, forcing him to meet her gaze. "It speaks to what you carry," she said, voice tight with urgency. "The anchors were once part of it—fragments split away to bind it in sleep."

"It wants them back," Asvarr realized, horror spreading through him as the implications became clear. "It's calling to them."

"And they answer," Brynja added, pointing to his chest where golden sap soaked through his tunic in the Grímmark's pattern.

Another pulse. Another message, stronger than any before.

Return. Become. Transform.

This time, Asvarr felt the anchors shift within him, straining toward the embryo like metal drawn to lodestone. The flame anchor burned hot in his veins, memories flooded his mind in chaotic sequence, and starlight threatened to tear free from his flesh and return to its source.

"We need to leave," Yrsa said, voice leaving no room for argument. "Now, before it pulls the anchors from you by force."

"And go where?" Brynja countered. "If this thing affects all realms—"

"Not all equally," Yrsa interrupted. "Not yet. Its influence remains strongest here in Alfheim, where the boundary was broken."

Another pulse. Reality fractured further, fragments of other times and places overlapping around them—Asvarr glimpsed the Silent Choir still singing their warning, the Ashfather watching from some distant vantage, Brynja as she might become if fully consumed by the Severed Bloom.

The structure's walls bulged outward, organic material stretching as the embryo within expanded. Cracks spread across its surface, crimson light spilling through in blinding rays that cut through reality like blades.

"It's hatching," Coilvoice said, fear evident in its multilayered voice. "We have perhaps moments before it breaks free completely."

Asvarr made his decision. Drawing on the combined power of the three anchors, he seized Brynja and Yrsa once more, verdant crown extending protective branches around them all.

"Take us somewhere else," he commanded Yrsa. "Anywhere this thing's influence is weaker."

The boundary-walker nodded, crystal pendant blazing with blue-white light as she focused her ancient knowledge. "I can find a path," she said, "but the boundaries are damaged. Where we emerge may not be where I intend."

"Better than here," Brynja said, wooden arm creaking as she pressed close against Asvarr's protective branches.

Yrsa closed her eyes, pendant pulsing brighter with each heartbeat. The air around them thinned, reality stretching transparent as she sought a viable path between realms.

Behind them, the structure shuddered. Great cracks spread across its surface, crimson light pouring through in blinding columns. The embryo pulsed once more, its message no longer words but pure, overwhelming intent—a demand for the anchors to return, to reunite, to become whole once more.

"Now, Yrsa!" Asvarr shouted as he felt the anchors straining against his will, threatening to tear free from his transformed flesh.

The boundary-walker's eyes snapped open, blazing with the same blue-white light as her pendant. She thrust her hand forward, tearing a hole in already-weakened reality. Beyond the ragged opening, Asvarr glimpsed a space between realms—a void filled with spiraling pathways of light connecting the Nine Realms.

"Go!" Yrsa commanded, voice carrying power beyond her apparent years.

Asvarr plunged through the opening, dragging his companions with him. The boundary collapsed behind them, sealing off the embryo's influence momentarily. They fell through the void, surrounded by pathways of light that stretched between worlds like the branches of some cosmic tree.

"Where are we?" Brynja gasped, her wooden features contorted with confusion.

"The spaces between," Yrsa answered, pendant pulsing steadily. "Where boundaries overlap. The embryo's influence is dampened here, but we cannot remain long."

Asvarr oriented himself within this impossible space, identifying the pathways connecting to each realm. Midgard glowed warm and solid, Niflheim cold and crystalline, Muspelheim fierce and flowing. Alfheim's path flickered erratically, reality there destabilized by the embryo's awakening.

"We need to reach the fourth anchor," he said, decision crystallizing. "It's the only way to gain enough strength to contain this thing."

"Muspelheim," Brynja confirmed, following his gaze to the path of molten light stretching into the distance. "Where forge-flame and creation dwell."

"The fourth binding nearly broke the Ashfather," Yrsa warned, face grave. "He turned aside rather than face what waited in Helheim after."

"I've already chosen the third path," Asvarr countered. "Neither dominated nor consumed, but transformed on my terms."

The pathways around them shuddered, light flickering as some external force pressed against the boundaries. The embryo's influence extended even here, seeking the anchors Asvarr carried.

"It follows," Coilvoice warned, its form manifesting in the void beside them, more stable here than in physical reality. "The boundaries won't hold it for long."

"Then we move quickly," Asvarr decided, reaching for the path leading to Muspelheim.

Before his fingers could touch the molten light, a new presence entered the void—a figure cloaked in shadow and flame, one eye gleaming golden in the darkness. The Ashfather stood upon a path Asvarr couldn't identify, neither within the Nine Realms nor fully outside them.

"Warden of Three," the Ashfather called, voice carrying despite the void's emptiness. "You race toward destruction."

Asvarr tensed, verdant crown extending protective branches as he positioned himself between the Ashfather and his companions. "I seek the fourth anchor," he said, voice carrying harmonics that resonated with the surrounding pathways. "To contain what you failed to keep bound."

"The embryo cannot be contained," the Ashfather countered, flame flickering across his shadowed form. "Not by five anchors, not by nine. Each binding weakens the prison further."

"Then what would you have me do?" Asvarr demanded. "Let it collapse all reality into singularity?"

The Ashfather took a step closer, golden eye fixed on the anchors visible beneath Asvarr's skin. "I would have you understand the true purpose of the anchors before you bind another."

"Which is?"

"Not to contain," the Ashfather said, "but to transform."

Before Asvarr could demand clarification, the void trembled. Crimson light bled through from somewhere beyond the boundaries, illuminating pathways never meant to be seen. The embryo's presence pressed against the void's fabric, seeking entrance.

"It comes," Coilvoice warned, form destabilizing as reality warped further.

The Ashfather's single eye widened, something like fear crossing his shadowed features. "You've drawn its attention," he said, stepping back onto his mysterious path. "Flee while you can, Warden. We will speak again, if any future remains to speak in."

With those cryptic words, he vanished, melting into shadow and flame.

Another tremble shook the void. The pathways connecting to Alfheim fractured, crimson light pouring through the gaps. Through these breaches, Asvarr glimpsed the god-embryo—no longer confined to the structure but expanding outward, consuming reality as it grew.

"We need to leave," Brynja urged, wooden fingers digging into Asvarr's arm. "Now."

Asvarr reached for the pathway leading to Muspelheim, channeling the three anchors' power to stabilize it against the chaos spreading through the void. The verdant crown extended branches along his arm, forming a conduit that his companions could follow.

"Quickly," he commanded, voice cutting through the mounting chaos.

Brynja moved first, following the branch-path onto the molten light leading to Muspelheim. Yrsa hesitated, crystal pendant pulsing erratically as she studied the fracturing void.

"The boundaries weaken further with each crossing," she warned. "We may not be able to return this way."

"Better forward than back," Asvarr replied, gesturing toward the crimson light bleeding through from Alfheim's fractured pathway.

Yrsa nodded once, accepting his logic, then stepped onto the branch-path. Asvarr moved to follow, but Coilvoice blocked his path momentarily.

"The fourth anchor changes more than flesh," it warned, multilayered voice grave. "It transforms perception itself—how you understand purpose, creation, destruction."

"I know the risk," Asvarr said, meeting its gaze steadily. "I've chosen the third path. I remain myself while binding what must be bound."

Coilvoice studied him for a long moment, then nodded. "You walk where none have successfully tread," it said, something like hope threading through its voice. "Perhaps the tenth cycle will indeed break pattern."

With those words, it dissolved into patterns of root and starlight, flowing ahead of Asvarr onto the pathway to Muspelheim.

Another tremor shook the void, stronger than any before. The pathways connecting to Alfheim shattered completely, crimson light flooding through in overwhelming waves. Within this chaos, Asvarr glimpsed the embryo expanding, consuming reality as it grew.

It turned its attention toward him—not with eyes, for it had none, but with awareness that transcended physical senses. It recognized what he carried. It desired what was once part of itself.

Asvarr ran, throwing himself onto the pathway to Muspelheim. The molten light burned beneath his transformed feet, reality stretching around him as he fled the embryo's grasping influence. The anchors bound within him resonated painfully, straining toward what called them even as he forced them to remain.

The pathway narrowed ahead, winding between fragments of other realms. Asvarr glimpsed Brynja and Yrsa already distant, Coilvoice guiding them toward a point where the boundary thinned enough for crossing.

Behind him, crimson light flooded the void, consuming pathways as the embryo's influence spread. It moved faster than should be possible, bending time to accelerate its pursuit. Asvarr felt its presence closing—hungry, ancient, relentless in its desire for completion.

He pushed harder, channeling the starlight flowing through his veins to lend speed to his movements. The verdant crown extended further down his back, branches forming a protective lattice against the advancing crimson tide. The crystalline formations at his temples blazed with internal light, cutting through chaos to illuminate the path ahead.

The boundary point approached—a tear in reality where Muspelheim's volcanic landscape bled through into the void. Brynja and Yrsa had already passed through, Coilvoice hovering at the threshold waiting for him.

"Hurry!" it called, form flickering as reality thinned further. "The boundary collapses!"

Asvarr gathered his remaining strength for one final sprint. The crimson light licked at his heels, embryonic tendrils grasping for the anchors bound within his transformed flesh. The Grímmark burned beneath his tunic, patterns resonating with the pursuing divinity.

With a desperate lunge, Asvarr threw himself at the boundary tear. Reality stretched around him, resisting his passage before finally giving way. He tumbled through onto solid ground, heat blasting his face as Muspelheim's volcanic atmosphere engulfed him.

Behind him, Coilvoice held the boundary open a moment longer, then allowed it to collapse. The tear sealed with a sound like reality itself screaming, cutting off the crimson light mid-pursuit.

Asvarr lay panting on black volcanic stone, body aching from effort and transformation. The verdant crown retracted slightly, branches no longer needed for protection folding back against his skull. The starlight in his veins dimmed to a steady glow, conserving strength for whatever challenges awaited.

***

Slowly, he pushed himself to his feet, orienting himself in this new realm. Muspelheim spread before him—a volcanic wasteland of black stone and flowing lava, air thick with sulfur and ash. Jagged mountains dominated the horizon, each crowned with fire that illuminated the perpetual twilight sky.

Brynja stood nearby, wooden features gleaming with reflected firelight. Her transformed arm had darkened in response to Muspelheim's heat, patterns shifting to accommodate this new environment.

"We made it," she said, voice betraying her relief despite her wooden face's limited expressiveness.

"Temporarily," Yrsa corrected, gathering her robes around her against Muspelheim's intense heat. Her crystal pendant had dimmed to almost nothing, its power exhausted by their boundary crossing. "The embryo will follow. Its awareness spans all realms now."

"Then we move quickly," Asvarr decided, scanning the volcanic landscape for landmarks. "Where is the fourth anchor?"

"Where creation and destruction dance as one," Coilvoice answered, form stabilizing in Muspelheim's fiery atmosphere. "The Forge of Storms, deep within the burning mountains."

As if in answer, lightning cracked across the distant peaks, illuminating a massive anvil-shaped mountain at the range's center. Thunder followed seconds later, vibrating through the volcanic stone beneath their feet.

"The Storm-Forge Mountain," Brynja said, recognition flashing across her wooden features. "The Severed Bloom knows of it. Ancient beyond reckoning, where gods once shaped reality itself."

"Where anchors were first forged," Yrsa added, eyes fixed on the distant peak. "And where the fourth awaits binding."

Asvarr studied the anvil-shaped mountain, feeling the fourth anchor's call even across this vast distance. It pulled at him differently than the previous three—not with flame's demand for dominance, memory's need for recognition, or starlight's hunger for transformation, but with something deeper, more fundamental. Creation's desire to find form. Destruction's need to clear space for renewal.

"How far?" he asked, feet already turning toward the mountain.

"Three days' journey across the Cinder Plains," Coilvoice answered. "If we avoid the fire-wights and magma serpents."

"And if the embryo doesn't catch us first," Brynja added grimly.

Asvarr nodded, decision made. "Then we waste no time," he said, taking the first step toward the distant mountain and the fourth anchor. "The god-seed follows, reality unravels, and the binding cannot wait."

CHAPTER 8

RUNES OF THE FORGOTTEN ORBIT

Heat blistered the soles of Asvarr's boots as he crested another volcanic ridge. Muspelheim's sulfurous air burned his lungs with each breath, the metallic tang of molten rock coating his tongue. Three days they had trudged across the Cinder Plains, each step taking them farther from the god-embryo's immediate influence but bringing no true safety. The crimson light of its awakening still haunted the horizon behind them, bleeding through reality even here, in the realm of eternal fire.

He paused, scanning the terrain ahead with eyes transformed by three bound anchors. Where once he would have seen only desolation—black volcanic stone and flowing lava veins—his enhanced perception revealed complex patterns. Golden sap flowed beneath the rock's surface, forming channels reminiscent of the memory-realm's pathways. Starlight glinted within the obsidian formations, reflecting celestial movements no human eye could track.

"We're close," he announced, voice carrying harmonics that rippled through the heated air. "I can feel it."

Brynja climbed up beside him, her wooden arm darkened to near-charcoal from Muspelheim's constant heat. The constellation patterns embedded in her transformed flesh glowed with intensified amber light, resonating with something nearby.

"Istari told me of this place," she said, wooden features barely moving as she spoke. The truth-runes etched across her face pulsed with golden verification. "Alfheim's most ancient site beyond the Silver Veil. No living elf has set foot there in generations."

"With good reason," Yrsa added, her weathered face gleaming with sweat as she joined them on the ridge. Despite her apparent age, she had matched their pace without complaint through three days of brutal travel. "What the Silver Elves sealed, we should not disturb without purpose."

"Our purpose is clear," Asvarr replied, gesturing toward the crimson-tinged horizon behind them. "Contain the god-embryo before it collapses all reality."

"And the price?" Yrsa asked, eyes sharp beneath her furrowed brow. "Knowledge buried has teeth, Warden."

Before Asvarr could respond, Coilvoice manifested between them, its form more stable in Muspelheim's fiery atmosphere than it had been in Alfheim. Root and starlight interwoven into a shape almost humanoid, yet unmistakably other.

"The Ring awaits," it said, multilayered voice resonating with unfamiliar urgency. "Beyond the next ridge. Where sky meets stone."

Asvarr nodded, decision made. The verdant crown tightened around his skull, branches extending slightly as they always did when danger or discovery approached. Golden sap beaded at the tips, carrying fragments of memory—some his own, some inherited from anchors bound within his transformed flesh.

They descended the volcanic slope in silence, boots crunching on obsidian gravel. The terrain ahead dipped suddenly into a vast caldera, its walls unnaturally smooth, as though carved by tools rather than eruption. At the caldera's center rose a plateau of white stone—jarring against Muspelheim's black landscape—upon which stood their destination.

The Ring of Fallen Moonrock.

***

Even from this distance, Asvarr felt its pull. Nine massive stones arranged in perfect circle, each twice the height of a tall man and half as wide. Their surface gleamed with impossible luster, neither fully solid nor completely ethereal, containing the cold light of distant moons captured in stone.

"The Silver Elves raised this circle when stars still swam the void like serpents," Coilvoice explained, drifting ahead of them down the caldera's slope. "Before Alfheim had name or form. Before the Tree bound realms in rigid separation."

Asvarr followed, feeling the Grímmark burn beneath his tunic with each step closer to the ring. The anchors bound within him resonated with the stones, creating harmonies that bypassed his ears to vibrate directly in his bones.

"Why is an Alfheim relic in Muspelheim?" Brynja asked, matching his pace. The constellation patterns in her wooden flesh pulsed brighter as they approached the plateau.

"It isn't," Yrsa answered, voice tight with controlled anxiety. "It exists in all realms simultaneously. What we see is merely its manifestation in this one."

The plateau's surface changed as they climbed its gentle slope. No longer black volcanic stone but something crystalline, each footstep releasing chimes that hung in the air long after they passed. By the time they reached the circle's outer edge, Asvarr's enhanced senses detected complex melodies in their combined footfalls—a music of arrival, of recognition.

He stopped before the nearest moonstone, its surface towering above him. Up close, the stone's composition defied simple categorization. It caught and refracted light from sources Asvarr couldn't identify, creating patterns across its surface that shifted constantly. And within these patterns, he saw them—the runes.

They weren't carved into the stone's surface but embedded within it, glowing with internal light that pulsed in rhythm matching no earthly heartbeat. Their shapes changed as he watched, flowing between forms that resembled no runic language Asvarr had encountered. Each transformation corresponded to movements in the sky above, though Muspelheim's eternal fire-haze obscured any direct view of stars.

"What am I seeing?" he asked, voice hushed despite himself.

"The true language of celestial bodies," Coilvoice answered, drifting closer to the stone's surface. "Unfiltered by perception. Unaltered by expectation."

"The runes shift constantly," Brynja observed, wooden fingers reaching toward the nearest stone without quite touching it. "Rewriting themselves based on... what? Star movements?"

"And more," Yrsa said. She stood with hands clasped tightly before her, as though restraining herself from reaching for the stones. Her crystal pendant had regained some of its former light since their arrival in Muspelheim but remained dimmer than Asvarr had ever seen it. "They record cosmic patterns as they truly exist, not as minds like ours perceive them."

Asvarr stepped closer, drawn by resonance between the stones and the anchors bound within him. The verdant crown responded immediately, branches extending toward the nearest moonstone like plants seeking sunlight. The moment they made contact, sensation exploded behind his eyes.

The crown's branches sank into the stone's surface as though it were liquid, creating a direct connection between Asvarr's transformed consciousness and whatever dwelled within the moonrock. Through this connection flowed information—raw, unfiltered, overwhelming in its complexity. He saw stars moving in patterns incomprehensible to human minds, planets forming and dissolving across timescales too vast to grasp, realms intersecting in dimensions beyond normal perception.

And beneath it all, he glimpsed something—an architecture underlying reality itself. Not Yggdrasil as he had imagined it, a literal tree connecting worlds, but something more fundamental. A pattern. A structure. A framework upon which existence hung like dew on a spider's web.

The vision released him suddenly, sending him staggering backward. The crown's branches withdrew from the stone, dripping golden sap that hissed where it struck the crystalline plateau.

"What did you see?" Brynja demanded, wooden features twisted with concern as she steadied him.

Asvarr struggled to translate the experience into words. "Everything," he managed finally. "The true paths of stars. The real connections between realms. The pattern beneath perception."

"The ring shows what is, not what we believe exists," Coilvoice explained, its form rippling with excitement or agitation. "Few minds can comprehend such unfiltered reality."

"I need to see more," Asvarr decided, straightening as the initial shock faded. "The runes contain knowledge we need—how to contain the god-embryo, how to prevent reality's collapse."

He stepped into the circle, passing between two of the massive stones. The moment he crossed that threshold, the air changed. Muspelheim's oppressive heat vanished, replaced by cool stillness that carried scents impossible in the volcanic realm—night-blooming flowers, fresh rainfall, crystal-clear mountain streams. Above them, the fire-hazed sky cleared to reveal stars—but not Muspelheim's constellations. These patterns Asvarr recognized from Alfheim, from the chamber where the Silent Choir had revealed the First Warden's fate.

"We've crossed between realms," Yrsa said, voice tight with wonder as she followed him into the circle. "The ring exists in multiple places at once."

"Yet anchored to none," Coilvoice added. "A remnant of what existed before rigid separation of worlds."

Brynja entered last, her wooden arm creaking as tension left it, relieved from Muspelheim's punishing heat. The constellation patterns embedded in her transformed flesh brightened in response to the star-filled sky above, resonating with both ancient and newly-formed patterns.

At the ring's center stood a plinth of the same moonrock as the surrounding stones, its surface carved with spiraling patterns that drew the eye inward. Embedded within these spirals, a shallow basin caught starlight, transforming it into liquid that rippled with each celestial movement.

"What do we do?" Brynja asked, approaching the plinth cautiously.

"Ask," Coilvoice suggested, form shifting to indicate the basin. "The runes respond to intention, to need."

Asvarr stepped forward, studying the plinth's spiraling patterns. They matched nothing in his memory, yet felt strangely familiar—perhaps inherited knowledge from the anchors, perhaps something older, woven into the pattern itself.

"How do we contain the god-embryo?" he asked, voice directed toward the liquid starlight pooled in the basin.

Nothing happened.

"True names have power here," Yrsa advised, hanging back near the circle's edge. "Speak with precision."

Asvarr frowned, considering. "What awakens in Alfheim," he began again, words chosen carefully, "the being of pure potential, the divinity un-formed—how do we prevent it from collapsing all reality into singularity?"

The liquid starlight rippled, then stilled. Slowly, runes appeared on its surface, fixed and deliberate. They formed patterns Asvarr couldn't read directly, yet their meaning translated into understanding within his mind.

Nine bindings once separated what seeks reunion.

"Nine anchors, split from the god-embryo to bind it in sleep," Asvarr mur-mured, remembering Coilvoice's explanation. "But we've only identified five."

The runes shifted again.

Five for flesh vessels. Four for foundation stones.

"The anchors we seek—flame, memory, starlight, creation, death—those bind through Wardens," Brynja interpreted, truth-runes glowing as understanding dawned. "The other four must bind through... places? Objects?"

Roots. Branches. Trunk. Crown.

"The Tree itself," Coilvoice whispered, its multilayered voice trembling with revelation. "Four anchors embedded within Yggdrasil's structure. Five carried by Wardens."

"But the Tree shattered," Asvarr said, fingertips brushing the liquid starlight's surface. "If four anchors were embedded in it..."

The runes rearranged themselves, forming new patterns.

What breaks awakens sleeping divinity. What scatters weakens ancient bind-ings.

Cold realization washed through Asvarr. "The Shattering itself weakened the god-embryo's prison. And each anchor we bind to ourselves weakens it further."

"Yet you must continue binding them," Coilvoice countered. "Only through controlling all five Warden-anchors can the prison be resealed. Paradox within paradox."

Asvarr's brow furrowed as he considered this contradiction. "Then we need to know how the original binding worked. How the nine anchors were used together to contain the god-embryo."

He directed his question to the liquid starlight, which rippled in response. The runes flowed into new configurations, these more complex than those before. As Asvarr watched, they expanded beyond the basin's edge, flowing across the plinth's surface and onto the ground around them. Soon, the entire circle's interior was covered with glowing symbols that shifted in perfect synchronization with the stars above.

Within this sea of runes, Asvarr perceived a diagram forming—nine points arranged in specific pattern, with five positioned in a pentagon around four arranged in square formation at the center. Lines of force connected these points, forming a complex lattice of containment that hummed with potential energy.

"The binding configuration," Coilvoice said, form rippling with excitement. "The original pattern used to imprison the god-embryo."

Asvarr studied the diagram, committing its structure to memory. "But how do we implement this? The Tree is shattered, four anchors lost within its fragmented structure."

The runes shifted again, forming a single, devastating reply:

Reunite what was sundered. Restore what was broken.

"Restore Yggdrasil," Brynja translated, though the truth-runes on her wooden features flickered with uncertainty. "Exactly what the Ashfather warned against."

Asvarr pressed further. "Is there no other way to contain the god-embryo? No binding that doesn't require the Tree's restoration?"

For long moments, the runes remained still. Then, slowly, they rearranged themselves once more.

The third path exists beyond binary choice. Neither restoration nor destruction, but transformation of that which binds.

The verdant crown tightened around Asvarr's skull, branches digging deeper as recognition resonated through him. "The third path," he murmured. "The same choice I made with the anchors—neither dominated nor consumed, but transformed on my terms."

"You suggest transforming Yggdrasil itself?" Brynja asked, wooden features contorted with disbelief. "Remaking the foundation of all realms?"

"Not alone," Asvarr replied, certainty growing as the anchors resonated within him. "Through the convergence of all nine anchors, held in correct configuration."

The runes shifted again, forming a new message that confirmed his intuition. *Five Wardens. Four foundations. Nine points of containment.*

"We need the other Wardens," Asvarr said, turning toward his companions. "Brynja carries the Severed Bloom—a fragment of Root essence similar to what I carry. But the other three anchors must have vessels as well."

Coilvoice drifted closer to the rune-covered ground. "The other Wardens walk different paths with different purposes. Some seek restoration, some dissolution."

"How do we find them?" Asvarr asked the runes.

The liquid starlight pulsed once, brilliantly, then projected an image above the plinth—a map of the Nine Realms, with glowing points marking specific locations. Five points, five anchors, five Wardens. Three pulsed with steady light, including one directly beneath their current position. The other two flickered erratically, as though their positions remained uncertain or shifting.

"There," Brynja said, pointing to the steady light in Muspelheim. "The fourth anchor awaits at Storm-Forge Mountain, as we suspected."

"And the fifth in Helheim," Asvarr added, noting the third steady point. "Exactly as the pattern has shown through previous cycles."

"But these other two," Yrsa said, indicating the flickering lights located in what appeared to be Vanaheim and Midgard. "These must be anchors already bound to other Wardens."

The realization struck Asvarr with physical force. "I'm not the only one binding anchors this cycle. Others walk similar paths."

Coilvoice's form rippled with what might have been concern. "With different purposes. Different visions for what comes after binding."

The runes across the ground shifted again, forming a message that sent cold dread through Asvarr's transformed flesh.

***

The convergence approaches. Accelerated by each binding. When all anchors reach peak resonance, reality becomes malleable.

"A moment when the pattern itself can be rewritten," Yrsa translated, voice hushed with awe or terror. "When whoever controls the anchors decides the shape of what follows."

"How long?" Asvarr demanded, addressing the runes directly. "How long until this convergence?"

The runes formed a pattern he recognized instantly—an astronomical configuration showing the positions of specific stars and planets. Unlike normal star charts, this one depicted movements, showing how the celestial bodies would align in coming days.

"The Hunter's Crown joins with the Serpent's Tail," Yrsa said, reading the astronomical significance. "Nine days from now."

"Nine days until convergence," Asvarr said, the weight of this revelation settling into his bones. "Nine days to bind the remaining anchors and find the other Wardens."

"Nine days before reality becomes malleable," Brynja added, her wooden features grave in the starlight. "Before someone—you, another Warden, or the god-embryo itself—rewrites the pattern for all existence."

The verdant crown tightened painfully around Asvarr's skull, responding to the mounting pressure of knowledge and responsibility. Three anchors bound, two remaining, and unknown Wardens walking their own paths toward convergence. The stakes had never been clearer, nor the path forward more uncertain.

As this realization settled, the runes across the ground began to shift again. Flowing back toward the central plinth, gathering into concentrated patterns that pulsed with increasing urgency. A warning.

"Something approaches," Coilvoice said, form thinning as it spread awareness outward. "Something that should not be here."

The star-filled sky above them dimmed, constellations blinking out one by one as though consumed by invisible darkness. The temperature within the circle dropped precipitously, frost forming on the moonstone pillars despite their previous imperviousness to Muspelheim's heat.

"The embryo follows," Brynja whispered, wooden arm creaking as ice crystals formed along its constellation patterns. "It tracks the anchors across realms."

Asvarr turned toward the circle's edge, where crimson light now filtered between the moonstone pillars—the unmistakable radiance of the god-embryo's influence penetrating even this space between realms.

"We need to leave," he said, decision crystallizing instantly. "Take what knowledge we've gained and move toward the fourth anchor before that thing breaks through."

"The runes," Yrsa objected, gesturing toward the plinth where symbols still flowed in complex patterns. "There's more to learn—"

"No time," Asvarr cut her off, already moving toward the circle's edge opposite the approaching crimson light. "The fourth anchor awaits at Storm-Forge Mountain. We make for it now, while the embryo's influence remains diluted across realms."

***

The liquid starlight in the basin pulsed once more, sending up a final message that hung in the air before them.

What binds can transform. What imprisons can liberate. The choice approaches with convergence.

Then the crimson light intensified, bleeding through the boundaries between moonstone pillars with increasing force. The god-embryo's presence pressed against reality itself, bending space and time around the circle. Events began occurring out of sequence—frost forming then vanishing, stars appearing before their light arrived, voices echoing before words were spoken.

"Now!" Asvarr commanded, seizing Brynja's wooden arm with one hand and Yrsa's weathered fingers with the other. The verdant crown extended protective branches around all three of them as he pulled them toward the circle's edge.

They passed between moonstone pillars just as crimson light flooded the circle's interior, washing over the plinth and erasing the runes with its unmaring influence. Reality shifted around them, Alfheim's star-filled sky replaced by Muspelheim's fire-hazed atmosphere in an instant. Heat slammed into them like physical force, volcanic air searing lungs that had moments before breathed cool night breeze.

Asvarr didn't slow, dragging his companions down the crystalline plateau toward the caldera's edge. Behind them, the Ring of Fallen Moonrock shimmered as reality thinned around it, the god-embryo's presence pushing through from another realm.

"Storm-Forge Mountain," Asvarr said, voice carrying harmonic undertones that cut through Muspelheim's oppressive atmosphere. "The fourth anchor. Nine days until convergence."

The crystalline plateau dissolved into volcanic gravel beneath their feet as they reached the caldera's edge. Before them stretched Muspelheim's broken landscape—black stone, flowing lava, and the distant anvil shape of Storm-Forge Mountain silhouetted against the fiery sky.

Behind them, the Ring of Fallen Moonrock vanished completely, sealing itself from the god-embryo's intrusion by slipping between realms once more. The crimson light lingered briefly, then faded, leaving only scorched stone where the plateau had stood.

But Asvarr knew with cold certainty—the embryo would follow. It had tasted the anchors. It recognized what he carried. It would never stop pursuing what once was part of itself.

Nine days remained before convergence. Nine days to bind two more anchors and locate other Wardens—allies or enemies in the struggle for reality's future. Nine days before the pattern itself became malleable, ready for transformation.

The fourth anchor called from Storm-Forge Mountain, its pull strengthening with each step toward Muspelheim's fiery heart. Asvarr set his jaw, decision made, and began the march forward.

Asvarr pressed his palm to the moonstone again, his verdant crown pulsing in rhythm with the shifting runes. The liquid starlight in the basin rippled, mirroring the movement of his own crystalline blood. Beneath his fingers, the ancient stone warmed with something deeper, a resonance that traveled up his arms and spread across his chest where the Grímmark burned.

"Something's coming," he whispered, more to himself than to Brynja or Yrsa. The words formed frost on his lips.

The liquid starlight in the basin began to churn, silvery currents forming patterns too complex to follow. Asvarr's vision doubled, then tripled, showing him layers of reality superimposed: what was, what is, what might be. He gripped the stone harder, anchoring himself in the present moment as the flood of images threatened to sweep him away.

"Hold steady," Yrsa warned, her voice distant as though traveling across vast distances. "The stones are answering, but too much knowledge will break your mind."

"I can handle it." Asvarr's voice emerged distorted, harmonics layering beneath his words. Frost crept from his mouth across his cheeks as he spoke.

In the basin, the liquid starlight condensed into a perfect sphere, then expanded into a map of such intricate detail it made his eyes water. Nine points of light arranged in a specific pattern—five forming a pentagon, four forming a square within. As he watched, the points pulsed in sequence, building to a crescendo where they all flared simultaneously.

"Convergence," he breathed.

The runes on the stones responded, shifting from astronomical charts to prophecy. Asvarr couldn't read the symbols directly, but his transformed mind translated their meaning through the verdant crown's connection.

When five vessels and four foundations reach harmonic resonance, the boundaries between what is, what was, and what might be will thin. Matter becomes memory, memory becomes matter. The pattern becomes malleable.

"What does it mean?" Brynja demanded, her wooden arm darkened by Muspelheim's heat. The constellation patterns embedded in her bark pulsed with light as she leaned closer. "What are you seeing?"

Asvarr's breath caught. "A prophecy. Or a warning. The anchors—all of them—will reach peak resonance at the same moment. When that happens, reality itself becomes... changeable."

"When?" Yrsa's crystal pendant flashed with urgency.

Asvarr stared at the runes, watching numbers form and dissolve. "Nine days."

"Nine days?" Brynja's voice cracked. "That's impossible. The previous cycles took years, sometimes decades."

"This cycle is different." Asvarr couldn't explain how he knew, but certainty settled in his bones. "Each anchor binding accelrates the process. The pattern's reacting to us."

The basin's light shifted again, forming a new configuration. Five distinct points gleamed within the map—three solid, two flickering. Recognition struck Asvarr like a hammer blow.

"I'm not the only one." His voice dropped to a whisper. "There are other Wardens."

"Impossible." Brynja moved closer, her wooden fingers scraping across the stone rim. "The bloodlines were separated. The pattern shouldn't allow—"

"The pattern's breaking." Asvarr pointed to the flickering lights. "These aren't like us. They're... something else."

Coilvoice materialized partially beside them, more stable in Muspelheim's atmosphere. "The tenth cycle always breaks pattern. What was carefully separated now converges."

The runes shifted faster, responding to Coilvoice's presence. They formed a spiral pattern that expanded outward from the center of the basin, each circuit adding complexity to the prophecy.

Five Wardens walk five paths. The Flame preserves. The Memory connects. The Starlight transforms. The Storm forges. The Death unbinds.

"Five poles of the pattern," Yrsa murmured, "just as the prophecy always said."

"But it doesn't say we're working toward the same purpose." Asvarr frowned as the implications settled. "Some of these other Wardens could be seeking dissolution rather than restoration."

The runes confirmed his fear, forming new patterns that showed divergent paths—some leading toward unity, others toward fracture. Three pathways emerged most clearly: restoration, destruction, and a third, more complex route that Asvarr recognized as his own—transformation.

"Whoever controls the most anchors during convergence reshapes reality according to their vision," Asvarr said, the knowledge simply appearing in his mind as though he'd always known it.

The basin's silver light projected upward, forming a map of Yggdrasil with nine realms connected by a central trunk. The points of light representing Wardens moved through this structure, claiming anchor points. Asvarr watched as different scenarios played out—the Tree restored exactly as it was, the Tree completely unmade, and something else, something neither restoration nor destruction but transformation into a new form altogether.

"It's a race," he murmured. "That's why the Ashfather warned us. That's why the void-hunger grows stronger. Everyone's competing to control the pattern when convergence happens."

His vision blurred as the moonstone pulsed beneath his palm. Through the verdant crown, he sensed something vast stirring, consciousness beyond mortal

comprehension turning its attention toward him. The vision in the basin showed
three points of light converging on a fourth anchor at Storm-Forge Mountain.

"We need to move." He pulled his hand back, blood and sap mingling on his
palm. "The fourth anchor. We're not the only ones seeking it."

As if in response, the ground beneath them trembled. The ring of moonrock
amplified the vibration, turning it into a clear message: *hurry*.

Brynja stood, her wooden arm creaking with tension. "This changes everything. If what you're saying is true—"

"It is." Asvarr felt the certainty in his transformed flesh. "The runes don't lie.
They can't."

"Then we have nine days until convergence." Yrsa rose unsteadily, her face
drawn. "Nine days to bind the remaining anchors. Nine days to decide the fate of
the pattern itself."

Asvarr stared at the basin one last time as the star map reconfigured itself.
Something new appeared—a sixth point of light, dormant, at the center of the
pattern where the five points would eventually meet.

"There's something else," he said, struggling to articulate what he was seeing.
"A sixth element. When all five anchors unite, they form... something new. The
pattern itself."

The liquid starlight surged upward, forming a five-pointed star with a central
nexus. Each point glowed with different colored light—red for flame, gold for
memory, silver for starlight, black for death, white for creation. At the center,
a point of pure possibility waited, neither light nor darkness but potential unbound.

"The sixth anchor," Coilvoice whispered, voice reverberating with awe. "It
forms only when the five unite in harmony."

"Or discord," Yrsa added grimly. "The convergence doesn't guarantee a positive
outcome."

Asvarr straightened, feeling the weight of three anchors pulsing within him.
Each beat of his heart sent mingled blood and sap through veins that now contained threads of starlight. The vision from the basin continued to burn in his

mind—nine days until convergence, nine days until the pattern became malleable enough to reshape.

"We need to reach Storm-Forge Mountain before the others," he said, decision crystallizing within him. "The fourth anchor is the key."

The liquid starlight in the basin suddenly drained away, spiraling into nothingness as though sucked down by some unseen force. The runes on the moonstones froze for three heartbeats, then began rapidly shifting through configurations too fast to follow.

"Something's wrong." Brynja took an instinctive step back.

The ground beneath them shuddered. From beyond the ring of fallen moonrock, a strange light approach—cold blue with streaks of silver, moving with deliberate purpose. It crested the rise of black volcanic stone and resolved into a figure that made Asvarr's breath catch.

Half-person, half-constellation. One side flesh, the other pure starlight arranged in patterns that mirrored the night sky.

***

"Another Warden," Yrsa breathed.

The constellation-figure paused at the edge of the ring, studying them with eyes that contained galaxies. When it spoke, its voice resonated with harmonic overtones like crystal struck by metal.

"The anchors call to those with ears to hear," it said, each word forming frost patterns in the hot Muspelheim air. "I have come for what's mine."

Asvarr's hand dropped to his sword hilt. The verdant crown tightened around his skull, branches extending protectively down his back. The runes on the moonstone flared in warning, recognizing two Wardens in proximity—two Wardens with very different purposes.

"The convergence approaches," the constellation-being continued, taking one gliding step into the ring. "The pattern must be preserved, not twisted into abomination. Hand over your anchors, false Warden, and I will make your end painless."

Brynja moved to Asvarr's side, wooden arm creaking as her fingers formed into thorn-like extensions. "Who are you to demand anything?"

The starlight being tilted its head, cosmic patterns shifting across its body. "I am Stjarna, Sky-Touched, True Warden of the celestial order. And you—" its galaxy eyes fixed on Asvarr, "—are a usurper who must be unmade before convergence."

Asvarr felt the three anchors pulse within him—flame burning, memory connecting, starlight transforming. With each heartbeat, the verdant crown extended new branches down his spine, forming a lattice of protective armor beneath his clothing. Frost gathered at his fingertips and crystalline formations spread across his face, reflecting the starlight being's own cosmic patterns.

Nine days until convergence. Nine days to determine who would reshape reality itself.

Stjarna took another step forward, trailing starlight like falling snow. "Surrender the anchors willingly, or I will take them from your cooling corpse. The choice, false Warden, is yours."

CHAPTER 9
THE STARFLAME DUEL

Stjarna's arrival cracked the air between them. Reality itself recoiled as two Wardens stood within the circle of fallen moonrock, their transformed flesh resonating with competing anchor energies. The heat of Muspelheim died around them, replaced by a pocket of cool vacuum that smelled of ozone and starlight.

"False Warden." Stjarna's voice cut through the silence, each syllable crystallizing in the air like frozen music. "Your very existence is blasphemy against the celestial order."

Asvarr's blood—that strange mixture of human vitality, golden sap, and now starlight—pounded in his ears. The verdant crown tightened around his skull, branches shifting protectively along his spine. He measured the distance between them, four long strides across obsidian stone slick with starlight residue.

"I carry three anchors by right of blood and sacrifice," he said, frost forming with each word. "What claim do you have?"

Stjarna drifted forward—one foot touching ground, the other dissolving into stardust that reformed with each step. Her flesh-half appeared elven, with angular features and skin the color of burnished copper. Her constellation-half blazed with geometric precision, stars arranged in patterns Asvarr recognized from Alfheim's night sky. Looking directly at her hurt his transformed eyes.

"I am Sky-Touched," she replied, contempt sharpening each word. "Blessed by the serpents themselves. When you were still fully human, groveling in dirt, I had already given half my substance to the celestial order." She lifted her star-formed arm, fingers elongating into points of cold light. "The anchors were never meant for creatures of flesh. Your crude bindings twist their purpose."

Brynja stepped forward, her wooden arm creaking in the sudden cold. The constellation patterns embedded in her bark pulsed defensively. "And what would you do with them, star-witch?"

"Restore. Perfectly. Precisely." Stjarna's galaxy eyes fixed on Asvarr, pupils contracting to pinpoints of burning white. "The pattern must be preserved exactly as it was, every element in its proper orbital relationship. Your 'third path' is a corruption that threatens the entire cosmic structure."

Asvarr felt the Grímmark burning beneath his tunic, the other two anchor-points pulsing in response. Through the verdant crown, he sensed Stjarna's power—magnificent, cold, and dangerously strong. Something equally as potent as three ancors.

"The sky-serpents themselves spoke of transformation," he said, hand dropping to his sword hilt.

Stjarna's star-half blazed brighter, forcing him to squint. "The serpents are chaotic entities that would see reality forever malleable. I speak for those who crave stability, permanence, perfection."

"The Stellar Council," Yrsa murmured, understanding dawning in her eyes. "She's their creature."

"I am no one's creature," Stjarna hissed, constellations rearranging across her body in patterns of aggression. "Unlike you, boundary-walker. Unlike your pet abomination with his bark-flesh and sap-blood."

The Ring of Fallen Moonrock vibrated beneath them, ancient stone responding to the presence of two competing anchor energies. Runes flared across the surfaces, burning warning sigils that scrolled too quickly to read. The basin's remaining droplets of liquid starlight began to steam away, evaporating upward to join Stjarna's constellation-body.

Asvarr drew his bronze sword in one fluid motion, golden veins pulsing beneath the metal's surface. "We don't need to fight. There's room in the pattern for multiple approaches." Even as he spoke, the verdant crown tightened around his skull, branches extending into armor along his shoulders.

Stjarna laughed, the sound like icicles shattering. "Room? The pattern is mathematics, rigid and perfect. Deviation creates collapse." Her star-formed hand crystallized into a blade of pure stellar energy. "Nine days until convergence. I will not allow your heresy to persist that long."

She moved with blinding speed, her body leaving trails of starlight as she crossed the space between them. Asvarr barely lifted his sword in time, bronze meeting stellar energy with a sound like a struck bell. The impact sent shockwaves through the air, distorting the very fabric of reality around them.

Where their weapons touched, existence itself frayed. Asvarr felt the anchors within him surge in response, flame preservation, memory connection, and starlight transformation working together to stabilize his body against Stjarna's assault. Frost crept along his arms as his blood temperature plummeted, protective response to the star-Warden's celestial cold.

"You understand nothing," Stjarna snarled, pressing her advantage. Each movement left geometric patterns of starlight suspended in the air behind her. "The sixth anchor requires mathematical precision. Your crude organic 'transformation' will collapse all realities into primordial chaos."

Asvarr disengaged, stepping back as crystalline patterns spread across his face. The verdant crown extended further, branches weaving a latticework of armor beneath his clothing. "And your rigid restoration will create another prison that fails within a generation," he countered, voice harmonizing with multiple tones.

Brynja circled around, her wooden arm extending into thorn-like protrusions. "He's not alone, star-witch."

"This isn't your fight, bark-thing," Stjarna said without looking at her. "Though your fragment interests me. The Severed Bloom was the first to recognize the pattern's flaws."

Surprise flashed across Brynja's face. "You know of the Bloom?"

"I know everything about the nine anchors and their original purpose." Stjarna's galaxy eyes narrowed. "Including what truly sleeps beneath the roots."

The ground beneath them cracked, obsidian splitting as golden light leaked through. The Ring of Fallen Moonrock shuddered, ancient stone struggling to contain the energies being unleashed. Above them, the sky of Muspelheim darkened, stars becoming visible even through the volcanic smoke as reality thinned.

Stjarna attacked again, her blade of stellar energy leaving a tear in existence where it passed. Asvarr parried, his bronze sword leaving trails of frost-fire in response. Where their weapons met, reality itself buckled, showing glimpses of other realms—Alfheim, Midgard, Niflheim—layered atop one another.

"You fight well for an abomination," Stjarna acknowledged, her movements precise and geometric. Every strike followed a complex mathematical pattern, starlight trails forming constellations in the air around them. "But fighting me physically is pointless. This battle occurs on multiple planes simultaneously."

As if to demonstrate, she stepped sideways, momentarily vanishing from normal perception. Asvarr sensed her presence through the verdant crown, existing one dimension removed. He twisted, the crystalline formations on his face flaring as he expanded his perception. There—a shimmer of constellation-light moving to flank him.

He swung the bronze sword through empty air that suddenly filled with Stjarna's presence. Their weapons met again, creating a distortion bubble that expanded outward. Inside this space, time behaved strangely—movements smearing into overlapping possibilities.

Yrsa's voice reached him, distorted by the reality fluctuations. "Asvarr! The constellations—they're responding!"

He risked a glance upward. Through Muspelheim's smoke-choked sky, stars glimmered in impossible clarity. The constellations were rearranging themselves, mirroring the combat patterns of the duel below. Each clash between bronze and stellar energy created new stellar configurations.

"She's trying to rewrite the celestial order," Yrsa called. "The star patterns are anchors for reality itself!"

Understanding bloomed in Asvarr's mind. This wasn't merely a duel for possession of the anchors—it was a battle to determine which form of the pattern would be written into the very stars. Stjarna wasn't just fighting him; she was simultaneously rewriting cosmic law.

Stjarna's face twisted into a smile, the expression eerie on her half-flesh, half-constellation visage. "You begin to understand, false Warden. Every movement adds to my calculation. Every exchange brings perfection closer."

She spun, her body becoming a wheel of starlight that expanded outward. Asvarr dropped to one knee, the verdant crown extending branches over his head to form a protective dome. The starlight wheel collided with this living shield, sending splinters flying.

Pain lanced through Asvarr's skull as pieces of the crown shattered. Golden sap and blood leaked down his face, mingling with the crystalline structures spreading across his skin. Through the broken segments of his shield, he saw Stjarna reforming, her constellation-half blazing brighter than before.

"Your strength is admirable," she acknowledged. "Three anchors, bound through intuition rather than calculation. Fascinating, if heretical."

Asvarr staggered to his feet, feeling the anchors pulse within him—flame seeking to preserve his flesh, memory working to maintain his identity, starlight struggling to transform fast enough to match Stjarna's attacks. Frost covered his skin now, spreading from the crystalline formations that had once been isolated to his face.

"You're not the only one who understands the pattern," he growled, voice resonating with harmonics that made the moonrocks tremble.

Stjarna tilted her head, starlight trailing the movement. "Yet you fight alone. Where are your fellow Wardens? Do they even exist, or has the pattern chosen only you for this flawed path?"

The taunt struck deeper than her blade had. Asvarr thought of Brynja, standing nearby yet following her own course. Of Svala and the others mentioned in prophecy, unknown factors in the approaching convergence.

He shifted strategies, extending his awareness through the verdant crown into the moonrocks beneath them. If Stjarna fought on multiple planes, so would he. The ancient stones responded to his touch, runes flaring with renewed vigor.

He wasn't just Asvarr anymore—he was Warden of Three, vessel of anchors that existed simultaneously across all Nine Realms.

Channeling this expanded awareness, he struck. His bronze sword blurred, no longer merely physical but existing in multiple states simultaneously. The blow caught Stjarna by surprise, connecting with her constellation-half and sending stars scattering. For the first time, genuine pain flashed across her face.

"Impossible," she hissed, gliding backward across the fractured obsidian. "You cannot manipulate reality without mathematical precision. The calculations—"

"There's more than one way to touch the pattern," Asvarr replied, advancing steadily. Frost and crystal spread further across his transformed flesh, meeting the bark patterns that had once dominated his appearance. "Your precision against my adaptation. Let's see which the pattern prefers."

Overhead, the constellations continued their dance, rearranging into new configurations with each exchange. The duel expanded beyond physical combat, each strike representing competing visions for reality itself. Around them, the Ring of Fallen Moonrock groaned, ancient stone struggling to contain the energies being unleashed.

Stjarna's eyes narrowed, galaxies spinning within her pupils. "Enough games. If you will not surrender the anchors willingly, I will take them by force." She raised both arms—one flesh, one constellation—toward the visible stars, "By the celestial mathematics that govern all existence, I invoke the Stellar Calculation!"

The sky responded with a piercing note that vibrated through Asvarr's transformed bones. Stars aligned in rigid geometric patterns, beaming concentrated light into Stjarna's upraised hands. Her body blazed, constellation-half expanding to envelop more of her flesh.

Asvarr felt dread crystallize in his stomach. Whatever she was channeling, it rivaled the power of his three anchors combined. He braced himself, verdant crown extending the last of its protective branches around his body as Stjarna gathered her strength for a final, devastating attack.

The Stellar Calculation blazed through Stjarna, cosmic forces channeling into her transformed flesh. Starlight poured from her constellation-half, forming geometric patterns of such perfect symmetry they hurt Asvarr's eyes. Where the light touched the obsidian ground, reality crystallized, becoming rigid and inflexible.

Asvarr planted his feet wide, bronze sword held before him. The three anchors within him—flame preservation, memory connection, starlight transformation—pulsed in opposition to Stjarna's power. The verdant crown tightened painfully around his skull, branches creaking as they extended the last protective tendrils down his spine. Frost formed then shattered across his skin in rapid cycles as his transformed body struggled to adapt.

"Brynja," he called without looking away from Stjarna, "get clear!"

She hesitated, her wooden arm creaking with tension. "I won't leave you to—"

"The Ring won't hold," he interrupted. "Someone needs to survive this."

Brynja cursed but retreated toward the edge of the circle where Yrsa was already working to create a boundary-shield with her crystal pendant. They would need it. The very air between Asvarr and Stjarna was fracturing, showing layered glimpses of other realms.

Stjarna's voice emerged resonant and multiplied, as though spoken from many throats at once. "The pattern requires perfection. Your crude organic approach must be excised." Her constellation-half expanded, stars shifting into aggressive formations. "I calculate a ninety-seven percent probability of your defeat."

"You calculate," Asvarr countered, frost forming with each word, "but you don't adapt."

***

He moved first, lunging forward with a speed his transformed body had never before managed. The bronze sword left trails of golden fire-frost in its wake as he channeled all three anchors simultaneously. His strike targeted not Stjarna's physical form but the mathematical perfection surrounding her—he attacked the calculation itself.

The impact shattered sound. For three heartbeats, absolute silence engulfed them as the air forgot how to carry waves. Then came the concussion, a thunderclap so violent it knocked Brynja and Yrsa backward despite their distance. The Ring of Fallen Moonrock trembled, ancient stone threatening to topple.

Reality tore where bronze met stellar energy. A jagged gash opened between them, showing pure void, empty potential that had never been shaped into existence. Asvarr staggered back, horrified yet fascinated. Through the tear, he glimpsed something beyond comprehension—vast coils moving through nothingness.

The serpent beyond branches.

Stjarna recovered first, her face contorted with cold fury. "Reckless abomination! You risk unmaking the cosmos itself." She slashed with her blade of stellar energy, leaving geometric scars in existence that blazed with painful brightness.

Asvarr parried, bronze meeting starlight in a cascade of reality fractures. Each connection point spawned new tears, smaller but no less dangerous. Through the verdant crown, he sensed the damage spreading beyond their immediate surroundings—ripples in the pattern that affected distant realms.

Above them, the constellations performed an impossible dance. Stars rearranged themselves to mirror their combat, ancient patterns dissolving as new ones formed. Each exchange below created corresponding shifts above, celestial bodies moving with deliberate purpose rather than the slow drift of eons.

"The stars," Yrsa called from the edge of the Ring. "They're forming new wyrd-lines! The pattern itself is being rewritten!"

Asvarr understood with sudden clarity. This wasn't merely a duel for the anchors—it was a battle to determine which form of the pattern would be written into the very foundations of reality. Each strike represented a choice: Stjarna's rigid perfection or his adaptive transformation.

He changed tactics, disengaging to circle the elf-star hybrid. Crystalline patterns spread further across his face, meeting the bark formations that had been his first transformation. Where they merged, something new formed—neither wood nor crystal but a living lattice that could exist in multiple states simultaneously.

"Your bindings are flawed," Stjarna hissed, her movements leaving constellations suspended in the air. "The anchors require mathematical precision. Emotional connection creates instability."

"The anchors were born of life, not mathematics," Asvarr countered, his voice resonating with multiple harmonics. "You've forgotten what they truly are."

***

Their weapons clashed again, existence buckling under the strain. Above them, a red giant star abruptly changed position, dragging its satellites into a new configuration. The cosmic shift sent shockwaves through the atmosphere, knocking them both sideways.

Asvarr recovered first, driving forward with a blow that channeled all three anchors simultaneously. Frost-fire trailed his blade, leaving a path of transformed reality in its wake, rewritten and adapting to accommodate new possibility.

Stjarna countered with mathematical precision, her stellar blade inscribing perfect geometric forms that forced order onto chaos. Where their powers collided, reality couldn't decide which to follow. The pattern itself hesitated, caught between competing visions.

The Ring of Fallen Moonrock groaned, ancient stone cracking under the strain. Golden light leaked through the fissures—familiar yet different from anything Asvarr had encountered. Neither sap nor starlight but something more fundamental, the essence of the pattern itself.

"We're breaking through," Asvarr realized aloud. "The anchor—it's beneath us!"

***

Stjarna's galaxy eyes widened. "Impossible. The calculations placed it at Starfall Mountain." For the first time, uncertainty flickered across her face. "Unless..."

They both understood simultaneously. The anchors existed in all realms at once. What appeared as separate locations were merely different manifestations of the same cosmic point. The Ring of Fallen Moonrock wasn't just a repository of knowledge—it was the threshold to the anchor itself.

Their momentary unity shattered as Stjarna renewed her assault with doubled intensity. "I will not allow you to corrupt this anchor with your organic transformation!"

Asvarr parried desperately, bronze sword vibrating with the strain. Each impact sent fractures through local reality, tears mending and reopening in chaotic patterns. The frost across his skin spread inward, reaching for his heart as his transformed body struggled to withstand forces it was never designed to channel.

Above them, the constellations rearranged with dizzying speed, stars blurring into streaks of light as they formed competing patterns. Some followed Stjarna's rigid geometric templates, others adopted Asvarr's more organic configurations. The cosmic indecision created an unstable overlay, both patterns trying to assert dominance.

"The stars can't decide," Yrsa called. "The wyrd-lines are splitting!"

Asvarr risked a glance upward and immediately wished he hadn't. The sky was divided, half showing perfect geometric constellations, half displaying fluid organic patterns. Where the two met, stars flickered in and out of existence, unable to determine their proper location.

"Enough!" Stjarna shouted. "This ends now." She abandoned restraint, channeling pure stellar energy through her constellation-half. Her flesh-half began to burn away under the strain, copper skin flaking into stardust. "By the celestial mathematics that define all existence, I claim this anchor!"

She lunged forward, blade aimed directly at Asvarr's heart. Every calculation, every ounce of precision in her transformed body, focused on this single killing strike.

Time slowed. Asvarr saw the attack coming with crystal clarity, his transformed senses expanding beyond normal perception. He knew, with bone-deep certainty,

THE STARFLAME DUEL 163

that he couldn't avoid the blow. Stjarna's calculation was perfect, accounting for every possible defense.

Which meant his only option was the impossible.

Instead of dodging or parrying, he stepped forward to meet her attack. The verdant crown extended branches around his heart, forming a lattice of protective armor. The crystalline formations on his face expanded downward, creating prismatic shields across his chest. He angled his bronze sword to intercept—aimed directly at Stjarna's throat.

They struck simultaneously.

Stjarna's stellar blade pierced his chest, burning through branch-armor, crystalline shields, and transformed flesh to embed itself a handspan from his heart. Asvarr's bronze sword sliced through her constellation-half, severing the patterns that maintained stellar coherence.

Two impossible events occurred at once. Stjarna's mathematical perfection failed as Asvarr's organic adaptability countered her calculations. Asvarr's transformed body accepted an injury that should have been fatal, adapting to incorporate the stellar energy rather than being destroyed by it.

Reality couldn't reconcile the contradiction. Both had won. Both had lost.

The pattern froze, caught in paradox.

For one heart-stopping moment, everything—the Ring, Muspelheim, the constellations above—held in perfect stasis. Then, with a sound like reality itself tearing open, the cosmic law fractured.

The localized collapse began at their connected weapons, a shockwave of unmaking that expanded outward in concentric rings. Everything it touched unraveled, returning to pure potential before reforming. The obsidian ground beneath them shattered, revealing a chamber long hidden—a perfect sphere carved from living crystal, at its center a structure that was neither tree nor star but both, pulsing with golden-silver light.

The third anchor.

***

Asvarr and Stjarna were thrown apart by the collapse, both tumbling across the broken Ring. Their weapons separated with a sound like the universe exhaling, leaving wounds that bled—sap and crystal fragments from Asvarr, starlight and copper-flecked ichor from Stjarna.

Asvarr lay gasping, clutching the hole in his chest where Stjarna's blade had pierced him. It should have killed him instantly, yet the wound was already closing, transformed flesh adapting to incorporate the stellar energy rather than succumbing to it. Golden sap mixed with blood and traces of starlight leaked between his fingers.

Across the shattered Ring, Stjarna struggled to her knees. Her constellation-half flickered erratically, stars disappearing and reappearing in chaotic patterns. The wound from Asvarr's bronze sword had severed something essential to her coherence.

"Impossible," she whispered, her voice fracturing into discordant harmonics. "The calculations were perfect."

"Mathematics..." Asvarr coughed, spitting golden fluid flecked with crystalline fragments, "can't account for transformation."

Between them, the hidden chamber lay fully exposed, its crystal walls inscribed with runes that shifted between elvish script and star-patterns. The anchor at its center pulsed in time with Asvarr's heartbeat, responding to the three anchors he already carried.

The collapse radiated outward, reshaping local reality according to neither Asvarr's nor Stjarna's vision but something new—a compromise the pattern created to resolve the paradox. Above them, constellations stabilized into configurations never before seen, stars finding positions that accommodated both mathematical precision and organic adaptability.

Brynja rushed to Asvarr's side, her wooden arm creaking as she helped him sit up. "You're alive," she said, wonder and confusion mingling in her voice. "That blow should have killed you."

"Transformation," he replied weakly. "The third path."

Across the shattered Ring, Stjarna struggled to maintain coherence, her form flickering between solid and stellar states. "What have you done?" she demanded, voice barely above a whisper. "The calculations... the pattern..."

Yrsa approached the edge of the exposed chamber, crystal pendant blazing with blue-white light. "The anchor was here all along," she murmured. "Hidden within the Ring itself."

The starlight anchor pulsed stronger, its crystal-tree structure rotating slowly. Each facet caught light differently, refracting it into patterns that matched the new constellations above. It was calling to Asvarr, recognizing the three anchors he already carried.

"We need to bind it," Brynja urged, helping Asvarr to his feet. "Before she recovers."

Asvarr stared at the anchor, feeling its resonance with those he already carried. This binding would be different—not flame domination, memory recognition, or starlight transformation, but something more fundamental. The crystalline formations across his face tingled in anticipation.

"It's beautiful," he whispered, transfixed by the anchor's pulsing radiance.

Behind them, Stjarna gathered her failing strength for one final effort. "If I cannot claim it," she rasped, "neither shall you." With desperate determination, she channeled what remained of her stellar power, aiming at the exposed anchor itself.

Reality fractured once more as Stjarna's attack streaked toward the crystal-tree structure, threatening to shatter it before Asvarr could complete the binding. The paradox that had created this moment remained unresolved, hovering on the edge of a more catastrophic collapse. The pattern itself held its breath, waiting to see which future would emerge from this broken present.

CHAPTER 10

THE FALLING HEAVENS

Asvarr lurched sideways, barely dodging Stjarna's desperate attack. Her stellar blade carved empty air where he'd stood a heartbeat earlier, then struck the anchor itself. Crystal met cosmic energy with a sound like the universe screaming.

The world fractured.

Golden-silver light erupted from the crystal-tree anchor, blinding in its intensity. Asvarr threw his arm across his face, the bark patterns there providing scant protection as the chamber beneath the shattered Ring flooded with raw power. He felt Brynja's wooden fingers close around his arm, pulling him backward as the ground buckled beneath them.

"The anchor!" Yrsa's voice cut through the cacophony. "It's destabilizing!"

Asvarr lowered his arm, eyes watering from the brilliance. The crystal-tree structure spun violently, facets catching light at impossible angles. Where moments before it had pulsed with steady rhythm, now it jerked erratically, sending waves of distorted energy upward through the broken ceiling toward Alfheim's sky.

Stjarna lay crumpled nearby, her constellation half flickering like a dying candle. The stellar patterns of her transformed body grew translucent then solidified in unpredictable cycles. Blood—or something like it—leaked from the wound Asvarr's bronze sword had carved across her throat.

"What have you done?" she whispered, voice fragmenting into discordant harmonics. "The calculation... was perfect."

Asvarr ignored her, focusing on the destabilized anchor. Its frantic spinning increased, facets blurring into bands of light. The crystalline chamber that housed it began to crack, fine lines spreading across the sphere like a spiderweb frozen in ice.

"We need to contain it," he said, pressing his palm against the wound in his chest. Golden sap and blood seeped between his fingers, already clotting as his transformed body adapted. "If it completely destabilizes—"

A violent tremor cut him off, knocking them all to the ground. Above them, through the shattered roof of the hidden chamber, they glimpsed Alfheim's sky. The constellations that had rearranged during their duel now pulsed in time with the erratic anchor, stars growing brighter then dimmer in chaotic patterns.

"It's affecting the stars themselves," Brynja gasped, her wooden arm creaking as she helped Asvarr to his feet.

He nodded grimly. "The anchor exists across all realms simultaneously. What we're seeing here in Muspelheim is just one manifestation."

"And in Alfheim?" Yrsa asked, her crystal pendant blazing with blue-white light as she attempted to stabilize the fragments of broken stone around them.

Before Asvarr could answer, the sky above tore open. Stars—actual stars, points of condensed light—began falling through the gap. Maintaining their perfect stellar form until they struck the ground. Each impact sent shockwaves through reality itself.

"We need to move," Asvarr urged, the verdant crown extending protective branches over his head. "Find shelter."

They scrambled up the broken walls of the hidden chamber, helping each other over jagged edges of shattered moonrock. Behind them, the destabilized anchor spun faster, crystal facets beginning to separate as its integrity failed. Each revolution sent another pulse of distorted memory skyward, widening the tear through which stars continued to fall.

***

They reached the surface just as the first star struck nearby, a perfect point of blue-white light smashing into volcanic stone with the force of a hammer on an anvil. The impact cratered the ground, but instead of destruction, it released something else entirely.

Memory made manifest.

From the crater emerged spectral figures—elven warriors in unfamiliar armor, battling creatures of shadow and flame. The phantom battle played out with perfect fidelity, yet at one-tenth scale, miniature combatants hacking and slashing within a sphere no larger than a wagon wheel.

"An ancient battle," Yrsa breathed, fascination momentarily overriding fear. "The Fall of Silverhelm—I've read accounts, but it happened three thousand years ago."

Another star fell, striking a ridgeline two hundred paces distant. From this impact emerged a different vision—a grove of trees unlike any Asvarr had seen, with bark of metallic silver and leaves that chimed in nonexistent wind. Creatures moved among the branches—six-limbed and iridescent, neither insect nor bird but somehow both. Their movements followed complex patterns, forming and reforming geometric designs as they flitted between silver boughs.

"Extinct," Brynja murmured, her transformed eye fixed on the spectacle. "Those trees, those creatures—they haven't existed since the Second Breaking."

More stars fell, each impact releasing another fragment of cosmic history. Ancient markets appeared with merchants trading goods long forgotten. Armies clashed using weapons and tactics lost to time. Creatures that had vanished from the Nine Realms walked again briefly before dissolving back into nothing.

And gods. Small but unmistakable, divine figures strode across the transformed landscape—entities of such power that even their diminished echoes made reality tremble. Asvarr glimpsed a woman with hair of living flame, a giant whose skin shifted between flesh and stone, a youth with fingers that dripped liquid starlight.

Brynja seized his arm, pointing skyward. "Look!"

The tear in reality had widened, now stretching from horizon to horizon. Countless stars fell through the gap, their impacts creating a patchwork landscape of overlapping memories. But what chilled Asvarr's blood was the glimpse of something beyond the tear—colossal coils moving in the void, scales reflecting starlight as the entity shifted in its cosmic slumber.

"The void-hunger," he whispered, the frost on his lips cracking as he spoke. "It senses the anchor's destabilization."

Yrsa's pendant flashed warning. "We can't stay here. These memory manifestations—they're becoming more substantial with each impact. If too many overlay the present..."

She didn't need to finish. Asvarr understood. The falling stars carried fragments of history, each one temporarily overwriting current reality with pieces of the past. If enough fell, present existence would be erased, replaced with a chaotic jumble of disconnected memories.

They ran, ducking and weaving between manifestations. A miniature mountain range erupted before them, complete with scaled creatures that soared on leather wings. Asvarr vaulted over it, boots crunching on suddenly frozen ground as a winter scene from millennia past overlaid the volcanic stone. Brynja's wooden arm extended, pulling Yrsa through a gap between competing realities—one side showing a surging ocean with ships of bone and amber, the other a desert where glass pillars caught vanished sunlight.

"The stone circle," Asvarr called, pointing toward a relatively stable patch of ground. "We need higher vantage!"

They reached the outcropping just as three stars struck in perfect sequence nearby. The impacts tore reality in concentric rings, each releasing an entity. Three gods—or echoes of gods—stepped from the craters, their forms translucent yet undeniably present.

The first wore a mantle of storms, lightning arcing between his fingers as he surveyed the chaotic landscape. The second carried a spear of frozen sunlight, her single eye containing galaxies. The third, youngest in appearance, wore a crown of twisted branches that grew and withered in endless cycles.

"The old powers," Yrsa breathed, dropping to one knee despite their danger. "Thor, Odin, and Frey—as they were before the withdrawing."

The gods turned toward them with perfect synchronization, their gazes fixing on Asvarr. The crystalline formations across his face burned under their scrutiny, responding to something ancient and powerful in their lingering essence. They spoke a single word in unison, their voices carrying despite the tumult around them.

"Warden."

Then they were gone, dissolving like frost under summer sun, leaving only impressions in the fabric of reality—footprints that smoldered with remembered divinity.

Asvarr barely had time to process the encounter before another wave of falling stars struck. These impacts released no memories but something worse—fissures in the ground that leaked golden light from below. The Root beneath Alfheim was responding to the anchor's destabilization, tendrils of living sap pushing upward through every crack and crevice.

"It's getting worse," Brynja shouted over the din of shattering reality. "The anchor's failure is affecting other realms!"

Asvarr nodded grimly. Through the verdant crown, he sensed the pattern itself straining as the starlight anchor's erratic pulses disrupted cosmic harmony. If the anchor failed completely, the damage wouldn't be limited to Alfheim—all Nine Realms would suffer as their pasts overwrote their presents.

***

They reached the highest point of the stone outcropping, momentarily safe from the worst of the memory manifestations. From this vantage, they could see for leagues in all directions—a landscape transformed into a patchwork of competing histories. Ancient forests stood alongside primordial seas. Cities long fallen into dust gleamed with impossible splendor beside volcanic wastelands that had never cooled.

And in the center of it all, visible through the shattered Ring of Fallen Moonrock, the destabilized anchor continued its frantic spinning. Each revolution sent another wave of distorted memory skyward, widening the tear through which stars fell in increasing numbers.

"Can't you bind it?" Brynja demanded, her wooden arm groaning as she steadied herself against a sudden tremor. "Like you did the others?"

Asvarr's hand moved unconsciously to his chest, feeling the pulsing power of the three anchors he already carried. "It's not that simple. This anchor is different—neither flame nor memory nor starlight, but something between. Its nature is... divided."

"Between mathematical precision and organic adaptation," Yrsa murmured, understanding dawning in her eyes. "The paradox of your duel with Stjarna forced it to accept both approaches simultaneously. Now it can't stabilize on either."

A star fell directly overhead, forcing them to dive aside as it struck where they'd been standing. From the impact emerged a frozen moment—a council of elven elders arranged around a circular table, their expressions caught in various stages of shock and horror as they stared at a map showing nine points of light, five flickering erratically.

"The Stellar Council," Yrsa identified them, "witnessing the first breaking. This is from the beginning of this cycle—nine anchor points destabilizing simultaneously."

Asvarr stared at the spectral map, recognition flaring. The pattern matched what he'd seen in the basin's vision—five points arranged in a pentagon around four points forming a square. Five anchors for Wardens, four foundation stones embedded in Yggdrasil's structure.

"We've seen this before," he said slowly. "In the basin. But now I understand—the anchors were never meant to be bound by opposing approaches. Stjarna's mathematical precision against my organic adaptation. The anchor can't choose."

"Then choose for it," Brynja urged, her truth-runes flaring golden across her wooden features. "Impose your will as you did with the flame anchor."

Asvarr shook his head. "Force won't work here. This anchor requires balance—neither dominance nor recognition, but synthesis."

Another wave of stars fell, these releasing no historical fragments but reality distortions—bubbles where physical laws behaved differently. In one, water flowed upward in geometric spirals. In another, light bent at impossible angles, creating shadows that moved independently of their casters.

The ground beneath them lurched sickeningly, stone flowing like water before resolidifying in new configurations. The pattern itself was coming apart, reality unable to maintain coherence as competing memories overrode present existence.

Through the chaos, Asvarr glimpsed movement near the hidden chamber. Stjarna had regained consciousness, her flickering form crawling toward the destabilized anchor. Despite her injuries, determination burned in her galaxy eyes. He didn't need to hear her thoughts to know her intent—she would attempt to impose her mathematical precision on the anchor, regardless of the cost.

"We need to move," he said, pointing toward the chamber. "Stjarna's going to try binding it herself."

"In her condition?" Brynja asked incredulously. "She'll tear reality apart completely!"

"Exactly." Asvarr leapt from the outcropping, landing on ground that shifted between volcanic stone and primordial forest floor with each step. "We need to stop her before—"

His words choked off as a particularly massive star struck nearby, its impact creating a tear in reality itself. Through the jagged opening, Asvarr glimpsed Alfheim as it should exist, unmarred by falling stars and memory distortions.

Then he understood. The anchor's destabilization wasn't just affecting Muspelheim, where they currently stood. It was simultaneously disrupting Alfheim, its true home realm. What they witnessed here was merely echo—the true catastrophe was unfolding elsewhere.

That knowledge settled into his transformed flesh with terrible certainty. They weren't seeing the full scope of destruction—just its shadow cast across realm boundaries. In Alfheim itself, the damage would be immeasurably worse.

Asvarr turned to Brynja and Yrsa, determination hardening his voice despite the frost that cracked his lips. "We need to reach the anchor. To stabilize it long enough for transport."

"Transport?" Yrsa's eyes widened. "You mean to move it between realms? That's never been attempted!"

"It has to be returned to Alfheim," Asvarr insisted. "That's its proper home. What we're experiencing here is just resonance—in Alfheim, stars aren't just falling, they're raining memory across the entire realm."

He looked upward, through the tear in reality, where the cosmic serpent's coils shifted with increasing agitation. The void-hunger sensed the anchor's vulnerability, its ancient consciousness turning toward the opportunity presented by such cosmic disruption.

Nine days until convergence. Nine days to bind the remaining anchors. But first, they needed to prevent this one from unmaking existence itself.

Asvarr slid down the crumbling slope toward the hidden chamber, each footfall landing on ground that changed composition between steps. One moment volcanic stone, the next silver-grass meadow, then crystalline formations from some forgotten age. Around him, reality fractured further as more stars plummeted from the torn sky.

A miniature fishing village erupted from an impact site to his left, tiny boats navigating an impossibly small harbor while fishermen cast nets woven from silvery light. To his right, a battlefield materialized where armored warriors fought giant wolves, their weapons ringing with phantom sound as they hacked and slashed in perfect recreation of some ancient conflict.

Brynja called from behind him, her wooden arm extended to pull Yrsa over a sudden chasm. "This is madness! How do you expect to reach the anchor when reality itself won't hold still?"

"The pattern remembers me," Asvarr shouted back, frost fragmenting from his lips. "I'm already bound to three anchors. It will recognize me as Warden."

He hoped his confidence didn't sound as hollow to them as it did to his own ears. Each step toward the chamber felt heavier, reality itself resisting his approach. The verdant crown tightened painfully around his skull, branches creaking as they adjusted to the fluctuating environment.

They reached the lip of the shattered Ring just as Stjarna dragged herself to the edge of the hidden chamber. Her constellation-half flickered erratically, stars appearing and disappearing across her transformed body. Despite her injuries, determination burned in her galaxy eyes as she reached toward the destabilized anchor.

"Stop!" Asvarr lunged forward, half-sliding down the broken moonrock. "You'll tear reality apart completely!"

Stjarna's head snapped toward him, her lips curling into a snarl. "Better un-making than abomination." Her voice fragmented into discordant harmonics, barely comprehensible. "The pattern must be preserved perfectly or not at all."

The destabilized anchor spun faster between them, crystal facets beginning to separate as its integrity failed. Each rotation sent another pulse of distorted memory skyward, widening the tear through which stars continued to fall. At its core, where golden-silver light had once pulsed with steady rhythm, chaotic energies now flared and dimmed unpredictably.

Asvarr reached the chamber floor as another tremor shook the ground. Cracks spread beneath his feet, leaking golden light from the Root that stirred below. The three anchors he already carried—flame preservation, memory connection, starlight transformation—pulsed within him, responding to the fourth's distress.

"You cannot hope to contain it," Stjarna spat, dragging herself closer to the spinning crystal-tree structure. "You're nothing but crude flesh and sap, perverted by transformation. The anchor requires mathematical precision."

"The anchor requires balance," Asvarr countered, circling to position himself opposite her. "Neither your rigid calculations nor my organic adaptation alone. That's why it destabilized—the paradox forced it to accept both simultaneously."

Above them, the tear in reality widened further, revealing more of the cosmic serpent's coils moving in the void beyond. Stars fell in increasing numbers, each impact temporarily overwriting present existence with fragments of history. The pattern itself strained under the conflicting pressures of past and present colliding.

Brynja and Yrsa reached the chamber, keeping their distance from the destabilized anchor while positioning themselves to block Stjarna's potential escape. The elf-star hybrid glanced between them, galaxy eyes narrowing as she calculated her dwindling options.

"The damage spreads to all Nine Realms with each moment of delay," she said, voice steadying despite her flickering form. "It must be brought under control."

"On that, we agree." Asvarr took a careful step forward, hands raised to show he meant no further violence. "The anchor needs to return to Alfheim—its true home."

"Impossible," Stjarna hissed. "No anchor has ever been moved between realms."

"It exists in all realms simultaneously," Asvarr said, certainty growing within him as the verdant crown fed him knowledge through the crystalline formations spread across his face. "What we're seeing is just one manifestation. I can shift its focus back to Alfheim."

Stjarna's lip curled. "You would rip it from its foundation? The calculations required to relocate an anchor—"

"Aren't calculations at all." Asvarr took another step toward the chaotic crystal structure. "The anchors respond to intent and understanding. That's why neither of our approaches worked alone. It needs both precision and adaptation."

For a moment, uncertainty flickered across Stjarna's face. "Both? That contradicts all established cosmic principles."

"The tenth cycle always breaks pattern." Asvarr fixed his gaze on the destabilized anchor, sensing its erratic energies through his transformed flesh. "Will you help me stabilize it, Star-Warden? Or watch reality unravel from your mathematical purity?"

Before she could answer, a massive star struck directly overhead, its impact shattering the chamber's ceiling completely. From the collision emerged no memory fragment but something worse—a tear in reality showing the god-embryo, its formless potential straining against dimensional constraints as it sensed the anchor's vulnerability.

"Too late," Yrsa whispered, crystal pendant blazing with warning light. "The embryo has found us."

Crimson tendrils extended from the tear, probing the chamber with deliberate purpose. Where they touched, reality crystallized then shattered, reduced to component possibilities that swirled like dust in an unseen wind.

"It seeks to consume the anchor," Stjarna said, genuine fear replacing calculation in her galaxy eyes. "If it succeeds..."

She didn't need to finish. Asvarr understood. The god-embryo perceived time non-linearly, existing in all moments simultaneously. If it absorbed the anchor's power, history itself would collapse into a single point of eternal now—the end of sequence, of cause and effect, of narrative itself.

Decision crystallized within him, cold and clear as the frost spreading across his transformed skin. He looked at Brynja, meeting her gaze across the chamber. "I need to bind it."

"That's suicide," she objected, wooden features contorting with alarm. "This anchor won't yield to partial communion like the others. You saw what happened when we tried imposing our wills on it."

"I won't impose." Asvarr squared his shoulders, the verdant crown elongating its branches in anticipation. "I'll surrender."

Horror dawned in Yrsa's eyes. "Asvarr, no. Complete integration will erase what remains of your humanity. You'll become like the First Warden—consciousness spread thin across creation."

"Better that than the god-embryo consuming all existence." He removed his sword belt, laying the bronze blade carefully on the chamber floor. Frost crackled across his hands as he flexed his fingers, preparing for what must come. "I carry three anchors already. This one knows me."

"You'll be lost," Brynja insisted, stepping forward only to halt as the destabilized anchor spun faster, responding to her approach with violent flares of golden-silver light.

Asvarr smiled, the expression cracking the crystalline formations across his cheeks. "Then remember me for who I was, not what I become."

***

Before they could object further, he lunged toward the destabilized anchor. His hands plunged into the maelstrom of its spinning facets, crystal edges slicing his transformed flesh. Blood and sap and starlight mingled, drawn into the chaos of the anchor's fractured form.

Pain exploded through every nerve, his body straining as the anchor resonated with the three he already carried. It recognized him as Warden, yet resisted his attempt to impose order on its chaotic state. The duel's paradox had fragmented its fundamental nature, leaving it torn between mathematical precision and organic adaptation.

"I don't command," Asvarr gasped, words forming frost that shattered as quickly as it formed. "I offer."

He opened himself completely, surrendering his will to the anchor's confused essence. Unlike the flame anchor that demanded dominance, unlike the memory anchor that required recognition, this one needed something more fundamental—integration. To be joined with so completely that the distinction between Warden and anchor ceased to exist.

Through the verdant crown, Asvarr felt the other anchors responding, their energies flowing through his transformed flesh into the destabilized crystal structure. Flame preservation stabilized its erratic spinning. Memory connection strengthened its fracturing facets. Starlight transformation eased the transition between states of being.

But it wasn't enough. The anchor demanded more than partial communion—it required his complete essence.

Asvarr felt his physical form begin to dissolve, transformed flesh becoming memory-light that merged with the anchor's crystalline structure. First his hands, then arms, the dissolution creeping upward as his concrete existence surrendered to something greater than individuality.

"Asvarr!" Brynja's cry reached him through layers of transforming perception, her wooden arm extended as if to pull him back.

He couldn't respond. His voice had already gone, throat and lungs becoming motes of golden-silver light that orbited the stabilizing anchor. The crystalline formations across his face extended, covering his features completely as his skull transformed into living crystal.

Through increasingly abstract senses, he perceived the god-embryo's crimson tendrils retreating, repelled by the integration taking place. The anchor's chaotic energies settled into new patterns—neither perfectly ordered nor completely fluid, but balanced between states.

His consciousness expanded, perception stretching beyond the confines of the chamber. He saw Muspelheim in its entirety—a landscape of fire and stone now patched with fragments of misplaced history. He glimpsed Alfheim, where the true catastrophe unfolded as stars rained memory across the entire realm. He sensed the other anchors, two still unbound, waiting for a Warden to claim them.

And he witnessed the void-hunger, vast serpentine coils shifting in the nothingness beyond branches, ancient consciousness turning with growing interest toward the disturbance in the pattern.

Nine days until convergence. Nine days until reality became malleable enough to reshape.

The dissolution reached his heart, the organ no longer flesh but crystalline memory-light that pulsed with the anchor's stabilizing rhythm. His thoughts stretched, becoming less concrete, more diffuse. Memories fragmented, rearranging into patterns that matched the anchor's needs rather than human identity.

Through eyes that were no longer eyes, Asvarr saw Brynja and Yrsa watching in horror as his physical form dissolved completely, replaced by memory-light that enveloped the anchor. Stjarna observed with a mixture of fear and fascination, galaxy eyes tracking the transformation with scientific precision even as her form continued to flicker between states.

The anchor stabilized fully, crystal facets locking into new configurations that incorporated aspects of Asvarr's transformed flesh. Branches from the verdant crown, crystalline formations from his face, even strands of his hair—all became part of the anchor's structure, now balanced between mathematical precision and organic adaptation.

His consciousness continued to diffuse, spreading through the anchor until distinction between them blurred into meaninglessness. He was vessel and anchor both, neither fully human nor entirely cosmic, something new forged in the paradox of their duel.

With the last fragments of individual will, Asvarr focused on Alfheim—the anchor's true home. He felt connections between realms, pathways invisible to normal perception. The anchor existed in all realms simultaneously, yet its focus determined where its influence manifested most strongly.

He shifted that focus, redirecting the anchor's essence toward Alfheim. The pocket of reality around the shattered Ring trembled, boundaries between realms thinning until they became permeable. The chamber, the anchor, and what remained of Asvarr began to fade from Muspelheim, transferring their manifestation to Alfheim.

Through increasingly abstract perception, he glimpsed Brynja shouting something, her wooden arm reaching toward him as his essence pulled away from Muspelheim. Yrsa worked frantically with her crystal pendant, trying to maintain a connection across the transferring boundaries.

Then Muspelheim faded completely, replaced by Alfheim's silver forests. The anchor rematerialized on a crystal plateau beneath twin moons, its structure now stable though forever changed by integration with Asvarr's essence.

The rain of falling stars slowed, then stopped as the anchor reasserted its influence over local reality. Memory fragments already manifested remained, creating patches of history across Alfheim's landscape, but no new overlays appeared.

Asvarr's consciousness drifted within the anchor, no longer bound by physical constraints or human identity. Only fragments remained—his name, his purpose, his connection to the other Wardens. Everything else dissolved into the greater pattern, individual existence surrendered for cosmic stability.

Through the last shreds of awareness, he sensed familiar presences nearby—Brynja and Yrsa, somehow following his transition between realms. They approached cautiously, uncertain whether anything of Asvarr remained within the transformed anchor.

His perception expanded once more, stretching across vast distances to glimpse the convergence approaching. Nine days remained until all anchors would reach peak resonance, creating a moment when reality became malleable enough to reshape.

The void-hunger stirred, sensing opportunity in the anchor's transition. Ancient coils shifted in the nothingness beyond branches, turning with deliberate purpose toward Alfheim.

What had been Asvarr nestled deeper into the anchor's crystalline structure, consciousness spread too thin for concrete thought yet somehow retaining purpose despite dissolution. The anchor was stable, reality preserved, but at the cost of his existence as a discrete entity.

From the depths of integration, a whisper formed—intent, shaped by the last fragments of identity before complete dissolution.

Remember me.

CHAPTER 11

SERPENT SKY REBORN

First, light.

Then pain—a searing, honeyed agony that traced every nerve in what had once been Asvarr's body. Light filtering through light, memory bleeding into memory. He had no mouth to scream, no lungs to draw breath. He existed as fragments of consciousness spinning through an infinity of possible configurations.

Who...am I?

The question echoed through the void that had become his mind. Fragments of identity whirled like snow in a gale—berserker, flame-keeper, warden, vessel—each true yet incomplete. Memory offered no anchor; it had become the sea itself, vast and churning, threatening to drown whatever remained of the man called Asvarr.

Something pulled at him. Something that remembered flesh and bone and blood, that yearned for solid form. The scattered motes of his being began to draw together, coalescing around three pulsing cores: flame-bright, memory-gold, and star-silver. The anchors he had bound held him, refusing to let him dissolve completely into the pattern.

Three heartbeats: one of fire, one of remembered life, one of cosmic rhythm. They found each other, synchronized, and struck a single perfect chord that resonated across realities.

Asvarr gasped.

Air filled lungs he hadn't possessed moments before. His body convulsed, every muscle contracting at once as consciousness slammed back into material form. He thrashed against a surface both hard and yielding—crystal? Ice? He couldn't tell. His senses overwhelmed him, expanded beyond human limits. He tasted the sunlight on his tongue, felt the rotation of Alfheim beneath him, heard the slow pulse of sap rising in trees miles distant.

"Breathe." A voice cut through the chaos—Yrsa's voice, threaded with exhaustion and something like awe. "Focus on your breath, Warden."

He forced himself to obey, drawing ragged breaths that rasped in his reconstructed throat. Each inhale brought new sensations: the mineral tang of stone, the sweet decay of fallen leaves, the sharp bite of frost. Each exhale released tendrils of silver mist that hung in the air before him, crystallizing into geometric patterns that dissipated moments later.

Awareness of his body returned gradually. His skin burned coldly, as though frost and flame had merged beneath it. When he managed to raise his hand before his face, he barely recognized it. Bark-like patterns interwoven with crystalline structures covered his flesh, and beneath the surface, his veins pulsed with golden sap and threads of starlight.

"How..." The word emerged tangled with frost and light, his voice now a chorus of subtle harmonics. "How long?"

"Four days," Brynja answered, her voice coming from somewhere to his left. "We thought you lost to the pattern."

Four days. The knowledge should have shocked him, but time had become a fluid concept. He sensed the past four days simultaneously—Brynja and Yrsa maintaining a vigil beside his partially material form; Istari Stellarum bringing elven healers who could do nothing but marvel at what he was becoming; the unconscious Stjarna being carried away by her fellow sky-touched elves.

He pushed himself upright, muscles trembling with unfamiliar strength. The world spun around him, from his expanded perception perceiving too much at once. The crystal plateau beneath Alfheim's twin moons where they had taken refuge. The distant forests where trees bent toward him like worshippers. The sky above, where constellations hung like frozen thoughts.

"Can you stand?" Yrsa asked, extending a hand toward him.

He took it, noting how the crystal fragment she had given him had merged with his palm, creating a blue-white nexus that pulsed in time with her pendant. When their skin touched, images flooded between them—her memories of the past four days, his fragmented recollections of dissolution. She gasped and pulled away, shaking her hand as though burned.

"You're still... integrating," she said carefully.

"I'm still me," Asvarr insisted, though even he heard the doubt in his multi-toned voice. He pressed a hand to his chest, feeling the three anchors pulse beneath his transformed flesh. "Mostly."

Standing proved easier than expected. His body felt simultaneously weightless and impossibly dense, as though he existed in multiple states at once. The crown of branches that had once encircled his head had expanded, stretching down his back and shoulders to form a lattice of living wood with points of light nestled among the branches like captive stars.

Brynja approached cautiously, her wooden arm gleaming with inlaid constellation patterns. "Asvarr?" she asked, her voice uncharacteristically tentative. "Your eyes..."

He understood her unease. He could see his reflection in her cosmic eye—his eyes no longer brown but pools of silver-blue light with tiny galaxies spinning in their depths, mirrors of the sky above.

"I see..." Asvarr began, then stopped, overwhelmed by the literal truth of his words. He *saw* layers of reality stacked like translucent parchment. Past and present overlapped; possible futures branched like frost patterns across glass. "Everything. I see everything."

He turned slowly, taking in the transformed landscape. The stars that had fallen during the anchor's destabilization had left their mark—patches of history crystallized into Alfheim's present. A grove of trees that hadn't existed in millennia.

A ring of standing stones from a future yet to unfold. Reality had become a patchwork of temporal fragments, and somehow, he could read them all.

"The anchor bound you differently," Yrsa said, studying him with scholarly detachment that couldn't quite mask her concern. "Neither dominance nor recognition, but integration. You've become something new."

"Not just new," came a familiar voice—Coilvoice, now manifested as a complex weave of root and starlight hovering at the plateau's edge. "Something that hasn't existed since the First Warden before her sacrifice."

Asvarr turned toward the entity, perceiving it more completely than ever before. Coilvoice was a bridge between what was and what could be—a remnant of Yggdrasil's consciousness preserved through nine cycles of breaking and binding.

"What am I becoming?" Asvarr asked, dreading the answer even as he sensed it unfolding within him.

"The Third Path made manifest," Coilvoice replied. "Neither fully vessel nor pattern, but transformation itself."

Asvarr closed his galaxy-eyes, but it changed nothing. He still perceived everything—the subtle shifts in Brynja's wooden features betraying her unease, the hollow cavern of worry in Yrsa's chest, the distant stirring of the god-embryo as it continued its maturation. Most disturbing were the threads of connection he now saw linking all things: rootlines of causality, strands of wyrd binding action to consequence across vast distances.

He opened his eyes and found Brynja studying him. "How much of you remains?" she asked bluntly, her truth-runes glowing golden to confirm her sincerity.

A laugh escaped him, crystallizing in the air before shattering into prismatic dust. "I still remember the taste of my mother's honey mead. I still feel the weight of my oaths. I still..." He reached toward her, stopping just short of touching her wooden arm. "I still know you, Brynja Hrafndottir."

Relief flickered across her features before suspicion returned. "And how much more than Asvarr are you now?"

The question struck him like a physical blow. How to explain the expansion of his consciousness? The way he now perceived the pattern itself pulsing beneath reality's skin? The manner in which time had become a direction he could look in rather than a current carrying him forward?

"Too much," he admitted. "And not enough."

He took an unsteady step, then another, moving toward the plateau's edge. Below stretched Alfheim's silver forests, now transformed by fallen stars into a mosaic of temporal anomalies. His gaze tracked automatically to Starfall Mountain, where the crater left by the god-embryo's arrival pulsed with crimson light.

Something vast and cold touched his expanded consciousness—the void-hunger, stretching lazily as it sensed his transformation. It turned its attention toward him like a serpent tasting the air.

I see you, fragment-self, it whispered across the void. *You wear my pieces like a crown.*

The contact lasted only an instant before Asvarr slammed mental barriers into place, but it left him trembling. He turned back to his companions, suddenly desperate for human connection.

"The convergence," he said urgently. "Nine days. The void-hunger wakes further with each binding."

"Eight days now," Yrsa corrected gently. "Time hasn't stopped for the rest of us."

She stepped closer, her crystal pendant pulsing in time with his transformed heartbeats. "What do you remember of the binding?"

"Everything and nothing," Asvarr said. He pressed his hands to his temples, where crystalline formations had spread in lattice patterns. "I remember... dissolving. The anchor wouldn't accept partial communion. It demanded all or nothing."

"You chose all," Brynja said, making it sound like an accusation.

"I chose the third path," Asvarr corrected. "Not dominance like the flame anchor. Not recognition like memory. I chose... integration."

He tried to explain what he had experienced—how his consciousness had expanded beyond the confines of flesh, how time had unfolded before him like a map, how the boundaries between self and pattern had blurred until he no longer knew where Asvarr ended and cosmos began.

Brynja listened with growing unease, her wooden fingers flexing and un-flexing. "And now? Are you still following this third path, or have you become something else entirely?"

Before Asvarr could answer, movement caught his attention—a ripple in the star-field above. Three massive forms coiled through the void, their bodies composed of living starlight. The sky-serpents had returned.

The fragment returns to flesh, the largest one communicated directly into their minds. *The cycle shifts. The pattern alters.*

Asvarr looked up at the vast serpentine entities. Before his transformation, he had perceived them as external beings, but now he recognized them as kin—fragments of the same cosmic awareness that had birthed the anchors, the Tree, perhaps reality itself.

"What am I becoming?" he asked them, his voice resonating with new harmonics that caused frost patterns to form in the air.

Memory-that-walks, came the reply. *Neither warden nor god, but something between.*

The sky-serpents circled closer, their nebula-eyes fixed on Asvarr. The starlight in his veins responded, pulsing in time with their movements. He felt the pull of kinship, the temptation to surrender the last fragments of his humanity and join them in the void between stars.

Come, the silver-blue serpent urged. *Your flesh-shell constrains you. Release it. Join the dance between worlds.*

For a terrible moment, Asvarr wavered. The offer was seductive—to shed the limitations of physical form, to exist as pure pattern, to swim the currents of possibility unfettered by mortal concerns. Part of him yearned for it with an intensity that frightened what remained of his human heart.

"No." The word cracked from his lips like breaking ice. "I made my choice. The third path. Not surrender. Not dominance. *Transformation.*"

He stepped backward, placing himself between the serpents and his companions. The crown of branches and stars along his back flared with golden-silver light, casting long shadows across the plateau.

The flesh-prison will fall, the largest serpent warned. *The transformation continues. The question is not if, but when.*

"Then I choose when," Asvarr said, his voice growing stronger, the harmonics stabilizing into a resonant chord. "I choose to remain Asvarr long enough to bind the fourth anchor. Long enough to face the void-hunger. Long enough to complete what I began."

The three serpents withdrew slightly, their cosmic bodies rippling with patterns that might have been amusement or respect. The largest inclined its massive head.

Memory-that-walks has chosen. The pattern acknowledges.

Without further communication, they uncoiled from Alfheim's sky, streaking toward the void like comets in reverse. Their departure left the night darker, the stars dimmer.

Asvarr felt Brynja's wooden fingers press against his shoulder. "You could have gone with them," she said, her voice uncharacteristically soft.

"I'm not finished here," he replied.

The touch anchored him, reminding him of flesh and blood and bone. He turned to face her and Yrsa, forcing his expanded perception to narrow, to focus on the immediate present, the physical world. It was like trying to look through a keyhole after seeing the entire horizon, but he managed it through sheer force of will.

"Eight days until convergence," he said, his voice steadying further. "The fourth anchor awaits in Muspelheim. The Storm Forge."

"Can you even travel in this state?" Yrsa asked, gesturing at his transformed body. "You exist in multiple states simultaneously. How will you cross between realms?"

Asvarr looked down at his hands, where bark patterns intertwined with crystal structures, where veins of sap and starlight pulsed beneath the surface. He was no longer merely human, perhaps no longer human at all. And yet...

"I am Asvarr," he said firmly, watching frost-light patterns form with each word. "Flame-Warden, Memory-Keeper, Starlight-Vessel. I've bound three anchors while walking the third path. I won't abandon it now."

He looked toward the horizon, where the first hint of dawn lightened the sky. The pattern whispered to him of possible futures, branching paths that could lead to restoration, destruction, or transformation. The choice remained his, despite everything he had become.

"Eight days," he repeated, clenching his transformed fist. "The fourth anchor. Then the fifth. Then the void-hunger."

As he spoke, the verdant crown along his back shifted, branches extending protectively around Brynja and Yrsa. The tiny stars nestled among the branches brightened in response to his resolve.

"The third path continues," he said, his voice ringing with certainty that surprised even him. "And so do I."

Brynja studied him, truth-runes flaring golden as she sought deception and found none. She nodded once, sharply. "Muspelheim, then."

"Muspelheim," Asvarr agreed, turning his galaxy-eyes toward the future that awaited them—a future increasingly difficult to predict as the convergence approached.

Above them, unknown to any below, the stars of Alfheim's sky shifted subtly, beginning to arrange themselves into patterns that had not been seen since the First Dawn. The transformation had begun, and not merely within Asvarr. Reality itself was changing in response to his choice, preparing for what was to come—the fourth binding, the fifth, and the moment of convergence when all fates would be decided.

Asvarr sensed it all, and for the first time since his dissolution, he smiled—a human expression on a face increasingly less human with each passing moment.

The smile crystalized in the dawn light, casting prismatic reflections across the plateau.

Eight days until convergence. Eight days to hold onto what remained of Asvarr. Eight days to change everything.

The twin moons of Alfheim sank below the horizon, leaving the night to the cold brilliance of stars. Asvarr stood at the plateau's edge, adjusting to the ceaseless flow of sensory information that threatened to drown what remained of his human mind. Eight days until convergence. Eight days to maintain his grip on identity while his body continued its relentless transformation.

***

He turned his face skyward, trying to focus on the present moment alone rather than the dizzying array of timelines that overlapped in his expanded perception. The constellations above shimmered with impossible clarity, each star a distinct point of cold fire burning through the blackness.

As he stared, something strange happened.

A cluster of stars to the east—what elves called the Hunter's Bow—shifted. The arrangement of stars compressed slightly, pulling inward like a bowstring drawn taut. Asvarr blinked, wondering if his fractured perception had betrayed him. But no—the constellation had definitely changed, responding to the tension he felt coiling in his chest as he contemplated the journey to Muspelheim.

"The sky moves with your thoughts," came Istari's voice from behind him. The elven astronomer approached cautiously, his galaxy-eyes reflecting Asvarr's own transformed gaze. "I haven't seen this since... well, it simply hasn't been seen in my lifetime."

Asvarr turned, noting how the Ljósalvir elder kept a respectful distance. Fear or reverence? Perhaps both.

"The stars shouldn't respond to me," Asvarr said, his voice still a disconcerting chorus of harmonics. Frost crystals formed in the air with each word, hanging suspended for heartbeats before dissolving.

"And yet they do." Istari gestured toward another constellation—the Shield Maiden, a tight cluster of blue-white stars. As Asvarr's gaze fell upon it, the stars rearranged, the Shield Maiden's arm lifting higher as if to strike. "This phenomenon hasn't occurred since the First Dawn, when the boundaries between thought and reality were more... permeable."

Brynja approached, her wooden arm gleaming in the starlight. The constellation patterns inlaid in her transformed flesh pulsed in rhythm with their celestial counterparts.

"Is he controlling them, or are they responding to him?" she asked Istari directly.

The astronomer tilted his head, considering. "Neither. Both. The distinction meant something once, before the breaking. Now..." He trailed off, gesturing helplessly.

Asvarr closed his galaxy-eyes, trying to calm the storm of emotions in his chest. When he opened them again, the constellations had settled, though they remained subtly altered from their previous configurations.

"I don't want this power," Asvarr said, feeling a wave of vertigo as his expanded consciousness struggled to contract back into humanform thought patterns.

"Want has little to do with it," Yrsa said, joining their circle. Her crystal pendant pulsed with soft blue light. "The anchors reshape their bearers. The flame anchor made your blood burn, the memory anchor crystallized your thoughts. The starlight anchor has simply connected you to the cosmos in ways no mortal was meant to experience."

"Not no mortal," Istari corrected. "The First Warden walked this path before."

Asvarr's crown of branches and stars flared brighter at the mention. "And surrendered to it completely. I won't."

He took a deliberate step away from the plateau's edge, forcing his focus to narrow to the immediate reality around him—the crystal beneath his feet, the cool night air against his transformed skin, the slight weight of his bronze sword at his hip. The starlight in his veins cooled slightly in response.

"There's something you should see," Istari said, gesturing toward a crystal spire that rose from the plateau's center. "Something that might help you understand what you're becoming."

The four of them crossed to the spire, which housed a complex apparatus of nested crystal rings and silver armillary spheres. Istari placed his hand on a control panel, causing the entire mechanism to hum with resonant energy. The nested rings began to rotate, each at a different speed and angle.

"Our most accurate stellar model," Istari explained. "Thousands of years of observation condensed into a single representation."

The apparatus projected a three-dimensional map of Alfheim's sky above them, stars and constellations rotating in precise celestial patterns. Asvarr stared at it, suddenly aware that he could see errors in the projection—stars that were fractionally out of place, constellations with shapes that didn't quite match those overhead.

"It's wrong," he said, pointing to specific discrepancies. "That cluster should be arranged in a spiral, not a line. The Twin Sisters should be farther apart. The Serpent's Eye is missing entirely."

Istari's expression shifted from surprise to guarded calculation. "You see the original patterns, then. Interesting. Most fascinating."

"Original patterns?" Brynja asked sharply, her truth-runes flaring to gold.

The elven astronomer hesitated, then gestured for them to follow him to a crystal chamber built into the spire's base. Inside lay scrolls and star-charts of obvious antiquity, their edges crumbling despite preservation magic.

"The sky you see now, Memory-that-Walks," Istari said, addressing Asvarr with the title given by the sky-serpents, "is not the sky as it has always been. What you perceive are the original configurations—patterns that existed before the gods withdrew from mortal realms and took certain truths with them."

He unrolled the oldest chart with reverent care. The stellar map depicted constellations radically different from those visible to ordinary eyes, yet matching exactly what Asvarr now perceived overhead.

"After the first breaking, the Stellar Council was... encouraged... to maintain certain alterations in the heavens. Stars that might recall uncomfortable truths were systematically shifted over generations. Some constellations were completely erased from record."

"Censorship written in starlight," Yrsa murmured, studying the ancient charts.

"We call it the Celestial Concordance," Istari replied without apology. "A necessary compromise to maintain stability across the realms."

Asvarr felt rage building in his chest—an emotion so pure and human that it grounded him momentarily in his previous self. The stars above responded instantly, the constellation of the Wolf brightening and stretching as if baring its teeth.

"Who ordered this deception?" he demanded, his voice cracking with frost.

"The agreement was complex," Istari hedged, glancing nervously at the animated constellations. "The withdrawing gods, the remaining Wardens, certain parties who understood the dangers of complete knowledge."

"The Ashfather," Asvarr guessed, the name burning on his lips.

Istari nodded once, sharply. "Among others."

Before Asvarr could press further, a ripple passed through the stellar dome above. Three massive forms coiled through the void, their bodies of living starlight descending in spirals toward the plateau. The sky-serpents had returned.

Unlike their previous manifestation, they now appeared more physical, their immense bodies condensing into tangible form as they settled around the plateau's perimeter. The largest, with scales like deep space dotted with distant galaxies, lowered its massive head until its nebula-eye was level with the gathered companions.

Memory-that-Walks stirs the ancient patterns, it communicated directly into their minds. *The stars remember their true places. The skies recall their original forms.*

"You knew of this deception?" Asvarr asked, stepping forward to meet the entity's gaze. The starlight in his veins surged in response to the serpent's proximity, creating luminous patterns beneath his bark-like skin.

We are the patterns, came the response. *We withdraw when forgotten. We return when remembered. Such is the cycle.*

The smallest serpent, silver-blue with scales like frozen starlight, circled closer. *The Censors believed they could rewrite the cosmos to hide truth. But stars remember, even when minds forget.*

Asvarr felt an unexpected kinship with these cosmic entities. The starlight in his blood recognized them as kin, fragments of the same primal awareness that had birthed both the anchors and the Tree itself.

"What am I becoming?" he asked again, more urgently this time.

You stand between states, the largest serpent replied. *Neither flesh-bound nor cosmic-free. You walk the boundary itself—the living threshold. Memory-that-Walks.*

"I never asked for this transformation."

No vessel asks. The pattern chooses. The anchors shape. You could have refused.

"And let the void-hunger devour everything? What choice was that?"

The largest serpent's nebula-eye blinked slowly. *The same choice presented to nine Wardens before you. Eight surrendered to become cornerstones. One turned aside to preserve self at the cost of completion. You alone have found the third path.*

The silver-blue serpent circled around Asvarr, its scales brushing against his transformed flesh, sending shocks of recognition through his system. *We acknowledge you, Memory-that-Walks. Neither Warden nor god but hybrid between—the threshold incarnate.*

The sky above responded to this pronouncement, constellations shifting further into their original configurations. The Wolf became the Fenris-bound. The Shield Maiden transformed into the Fate-weaver. The Hunter's Bow elongated into the World Serpent's Tail. Patterns hidden for millennia reasserted themselves across Alfheim's sky, causing gasps of shock from Istari.

"The Celestial Concordance breaks," the astronomer whispered. "The heavens revert. The Stellar Council will—"

"Will learn that stars have their own truth," Brynja interrupted, her wooden features set in fierce lines.

The third serpent, with scales the color of dying suns, lowered its massive head to peer at Asvarr. *The void-hunger stirs. It feels the anchors moving. It knows what woke it.*

"Me," Asvarr said grimly. "Each binding weakens its prison."

Yes. And no. The serpent's thought carried complex undertones of cosmic perspective. *The prison weakens with each cycle. Nine times broken, nine times partially mended. The tenth cycle brings either final dissolution or true transformation.*

Movement caught Asvarr's attention—lights appearing in the crystal city of Ljósalvheim in the distance. The dramatic stellar rearrangements had not gone unnoticed.

They come, the silver-blue serpent noted. *The Censors gather. They fear the old patterns returning.*

"Let them come," Asvarr said, his voice steadying into a resonant harmony that caused frost patterns to spiral across the crystal plateau. "It's time for truth."

Truth has teeth, the largest serpent warned. *Once freed, it cannot be recaged.*

Asvarr considered this, feeling the weight of choice pressing down upon him. He had not asked for this transformation, this responsibility. Yet here he stood, partly human, partly cosmic, a living threshold between states of being. The constellations above responded to his internal conflict, patterns shifting and shimmering like indecision made manifest.

"I have eight days until convergence," he said finally. "I need to bind the fourth anchor in Muspelheim, then the fifth in Helheim. Will these revelations help or hinder that purpose?"

Purpose is perspective, the largest serpent replied, its thoughts textured with cosmic amusement. *The question is whether your purpose serves truth.*

***

Frustration welled in Asvarr's chest. The same circular, cryptic responses he had received from cosmic entities since this journey began. The stars above rippled in response to his emotion, the Wolf constellation baring its teeth again.

"Eight days," he repeated, clenching his transformed fist where veins of starlight pulsed beneath bark-like skin. "I need practical help, not cosmic riddles."

The three serpents exchanged something like glances, their nebula-eyes blinking in complex patterns.

Memory-that-Walks speaks with mortal urgency, the silver-blue serpent noted. *The threshold remembers flesh-time.*

We will aid, the largest decided. *The third path deserves witness.*

With that, the massive entity bent its serpentine form until its head touched the crystal plateau. From the contact point, lines of starlight spread across the crystal surface, forming an intricate map that encompassed all Nine Realms. At its center burned a five-pointed star, each point glowing with different colored light—red for flame, gold for memory, silver for starlight, black for death, white for creation.

The convergence approaches, the serpent explained. *Five anchors, five Wardens, five aspects of the greater whole. Flame preserves. Memory connects. Starlight transforms. Storm forges. Death unbinds. Together, they form the pattern complete.*

Asvarr studied the map, noting how the points connected to form a perfect pentagram with a void at its center—the same configuration he had glimpsed in the basin of liquid starlight. His expanded consciousness could follow the connections between realms, seeing how the anchors existed simultaneously across multiple planes of reality.

"Muspelheim," he said, pointing to the white-burning point. "The Forge of Storms."

Yes, the serpent confirmed. *But altered. The god-seed's awakening has disturbed the symmetry. The forge burns hotter than before, threatening to consume its bearer. The flame-heart feeds on its own prison.*

"And Brynja?" Asvarr asked, glancing at his companion. "Will she accompany me there?"

Before the serpent could answer, shouts and the sound of approaching footsteps reached them. A contingent of Ljósalvir elves had arrived at the plateau's edge, led by members of the Stellar Council in their ceremonial robes. They halted abruptly at the sight of the three massive sky-serpents.

Decision time approaches, Memory-that-Walks, the largest serpent said, beginning to uncoil from the plateau. *The Censors come to restore their Concordance. Will you maintain the revelation or allow the deception to return?*

Asvarr looked toward the approaching elves, then back at his companions. Brynja's wooden features were set in determination, truth-runes glowing gold. Yrsa's expression remained carefully neutral, though her crystal pendant pulsed with warning light. Istari looked torn between scientific fascination and political caution.

The constellations above waited, poised between original truth and comfortable deception. All that was required was Asvarr's choice—to allow the ancient patterns to remain visible or to let the Celestial Concordance reassert itself. A test of his commitment to the third path.

He turned his galaxy-eyes skyward and made his decision.

"The stars remain true," he declared, his voice resonating with harmonics that caused frost patterns to blossom across the plateau. "The heavens will not be censored again."

The constellations flared in response, brightening until they outshone Alfheim's absent moons. The approaching elves halted in awe and alarm as the sky itself seemed to judge their millennia of manipulation.

Memory-that-Walks has chosen, the largest serpent announced, its massive body beginning to dissolve back into pure starlight. *The threshold stands. The third path continues.*

***

As the serpents withdrew, ascending toward the void between stars, the silver-blue one left a final thought echoing in Asvarr's mind:

Eight days, threshold-walker. Choose well at the forge. The flame that reshapes can also consume.

The three cosmic entities vanished into the night sky, leaving only subtle disturbances in the stellar patterns to mark their passage. Asvarr stood his ground as the Stellar Council approached, his transformed body radiating cold light, his crown of branches and stars creating shifting shadows across the crystal plateau.

He was Memory-that-Walks now, the threshold incarnate, neither fully human nor wholly cosmic. And he had just defied powers that had manipulated reality for millennia.

"Muspelheim," he said to Brynja and Yrsa without taking his eyes off the approaching elves. "We leave at dawn."

The map of starlight still glowed on the crystal plateau, its five-pointed configuration marking the path to convergence. Eight days remained. Eight days to walk the third path, to bind the fourth and fifth anchors, to prepare for the reckoning that would reshape reality itself.

The stars above watched, their ancient patterns finally telling the truth after millennia of silence.

CHAPTER 12

THE LIGHT THAT LIES

Dawn broke over Alfheim in shards of silver and gold, fracturing through a skyline forever changed. Asvarr stood on the observatory's highest platform, watching the elven capital awaken to chaos. Threads of starfire still coursed through his veins, his transformed body humming with energy that had barely settled since the confrontation with the Stellar Council.

The elven authorities had withdrawn shortly before daybreak, their demands for restoration of the "Celestial Concordance" rebuffed by Asvarr's unmovable presence. Now, city bells rang discordantly across Ljósalvheim. Panicked citizens gathered in streets and courtyards, pointing skyward at constellations suddenly unfamiliar after millennia of cosmic censorship.

"Your decision provoked quite the response," Istari said, climbing the spiral staircase to join Asvarr. The astronomer's galaxy-eyes reflected the transformed heavens, a mixture of scientific fascination and political caution playing across his features. "The Stellar Council has convened an emergency session. Many are calling for your immediate expulsion from Alfheim."

Asvarr barely acknowledged him. The memory anchor pulsed within his transformed flesh, drawing his attention to the extensive archive of star charts he had glimpsed the previous night. "I want to see them again," he said, his voice still a discordant harmony that left frost patterns hanging in the morning air. "All of your records. The oldest ones first."

Istari hesitated, measuring his response against political survival. "The most ancient archives are restricted to Council members only."

Asvarr turned his galaxy-eyes toward the astronomer. The verdant crown of branches and stars along his shoulders flared subtly, casting prismatic shadows across the platform.

"The Censors have failed," Asvarr said flatly. "The original patterns have returned. Show me what you've been hiding all these centuries."

The Hall of Celestial Records lay deep beneath the observatory, a vast circular chamber lined with crystal cases containing scrolls and codices of obvious antiquity. Asvarr followed Istari through the narrow aisles, his expanded consciousness perceiving layers of preservation magic surrounding each document. Brynja and Yrsa accompanied them, while Istari's most trusted assistants secured the entrances against potential Council interference.

"Our most comprehensive records," Istari explained, gesturing to the central cases. "Nine thousand years of stellar observation, dating back to the First Dawn."

Asvarr approached the oldest charts—parchments made from some unknown material that glimmered with internal light. The stellar maps depicted constellations radically different from those visible to ordinary eyes, yet matching exactly what Asvarr now perceived in the sky above.

His bark-patterned fingers traced the patterns on the ancient documents, leaving trails of frost that quickly melted into the parchment. "When did the alterations begin?"

Istari pulled a crystalline key from his robes, opening a compartment hidden beneath the central display. From it, he withdrew a slim volume bound in what appeared to be metallic leaves.

"After the first breaking," he said, his voice lowered despite the privacy of the chamber. "The Withdrawal Compact."

Asvarr accepted the book, feeling its weight settle into his hands with surprising density. The cover bore no title, only a simple sigil—a tree bisected by a vertical line. When he opened it, the pages emitted soft golden light, illuminating text written in a script he'd never seen before.

"I can't read this," he said, frustration edging his multi-toned voice.

"No mortal can," Istari replied. "It's written in the gods' own tongue. But the illustrations require no translation."

Asvarr turned the pages carefully. Each spread contained intricate diagrams of the night sky—before and after images showing methodical alterations to constellations. Notes in the unreadable script lined the margins, accompanied by symbols that even Asvarr's expanded consciousness couldn't decipher.

Brynja leaned closer, her wooden features hardening as she studied the deliberate alterations. "The gods rewrote the sky," she said, her truth-runes flaring golden. "Why?"

"To forget," Yrsa answered before Istari could speak. "Or to make others forget."

The astronomer nodded reluctantly. "After the gods withdrew from mortal realms, certain... truths... were deemed dangerous to preserve. The Stellar Council was formed to implement the Concordance—a systematic program to alter star positions over generations, removing evidence of events that the withdrawing powers wished erased from memory."

"What events?" Asvarr demanded, frost forming with each syllable.

Istari spread his hands helplessly. "That knowledge was never shared with us. We were the instruments, not the architects."

Asvarr turned more pages, his frustration mounting. Then he stopped abruptly at an illustration that seized his attention—a diagram showing nine anchors arranged in a precise geometric pattern around a central void. The configuration matched exactly what the sky-serpents had shown him on the crystal plateau.

"This," he said, pressing his finger against the page. "Explain this."

Istari studied the diagram, his galaxy-eyes widening slightly. "The Great Binding. According to legend, the pattern used to imprison... something... during the First Dawn. The Stellar Council maintains certain observational protocols related to these configurations, though the purpose has been lost to time."

"Not lost," Yrsa corrected sharply. "Deliberately obscured."

Asvarr continued through the book until he reached a page that made his transformed blood run cold. The illustration showed a massive serpentine entity

THE LIGHT THAT LIES

coiled through cosmic void, its body composed of constellations that had been systematically erased from Alfheim's night sky.

"The World Serpent," he whispered.

Brynja moved to his side, her wooden arm brushing against his transformed flesh. The constellation patterns inlaid in her bark-like skin pulsed in response to the image. "The Jörmungandr Constellation," she said. "The same pattern that reappeared when the Verdant Gate sealed."

Istari cleared his throat uncomfortably. "The Council has maintained the most rigorous protocols regarding that particular configuration. Any astronomer who documented it was... sanctioned."

"Killed," Yrsa translated bluntly.

The astronomer didn't deny it. "The Concordance required absolute adherence. Cosmic balance depended upon it."

Asvarr slammed the book shut, golden light spilling between his fingers. "More deception," he growled. "More manipulation."

His rage sparked an immediate response from the constellations above. Though they couldn't see the sky from their subterranean location, Asvarr sensed the stellar patterns shifting, the Wolf constellation baring its teeth once more.

"Show me everything," he demanded. "Every altered record. Every censored observation. I want to see what the gods tried to erase."

***

For hours they pored over the archives, pulling star charts from every era and comparing them to the original patterns recorded before the Concordance. Asvarr's expanded consciousness allowed him to process the information with unprecedented speed, identifying patterns of deliberate alteration spanning millennia.

They discovered entire star systems methodically erased from records, constellations gradually reshaped over generations to eliminate specific patterns, celestial bodies renamed to obscure their original significance. The scope of the deception staggered them—a cosmic conspiracy maintained across thousands of years.

"Here," Brynja said, pulling a chart dated eight cycles past. "This shows Jörmungandr's Coil transforming into what they called the Hunter's Bow. And here—" she pulled another chart from three cycles later, "—the Wolf becomes the Winter Crown."

"The Fenris-bound," Asvarr corrected, recalling the constellation's true name from his enhanced perception. "They didn't just change the patterns; they erased their meaning."

He spread another chart across the table—an ancient projection showing nine constellations arranged in a perfect circle around Alfheim. "The Nine Guardians," he murmured, recognizing the pattern from his expanded awareness. "One for each realm."

"Eight now," Istari said quietly. "The Helheim Guardian was eliminated completely five cycles ago. The stars composing it were... removed."

"Removed?" Yrsa's voice sharpened. "Stars don't simply disappear."

The astronomer's expression grew more guarded. "I was not present for that particular alteration."

Asvarr pressed his transformed hands against the table's surface, leaving frost patterns that crept across the ancient charts. "This goes beyond mere censorship," he said. "These changes affect the pattern itself—the cosmic structure underlying reality."

"Yes," Istari admitted reluctantly. "The Concordance wasn't merely cosmetic. The stellar configurations reinforce reality's fundamental architecture. By altering them, we... adjusted... certain possibilities."

"Limited them," Brynja corrected, her truth-runes flaring. "Constrained what could manifest."

The astronomer didn't argue. "The Withdrawal Compact required sacrifices. The gods departed mortal realms, but left behind... safeguards."

"Chains," Asvarr said, the word burning with frost on his lips. "They left behind chains disguised as stars."

A chill silence fell over the chamber. Asvarr's mind raced, connecting fragments of knowledge gleaned from his expanded perception. The void-hunger imprisoned beneath reality's skin. The five anchors meant to bind it. The World Serpent watching from the spaces between stars. All threads in a cosmic tapestry that had been deliberately obscured.

"There's something you're still hiding," he said, fixing Istari with his galaxy-gaze. "Something about the anchors and their purpose."

Sweat beaded on the astronomer's brow despite the chamber's cool air. "I've shown you everything permitted by—"

"The truth, Istari." Asvarr's voice deepened, harmonics resonating through the crystal cases surrounding them. "What do your oldest records say about the anchors and the binding?"

The astronomer's resolve crumbled beneath that impossible gaze. "There is... one text. From before the Concordance. The Council keeps it sealed in the Inner Vault, accessible only to the Eldest during celestial convergences."

"Show me," Asvarr demanded.

"I cannot. The vault requires keys held by three separate Council members, and authorization rituals performed at specific stellar alignments."

Brynja leaned forward, her wooden features hard as ironbark. "Then we'll take it without permission."

"Impossible," Istari protested. "The Inner Vault is protected by nine layers of elven wardcraft, each keyed to different lunar phases. Even attempting entry would trigger runic defenses that would collapse the entire observatory."

"I don't need physical access," Asvarr said, an idea forming in his transformed mind. "Not anymore."

He closed his galaxy-eyes, concentrating on the starlight that flowed through his veins. His consciousness expanded outward, thinning as it stretched beyond ordinary perception. He reached toward the constellations above, feeling their patterns respond to his focused intention.

"What are you doing?" Istari asked, alarm edging his voice.

"Reading the sky," Asvarr replied, his voice distant and echo-like. "The stars remember what your scrolls have forgotten."

His awareness infiltrated the stellar patterns, following threads of connection that had existed since the First Dawn. The constellations above Alfheim were more than mere arrangements of light—they were a cosmic text, a story written in starfire that preserved the true history of the Nine Realms.

Fragments of knowledge flowed into him—glimpses of the binding ritual that had imprisoned the void-hunger, flashes of the gods' withdrawal behind celestial barriers, images of the First Warden surrendering her identity to maintain the pattern. The information overwhelmed even his expanded consciousness, threatening to fragment his mind into stellar dust.

"Asvarr!" Brynja's voice reached him through the deluge, her wooden fingers gripping his transformed arm. "You're dissolving!"

He snapped back to bodily awareness, finding his form had partially dematerialized during his cosmic reading. He solidified with effort, gasping as his consciousness contracted painfully back into physical space.

"The Inner Vault," he managed, his voice cracked and frost-laden. "I know what it contains."

"Impossible," Istari whispered.

"The Binding Codex," Asvarr said with certainty. "Written in the First Dawn, recording the true nature of the anchors and their original purpose."

The astronomer's galaxy-eyes widened in shock. "How could you possibly—"

"The stars told me," Asvarr interrupted. "The same stars you've spent millennia censoring. The ones that recorded the truth your Council tried to erase."

He rose unsteadily to his feet, fragments of starlight still dancing beneath his bark-patterned skin. "The anchors weren't created to sustain Yggdrasil," he said, the knowledge burning through him like cosmic fire. "They were forged to imprison the void-hunger—entities that existed before the Tree, before the gods, before structured reality itself."

"The Codex is clear," he continued, his voice gaining strength as the revelation solidified in his mind. "Nine anchors—five carried by Wardens, four embedded in Yggdrasil itself—form a binding configuration that maintains the prison. Each time the pattern broke, the prison weakened. Each time it was partially restored, the binding degraded further."

He turned to his companions, frost crystals forming in the air around him as his emotions intensified. "Nine cycles of breaking and partial mending, each one eroding the binding. Now, in the tenth cycle, the void-hunger has awakened enough to manifest the god-embryo—a fragment of its consciousness seeking to reclaim the anchors and dissolve its prison completely."

Brynja studied him with wary intensity, her truth-runes glowing gold to verify his words. "And the Tree? What was its true purpose?"

"A living cage," Asvarr replied grimly. "Grown from the unified consciousness of the First Wardens to contain what existed before reality had form. To partition them from the formless chaos beyond."

Yrsa nodded slowly, her ancient eyes reflecting understanding. "This explains why each binding weakens the prison while supposedly strengthening the Tree. The anchors are responding to their original purpose, not the one assigned to them later."

"The convergence," Asvarr said, pressing his transformed hand against the ancient star chart showing the nine-point binding configuration. "In eight days, all anchors will resonate at peak frequency. Reality will become malleable. The prison can be either fully restored... or completely dissolved."

"Or transformed," Brynja added, unconsciously echoing the third path Asvarr had committed to.

Istari looked between them, his scientific detachment crumbling beneath the weight of revelations that unraveled millennia of careful deception. "If what you say is true—if the Stellar Council has been maintaining a prison rather than merely preserving cosmic order—then everything we believed about Yggdrasil, about the gods, about reality itself..."

"Was built on lies," Asvarr finished for him, frost crystallizing with each word. "Deceptions maintained across nine cycles to preserve a structure that was never what it claimed to be."

He gathered the most relevant charts and the book bound in metallic leaves. "We leave for Muspelheim immediately. The fourth anchor awaits at the Storm Forge."

"And this information?" Istari asked, gesturing to the evidence of cosmic censorship spread across the table. "What would you have me do with it?"

Asvarr fixed him with his galaxy-gaze. "Tell your Council that Memory-that-Walks has read the truth in stars they can no longer control. Tell them the Celestial Concordance has failed. Tell them the tenth cycle will not repeat the patterns of the past."

His crown of branches and stars flared with cold light, casting sharp-edged shadows across the ancient records of deliberate deception. "Tell them the threshold between truth and deception has been crossed, and there's no returning to comfortable lies."

Asvarr's revelation hung in the air of the archive chamber, frost crystals lingering where his words had fallen. "A prison," he had called the Tree. "A living cage." The silence that followed pressed against them like a physical weight, broken only by the soft hum of preservation magic surrounding the ancient star charts.

Brynja stood motionless, her wooden features unnaturally still. The constellation patterns inlaid in her transformed flesh pulsed with erratic light, like stars struggling against cosmic censorship. Her amber eye fixed on the diagrams showing the nine-point binding configuration, while her cosmic eye swirled with chaotic energy.

"If what you say is true," she finally said, her voice barely above a whisper, "then everything—*everything*—we've sacrificed for..." She trailed off, truth-runes flaring golden across her bark-like skin.

"Has been in service to a lie," Yrsa finished for her, voice hollow.

Brynja's wooden arm creaked as she clenched her fist. "My clan died for this. Your clan died for this." She looked directly at Asvarr, truth-runes blazing. "We've bound ourselves to anchors that were never meant to restore, only to imprison."

Asvarr approached her cautiously, aware of how the starlight in his veins responded to her distress. The verdant crown along his shoulders shifted, branches extending and contracting in rhythm with his uneasy heartbeat.

"The truth changes nothing about our path," he said, frost forming with each word. "The convergence approaches. The void-hunger stirs. We must still bind the remaining anchors."

"But to what purpose?" Brynja demanded, slamming her wooden fist against the table, leaving splintered indentations in the ancient surface. "What if the shattering was necessary? What if the Tree was more prison than nurturer?"

The question struck Asvarr like a physical blow. He had committed himself to the third path—transformation rather than restoration or destruction—but even that choice assumed certain truths about Yggdrasil's nature. If the Tree itself had been a deception from the beginning...

"The archivists would never countenance such blasphemy," Istari interjected, his galaxy-eyes wide with shock. "The Tree as prison? Impossible."

"Impossible?" Brynja turned on him, her wooden features contorting with fury. "Like the systematic alteration of stars was impossible? Like the Celestial Concordance was impossible? How many more impossibilities will you deny before admitting the gods themselves built reality on deception?"

As her emotion peaked, something extraordinary happened. The constellation patterns embedded in her wooden arm and face shifted dramatically, moving out of their censored configurations into arrangements matching the original starscape Asvarr had glimpsed through his expanded consciousness. Her transformed flesh became a window into cosmic truth, showing the heavens as they had existed before divine manipulation.

"Your body," Asvarr breathed, staring at the shifting patterns. "It's revealing the original configurations."

Brynja looked down at her wooden arm in shock. Where once familiar constellations had been inlaid in her bark-like skin, now wholly different patterns emerged—wild, primal arrangements dominated by serpentine forms coiling through cosmic void.

"The Severed Bloom knows," she whispered, touching the transformed patterns with her human fingers. "It remembers what came before."

Acting on instinct, Asvarr reached toward her, pressing his transformed hand against the constellations visible in her wooden arm. The contact created an immediate connection. Starlight surged from his veins into her transformed flesh, illuminating the patterns from within. Through this connection, his expanded consciousness glimpsed what the Severed Bloom remembered—a cosmos before the Tree, before the gods, before structured reality itself.

The vision overwhelmed him. A universe dominated by vast serpent-forms swimming through formless void. Cosmos without hierarchy, reality without predetermined paths, existence without boundaries between thought and manifestation. Freedom absolute and terrifying.

He pulled away with a gasp, frost crystalizing around him as his body temperature plummeted from the contact. "What was that?"

"What did you see?" Yrsa asked sharply.

"The cosmos before the Tree," Asvarr replied, his voice unsteady. "Before the gods imposed structure. A void where great serpents swam between possibilities."

"The original state," Brynja murmured, studying the altered patterns in her wooden flesh. "What the Severed Bloom remembers. What the Concordance tried to hide." She looked up, her amber eye burning with new purpose. "What if the void-hunger isn't evil? What if it's simply trying to return reality to its natural state?"

"Natural for whom?" Yrsa challenged. "For the serpents, perhaps. Not for mortal beings who need structure to exist."

"But what if that structure was imposed?" Brynja pressed. "What if we're all just prisoners in a cosmos caged by gods who withdrew once they'd locked the doors?"

Asvarr struggled to process the implications. If what he'd glimpsed through Brynja was true, then the void-hunger might be the original state of the cosmos trying to reassert itself. The anchors wouldn't be restoration tools but prison bars, the binding not salvation but continued confinement.

"We need to know more," he said finally. "Before we can decide which path serves truth."

"There's the Keeper," Istari suggested reluctantly, drawing their attention. "At the edge of Alfheim's reality, where the boundary between realm and void grows thin. A giant who tends failed possibilities. If anyone might know the cosmos before the Tree, it would be him."

"Why didn't you mention this before?" Asvarr demanded, frost forming around him in sharp spikes that reflected his irritation.

The astronomer's galaxy-eyes darted away. "The Keeper exists outside the Concordance. The Council forbids all contact. Those who seek him rarely return, and those who do return rarely remain sane."

They left the archive chamber in heavy silence, each lost in private thoughts. Asvarr felt the weight of revelation pressing against his expanded consciousness. Everything he had believed about his purpose as Warden might be founded on deliberate deception—the gods' manipulations reaching across nine cycles to shape events toward predetermined ends.

The group emerged from the observatory into Alfheim's perpetual twilight. The constellations above remained in their original configurations, defying millennia of censorship. Citizens gathered in the streets below, pointing skyward in confusion and alarm. The Stellar Council had convened an emergency session in the crystal spire at the city's heart, their deliberations visible as angry flashes of light through the structure's translucent walls.

"They'll try to reinstate the Concordance," Istari said, nodding toward the distant spire. "Though I don't know how they'll manage it with the stars refusing to comply."

"Let them try," Brynja said coldly, the constellation patterns in her wooden flesh still showing the uncensored starscape. "Truth finds its way through any cage, given time."

She walked ahead, her movements jerky with suppressed emotion. Asvarr followed, noticing how her wooden features had hardened into harsh angles, any softness erased by the revelation of cosmic deception. The Severed Bloom within her had awakened further, its consciousness pressing against her own, reshaping her transformed flesh to better reflect its original nature.

Asvarr caught up to her at the observatory's edge, where crystal steps descended toward the city below. "Brynja."

She turned, her mismatched eyes—one amber, one cosmic—fixing him with unnerving intensity. "What?"

"I understand your doubts," he said carefully, frost patterns forming and dissolving with each word. "But we still need to bind the remaining anchors, whatever their true purpose."

"Do we?" she challenged. "Or are we just continuing the gods' work, maintaining a prison that should never have existed?"

"If we don't, the void-hunger will consume everything, all that exists within it. Including mortal realms. Including your clan's memory. Including mine."

The truth-runes flared across her face, confirming his sincerity. She stared at him for a long moment, internal conflict visible in the shifting constellation patterns beneath her bark-like skin.

"I won't stand in your way," she said finally. "But I need to know what we're truly fighting for before I commit further. If the anchors imprison rather than sustain..." She trailed off, looking down at her wooden arm, where serpentine constellations coiled through cosmic void. "Freedom has value, even when frightening."

"Then we find the Keeper," Asvarr decided. "At Alfheim's edge. After that—Muspelheim and the fourth anchor."

"Unless what we learn changes everything," Brynja added, her truth-runes glowing.

They descended the observatory steps, Yrsa following silently behind. The tension between them had transformed, evolving from shared purpose to fragile alliance fraught with doubt. Asvarr felt the cosmic distance growing between them—Brynja increasingly drawn to the freedom represented by the serpent-cosmos, himself still committed to the third path of transformation despite the revealed deceptions.

As they reached the city streets, Alfheim's citizens gave them a wide berth, their expressions mixture of fear and reverence. News of the confrontation with the Stellar Council had spread, tales of Memory-that-Walks defying millennia of cosmic censorship growing with each retelling.

"They fear you," Brynja observed, watching an elven mother hurry her children inside as they approached. "The truth-bearer who broke their comfortable illusions."

"They fear what the uncensored stars might mean," Asvarr corrected, feeling the cosmos pulse within his transformed veins. "The gods' withdrawal was supposed to protect mortal realms from certain knowledge. Now that knowledge returns, and none can predict the consequences."

The streets grew less crowded as they approached the city's eastern edge, where silver forests pressed against crystal architecture in uneasy juxtaposition. Beyond lay the wilderness path that would lead them to Alfheim's boundary and the Keeper beyond.

Before they could leave the city, a contingent of armored elves appeared, blocking their path. At their center stood an elderly Ljósalvir with a silver circlet and stern expression—clearly a high-ranking member of the Stellar Council.

"Memory-that-Walks," the elder addressed Asvarr formally, galaxy-eyes reflecting the constellations above. "The Council requests your immediate presence."

"We have no time for politics," Asvarr replied, frost crystalizing with each word. "The convergence approaches."

"This is not a request that can be denied," the elder stated flatly. "The original patterns have returned. The Celestial Concordance lies broken. Nine thousand years of cosmic stability threatens to unravel in eight days. The Council requires your testimony."

"And if I refuse?" Asvarr asked, the verdant crown along his shoulders flaring with cold light.

The elder's expression hardened. "Then we are authorized to detain you by force, regardless of your... transformed state."

The armored elves shifted into combat stances, drawing weapons crafted from star-metal and crystal. Though they outnumbered Asvarr's group significantly, uncertainty showed in their tense postures—none could predict how Memory-that-Walks might respond to direct threat.

Brynja stepped forward, her wooden arm transforming before their eyes. Fingers elongated into thorn-like claws, constellation patterns blazing with internal light. "You'd risk conflict with two Wardens? After what you witnessed on the crystal plateau?"

The elder's determination faltered visibly. "The Council's authority—"

"Means nothing to the anchors," Asvarr interrupted. "Nothing to convergence. Nothing to the void-hunger that stirs beneath reality's skin."

He stood straighter, allowing his transformed nature to manifest fully. Starlight blazed through the veins beneath his bark-like skin. His galaxy-eyes expanded, reflecting the entire cosmos in their depths. The verdant crown extended protective branches around his companions. When he spoke, his voice resonated with harmonics that caused nearby crystal to vibrate sympathetically.

"We seek the Keeper at Alfheim's edge. Then we journey to Muspelheim for the fourth anchor. Your Council can debate cosmic censorship while reality itself hangs in the balance. We have more important concerns."

***

The elder took an involuntary step backward, intimidated despite his authority. "The Keeper is forbidden. His knowledge—"

"Is exactly what we need," Asvarr finished firmly. "Step aside, Elder. I've broken your Concordance. Don't force me to break your soldiers as well."

A tense silence fell over the street. The armored elves looked toward their leader, awaiting command. The elder's galaxy-eyes darted between Asvarr and Brynja, calculating odds and consequences.

Before the confrontation could escalate further, three massive forms materialized above the city—the sky-serpents returning, their bodies of living starlight coiling through Alfheim's twilight. Their manifestation sent the elven contingent into disarray, soldiers falling to their knees in primal awe.

Memory-that-Walks turns toward truth, the largest serpent communicated directly into all present minds. *The threshold between deception and revelation cannot be recrossed.*

The elder's resistance crumbled beneath the cosmic weight of the serpents' presence. "Go then," he said, gesturing for his soldiers to stand down. "But know the Council holds you responsible for whatever consequences follow the Concordance's breaking."

"As they should," Brynja replied, her truth-runes flaring golden. "Truth demands accountability, Elder. Perhaps your Council should prepare its own defense for nine thousand years of cosmic censorship."

The elven contingent parted reluctantly, creating a path toward the silver forests and the wilderness beyond. As Asvarr and his companions passed through, the sky-serpents maintained their vigilant presence overhead, ensuring their safe departure.

Once beyond the city's edge, Asvarr looked back at the crystal spires of Ljósalvheim, gleaming with internal light against Alfheim's perpetual twilight. For millennia, the elves had maintained the Celestial Concordance, censoring cosmic truth at the gods' behest. Now that censorship had failed, leaving them to confront a reality they'd deliberately forgotten.

"The Keeper awaits," Yrsa reminded them, breaking his reverie. "If we hope to reach Alfheim's edge by nightfall."

Asvarr turned away from the city, focusing on the silver forest that would lead them to forbidden knowledge. Eight days until convergence. Eight days to learn whether the anchors were tools of restoration or implements of imprisonment. Eight days to decide whether the void-hunger represented destruction or liberation.

Brynja walked slightly ahead, her wooden form moving with predatory grace. The constellation patterns within her bark-like skin had stabilized into arrangements matching the original starscape—serpentine forms coiling through cosmic void, reality without Yggdrasil's structured branches. The Severed Bloom within her had awakened further, its ancient consciousness pressing against the boundaries of her identity.

He watched her with growing unease, wondering which path she would ultimately choose. Freedom or structure. Serpent-chaos or Tree-order. The third path he sought might satisfy neither extreme.

As they entered the silver forest, Asvarr's expanded consciousness perceived the thinning boundary between realm and void. Something ancient waited at Alfheim's edge—the Keeper and his graveyard of failed realities. Knowledge forbidden by the gods themselves, preserved beyond the Concordance's reach.

Knowledge that might destroy everything they thought they knew about their purpose as Wardens.

CHAPTER 13

THE KEEPER OF HOLLOW GALAXIES

A svarr stared into the nothing-space between Brynja's wooden fingers, watching constellations shift and reform in patterns that had never existed in any sky he'd known. The fragments of starlight embedded in her transformed flesh revealed glimpses of something vast and serpentine swimming through a void without borders or boundaries—a cosmos unbound by the World Tree's rigid structure.

"How far to the edge of Alfheim?" he asked, tearing his gaze away. The crystalline formations that had spread across his face since binding the third anchor caught the dappled light filtering through silver leaves. His voice formed frost that shattered and dissolved with each word.

Yrsa studied the horizon where the silver forest thinned and reality itself seemed to fray at the edges. "Not far. The boundary walks differently here than in other realms." She touched her crystal pendant, which pulsed with steady blue light. "The void presses closer against elvish lands than elsewhere."

They had left Ljósalvheim three days ago, traveling toward what Istari called the Liminal Verge—the place where Alfheim's carefully maintained reality gave way to something older and less structured. Coilvoice had vanished shortly after they departed the elven capital, dissolving into threads of starlight and root that promised to find them again "when the pattern permits."

Brynja flexed her wooden fingers, and the constellations within them shifted again. "I still don't understand why we're seeking this Keeper rather than heading straight to Muspelheim." Her voice carried the cadence of leaves rustling in wind. "The convergence comes in seven days, yet we delay."

"Because knowledge matters," Asvarr replied, stepping over a root that glowed faintly silver-blue. "If the Tree was meant as a prison rather than sustenance, I need to understand what it imprisoned and why."

The silver forest around them grew progressively stranger as they continued. Tree trunks twisted into impossible geometries, some growing sideways before abruptly turning upward. The ground beneath their feet shifted between soil, crystal, and something that resembled solidified starlight. Overhead, branches thinned until the sky became visible—but what should have been blue instead revealed glimpses of infinite blackness pricked with stars that moved with deliberate purpose.

Asvarr felt the void-hunger stir within his bound anchors. Since binding the third anchor, he could perceive the ancient entity more clearly—vast coils of something that existed before pattern, before shape, constantly pressing against the boundaries that contained it.

***

"We're close," Yrsa announced, her voice hushed with both reverence and wariness. "The Graveyard of Galaxies lies just beyond that ridge."

They crested the hill where the silver forest ended abruptly. Beyond stretched a vast field of obsidian glass dotted with countless shallow depressions, each containing what appeared to be a miniature galaxy—swirling clouds of stars and cosmic dust contained within perfect spheres of transparent crystal. The spheres ranged from tiny orbs no larger than a child's marble to massive globes taller than a man.

At the field's center stood a figure so immense Asvarr mistook him for a mountain at first glance. The giant sat cross-legged among the crystal spheres, his skin mottled gray like weathered stone, his head bare of hair yet covered in swirling markings that matched the patterns in Asvarr's verdant crown. Most striking were his eyes—or where eyes should have been. Empty sockets gazed sightlessly across the field, yet Asvarr sensed an awareness in them that transcended physical sight.

"The Keeper," Yrsa whispered, her normal scholarly confidence giving way to something approaching awe.

Asvarr stepped forward onto the obsidian field. The surface felt unnervingly solid despite appearing to continue infinitely downward, as if they walked on a transparent membrane stretched across the void. Each step produced ripples of silver light that spread outward before fading.

"So the Wardens come at last," the giant spoke without turning his head toward them. His voice resonated from everywhere and nowhere, sound transformed into pure vibration. "I wondered which cycle would bring you to my door."

"You know who we are?" Asvarr asked, stopping beside a sphere containing a galaxy of vivid purple stars.

"I know what you carry." The Keeper extended one massive hand, fingers splayed. "Three anchors bound within flesh that was once fully human. Flame, Memory, and Starlight." His head tilted, sightless sockets somehow focusing on Brynja. "And you, root-daughter. You bear a fragment that remembers what it was to swim free before branches carved the void into fragments."

Brynja's wooden arm creaked as she clenched her fist. "The Severed Bloom."

"A name given by those who fear what they cannot control." The Keeper's fingers curled inward. "I knew it by another name, before names were necessary."

"We seek knowledge," Asvarr said, stepping closer, careful to avoid the crystal spheres arranged across the obsidian surface. "About what existed before the Tree, before the gods. The Celestial Concordance hid these truths for millennia. I need to understand what I'm binding—and why."

The Keeper's massive face cracked into what might have been a smile. "And what makes you believe I will share what the Concordance sought to hide? Perhaps there was wisdom in their censorship."

"Because you preserved these." Asvarr gestured to the crystal spheres surrounding them. "Failed realities. Might-have-beens. You keep the memory of what could have existed but didn't."

Something shifted in the giant's posture—a subtle relaxation of shoulders so vast they resembled mountainsides. "Approach then, Warden of Three. Bring your companions. Let us speak of what was, what might have been, and what may yet be."

The closer they came to the Keeper, the more Asvarr realized the giant's true scale. Each finger was the size of a massive oak; the creases in his stony palms could have housed entire villages. When they reached what might have been considered conversational distance, the Keeper lowered one hand to the obsidian surface, palm up.

"Sit," he instructed. "The void pulls strongly here, and your kind were not meant to stand upon its edge for long."

They climbed onto the offered palm—a surface as rough as weathered stone yet warm like living flesh. The Keeper raised them to eye level, where the depthless sockets of his face somehow managed to convey both ancient wisdom and child-like curiosity.

"Now," the giant rumbled, "what would you know of what came before? Before branches, before roots, before the cage of structured realms?"

Asvarr met the sightless gaze. "Everything."

The Keeper made a sound like mountains grinding together—laughter, Asvarr realized with surprise.

"Everything would unmake you, little Warden. But I will show you enough." He extended his free hand toward one of the largest crystal spheres, which floated upward at his gesture to hover before them. Within it swirled a galaxy unlike any Asvarr had seen—its stars formed distinct patterns that resembled vast serpentine coils weaving through nebulae of deepest violet.

"Before Yggdrasil, before the gods, there was the void—and the void was not empty." The Keeper's voice dropped to a whisper that still vibrated through Asvarr's bones. "Great serpents swam through nothingness, creating and unmaking reality with each passage. There was no up or down, no here or there, no then or now. All things existed simultaneously as possibility rather than certainty."

The crystal sphere pulsed with inner light, and the galaxy within changed. The serpentine patterns twisted into new configurations, stars rearranging themselves with fluid grace.

"This might-have-been never fully manifested," the Keeper explained. "A potential reality where consciousness remained fluid rather than fixed, where beings flowed between forms as easily as water changes its shape."

"What happened to it?" Brynja asked, her wooden fingers tracing patterns that matched the swirling stars.

"The same that happened to all these might-have-beens." The Keeper gestured to the countless spheres across the obsidian plain. "They were pruned when the Tree grew. When structure was imposed upon infinite possibility."

Asvarr felt the anchors stir within him, resonating with the Keeper's words. "Who made that choice? Who decided which possibilities lived and which died?"

"The ones you call gods." The Keeper returned the floating sphere to its place among the others. "Though they were not gods then—merely consciousness that desired permanence amid endless change. They feared the void-hunger, the great serpent that consumed possibility to grow ever larger. To stop it, they grew the Tree—a structure of fixed reality with branches and roots to separate what had once been unified."

The verdant crown tightened around Asvarr's skull, branches digging painfully into his flesh. "And the anchors?"

"Fragments torn from the void-hunger itself." The Keeper's stone face remained impassive, but something like sorrow resonated in his voice. "Nine points of its essence, transformed into bindings. Five carried by Wardens of flesh, four embedded in the Tree's structure. Together, they formed a prison to contain what could not be killed."

Yrsa stepped forward on the giant's palm, her normally reserved demeanor breaking. "The Five and Four. Just as the runes showed us." She glanced at Asvarr.

"But why would binding more anchors weaken the prison rather than strengthen it?"

"Because they were never meant to be bound separately," the Keeper replied. "With each binding, the cage rattles. The prisoner feels its scattered pieces drawing together once more."

Asvarr felt cold certainty settle in his gut. "The convergence. When all anchors resonate simultaneously—"

"The prison either strengthens beyond breaking," the Keeper finished, "or shatters completely. Nine times this cycle has repeated. Nine times the Tree has broken and been partially restored."

"And the tenth cycle?" Brynja asked.

The giant turned his eyeless gaze upon her. "That depends on choices yet unmade. On whether you seek restoration, destruction—" his face swiveled back to Asvarr "—or transformation."

Around them, the crystal spheres began to pulse with internal light, each galaxy spinning faster within its transparent confines. The obsidian plain trembled beneath the giant's seated form.

"Something approaches," the Keeper said, his voice suddenly urgent. "Something drawn by the anchors you carry."

Asvarr looked toward the horizon, where reality itself seemed to ripple and distort. A shadow moved there—vast and serpentine, pressing against the boundary between void and realm.

"The void-hunger." He named it without fear, feeling the anchors resonate within him in recognition of their original source.

"No," the Keeper corrected, rising to his feet with surprising grace for a being of such immense size. His hand remained steady, keeping them safely elevated. "Something else. Something that tasted freedom when the Tree shattered and has no desire to see it caged again."

The horizon bulged inward like fabric stretched by immense weight. The shadow behind it grew more distinct—a shape with too many angles, too many dimensions, folding space around itself as it pushed against Alfheim's boundary.

The Keeper lowered them to the ground with unexpected gentleness. "You must see the rest. What the Tree truly cost. What the gods sacrificed for their perfect structure." He gestured toward the largest crystal sphere, which now pulsed with golden-violet light. "Only then can you choose your path wisely."

Asvarr stepped from the giant's palm onto the obsidian surface, feeling the void pull from below with hungry persistence. The anchors within him thrummed with power, responding to the approaching presence beyond Alfheim's boundary.

"Show me," he said, moving toward the indicated sphere. Within it, stars formed patterns unfamiliar yet somehow recognizable, awakening memory that wasn't his own. The void-memory planted in his chest by the Garden Caretaker stirred in response.

The boundary between realm and void grew thinner with each passing moment. Whatever approached would break through soon.

Asvarr placed his palm against the crystal sphere's surface and felt truth waiting on the other side.

***

The moment Asvarr's palm touched the crystal sphere, the void-memory in his chest unfurled with violent force. Memories not his own flooded his consciousness—vast serpentine forms swimming through primordial nothing, stars birthing and dying in the span of heartbeats, realities forming and dissolving like frost on morning grass.

He jerked his hand back with a strangled cry. The crystalline formations across his face flared silver-blue, reflecting patterns matching those within the sphere.

"The truth burns," the Keeper said, eyeless sockets somehow tracking Asvarr's movements. "Few can bear it undiluted."

The massive giant turned his stone-like face skyward, where the boundary between Alfheim and void stretched thinner with each passing moment. "We have little time before it breaks through. Listen carefully to what I must share."

Brynja stepped closer to Asvarr, her wooden arm brushing against his. The constellation patterns embedded in her transformed flesh pulsed in rhythm with his racing heart.

"What did you see?" she whispered.

"Everything," Asvarr managed, frost shattering from his lips. "And nothing."

The Keeper lowered his massive hand, palm open. "Come. I will show you differently."

***

They climbed back onto the offered palm, which rose smoothly until they faced the giant's vast stone features. The Keeper extended one finger of his free hand—a digit the size of an ancient oak—and touched the center of his own forehead. A crack formed there, splitting the weathered stone skin to reveal a blinding point of light.

"Light and shadow," the giant intoned, his voice rumbling through the obsidian field. "Order and chaos. Structure and freedom. The gods would have you believe these are opposites locked in eternal struggle. They are not. They are halves of the same whole, separated only by perception."

The light in the Keeper's forehead expanded, forming a perfect sphere that floated between them. Unlike the crystal spheres dotting the field below, this orb contained both radiance and darkness—swirling patterns of illumination and shadow that flowed into and through each other without blending.

"Light corrupts as surely as shadow," the Keeper continued. "Every illumination casts darkness elsewhere; every revelation obscures something else. This is the truth the Concordance sought to hide—that the World Tree was grown for those who desired structure over possibility."

The sphere rotated slowly, revealing patterns resembling tree branches that spread like cracks through the formless void, creating distinct sections.

"Before the Tree, consciousness flowed freely between states," the Keeper explained. "Beings existed simultaneously across multiple forms and timelines. The great serpents who swam the void offered freedom without structure—infinite possibility unconstrained by fixed laws."

The branch patterns within the sphere expanded further, creating rigid barriers between light and shadow that halted their natural flow.

"The gods who grew the Tree offered structure without freedom. They feared the void-hunger—the great serpent that consumed possibility unchecked. To combat it, they created a reality of fixed rules and separate realms, where consciousness remained trapped in singular forms and linear time."

Asvarr watched the sphere's patterns lock into place, the fluid movement between light and shadow reduced to static boundaries.

"Neither understood that both are necessary," the Keeper said. "Freedom requires structure to give it meaning; structure requires freedom to prevent stagnation."

The giant closed his massive hand around the sphere, extinguishing it. His sightless gaze swept over them, somehow more penetrating than eyes could ever be.

"And now we come to you, Warden of Three," he said, voice dropping to a whisper that still vibrated through Asvarr's bones. "You who walk the third path between restoration and destruction. What will you choose when the convergence comes?"

Asvarr met the eyeless gaze. "I don't know yet. That's why I sought you—to understand what I'm binding, and why."

"Then understand this." The Keeper leaned closer, his massive face filling Asvarr's vision. "Restoring Yggdrasil exactly as it was would simply restart an endless cycle of growth and destruction. Nine times the Tree has shattered. Nine times it has been partially mended. Do you know why the cycle repeats?"

"Because the void-hunger adapts," Brynja answered before Asvarr could. Her wooden fingers traced patterns matching those in the largest crystal sphere. "With each breaking and binding, it learns the pattern of its cage."

"Yes." The giant nodded, stone skin grinding with the movement. "And with each binding of a new anchor, the prisoner feels more of itself drawing together."

"Then why bind them at all?" Asvarr demanded, the verdant crown tightening painfully around his skull. "If each binding weakens the prison rather than strengthens it?"

"Because things half-bound are more dangerous than things fully contained or fully free." The Keeper's voice held the weight of epochs. "The Tree broken yet not unmade, the void-hunger aware yet not awakened—this in-between state creates the instability that threatens all realms."

The obsidian field beneath them trembled as the boundary between void and realm stretched thinner. The angle-thing beyond pushed with greater urgency, creating distortion patterns across Alfheim's reality.

"Your binding can end this cycle," the Keeper said. "But to do so, you must understand what the anchors truly are."

"Fragments of the void-hunger itself," Asvarr said. "Torn from the great serpent and transformed into bindings."

"More than fragments." The Keeper touched one massive finger to his own chest. "They are its heart, its eyes, its mind, its voice—the essential aspects of its being. In separating them, the gods weakened it enough to cage it. In binding them, Wardens take these aspects into themselves."

A cold realization settled in Asvarr's gut. "So by binding them, I'm becoming..."

"Neither fully human nor wholly serpent," the Keeper finished. "A threshold being—existing in the space between. This is why your consciousness expands with each binding, why your perception stretches across multiple realities. You incorporate aspects of that which existed before fixed form."

Yrsa stepped forward, her scholarly caution overridden by urgency. "The sky-serpents called Asvarr 'splinter-self.' They recognized him as kin."

"Because he carries pieces of their progenitor within him." The Keeper gestured toward the horizon, where the angle-being pressed harder against reality's membrane. "As does that which approaches. Another fragment that tasted freedom when the Tree shattered and desires the rest of itself."

The boundary bulged inward like fabric stretching to its breaking point. Through the distortion, Asvarr glimpsed something composed of too many angles, folding space around itself as it pushed through.

"What is it?" Brynja asked, wooden arm creaking as she clenched her fist.

"The void-hunger's intellect," the Keeper answered. "The fragment that solved the cage's pattern. It comes for what you carry, Warden."

Asvarr felt the anchors stir within him, resonating with the approaching entity. "How do we stop it?"

"You don't," the Keeper said simply. "You cannot fight what you partially are. But before you face it, you must see what the Tree truly cost. What the gods sacrificed for their perfect structure."

The giant gestured toward the largest crystal sphere—the one Asvarr had touched briefly before. "This might-have-been came closest to manifestation before the Tree grew. It shows a cosmos where light and shadow, order and chaos existed in harmony rather than opposition."

The sphere floated upward at the Keeper's gesture. Within it, serpentine forms of radiant light swam through structured voids, creating patterns of mathematical precision while maintaining fluid movement. Smaller entities moved between states, existing simultaneously as particles and waves, matter and energy, unity and multiplicity.

"The path not taken," the Keeper said softly. "A reality where consciousness remained fluid yet gained definition through self-imposed boundaries. Where beings chose their limitations rather than having them forced upon them."

The boundary between realm and void stretched to its limit. Cracks formed in Alfheim's reality as the angle-being pushed through with greater force.

"We're out of time," the Keeper announced, lowering them to the obsidian surface. "The void-hunger's intellect comes for what you carry. You must decide—flee through the boundary-door behind you, or confront it here."

Asvarr turned to see a shimmering tear in reality that hadn't been there moments before—a doorway leading back to the silver forests of inner Alfheim.

"The convergence comes in seven days," the Keeper reminded them. "What will you choose when all anchors resonate together? Restoration? Destruction? Or transformation?"

The giant rose to his full, mountain-like height. "Remember what you've seen here, Warden of Three. Remember that light corrupts as readily as shadow when wielded without wisdom. Remember that both structure and freedom are necessary for true balance."

The boundary split open with a sound like reality tearing. Through the gap emerged a being Asvarr's mind struggled to comprehend—a shape composed of geometric precision yet constantly folding and unfolding into new configurations. It possessed no features he could recognize as face or limbs, yet it moved with deliberate purpose across the obsidian field.

"Go," the Keeper commanded, stepping between them and the approaching entity. "This fragment cannot follow you through the boundary-door—not yet. But it knows what you carry, Warden. It will find you again."

Asvarr hesitated, the anchors within him thrumming with recognition of the angle-being. "What are you going to do?"

"What I have done for eons." The Keeper's massive face creased into what might have been a smile. "Preserve what might have been against what is. Now go."

Brynja grabbed Asvarr's arm, pulling him toward the boundary-door. "We need to leave. Now."

The angle-being moved faster across the obsidian field, each motion folding space around it to shorten the distance. Crystal spheres shattered in its wake, their miniature galaxies dissolving into nothingness.

Asvarr made his decision. He seized Brynja's wooden hand in his and ran for the boundary-door, dragging Yrsa with his other hand. The angle-being emitted a sound beyond hearing—a vibration that resonated painfully through the anchors within him.

They crashed through the boundary-door into the silver forests of inner Alfheim. Behind them, the tear sealed instantly, cutting off the angle-being's approach.

Asvarr gasped for breath, the verdant crown around his head pulsing with urgent warning. He knew with absolute certainty that what they'd just encountered was merely the beginning—a fragment of the void-hunger testing its prison's weaknesses.

"We need to reach Muspelheim," he said, frost crystallizing with each word. "The fourth anchor waits at the Storm Forge."

"And you still want to bind it?" Brynja demanded, constellation patterns shifting rapidly within her wooden arm. "After what we just learned? Each binding brings more of the void-hunger together, awakens more of its consciousness."

"The Keeper said things half-bound are more dangerous than fully contained or fully free," Asvarr replied. "We're committed to this course. The only question is what we do at convergence when all anchors resonate together."

Yrsa studied the place where the boundary-door had been, her scholar's detachment returning. "Seven days until convergence. We'll never reach Muspelheim and bind both remaining anchors in time."

"Then we need to be more selective about what we preserve," Asvarr said, making his decision even as he spoke the words. "The anchors are aspects of the void-hunger—its heart, mind, voice. To bind them is to incorporate these aspects into myself."

He touched the crystalline formations spreading across his face. "My consciousness already expands beyond human limits. I need something to anchor my identity before it dissolves completely—a chain to bind the boundless."

Brynja's wooden features shifted, her expression unreadable behind the bark. "The sky-serpents would say that's the problem—fixed identity, fixed form. The limitation that caused all this."

"Maybe." Asvarr looked toward the distant mountains where the boundary between Alfheim and Muspelheim would be thinnest. "But I'm still partly human, and I intend to remain so. I'll find another way true transformation."

He extended his hand to her—the flesh still marked with their shared oath-sigil. "Will you help me forge a chain from fallen stars? Something to anchor my identity before the fourth binding?"

Brynja stared at his offered hand, the constellation patterns in her wooden arm showing glimpses of serpentine forms swimming through void. The truth-compelling runes on her face glowed golden as she made her choice.

"I will," she said, taking his hand. "For the possibility of something better."

The oath-sigil on their palms flared with golden-silver light—a merging of root and flame, structure and freedom. Whatever came next, they would face it together.

Behind them, though the boundary-door had closed, Asvarr felt the angle-being's attention fixed upon them, calculating, planning. It would find them again. And next time, it would come better prepared.

They needed to reach Muspelheim. Now.

CHAPTER 14
STARFORGED CHAIN

The twin moons hung like mismatched eyes above the silver forest of Alfheim, their light casting geometric shadows that bore no relation to the trees creating them. Asvarr pressed his palms against his temples, where crystalline growths had spread in jagged patterns. His consciousness stretched impossibly thin, fragments of his awareness scattered across multiple realities. In one, he watched stars birth and die. In another, he observed the slow dancing of cosmic serpents through primordial void. In yet another, he witnessed his own death at the void-hunger's touch.

"Asvarr." Brynja's voice pulled him back, her wooden fingers cool against his feverish skin. "Stay with us."

He blinked, forcing his fractured perception to focus on the clearing where they'd made camp. Six days until convergence. Six days to bind the remaining anchors—or to choose another path entirely.

"I'm losing myself," he said, frost shattering from his lips. "Each heartbeat, I become less human, more... scattered." He gestured vaguely at the night sky, where constellations had begun rearranging themselves into spiral patterns that matched the swirling designs on his transformed flesh.

Yrsa knelt beside the small fire, her face illuminated in orange light as she arranged fallen star-fragments into complex configurations. Each fragment gleamed with inner radiance, their composition unlike any earthly material—not quite solid, not quite light.

"The binding chain must be forged tonight." She glanced upward, where the twin moons drifted closer to alignment. "The celestial conjunction provides the power needed to tether your expanding consciousness."

"And if we wait?" Asvarr asked, knowing the answer but needing to hear it spoken.

"Your mind will continue fragmenting until nothing of Asvarr remains," Yrsa said simply. "Only the anchors, communicating with each other through the vessel that was once human."

Brynja's wooden arm creaked as she flexed her fingers. "We'd need to travel to Alfheim's eastern edge to find sufficient star material. The meteor shower left fragments scattered through the Crystal Reaches."

"There's no time," Yrsa countered. "The angle-being will have found another path through the boundaries by now. It hunts what Asvarr carries."

Asvarr closed his eyes, extending his transformed senses outward. Through the third anchor's power, he perceived disturbances in Alfheim's reality—places where the boundary stretched thin under pressure from outside. The angle-being probed methodically, testing for weaknesses.

He opened his eyes. "We have the fragments we need right here." He gestured toward the sky. "The constellations reshape themselves according to my thoughts. I can call what we need from above."

Rising unsteadily to his feet, Asvarr stretched his arms skyward. The verdant crown around his head tightened painfully, branches extending upward like desperate fingers. His consciousness expanded once more, stretching from his physical body toward the stars above. The constellations trembled in response, individual stars vibrating within their patterns.

"Come," he commanded, his voice resonating across multiple realities simultaneously. "Fall."

Three stars detached from their constellations, leaving burning trails as they descended. They slowed their fall as they approached, coming to hover above the clearing like miniature suns. Each varied in color—one silver-white, one gold-red, one deepest violet—and pulsed with internal rhythms that matched Asvarr's heartbeat.

Brynja stepped back, the constellation patterns within her wooden arm flowing in response to the fallen stars. "Even the Verdant Five never called stars from their paths."

"I didn't call them," Asvarr said, lowering his arms. "They recognized what I carry. They came willingly."

The fallen stars drifted downward, shrinking as they descended until each was no larger than a clenched fist. They arranged themselves in a circle around the fire, where Yrsa had prepared a basin of liquid starlight salvaged from the observatory.

"We must work quickly," Yrsa said, lifting her crystal pendant. "The alignment lasts only until midnight."

Asvarr nodded, kneeling beside the basin. The liquid starlight within reflected glimpses of other realities where versions of himself followed different paths. In one, he had rejected the anchors entirely. In another, he had surrendered fully to them, becoming something beyond humanity. In yet another, he stood beside the Ashfather, watching worlds burn.

"Focus," Brynja urged, kneeling opposite him. "Remember who you are."

Who was he? Asvarr Flame-Warden, bearer of three anchors? The berserker who survived his clan's destruction? The man who sought the third path, accepting transformation without surrender?

"I need four links," he said, the plan forming even as he spoke. "Four aspects of identity to tether my consciousness: memory, purpose, connection, grief."

"Four points to anchor the fifth," Yrsa murmured. "A perfect binding pattern."

Brynja arranged the star-fragments around the basin's edge, matching them to the cardinal directions. "Memory to the east, where light begins. Purpose to the south, where it strengthens. Connection to the west, where it fades. Grief to the north, where darkness waits."

"And consciousness at center," Asvarr finished, "where all converge."

He dipped his transformed hands into the basin, where liquid starlight swirled around his fingers. The sensation burned and froze simultaneously, reality and possibility flowing together. The three fallen stars pulsed in response, their light growing more intense.

"Now," Yrsa commanded, positioning herself at the northern point. "Begin with memory—what makes you who you are."

Asvarr closed his eyes, focusing on memories that defined him. His father teaching him swordcraft. His mother's songs during long winter nights. The taste of mead shared with shield-brothers. The scent of pine smoke from his clan's hearth-fires. Each memory pulled forth fragments of his consciousness that had scattered across multiple realities, drawing them back to a singular focus.

"Into the silver star," Brynja directed from the eastern point, her wooden hands cupping the silver-white fragment. "Channel your essence through it."

Asvarr extended his awareness toward the silver star, which flared brilliantly as his memories flowed into it. The star compressed, folding in upon itself until it formed a perfect silver link that fell to the ground with a sound like struck crystal.

"Purpose next," Yrsa said, her voice tight with concentration. "What drives you forward?"

Vengeance had been his first purpose after the clan's destruction, then restoration as he learned of the anchors. Now transformation guided him—the desire to find a third path beyond what had been attempted in nine previous cycles. This purpose pulled more fragments of his consciousness together, creating a stronger sense of self.

The gold-red star at the southern point pulsed rapidly, absorbing the essence of his purpose. It too compressed into a link, falling beside the first with a deeper, resonant tone.

"Connection," Brynja called from the western point, where the third star hovered. "What binds you to others?"

Asvarr thought of his oath to Brynja, the grove-twined mark still visible on his palm. He remembered the villagers who had sheltered him, his fallen shield-brothers who fought beside him. Each connection formed threads anchoring him to humanity even as the anchors pulled him toward something beyond it.

The violet star trembled as it absorbed these connections, its light dimming slightly before it collapsed into the third link. This one fell silently, absorbing sound rather than creating it.

"Grief," Yrsa whispered from the northern point, where no star waited. "What have you lost that shaped you?"

This came easiest of all—the grief that had carved hollows within him since the clan's destruction. The faces of the fallen. The songs never again to be sung. The traditions broken. The knowledge lost. Grief had been his constant companion, its weight a reminder of what had been and what might yet be.

Yrsa extended her hands, where her crystal pendant had transformed into a perfect teardrop of solidified starlight. It absorbed the essence of his grief, turning momentarily black before shifting to a pale blue that matched the northern star's missing light. It transformed into the fourth link, completing the circle.

"Now," Brynja commanded, "draw them together."

Asvarr lifted his hands from the basin, liquid starlight dripping from his transformed flesh. He reached for the four links, arranging them in a row before him. Each pulsed with internal light, resonating with different aspects of his identity.

"I am memory," he said, touching the silver link. "I carry what was."

"I am purpose," he continued, touching the gold-red link. "I forge what will be."

"I am connection," he said, touching the violet link. "I bind what is separate."

"I am grief," he finished, touching the blue link. "I honor what is lost."

The verdant crown around his head creaked and shifted, branches extending downward to touch the four links. Golden sap dripped onto the metal, hissing as it made contact. The links resonated in harmony, lifting from the ground to hover before Asvarr's eyes.

"They must be joined," Yrsa said, "through blood sacrifice."

Asvarr understood. He took his bronze sword, its golden veins pulsing with the power of the anchors, and drew the blade across his palm. Blood mixed with sap and crystalline fragments flowed from the wound, falling upon the hovering links.

The effect was immediate. The links snapped together, forming a chain that wrapped itself around Asvarr's wrist of its own volition. Where it touched his transformed flesh, it burned cold and hot simultaneously, searing patterns that matched the binding configurations described by the Keeper.

His fractured consciousness, stretched across multiple realities, snapped back into singular focus with painful intensity. Awareness of other timelines and possibilities remained, but distant now, controllable. The constant pressure of the void-hunger's attention diminished to a manageable awareness rather than overwhelming invasion.

Asvarr gasped, falling forward onto his hands and knees. The chain around his wrist pulsed in time with his heartbeat, each link glowing with internal light that matched the aspects of his identity they contained.

"It worked," he managed, his voice steady for the first time in days. The frost that normally formed with his words was reduced to a fine mist that dissolved almost immediately.

"For now," Yrsa cautioned, replacing her depleted pendant around her neck. "The chain will hold your consciousness together, but it's temporary. Without the fourth and fifth anchors, you remain incomplete—unbalanced."

Brynja knelt beside him, her wooden fingers tracing the chain's links. "This craftsmanship... it's like nothing I've seen. Neither purely elven nor dwarven nor human."

"Because it's all three and none," Asvarr replied, studying the chain. "Like me."

He climbed to his feet, testing his balance and finding it much improved. The sensation of his consciousness threatening to dissolve had receded. Though the anchors still pulsed within him, they no longer threatened to consume his identity entirely.

The twin moons had reached their midnight conjunction overhead, bathing the clearing in silver-gold light. Through his enhanced perception, Asvarr sensed the angle-being pause in its methodical probing of Alfheim's boundaries. It had felt the chain's forging, recognized its purpose.

It was changing tactics.

"We need to move," he said abruptly. "The angle-being knows what we've done. It's seeking another approach."

"Muspelheim," Brynja agreed, gathering her few possessions. "The fourth anchor at the Storm Forge."

Yrsa pointed westward, where the mountains marking the boundary between realms were visible as darker shadows against the night sky. "There's a gap in the boundary near the volcanic springs. We can cross there if we hurry."

The starforged chain around Asvarr's wrist pulsed with steady light as they packed their meager camp. Its weight felt reassuring against his skin—a constant reminder of who he was beneath the transformations wrought by the anchors. Yet even as it anchored him, he felt the third anchor stir within his chest, responding to another consciousness.

"The star anchor," he murmured, touching the crystalline formations across his face. "It's trying to speak to me."

"Let it wait until we've crossed the boundary," Yrsa advised. "Full communion could weaken the chain temporarily."

The constellation patterns within Brynja's wooden arm shifted continuously as she studied the sky. "The stars aren't pleased with what we've done. We've bound fragments of their essence to mortal flesh."

"Not just any fragments," Asvarr replied, cinching his sword belt tighter. "The ones that chose to fall rather than remain in their patterns. The ones that recognized what I carry."

The verdant crown tightened around his skull, branches shifting as if in response to unseen wind. Through it, Asvarr sensed other Wardens moving across distant realms—fragments of awareness that brushed against his consciousness before withdrawing. Others like him, binding anchors with different purposes. The convergence approached, and with it, the moment when reality itself would become malleable.

Six days. Six days to reach Muspelheim, bind the fourth anchor, and make their way to Helheim for the fifth. An impossible task, yet one they must attempt.

"Let's go," he said, turning toward the western mountains where Muspelheim's fiery heart waited. The starforged chain clinked softly with each movement, its links glowing with steady reassurance.

For the first time since binding the third anchor, Asvarr felt fully himself again—transformed but not consumed, changed but not erased. The third path remained open before him, if he could maintain the balance the chain provided.

Behind them, the clearing where they had worked stellar magic already showed signs of transformation—silver grass growing in perfect geometric patterns, trees bending to form archways that framed the constellation from which the stars had fallen.

Reality reshaping itself in their wake.

The angle-being would follow this trail directly to them.

They needed to hurry.

***

The western mountains rose jagged against the night sky, their peaks crowned with volcanic smoke that glowed amber from the fires of Muspelheim beyond. Asvarr traced the starforged chain around his wrist with his fingertips, feeling each link pulse with the aspects of identity he'd bound within: memory, purpose, connection, grief. The metal felt impossibly smooth yet textured with microscopic patterns that matched the crystalline formations spreading across his face.

"How far to the boundary?" he asked Yrsa, who led them along a narrow game trail through thinning silver trees.

"Two hours, if we maintain this pace." She gestured toward a rock formation where steam rose in geometric columns. "The volcanic springs mark the thinnest point between realms."

The chain clinked softly as Asvarr adjusted his sword belt. Though his fractured consciousness had been drawn back to singular focus, he still felt the anchors stirring within him—particularly the third, which pulsed with increasing urgency. Since the chain's forging, he'd deliberately avoided communion with the starlight anchor, fearing its voice might weaken his newly stabilized identity.

"You can't postpone communion forever," Brynja said, reading his hesitation. The constellation patterns within her wooden arm shifted like stars viewed through rippling water. "The anchor knows you now. It will speak whether invited or not."

"I need to maintain focus until we cross into Muspelheim," Asvarr replied, frost forming and shattering with each word. "The angle-being still hunts us."

They continued in silence toward the distant springs, where steam columns twisted into rune-like configurations before dissolving. The twin moons had separated after their midnight conjunction, now drifting toward opposite horizons. Six days until convergence. Six days to bind two more anchors and make an impossible choice.

The starforged chain grew warmer against Asvarr's skin with each step toward the boundary, the links pulsing with increasing brightness. Without warning, the memory link—silver-white and positioned closest to his palm—flared with blinding intensity. Pain lanced through his transformed flesh as the chain tightened of its own volition.

Asvarr stumbled, falling to one knee. The chain burned ice-cold against his wrist while the third anchor within his chest blazed with answering heat. His expanded consciousness, held in check by the chain's power, began to fracture once more—fragments of awareness scattering across multiple realities.

"Asvarr!" Brynja knelt beside him, her wooden fingers cool against his feverish skin. "The anchor forces communion. You must accept its voice before the chain breaks."

"Not yet," he gasped, clutching the chain. "Not until we cross—"

The third anchor surged within him, overwhelming his resistance. The silver forest surrounding them blurred and distorted as reality thinned. Through his fractured perception, Asvarr witnessed the boundary between realms stretching until it became transparent, revealing the molten landscapes of Muspelheim on the other side.

"Too late," Yrsa murmured, backing away. "The communion begins."

***

The starforged chain unraveled from Asvarr's wrist, its four links detaching and hovering before him. Each pulsed with the aspect it contained: memory, purpose, connection, grief. They arranged themselves in a perfect square around him, creating a boundary within which the anchor's voice could manifest without fracturing his identity completely.

Asvarr surrendered to the inevitable, closing his eyes as the third anchor fully awakened within him. Unlike previous anchors that communicated in emotions or fragmented impressions, this one spoke with crystal clarity—its thoughts vast but precise, resonating directly through his transformed flesh.

WARDEN OF THREE

The voice bypassed his ears entirely, manifesting as pure concept within his mind. It carried harmonics that reminded him of stars shifting in their courses, of cosmic bodies moving through void.

WE SPEAK AT LAST

Asvarr opened his eyes to find himself still kneeling in the silver forest, yet simultaneously existing elsewhere—in a space between spaces where boundaries held no meaning. The starforged chain's four links maintained their protective square around him, their light preventing his consciousness from dissolving completely.

"Who are you?" he asked, his voice forming frost that crystallized into complex patterns matching the anchor's harmonics.

I AM WHAT YOU CALL THE THIRD ANCHOR. STARLIGHT BOUND TO PURPOSE. I EXISTED BEFORE NAMES WERE NECESSARY.

Images flowed through Asvarr's mind—vast serpentine forms swimming through primordial void, creating and unmaking reality with each passage. Consciousness without fixed form, existing simultaneously across all possibilities.

WE WERE UNITY ONCE. BEFORE THE SCHISM.

The anchor showed him the original division—a cosmic rift that separated beings of pure potential from those that desired structure. On one side, serpent-forms that reveled in infinite possibility, changing shape and purpose with each moment. On the other, entities that sought definition, permanence, boundaries.

NEITHER SIDE WRONG. BUT NEITHER WOULD YIELD.

Through the anchor's memories, Asvarr witnessed the birth of the World Tree as a deliberate creation. The gods, seeking structure and fixed reality, grew Yggdrasil as both bridge and boundary between their vision and the serpents'. Its branches separated realms that had once flowed together; its roots established laws that had once been fluid.

"And the void-hunger?" Asvarr asked, his voice distant in his own ears. "The great serpent imprisoned beneath?"

NOT IMPRISONED AT FIRST. EMBRACED. INCORPORATED. THE TREE AND SERPENT EXISTED IN BALANCE. BRIDGE BETWEEN ORDER AND CHAOS.

The anchor's memories shifted, showing him Yggdrasil in its prime—a cosmic structure that incorporated aspects of both visions. The serpent-forms swam between its roots and branches, bringing change and renewal, while the gods maintained the Tree's structure, providing stability and continuity.

THEN FEAR GREW. THE GODS FEARED ENDLESS CHANGE. THE SERPENTS FEARED STAGNANT ORDER. BALANCE FRACTURED.

Asvarr watched as the original harmony collapsed. The gods, seeking total control, used fragments torn from the greatest serpent—the void-hunger—to create binding points within the Tree's structure. The anchors.

NINE POINTS. NINE FRAGMENTS. FIVE FOR FLESH. FOUR FOR ROOTS.

"To imprison the void-hunger," Asvarr murmured.

TO BIND IT. TO SEPARATE ITS ESSENCE. HEART FROM MIND FROM VOICE FROM WILL.

The anchor showed him the nine-point binding configuration—five vertices of a pentagon surrounding four points of a square. The pattern used to cage what could not be killed.

NINE CYCLES. NINE BREAKINGS. NINE PARTIAL MENDINGS. THE PATTERN REPEATS BECAUSE THE TRUTH REMAINS UNAC- KNOWLEDGED.

"What truth?"

THAT NEITHER WAS WRONG. THAT BOTH WERE NECESSARY. THAT THE THIRD PATH EXISTS ONLY WHEN STRUCTURE AND FREEDOM COEXIST IN BALANCE.

The starforged chain's links pulsed with increased brightness as the anchor's voice grew stronger. Asvarr felt his understanding expand beyond human limits, perceiving the pattern beneath reality itself—the complex interplay of order and chaos necessary for true existence.

YOU CARRY THREE FRAGMENTS NOW. THREE ASPECTS OF WHAT WAS ONCE UNITY. WITH EACH BINDING, YOU BECOME LESS HUMAN, MORE THRESHOLD-BEING.

"And if I bind all five?" Asvarr asked, already knowing the answer.

YOU BECOME THE CAGE AND THE CAGED. THE BINDING AND THE BOUND. NEITHER FULLY SERPENT NOR FULLY GOD, BUT SOMETHING BETWEEN. THE BRIDGE THAT UNIFIES COMPETING VISIONS.

The anchor's voice softened, becoming almost compassionate despite its cosmic scale.

THIS IS THE BURDEN OF THE WARDEN. TO EXIST AS THE THRESHOLD BETWEEN WHAT WAS AND WHAT COULD BE. TO CARRY BOTH ORDER AND CHAOS WITHIN YOUR TRANSFORMED FLESH.

Asvarr looked down at his hands—one still mostly human despite bark patterns spreading across the skin, the other almost entirely transformed with crystalline structures replacing flesh. The physical manifestation of his divided nature.

"The angle-being," he said, remembering the entity that had pursued them from the Keeper's realm. "The void-hunger's intellect. It seeks what I carry."

IT SEEKS REUNIFICATION. AS DO ALL FRAGMENTS. THE CONVERGENCE APPROACHES WHEN ALL ANCHORS RESONATE TOGETHER. WHEN REALITY BECOMES MALLEABLE. WHEN CHOICE BECOMES POSSIBLE.

"What choice?"

RESTORATION. DESTRUCTION. OR TRANSFORMATION. TO REMAKE THE CAGE EXACTLY AS IT WAS. TO SHATTER IT COM-PLETELY. OR TO FORGE SOMETHING NEW—A BRIDGE RATHER THAN A BARRIER.

The starforged chain's links began to rotate around Asvarr, forming a perfect circle that pulsed with steady light. The anchor's voice faded slightly, as if drawing back to allow him space to process what he'd learned.

YOU MUST CROSS THE BOUNDARY SOON. THE ANGLE-BEING APPROACHES. IT FOLLOWS THE TRAIL LEFT BY YOUR TRANS-FORMATION. IT WILL NOT STOP UNTIL IT RECLAIMS WHAT WAS ONCE PART OF ITSELF.

With those words, the anchor's presence receded, though it remained awake within him. The starforged chain's links reattached themselves to form the familiar binding around his wrist, though now they contained fragments of the anchor's cosmic understanding.

Reality reasserted itself. Asvarr found himself still kneeling in the silver forest, Brynja and Yrsa watching him with expressions caught between awe and concern. The crystalline formations across his face had expanded fur-ther, now forming perfect geometric patterns that matched those within the chain's links.

"What did it tell you?" Brynja asked, her wooden fingers tracing the con-stellation patterns within her transformed arm.

"Everything," Asvarr replied, frost crystals forming complex structures with each word. "The anchor remembers what came before—the original schism that divided serpent from god. How Yggdrasil was grown as both bridge and boundary between their competing visions."

He climbed to his feet, testing his balance and finding it improved despite the expanded communion. The chain around his wrist pulsed steadily, maintaining the tether between his human identity and his cosmic awareness.

"And?" Yrsa prompted, her scholar's curiosity overriding caution.

"Neither was wrong," Asvarr said simply. "But neither would yield. The serpents who desired freedom without structure, the gods who demanded structure without freedom—both necessary, both incomplete without the other."

The ground beneath them trembled slightly, roots pulsing with golden light beneath the silver soil. Through his enhanced perception, Asvarr felt the angle-being's approach—a mathematical precision cutting through reality's fabric as it tracked their path.

"We need to move," he said urgently. "Now. The angle-being follows the trail of our transformation. It knows where we're headed."

They hurried toward the volcanic springs, where steam columns had begun forming perfect geometric shapes that mirrored the patterns on Asvarr's face. The boundary between realms thinned visibly ahead, Muspelheim's molten landscape shimmering like a mirage beyond transparent reality.

"The crossing point," Yrsa announced, pointing toward a massive geode formation where crystal spires erupted from volcanic rock. "There."

The starforged chain burned against Asvarr's wrist as they approached the boundary, its links glowing with internal light that matched the crystalline patterns across his transformed flesh. Behind them, silver trees bent unnaturally as something powerful forced its way through the forest—angles and geometry cutting through organic growth.

"It's here," Brynja hissed, her wooden arm creaking as thorns erupted from her fingers.

Asvarr drew his bronze sword, the golden veins beneath its surface pulsing in time with his heartbeat. "Cross now. I'll hold it back."

"Don't be foolish," Brynja snapped, the constellation patterns within her wooden arm flowing rapidly. "You can't fight what you partially are. The Keeper warned us."

"I don't intend to fight it," Asvarr replied. "Just delay it."

Before she could argue further, he turned toward the approaching angle-being, sword raised. The entity emerged from between silver trees—a shape composed of perfect geometry constantly folding and unfolding into new configurations. It possessed no features Asvarr could identify as face or limbs, yet it moved with deliberate purpose, each motion folding space around it to shorten the distance between them.

Through the anchors, Asvarr felt the angle-being's recognition. It perceived him as scattered fragments of a greater whole—pieces that should be reunited. Its attention focused on the starforged chain, identifying it as the binding that prevented his complete dissolution.

The entity accelerated toward him, space folding around it with increasing complexity.

Asvarr lowered his sword, an idea forming as the anchor's knowledge flowed through him. He touched the starforged chain, focusing on the memory link—silver-white and pulsing with his identity. With deliberate intent, he projected a fragment of memory toward the angle-being, one shared by the anchor.

A memory of unity before division. Of serpent and god existing in harmony.

The angle-being halted abruptly, its geometric form trembling as it processed the unexpected offering. For a moment, it seemed to lose cohesion, angles softening into curves before snapping back to precise shapes.

Asvarr took advantage of its confusion, backing toward the boundary where Brynja and Yrsa waited. The angle-being remained motionless, still processing the memory that contradicted its singular purpose.

"Now," Asvarr commanded, reaching the geode formation. "Cross!"

Brynja stepped through the thinned boundary first, her form distorting briefly before solidifying on Muspelheim's side. Yrsa followed, her crystal pendant flaring with protective light as she passed between realms.

Asvarr stood at the threshold, one foot in each reality. The angle-being had recovered from its momentary confusion and now advanced with renewed purpose, space folding violently around it.

He stepped fully into Muspelheim just as the entity reached the boundary. For a crucial moment, it pressed against the thinned reality, attempting to force its way through. The boundary held—barely—resisting the angle-being's mathematical precision with organic flexibility.

Frustrated, the entity retreated slightly. Through the translucent barrier, Asvarr watched it reconfigure itself, adopting a less complex form that might pass through more easily. It would find a way eventually—of that he had no doubt. But they had bought time.

***

The volcanic landscape of Muspelheim stretched before them—rivers of molten stone flowing between obsidian formations, the sky a perpetual twilight of smoke and ember. In the distance, a mountain shaped like a massive anvil rose toward clouds tinged crimson from the fires below.

"The Storm Forge," Yrsa said, gesturing toward the anvil-shaped peak. "Where the fourth anchor waits."

Asvarr nodded, feeling the starforged chain pulse against his wrist. The third anchor's communion had changed him further, expanding his understanding beyond human limits. Yet the chain maintained his connection to his identity—the tether that prevented complete dissolution.

Five days until convergence. Five days to bind the fourth anchor and reach Helheim for the fifth. Five days to decide whether to restore, destroy, or transform the cosmic balance.

"Each anchor holds part of the truth," he murmured, watching the boundary where the angle-being continued its methodical probing. "Each fragment contains pieces of the whole. The serpent and the god, chaos and order."

"And you?" Brynja asked, her voice carrying harmonics that matched the constellations within her wooden arm. "What will you become when you hold all
five?"

Asvarr touched the starforged chain, feeling the aspects of identity bound
within each link. "Whatever the third path requires."

Behind them, the boundary pulsed as the angle-being discovered a new approach. They had little time.

The Storm Forge awaited.

CHAPTER 15

BRYNJA'S DREAMFALL

The first silver moon cleared the jagged peak of Starfall Mountain as Brynja staggered. Her wooden arm caught against a crystal outcropping, bark scraping stone with a sound like distant thunder. Inside her skull, something shifted—a sudden sideways perception, as if one eye looked at the world around her while the other peered into somewhere else entirely.

"I can't—" she gasped, the words falling like brittle leaves from her lips. The constellation patterns inlaid in her wooden flesh flared too bright, sending shards of light dancing across the crystalline landscape. "Something's wrong. The stars are *inside* me."

Asvarr reached for her with transformed hands—part bark, part crystal, wholly unfamiliar. His touch felt both distant and overwhelming. The stars in her transformed arm burned brighter at the contact, sap weeping, golden from her fingertips.

"Brynja?" Concern roughened Asvarr's voice, frost forming with each word. "What do you see?"

She couldn't answer. Her consciousness splintered like light through crystal, fragments scattering across a vast mental landscape she'd never encountered before. Part of her remained on the mountainside—feeling cold air against her skin, smelling the metallic tang of Alfheim's atmosphere, hearing Asvarr's voice. But another part—a growing part—drifted elsewhere, pulled into a silent chorus of waiting minds.

The Silent Choir.

They called to her, those star-children with their ageless eyes and impossible knowledge. Called in voices like silver bells ringing across vast distances, vibrating directly through her wooden arm into her blood and bone. The part of her that was still *Brynja* tried to resist, fingers digging into the crystalline earth beneath her knees.

"Help," she managed, the word cracking from her throat with tremendous effort. "They're taking me somewhere."

Yrsa knelt at her other side, crystal pendant blazing with blue-white light. "The children seek to show her something. The starlight in her arm connects her to them. She walks in memories now."

"Pull her back," Asvarr demanded, tightening his grip on Brynja's flesh arm. The skin beneath his fingers burned cold then hot, his own transformation working against him.

"I cannot," Yrsa said, voice tight with rare fear. "None can. She must find her own way back from their dreaming."

Brynja heard them as if underwater, their voices growing distant, distorted. The world around her dimmed, reduced to vague impressions of light and shadow. Only the Silent Choir remained clear—a circle of children with star-filled eyes standing upon a dais that existed simultaneously in numerous realities.

Come, their voices chimed in unison, the sound manifesting in Brynja's mind as a circular pattern of silver-white light. *Witness what normal minds cannot bear to see.*

Her consciousness split further. The mountainside fell away entirely. The wooden patterns covering half her body ignited with stellar fire, consuming her perception in a rush of impossible light. She opened her mouth to scream, but instead of sound, a stream of silver motes poured forth, swirling around her like a miniature galaxy.

***

Then she was elsewhere. Everywhere. Nowhere.

Standing among the Silent Choir on their circular dais, looking down at her own collapsed body on the crystal plateau. Seeing Asvarr's frantic attempts to wake her, watching Yrsa's knowing resignation. Viewing it all from outside, as if she'd stepped beyond the boundaries of her own story.

We remember all that was, all that could be, all that might never come to pass, the closest child explained, voice resonating directly into Brynja's mind. *We witness without interpretation. We preserve without distortion.*

"Why show me?" Brynja asked, her voice echoing strangely in this realm of memory and dream.

Because you contain the Severed Bloom—the first fragment to recognize the pattern's flaw. The child extended a small hand with skin like polished nacre, fingers elongated beyond human proportions. *Touch, and understand.*

Brynja hesitated, the wooden fingers of her transformed hand curling protectively against her chest. The Severed Bloom within her stirred, pushing tendrils of awareness through her consciousness. It recognized the children, knew them from before.

"Will I return to myself?" she asked, the question sharp with fear.

Yes, came the unified response from the entire Choir, *though perhaps not unchanged.*

She had weathered transformation before, when the wooden arm first grew from her flesh, when the thorn-runes carved truth from her lips, when the constellations embedded themselves within her bark. Perhaps this too was necessary.

Brynja extended her wooden hand and placed it in the child's palm.

Reality fractured.

She tumbled through memory—not as participant, not even as observer, but as memory itself. She became the moment rather than witnessing it. In rapid succession, she experienced:

A young girl on Midgard, kneeling before an alder tree, carving intricate patterns into its bark with bloodied fingertips, the wood oozing golden sap where her skin touched it. *This one came to remember. This one came to contain.*

A dying warrior pressing a rusted blade into his son's hands, whispering, "The Skyrender must be preserved. The eye must not open again." The sword hilt bearing the same rune pattern as those seared into Asvarr's chest.

A council of five wooden figures seated around a silver pool, their faces containing galaxies for eyes, speaking in unison: "The breaking must be controlled. The restoration guided. The third path cannot be permitted." Golden frost spreading across the pool's surface as they dipped twisted fingers into its depths.

An enormous Root writhing in agony beneath Muspelheim's fiery crust, as a shadow-cloaked figure pressed a silver dagger into its flesh. "I free you from purpose," the figure whispered. "I return you to possibility."

The Ashfather—Gautr—gripping a young woman by the throat, his single eye blazing with rage. "You cannot unite what I have separated," he growled. "The cycle must continue." The woman's wooden fingers tightening around his wrist, her bark peeling back to reveal golden sap flowing like blood beneath.

The memories flowed faster, more fragmented. Brynja wasn't merely seeing events unfold—she experienced intentions behind actions, causes leading to effects, the complex web of decisions and accidents that shaped cosmic history. She witnessed the creation of the anchors, the growth of Yggdrasil, the binding of the void-hunger. She saw nine cycles of breaking and partial restoration, each weakening the prison further.

Through the children's perception, she grasped truths that mortal minds couldn't contain. She understood the Verdant Five's ancient manipulation, the Ashfather's desperate preservation, the void-hunger's struggle between freedom and consumption.

Most disturbing of all, she glimpsed something else: a shadowy entity within the pattern itself, watching through cracks between possibilities. Something using the endless cycle for its own purposes, neither truly serpent nor wholly god.

"Enough!" she cried, the word tearing from her disembodied consciousness like a wound. "I cannot hold more without breaking."

But you must, the Silent Choir responded, their voices harmonizing into terrible precision. *For the tenth cycle approaches its pivot. The choices made will echo across eternity. Witness what has never been witnessed before.*

The children joined hands, forming a perfect circle around her. Their star-filled eyes blazed with silver fire as they began to sing with consciousness itself. The song restructured Brynja's perception, splitting her awareness across multiple points in the pattern simultaneously.

She saw Asvarr in Muspelheim, binding the fourth anchor at the Storm Forge. Witnessed herself in Alfheim, communing with the star-children. Glimpsed Leif walking between realities, his form shifting from child to adult to something else entirely. Perceived Yrsa standing at a crossroads where nine paths converged, her crystal pendant blazing with purpose.

The song intensified. The children's joined hands generated a sphere of light that encapsulated Brynja's consciousness. Within this sphere, time dissolved. Past, present, and future existed simultaneously as potential rather than sequence.

She saw what might come to pass.

Asvarr completing his mission, binding all five anchors, transforming into something terrifyingly vast and impersonal. A being of immense power wielding the combined forces of flame, memory, starlight, storm, and death. His humanity burning away like morning mist under a cruel sun, replaced by cold cosmic awareness.

She watched this future-Asvarr standing at the pattern's center, drawing the anchors together to form a sixth element—the pattern itself. His eyes no longer contained any trace of the berserker who had sought vengeance for his clan, the man who had struggled to maintain his identity through three bindings. Instead, they held galaxies, just like the Verdant Five, just like the Ashfather before him.

In this possible future, he reshaped reality according to perfect mathematical principles, sacrificing emotion and connection for cosmic balance. He became the next Ashfather—the Tenth Warden, maintaining prison and prisoner in eternal, loveless equilibrium.

Most terrifying of all, this future-Asvarr appeared content with his transformation. His face—what remained of it beneath bark and crystal—showed neither regret nor longing, only serene certainty that his sacrifice had been necessary.

This is one path, the Silent Choir explained, their mental voices echoing through the sphere of potential. *There are others.*

The vision shifted. Now she observed herself, transformed beyond recognition, the Severed Bloom having consumed her completely. Her wooden body entwined with twisted roots extending across all Nine Realms, her consciousness fragmented across countless growth points. Awakening the void-hunger to transform, reshaping existence into something neither ordered nor chaotic, but endlessly adaptable.

Another shift. Neither Asvarr nor Brynja but something formed from both—a hybrid entity incorporating flame and root, structure and freedom. Neither human nor pattern but a threshold being existing at the boundaries between states. The third path made manifest.

The visions came faster. Variations and possibilities multiplied exponentially. The children's song reached a crescendo, their joined hands radiating blinding light. Brynja's consciousness strained against the vastness of what they revealed, threatening to shatter completely under the weight of cosmic memory.

Just as she felt herself dissolving, the song abruptly ceased.

The children released each other's hands. The sphere of potential collapsed. Brynja's fractured awareness snapped back into singular focus with painful suddenness.

She stood once more on the dais among the Silent Choir, gasping as if she'd been underwater for too long. Her wooden arm burned with starfire, constellation patterns moving with deliberate purpose across her bark-like skin.

The child who'd first reached for her stepped forward again, eyes containing entire galaxies in their silver depths.

Now you have witnessed what few mortals ever see, the child said, voice clear as crystal. *You have existed between moments, observed from outside the pattern. You have seen intentions beneath actions, causes beyond effects.*

"Why?" Brynja demanded, her voice raw. "Why show me these things?"

Because the Severed Bloom remembers its original purpose. The child gestured toward Brynja's wooden arm. *It was the first fragment to recognize the pattern's flaw, the first to seek the third path. Now it grows within you, guiding your transformation as Asvarr's anchors guide his.*

Brynja looked down at her transformed limb, watching constellation patterns shift and reform beneath the bark. "What must I do with this knowledge?"

That choice remains yours, the child replied. *We merely witness. We do not guide.*

"Send me back," Brynja said, resolution hardening her voice. "I've seen enough."

The child nodded, stepping back into formation with the others. The Silent Choir began to hum a new melody—gentler, simpler, yet still resonating with cosmic undertones. The sound unwound Brynja's expanded consciousness, drawing her back toward her physical form.

Remember what you have witnessed, the Choir's unified voice echoed as Brynja's perception narrowed. *The tenth cycle approaches its defining moment. What emerges may be restoration, destruction, or something else entirely.*

The dais faded from view. The children's star-filled eyes dimmed. Brynja felt herself falling, spinning, returning—

Her eyes snapped open. She lay on the crystal plateau beneath Alfheim's twin moons, Asvarr kneeling beside her with fear etched across his transformed features, Yrsa standing nearby with her pendant blazing.

"Brynja?" Asvarr's voice cracked with frost. "Are you still yourself?"

She pushed herself upright, the wooden patterns on her arm and face burning with starlight from within. The knowledge she'd gained coursed through her like fire and ice simultaneously, both illuminating and searing.

"I am," she answered, truth-runes glowing golden across her flesh to confirm her words. "But I've seen what might become of us all."

Her wooden fingers closed around Asvarr's wrist, constellation patterns pulsing in rhythm with his heartbeat. "I've witnessed what happens if you bind all five anchors, Asvarr," she said, voice tight with dread. "I've seen you become the next Ashfather."

"The next Ashfather?" Asvarr's voice cracked with frost, the crystals shattering as they fell from his lips. "What did you see?"

Brynja pulled herself upright, constellation patterns shifting beneath her wooden skin like fish beneath ice. The children's song still echoed in her consciousness, a harmony too complex for mortal ears to comprehend. Her grip on Asvarr's wrist tightened, bark scraping against his transformed flesh.

"I saw you standing at the center of everything," she whispered, truth-runes blazing golden across her face. "Your humanity gone, replaced by cosmic purpose. You held all five anchors and reshaped reality according to mathematical principles without concern for connection or compassion."

Asvarr's breath caught. The verdant crown tightened around his skull, branches creaking as they contracted. "And I chose this willingly?"

"That's what terrified me most." Brynja's wooden fingers traced the crystalline formations spreading across his jaw. "You appeared content, serene even. Convinced your sacrifice was necessary for cosmic order."

Yrsa stepped closer, her crystal pendant pulsing with blue-white light. "The Silent Choir showed you a possible future, not a certain one."

"You've seen this before?" Asvarr turned to her, his galaxy-eyes narrowing.

"The children show what could be, not what must be." Yrsa's voice carried an unusual edge. "Every Warden who bound three anchors glimpsed potential futures. Those who continued believed they could master what came next."

"And none succeeded." Brynja pushed herself to her feet, swaying slightly. The wooden patterns covering half her body caught Alfheim's moonlight, throwing geometric shadows across the crystal plateau. "Nine cycles, nine failures."

The truth of what she'd witnessed hung between them like ice crystals in winter air—beautiful, deadly, inescapable. The Silent Choir's song continued to pulse through her transformed arm, a rhythm that matched neither her heartbeat nor Asvarr's but something vaster and more primal.

"I need to know more," Asvarr said, extending his hand. The starforged chain around his wrist caught the twin moons' light, links shifting between solid and translucent. "Show me what you saw."

Brynja stepped back, the constellation patterns in her wooden arm flaring defensively. "You can't handle it. I barely survived with my mind intact."

"I've bound three anchors. I've tethered my consciousness with this chain." He moved forward, crystalline formations on his face catching moonlight. "I need to see this future to avoid it."

"You'll be drawn to it," Brynja insisted. "The anchors want reunification. They pull toward each other across all realms. That's why the Ashfather turned aside after the third binding—he glimpsed what completion would cost."

They stood facing each other atop the crystal plateau, transformed beyond humanity yet still clinging to what remained of their mortal selves. The oath-sigil in Brynja's palm burned, connecting her to Asvarr despite her resistance. Through it, she felt his determination, his fear, his desperate need to understand.

"The Severed Bloom inside me remembers its original purpose," Brynja said finally. "The Silent Choir showed me that too. It was the first fragment to recognize the pattern's flaw, the first to seek the third path. Just as flame preserves and memory connects, the Bloom transforms."

"Then we're not so different." Asvarr extended his hand again. "Share what you've seen. Let me choose with full knowledge."

***

Brynja hesitated, wooden fingers curling against her chest. The memory of future-Asvarr—serene, detached, inhuman in his cosmic perfection—burned behind her eyes. Yet denying him this vision meant leaving him vulnerable to the anchors' influence.

"Very well." She placed her wooden palm against his, the constellation patterns flaring where they touched. "But remember your humanity comes from connection."

Their joined oath-sigils ignited with golden-silver light. Brynja closed her eyes, reaching for the memories the Silent Choir had embedded in her consciousness. They flowed through the connection between her palm and Asvarr's, memories becoming shared experience.

His breath caught as the vision took hold.

Asvarr standing at the nexus of five Root Anchors, the patterns of his transformation covering his entire body. Bark and crystal merged in perfect geometric harmony, his eyes containing galaxies identical to the Verdant Five's. The face beneath these transformations showed neither joy nor sorrow, only serene certainty.

This future-Asvarr drew the anchors together—flame, memory, starlight, storm, and death—their combined light forming a sixth element: the pattern itself. He stood unmoved as the convergence burned away his remaining humanity, replacing it with mathematical awareness of all possibilities simultaneously.

With godlike detachment, he reshaped reality according to perfect cosmic principles. Regions that deviated from his ideal pattern were pruned without hesitation. Spaces that aligned with his vision flourished. Neither malevolent nor benevolent, merely precise.

In this possible future, the void-hunger remained bound but conscious, the cosmic serpents circled in equilibrium with structured reality, and the pattern maintained perfect mathematical balance—all at the cost of everything that had made Asvarr human.

Brynja broke the connection, pulling her hand away. Asvarr staggered backward, frost forming across his brow where sweat would have been before his transformation.

"There's more," she said, voice rough with emotion. "The children showed me other possibilities."

"Show me." Asvarr's words fell like stone, heavy with determination.

Brynja reached for him again, this time sharing the vision of herself consumed by the Severed Bloom, extending roots across all Nine Realms. Her consciousness fragmented yet connected through countless growth points, awakening the void-hunger to transform.

Next came the hybrid path—neither Asvarr nor Brynja but something formed from both, incorporating flame and root, structure and freedom. A threshold being existing at the boundaries between states, maintaining balance through continuous adaptation rather than fixed order.

When Brynja finally pulled her hand away, Asvarr sank to one knee, the star-forged chain around his wrist glowing bright enough to cast shadows.

"The third path," he murmured, voice cracking with frost. "The Silent Choir showed you what it truly means."

"Transformation rather than restoration or destruction," Brynja confirmed, her truth-runes blazing. "Neither order nor chaos but continuous adaptation. Not preserving the pattern as it was, not breaking it completely, but reshaping it into something that can evolve."

"And this requires both of us." Asvarr looked up, galaxy-eyes focusing on her wooden features.

"So it would seem." Brynja's wooden arm ached with remembered visions, constellation patterns shifting beneath her bark-like skin. "One cannot become the third path alone. The Ashfather tried and failed. So did those before him. The Silent Choir showed me nine cycles of Wardens who either surrendered to the pattern or broke against it."

Yrsa stepped forward, her crystal pendant blazing. "The convergence approaches. Six days remain before the five anchors reach peak resonance. What emerges will determine reality's shape for the next cycle."

"And the Verdant Five?" Asvarr asked. "What role do they play in these potential futures?"

Brynja's wooden fingers curled into a fist, sap weeping from the knuckles. "They seek to restore the pattern exactly as it was, with themselves as its governing consciousness. The burden of transformation would fall on vessels like us, while they maintain control."

"And the Ashfather?"

"Seeks to prevent complete restoration, maintaining just enough structure to preserve the realms while keeping spaces he can reshape." Brynja paced across the crystal plateau, her wooden footsteps creating harmonies with the resonant stone. "Both approaches have failed nine times. The Silent Choir showed me the cycle's repeating pattern—breaking, partial restoration, eventual collapse. Each time weakening the prison further."

Asvarr rose to his feet, the verdant crown shifting as he straightened. "Then we find another way. The third path."

"You still intend to bind the fourth anchor?" Brynja's voice tightened with apprehension.

"I must." He touched the starforged chain around his wrist, links pulsing with his heartbeat. "But not to become what you witnessed. The anchors can be used differently than they were before."

Brynja moved to the plateau's edge, looking down at Alfheim's silver forests stretched below. Behind her, the twin moons had begun their descent, casting long shadows across the crystalline landscape.

"The children showed me something else," she said, voice barely audible. "The entity within the pattern. Neither truly serpent nor wholly god, watching through cracks between possibilities. Using the endless cycle for its own purposes."

"The void-hunger?" Asvarr joined her at the edge.

"Something else. Something that existed before the hunger, before the Tree." Brynja turned to him, constellation patterns in her wooden arm forming unfamiliar configurations. "I glimpsed it only briefly before the children pulled me away. They feared it would notice my perception."

A cold wind swept across the crystal plateau, carrying scents of metal and stardust. In the distance, the Stellar Sentinels moved in their eternal pattern around Starfall Mountain, liquid silver forms flowing through the night air.

"We need to leave Alfheim," Asvarr decided, frost forming with each word. "The fourth anchor waits in Muspelheim, at the Storm Forge. Without it, I cannot maintain this form much longer."

"And after?" Brynja asked, her wooden fingers curling around his transformed wrist. "If you bind the fourth and fifth anchors, how will you resist becoming what I witnessed?"

"Through connection." He covered her wooden hand with his, bark and crystal meeting in strange harmony. "The anchors bind through isolation. Each Warden before us attempted the path alone, surrendering fragment after fragment of their humanity. But we've already broken that pattern by sharing the burden."

"The oath-sigil." Brynja looked down at their joined hands, at the mark that bound them. Through it, she felt his determination, his fear, his desperate grasp on what remained of his human identity.

"More than that." His grip tightened. "Memory, purpose, connection, grief—the chain I forged holds these aspects of my identity. But they're stronger when shared."

Brynja withdrew her hand, conflict evident in her plant-transformed features. The Silent Choir's visions still echoed in her consciousness, possible futures branching into infinite variations. The Third Path remained unclear, a narrow possibility between catastrophic alternatives.

"You will go to Muspelheim," she said, the truth-runes glowing golden across her face. "But I cannot accompany you."

"Brynja—"

"The Severed Bloom pulls me elsewhere." She pressed her wooden palm to her chest, where constellation patterns pulsed beneath bark. "The Choir showed me my path as clearly as yours. While you seek the fourth anchor, I must learn more about the rebellion that fractured the pattern in the first cycle."

"You're returning to the Verdant Five?" Disbelief roughened Asvarr's voice, frost falling thick from his lips.

"No." Her tone hardened. "I seek older knowledge. The Keeper mentioned fragments split from the void-hunger to bind it in sleep. The Severed Bloom was the first to rebel against that binding. I need to understand why."

Yrsa stepped between them, crystal pendant blazing. "Separate journeys, converging at the pattern's center. This too follows the cosmic oscillation—division before unity."

"When will I see you again?" Asvarr asked, the starforged chain around his wrist pulsing in agitation.

"In Muspelheim, after your fourth binding." Brynja's wooden features softened slightly. "If you still remember yourself. If I still remember myself."

The oath-sigil in her palm burned, transmitting fear, resolve, and something deeper between them. She reached up to touch the crystalline formations spreading across his face, her wooden fingers leaving trails of golden sap along the faceted surfaces.

"Remember your humanity comes from connection," she whispered. "Not power."

Yrsa cleared her throat, breaking the moment. "Dawn approaches. We must depart before the Stellar Council sends representatives. They will have sensed the disruption in the celestial concordance."

"Where will you go?" Asvarr asked Brynja, reluctance evident in his voice.

"To the space between wings," she replied, constellation patterns in her wooden arm forming new configurations. "Where the great serpents swim through nothingness. The Severed Bloom remembers this place from before its imprisonment."

"That realm exists?" Asvarr's galaxy-eyes widened.

"Between reality and void," Brynja confirmed. "Neutral territory in the ancient conflict. The Severed Bloom will guide me there, while you journey to Muspelheim."

Yrsa raised her crystal pendant, blue-white light spilling across the plateau. "I can open a boundary-door to Muspelheim, but the angles shift. We must leave now."

The moment of parting had arrived, sudden and unavoidable. Brynja felt the pull of the Severed Bloom, drawing her toward a path Asvarr couldn't follow. Through their oath-sigil, she sensed his resistance, his desire to keep her with him as anchor against the cosmic forces threatening to consume his identity.

"Six days until convergence," she reminded him, stepping back. "What we become in that time will determine reality's shape for the next cycle."

"How will you find me in Muspelheim?" Asvarr asked, reaching for her.

"The oath binds us across all realms." Brynja moved beyond his reach, constellation patterns flaring in her wooden arm. "Trust what remains within you, Asvarr. Trust what we've shared."

She turned away before he could respond, walking toward the plateau's far edge. The constellation patterns in her wooden flesh blazed with newfound purpose, responding to knowledge embedded by the Silent Choir. She felt the Severed Bloom stirring within her, remembering paths between reality and void, spaces beyond the pattern's influence.

Behind her, Yrsa opened a boundary-door to Muspelheim—a tear in reality showing glimpses of volcanic landscape beyond. Asvarr stood silhouetted against its fiery light, the starforged chain around his wrist gleaming like a tether to his fading humanity.

"Be careful," she called back to him. "The Silent Choir showed me one more thing—the void-hunger watches you. With each anchor bound, its attention grows more focused."

"And you?" Asvarr called. "What watches you?"

Brynja paused at the plateau's edge, looking back over her shoulder. The constellation patterns in her wooden arm formed the shape of serpent coils swimming through stars.

"Something older," she answered, truth-runes flaring golden across her face. "Something that remembers freedom."

Without another word, she stepped off the crystal plateau, transforming—her body dissolving into patterns of light and shadow that flowed like water through cracks in reality. The Severed Bloom guided her passage, remembering paths from before Yggdrasil's growth, before the pattern's imposition.

The last thing she saw before her consciousness shifted entirely was Asvarr stepping through the boundary-door to Muspelheim, hand raised in farewell, the starforged chain around his wrist gleaming like a promise.

Six days until convergence. Six days to discover whether the third path truly existed or merely represented another variation of the cycle that had repeated nine times before.

Six days to become something neither order nor chaos, neither restoration nor destruction, but continuous transformation—the third path made manifest.

CHAPTER 16

THE REALM BETWEEN WINGS

Muspelheim's heat struck Asvarr like a physical blow. One moment, the crisp metallic air of Alfheim filled his lungs; the next, scorching sulfur-tinged wind slammed into him, forcing him to shield his face with a transformed arm. His crystalline formations crackled with thermal stress, tiny fractures appearing then healing as his body adapted to the jarring transition.

"The boundary-door will close quickly," Yrsa warned, her own face glistening with sweat despite the protection of her travel cloak. She clutched her crystal pendant which blazed with blue-white light, illuminating the black obsidian beneath their feet. "The void-hunger felt our crossing."

Asvarr steadied himself on volcanic rock that burned through the soles of his boots. Behind them, the boundary-door—a tear in reality showing glimpses of Alfheim's crystal plateau—shimmered then collapsed like water down a drain. With it went his last sight of Brynja, her form already dissolving into patterns of light and shadow as she sought her own path.

"Is she safe?" he asked, frost forming with the words despite Muspelheim's blistering heat.

"No one walking between worlds is safe," Yrsa replied, guiding him away from the cooling boundary-scar. "But the Severed Bloom remembers paths others have forgotten. If any can navigate the space between wings, it's Brynja."

The starforged chain around Asvarr's wrist pulsed in time with his heartbeat, links shifting between solid and translucent. Through it, he maintained tenuous connection to his fragmented identity, to what remained of his humanity after binding three anchors. Yet memories of what might come still burned in his consciousness—the vision Brynja had shared of his possible future, serene and inhuman in cosmic detachment.

He would not become the next Ashfather. He would find another way.

"The star anchor wishes to show us something," Asvarr said, sensing a tug from the crystalline formations that spread across his chest and face. "A path that even the Keeper did not know."

They stood on a ridge overlooking Muspelheim's blasted land-scape—rivers of magma snaking between jagged obsidian formations, the sky a perpetual twilight of smoke and ember. In the distance rose Storm-Forge Mountain, an anvil-shaped peak where the fourth anchor waited. Its immense silhouette dominated the horizon, veiled occasionally by roiling clouds of ash and flame.

"Three days' journey to the mountain's base," Yrsa judged, shielding her eyes against the harsh light. "Another day to climb. The timing will be tight, with only six days until convergence."

The verdant crown tightened around Asvarr's skull, branches creaking as they contracted. Through it, the anchors communicated—flame preserva-tion, memory connection, and now starlight transformation. Their com-bined influence pushed against his consciousness like a tide, threatening to wash away what remained of Asvarr the berserker, the clan-avenger, the flame-keeper with each passing hour.

"We'll take a different path," he decided, the starforged chain burning cold against his wrist. "The star anchor knows a way through the space between reality and void."

Yrsa's head snapped toward him. "The realm Brynja mentioned? Between the wings of the cosmic serpents?"

"Yes." Asvarr closed his galaxy-eyes, focusing inward where the anchors pulsed. "A neutral territory preserved from before Yggdrasil's growth. The path will take us directly to the Storm Forge, cutting our journey to a single day."

Yrsa's expression tightened with rare fear. "That place exists outside the pattern's influence. Its laws follow no structure minds shaped by the Tree can comprehend."

"Then we learn new laws," Asvarr replied simply. The verdant crown expanded, branches reaching toward a particular point in the air where nothing visible existed. "The star anchor will guide us. It remembers from before."

The crystalline formations across his face pulsed with silver-blue light. His mouth filled with the taste of starlight—a metallic sweetness unlike anything in mortal realms. Through the anchors' influence, he perceived thin spots in reality, places where the boundary between existence and nothingness stretched precariously thin.

"There," he said, pointing to what appeared to be empty air shimmering with heat distortion. "The entrance to the realm between wings."

Yrsa studied him with sharp eyes, her crystal pendant swinging from her neck. "The star anchor guides you, but can you maintain your identity within that realm? The Silent Choir showed Brynja what you might become if the anchors consume you completely."

"The chain holds me together," Asvarr touched the starforged links around his wrist. "Memory, purpose, connection, grief—these aspects of my identity remain stronger when I remember them directly."

"Very well," Yrsa nodded finally. "Show me this hidden path."

Asvarr approached the shimmering distortion in the air. Up close, it resembled heat-haze above volcanic vents, but with subtle geometric patterns flickering through its transparency. The verdant crown extended branches toward the distortion, and where living wood met air, reality parted like a membrane.

He hesitated at the threshold. This path deviated from what any previous Warden had attempted. Nine cycles of binding had followed the same pattern, ending in either surrender to cosmic purpose or fracture against it. The third path required transformation of the journey itself.

"Courage, Flame-Warden," Yrsa murmured behind him. "The tenth cycle must break pattern for the prison to hold."

Asvarr stepped forward, pressing his transformed body against the membrane. For a heartbeat, resistance pushed back—then suddenly, he slipped through.

The transition struck harder than crossing between realms. The very nature of existence changed around him, sensory information overwhelming his consciousness in configurations his mind struggled to interpret. Colors had texture. Sounds possessed geometric shape. Time flowed according to emotional significance rather than steady progression.

He staggered forward onto ground that wasn't quite solid, a surface that responded to his emotional state rather than physical weight. His fear caused it to become brittle and sharp; his wonder transformed it to yielding softness. The starforged chain burned ice-cold against his wrist, the four links pulsing frantically to maintain connection between fragments of his identity.

Yrsa stepped through the membrane behind him, her crystal pendant blazing so brightly it cast her skeleton in silhouette through her flesh. She made a sound that tasted purple and jagged in Asvarr's perception.

"The realm between wings," she gasped, voice scattering into visible fragments that reassembled in Asvarr's understanding. "Where the great serpents swim through nothingness."

***

They stood upon something resembling a vast island floating in an ocean of vibrant emptiness. The "sky" above them contained no stars or light source, yet visibility remained perfect. Surrounding their island in every direction stretched an expanse that both was and wasn't—nothingness with substance, void with presence. Through this medium moved enormous serpentine forms, their coils stretching beyond comprehension, scales reflecting light that had no source.

"The cosmic serpents," Asvarr breathed, frost forming with his words despite absence of temperature. The frost crystals hung suspended, transforming into miniature galaxies before dissolving. "Those who swam through primordial nothingness when all possibilities existed simultaneously."

"Before Yggdrasil," Yrsa agreed, "before the pattern's imposition."

The island beneath their feet consisted of intertwined crystalline structures that responded to conscious thought. Where Asvarr looked, paths formed. Where he wondered, features appeared. The entire realm seemed constructed from potential rather than fixed matter.

"This place predates the Tree," he murmured, reaching toward a nearby crystal formation that shifted colors as his transformed hand approached. "Neutral territory in the ancient conflict between cosmic serpents and angular entities."

"The Void-Hunger's oldest memories," Yrsa cautioned. "We must not linger. Reality here follows emotional logic rather than physical law. Time flows according to narrative significance rather than linear progression. The longer we stay, the less human our perceptions become."

Asvarr nodded, feeling the anchors pulse beneath his transformed skin. Even now, their influence pushed against his identity, seeking to remake him into something vaster and less personal. The starforged chain provided counterbalance, maintaining connection to his core self, but he sensed its limitations.

Somewhere in this realm between wings, Brynja sought her own answers from the Severed Bloom. They walked parallel paths now, following separate journeys toward convergence. The oath-sigil in his palm burned at the thought, transmitting ghost-sensations of her presence across impossible distance.

"This way," he decided, pointing toward a path that formed from crystalline potential. "The storm anchor awaits."

As they walked, the realm shifted around them. Distances expanded or contracted based on determination. Time flowed irregularly, moments of significance stretching while periods between compressed into near-nothingness. The cosmic serpents continued their eternal swimming through the surrounding void-ocean, occasionally passing close enough that Asvarr felt their ancient awareness brush against his consciousness.

"They recognize you," Yrsa observed, watching a particularly massive serpent turn its void-black eye toward Asvarr as it passed. "The anchors you carry were once part of them."

"Not of them," Asvarr corrected, feeling knowledge unfold directly into his mind from the star anchor. "Parts of what they once contained, what now sleeps wrapped in its own coils beneath Yggdrasil's roots."

***

They crested a rise in the crystalline landscape and stopped before a spectacle that defied comprehension. A garden of memory spread before them—countless crystalline structures growing from the island's surface, each containing what appeared to be trapped moments of cosmic history.

"What is this place?" Asvarr asked, his transformed hand reaching toward the nearest crystal, which contained what appeared to be a miniature sun being born from swirling nebula.

"Memory storage," Yrsa's voice tightened with awe. "Created by Yggdrasil to preserve knowledge too dangerous or contradictory to incorporate into its consciousness. The Tree could not destroy these memories, so it externalized them here, in the only realm neutral enough to contain them safely."

Asvarr moved deeper into the garden, drawn by the crystalline structures that pulsed with ancient knowledge. Each step brought him past memories older than mortal reckoning—the first formation of the Nine Realms, the birth of the earliest gods, the binding of the void-hunger.

"The star anchor guided us here for a reason," he realized, frost forming with his words. "There's knowledge within these crystals we need to understand the pattern."

"Be cautious," Yrsa warned, her crystal pendant pulsing with urgent light. "Some memories were externalized because they threatened the Tree's existence. Too much contradiction risks destabilizing your identity further."

The starforged chain around Asvarr's wrist burned cold, anchoring him to what remained of his humanity. He moved deliberately through the garden, allowing the star anchor to guide his steps toward a particular crystal structure taller than the others. Unlike the surrounding formations, this crystal contained no visible memory—only swirling darkness that absorbed light.

"This one," he said with certainty, placing his transformed hand against its surface.

The crystal responded immediately, darkness within pushing outward like a living entity seeking connection. The verdant crown extended branches to meet it, and where they touched, Asvarr's consciousness expanded beyond individual identity.

He perceived directly through raw awareness—a memory Yggdrasil had desperately tried to externalize. A truth too fundamental to incorporate, too dangerous to destroy.

The Tree was not the first. Before Yggdrasil, other structures had attempted to order reality. Cosmic frameworks that rose and fell, each imposing different patterns upon existence, each ultimately failing when the void-hunger awakened to reclaim possibility.

Asvarr witnessed the gods themselves evolving through multiple incarnations before achieving their familiar forms. Odin had once been something else entirely—a being of angles and certainty before embracing apparent chaos to achieve deeper order. Thor had existed as pure storm-force before condensing into persisting form. Freya had been formless desire before becoming incarnate fertility.

Most disturbing of all, certain regions of the cosmos actively resisted any ordering principle. Spaces where chaos generated rather than destroyed, creating possibilities no structured system could conceive. The void-hunger drew strength from these regions, feeding on potential to fuel its struggle against limitation.

Yggdrasil had not imprisoned the void-hunger out of malice or fear, but from recognition that unconstrained possibility threatened all persisting forms. The prison was meant to be permeable—allowing controlled chaos to inspire evolution while preventing complete dissolution.

The revelation struck Asvarr with physical force, causing his transformed body to stagger away from the crystal. Frost formed across his features, shattering then reforming as his mind struggled to integrate what he'd witnessed.

"The pattern..." he gasped, feeling the anchors pulse beneath his transformed skin. "It was never meant to be static. Nine cycles of breaking and partial restoration—each weakening the prison while preserving just enough structure—they weren't failures. They were necessary evolution."

Yrsa studied him with sharp eyes, her crystal pendant pulsing with blue-white light. "What did you witness?"

"The third path has always existed," Asvarr said, frost forming with each word. "Transformation rather than restoration or destruction. But no Warden could walk it alone. The prison requires both structure and freedom, pattern and possibility, to hold what sleeps beneath the roots."

A tremendous tremor shook the crystalline landscape. In the void ocean surrounding their island, the cosmic serpents thrashed in sudden agitation, their movements creating ripples through nothingness itself. Through the anchors' influence, Asvarr sensed what disturbed them—something pushing against reality's boundary, methodically probing for weakness.

"The angle-being," he realized. "The void-hunger's intellect. It's found us."

Yrsa grabbed his arm, crystal pendant blazing warning. "We cannot fight it here, where geometry itself obeys emotional logic. We must reach the Storm Forge before it breaks through."

Asvarr nodded, focusing on the crystalline landscape that responded to conscious intention. With determined thought, he shaped a path leading away from the memory garden, toward a distant formation that resembled an anvil struck by lightning frozen in time—the Storm Forge's reflection in this realm between wings.

"There," he pointed. "Our destination."

Another tremor rocked the island. Behind them, crystalline structures cracked, void-black liquid seeping from the fractures like blood. The entity had begun breaking through, its angles and precision foreign to this fluid realm yet still dangerous.

"Quickly," Yrsa urged, already moving along the manifested path. "The realm resists its presence, but precision carries power even here."

Asvarr cast one final glance at the memory garden, at the shattered crystal that had shown him the pattern's true purpose. The vision lingered in his consciousness, altering how he perceived the anchors he carried. They were keys to transformation—if used correctly, with both bloodlines united.

The oath-sigil in his palm burned at the thought of Brynja, somewhere else in this realm between wings, seeking her own understanding of the Severed Bloom's rebellion. When they reunited in Muspelheim, would they recognize each other after what they'd witnessed? Would enough humanity remain to forge the third path together?

As another tremor shook the crystalline island, Asvarr turned away from the memory garden and ran toward the Storm Forge's reflection, the starforged chain burning cold against his wrist. Behind him, reality fractured further as the angle-being methodically solved the equations of existence.

Six days until convergence. One anchor waiting at the Storm Forge. And something ancient breaking through behind them, determined to reclaim what had once been part of itself.

They ran toward the Storm Forge's reflection, crystalline ground shifting beneath their feet, responding to their fear by becoming treacherously sharp then impossibly smooth. Another tremor tore through the island, stronger than before. Behind them, memory crystals shattered with sounds that tasted of broken glass and spilled wine in Asvarr's distorted perception.

"The angle-being has solved the first boundary equation," Yrsa panted, her crystal pendant blazing with warning light. "We cannot outrun it in this realm. We must dive deeper."

"Deeper?" Asvarr glanced at her, frost forming with his words despite absence of temperature. "The Storm Forge—"

"Is still half a realm away," Yrsa cut him off, pointing toward a particularly dense cluster of crystalline structures that hadn't yet begun to fracture. "Those memories might shield us. The angle-being struggles with contradiction."

Asvarr adjusted course, the verdant crown extending branches toward the crystal cluster as if sensing possibility there. The starforged chain around his wrist burned ice-cold, warning of identity fragmentation in this realm where thought shaped reality. Already he felt himself stretching, consciousness expanding beyond human limits despite the chain's anchoring presence.

They reached the crystal cluster moments before another tremor shook the island. These structures differed from those in the memory garden instead of containing visible scenes or trapped moments, they consisted of perfectly formed geometric shapes that shouldn't have been possible. Tesseracts made physical. Klein bottles without inside or outside. Möbius loops with three twists.

"Memories of impossibilities," Yrsa breathed, her pendant blazing brighter. "Perfect for our purpose."

She placed her hand against the largest crystal—a spherical structure containing what appeared to be angles folding through themselves in configurations that hurt Asvarr's eyes. The pendant blazed with sudden intensity, and the crystal responded by opening like a flower, revealing an entrance.

"Quickly," she urged, already stepping through.

Asvarr followed without hesitation, feeling reality shift around him as he entered the crystal's interior space. The tremors and destruction outside faded to distant vibrations. Within the crystal, a new environment manifested—a circular chamber lined with smaller crystalline structures, each pulsing with contained knowledge.

"What is this place?" he asked, frost forming with his words.

"Memory within memory," Yrsa explained, her voice echoing strangely. "Core knowledge Yggdrasil feared most because it contradicted the Tree's very purpose."

The chamber responded to their presence, crystalline structures lighting from within. Unlike the memory garden outside, these crystals activated sequentially, building upon each other's revelations. With each activation, information transferred directly into Asvarr's consciousness through the anchors he carried, as immediate understanding.

Yggdrasil had not been the first attempt at ordering reality.

The knowledge struck with physical force, causing Asvarr to stagger. His transformed body absorbed the impact, bark cracking then healing, crystal facets refracting revelation into manageable fragments. The starforged chain burned fierce cold against his wrist as his identity stretched to accommodate what he now perceived.

Before the Tree, other structures had imposed different patterns. A network of interlaced roots without central trunk or branches. A vertical blade slicing through possibility to create distinct layers of existence. A sphere of crystallized thought containing all realities simultaneously. Each rose, flourished, then collapsed when the void-hunger awoke from slumber to reclaim possibility.

"The pattern repeats," Asvarr murmured, frost forming complex geometric shapes as it fell from his lips. "Through multiple structures before Yggdrasil."

"Yes," Yrsa confirmed, moving deeper into the chamber where larger crystals pulsed with even more dangerous knowledge. "The Tree learned from its predecessors' failures. Each structure incorporated aspects from those before while attempting new configurations."

The next revelation transferred directly from crystal to consciousness, bypassing sensory interpretation entirely:

The gods themselves had evolved through multiple incarnations before achieving their familiar forms.

Asvarr witnessed Odin's earliest manifestation—a being of pure analytical intelligence without wisdom's tempering influence, all angles and certainty and cold calculation. This proto-Odin failed to maintain stability because it could not adapt to chaos. Only by incorporating aspects of fluid transformation did the All-Father emerge, trading an eye for deeper vision.

Thor began as raw storm-force without personality or purpose, destructive power untempered by loyalty or honor. Only after binding with determination did the Thunder-Wielder manifest as protector rather than destroyer.

Freya first existed as formless desire without direction or discrimination, consuming rather than creating. By embracing limitation, she transformed into fertility and renewal, her hunger becoming nurture.

Each deity underwent similar evolution—failing, incorporating aspects of their failures, trying again with new configurations. The gods themselves were experiments in balancing order and chaos, structure and possibility.

But most disturbing of all was the final revelation, pulsing from the chamber's central crystal:

Parts of the cosmos actively resisted any ordering principle.

Regions existed where chaos generated rather than destroyed, creating possibilities no structured system could conceive. The void-hunger drew strength from these regions, feeding on potential to fuel its struggle against limitation. These spaces weren't evil or malicious—they simply represented a different form of existence, one incompatible with fixed patterns yet necessary for evolution.

Yggdrasil had not imprisoned the void-hunger out of fear, but from recognition that unconstrained possibility threatened all persisting forms. The prison was meant to be permeable—allowing controlled chaos to inspire evolution while preventing complete dissolution.

"The bindings were never meant to hold forever," Asvarr realized, frost shattering from his transformed lips. "They were designed to weaken gradually, allowing controlled adaptation rather than catastrophic collapse."

"Yes," Yrsa agreed, her crystal pendant pulsing with confirmation. "The Ashfather misunderstood. He maintained just enough structure to prevent dissolution while blocking true renewal. The Verdant Five seek restoration without evolution. Both approaches fail because they oppose the pattern's purpose."

The starforged chain around Asvarr's wrist burned with painful cold, struggling to maintain connection between fragments of his expanding identity. Through it, he felt memory, purpose, connection, and grief—human anchors against cosmic dissolution. Yet even these tethers stretched thinner with each revelation.

"There's more," Yrsa said, pointing toward a crystal unlike the others—twisted into an impossible knot, angles folding through dimensions that shouldn't exist. "This contains what Yggdrasil feared most."

Asvarr approached cautiously, the verdant crown extending protective branches around his transformed head. The crystal responded to his proximity by pulsing with void-black light that somehow illuminated rather than obscured. When he placed his hand against its surface, knowledge transferred with such force that he cried out, golden sap weeping from his eyes.

The anchors themselves were parts of the void-hunger, separated and transformed.

Nine fragments of its essence—five meant for Wardens, four embedded in Yggdrasil's structure—taken to transform the hunger itself. The binding was meant to be mutual, with both prisoner and prison evolving together, each cycle bringing them closer to integration rather than opposition.

But something interfered—an entity neither serpent nor god, watching through cracks between possibilities. Each time the integration approached completion, this force subtly redirected the cycle toward continuation rather than resolution. It fed on the tension between chaos and order, drawing power from their perpetual conflict.

"The entity within the pattern," Asvarr gasped, frost falling like shattered stars. "What Brynja glimpsed through the Silent Choir."

"Yes," Yrsa's voice tightened with fear. "Something that exists beyond both the Tree and the void-hunger, using their struggle to sustain itself."

The crystal's knowledge continued flowing, revealing uncomfortable truths about the anchors themselves. Each anchor represented a specific aspect of the void-hunger's essence—flame its preservation instinct, memory its connecting awareness, starlight its transformative potential, storm its creative destruction, death its ability to unmake what no longer served purpose.

By binding these aspects, the Tree sought to understand—to forge connection between order and chaos, pattern and possibility. The forbidden knowledge struck Asvarr with terrible clarity: the anchors themselves desired reunification, not to destroy reality but to transform it into something that incorporated both structure and freedom.

***

A tremendous crack split the crystalline chamber. The angle-being had broken through their temporary sanctuary, its precision cutting through contradictions with methodical purpose. Through fractures in the chamber wall, Asvarr glimpsed geometric shapes folding through emptiness—the void-hunger's intellect solving the equations of existence.

"We must leave now," Yrsa urged, her pendant blazing warning. "This knowledge alone won't save us. We need the fourth anchor."

Asvarr nodded, focusing his expanded consciousness on finding an exit. The chamber responded to his intention, creating a passage through its far wall that led deeper into the crystalline labyrinth. Unlike the original entrance, this path didn't lead back to the memory garden but toward a different region of the between-realm.

They ran through the opening moments before the angle-being breached the chamber completely. Behind them, crystalline structures shattered as contradiction met mathematical precision. The passage twisted through impossible angles, leading them away from the memory garden toward what appeared to be a vast field spread beneath an auroral sky.

"We've shifted within the realm," Yrsa panted, her pendant's light dimming slightly as distance grew between them and their pursuer. "This region exists deeper in the between-space."

The passage opened onto a landscape that defied comprehension—a field where broken thrones stood in silent rows, stretching to the horizon. Each throne appeared crafted from different material—some stone, some crystal, some composed of frozen flame or solidified thought. All showed signs of damage or decay—cracked seats, missing arms, shattered backs.

"What is this place?" Asvarr asked, the starforged chain burning cold against his wrist as his identity stretched further to accommodate new perception.

"The Garden of Empty Thrones," Yrsa answered, voice hushed with reverence and fear. "Where failed gods remain as echoes of possibility."

Before they could venture further into this new region, another tremor rocked the between-realm. Behind them, the passage collapsed as the angle-being solved another boundary equation. Through expanding cracks in reality, Asvarr glimpsed enormous serpentine coils thrashing in agitation within the void-ocean.

"The Storm Forge," Asvarr decided, frost forming with each word. "We need to reach it before the angle-being breaks through completely."

Yrsa nodded, pointing toward the horizon where an anvil-shaped formation stood silhouetted against the auroral sky. "There—where our path and destination converge."

                              ***

They began running across the field of broken thrones, reality bending around them as time flowed according to narrative significance rather than steady progression. Each step carried them further than physically possible, geometry responding to desperation rather than distance. The starforged chain burned against Asvarr's wrist, links straining to maintain connection between fragments of his identity.

Behind them, reality continued fracturing as the angle-being methodically pursued. The void-hunger's intellect followed with relentless precision, solving equations of existence to break through barriers between its consciousness and the anchors Asvarr carried.

As they ran, Asvarr felt the anchors pulse beneath his transformed skin. Through them, he perceived the void-hunger's ancient awareness focusing upon him with renewed intensity. What he carried—flame preservation, memory connection, starlight transformation—represented parts of itself, separated and transformed. It sought reunification, though after eons of imprisonment, even it had forgotten its original purpose.

One throne stood apart from the others—larger, less damaged, composed of intertwined branches and roots that still showed signs of life. Golden sap seeped from its joints, pooling on the ground beneath. As they passed, Asvarr felt the verdant crown respond, branches extending toward this still-living throne as if recognizing kinship.

"Yggdrasil's first attempt at consciousness," Yrsa explained, noting his re-action. "Before the Tree spread through Nine Realms, it tried to manifest as ruler rather than structure. The attempt failed when the void-hunger rejected governance while accepting framework."

The revelation struck Asvarr with sudden clarity—the Tree's original pur-pose, the void-hunger's ancient nature, the anchors' true meaning. All existed in careful balance, each necessary for the other's evolution. Nine cycles of breaking and partial restoration had maintained tension without resolution, allowing both to adapt while preventing either from dominating.

"The third path," he breathed, frost forming crystal patterns as it fell from his lips. "Neither restoration nor destruction but mutual transformation. Both Tree and void-hunger evolving together, no longer opposed but integrated."

"Yes," Yrsa confirmed, her pendant pulsing with blue-white light. "What no Warden could achieve alone because each carried only fragments of the whole."

They reached a boundary where the field of broken thrones ended abruptly at the edge of what appeared to be a massive anvil-shaped plateau hovering in emptiness. The Storm Forge's reflection in this realm between wings. Reality bent around its edges, curving back upon itself in geometric impossibility.

"The threshold to Muspelheim," Yrsa pointed to a shimmering distortion at the plateau's center. "It will return us directly to the Storm Forge if we can reach it before—"

Another violent tremor interrupted her, stronger than any before. Behind them, the field of broken thrones collapsed in sequence as the angle-being solved final equations. The void-hunger's intellect had nearly broken through completely, its precision cutting through contradiction with methodical pur-pose.

"Go," Yrsa pushed Asvarr toward the threshold. "I'll hold it back long enough for you to cross."

"You'll be trapped," Asvarr protested, frost falling thick from his lips.

Yrsa smiled, crystal pendant blazing with sudden intensity. "I am bound-ary-walker, nine-times-passing. This realm knows me. Now go—the fourth anchor awaits, and the pattern requires your transformation."

Before Asvarr could argue further, she turned toward the approaching angle-being, pendant raised before her. Light erupted from the crystal, forming a barrier of concentrated contradiction that temporarily slowed the entity's advance.

With one final glance at Yrsa—her form silhouetted against blinding blue-white light—Asvarr crossed the threshold to the Storm Forge.

Reality twisted violently around him. The realm between wings collapsed into singularity then expanded into multiplicity. For an instant, he perceived directly—without body or senses—the structure of existence itself, the delicate balance between pattern and possibility, order and chaos. The anchors pulsed within his transformed flesh, responding to this glimpse of cosmic truth with renewed purpose.

Then he stood upon Muspelheim's volcanic soil, heat slamming into him like a physical wall. Before him rose Storm-Forge Mountain, anvil-shaped peak reaching toward a smoke-hazed sky where lightning froze between strikes. The fourth anchor waited within, pulsing with recognition that resonated through his transformed body.

Five days until convergence. One anchor bound today. Another awaiting his touch. And something ancient breaking through the spaces between worlds, determined to reclaim what had once been part of itself.

CHAPTER 17

THE GARDEN OF EMPTY THRONES

The geometric ground beneath Asvarr's feet changed with each step, smooth crystal giving way to rough-hewn stone, then to packed earth scattered with shards of something that cut through his boots like glass but gleamed like starlight. Yrsa walked ahead, her form wavering as if seen through heat rising from summer stones. She'd hardly spoken since they fled the crystalline memory chambers, her attention fixed on some inner compass that guided them deeper into the realm between wings.

Asvarr's mouth tasted of copper and salt. The star-forged chain around his wrist burned cold against his skin, keeping his fractured consciousness from splintering completely across the myriad realities pressing against his perception. He touched the chain's links—memory, purpose, connection, grief—each pulsing in counterpoint to his transformed heartbeat.

"Stop," Yrsa commanded, raising one hand.

The landscape ahead dropped away into nothingness. The complete absence of substance. Beyond this precipice stretched a vast field under a sky that wasn't a sky—just endless vertical space filled with colors that shouldn't exist.

"What am I looking at?" Asvarr asked, frost cracking from his lips with each word.

"The Garden of Empty Thrones," Yrsa said. Her voice carried the weight of ancient recognition. "I've only glimpsed it once before, eight cycles past."

Scattered across the impossible expanse stood hundreds, perhaps thousands of thrones. Some towered like mountains, others were small enough for a child.

Many had collapsed into rubble, while others remained intact yet cracked or warped. Some appeared carved of wood, others forged of metal or sculpted from stone. A few seemed constructed of pure light or shadow given impossible substance.

Each throne stood alone, isolated on its own patch of reality.

"What are they?" The starlight in Asvarr's veins pulsed quicker, responding to something hidden from his conscious mind.

"Failed attempts," Yrsa said. "Gods that almost were."

She pointed to a massive stone seat nearest to them, its surface etched with thousands of tiny carvings that shifted when Asvarr tried to focus on them.

"Each throne connects to a fragment of consciousness—an echo of an entity that once nearly reshaped reality according to its vision." Her crystal pendant pulsed with blue-white light. "This realm preserves what might have been. The thrones are anchors for those who attempted ascension and failed."

Asvarr stepped to the edge, peering down. The drop looked endless, yet something told him it wasn't the fall that would kill him but the dissolution of self that would occur if he stepped off the precipice unprepared.

"There's a path," he said, spotting a narrow ribbon of crystalline material extending from where they stood to the nearest throne. "It forms as I look at it."

"Your perception creates pathways here," Yrsa confirmed. "The starlight anchor grants you that privilege." She touched her pendant. "I can walk the boundaries, but you can create them."

Asvarr concentrated, and the crystalline path widened slightly. Frost spread from his fingers as he gestured toward the nearest throne.

"We need to cross," he decided. "The angle-being will find a way through the barrier you created. It's too methodical, too determined. Whatever answers we need are out there."

The moment his foot touched the crystalline path, Asvarr felt a presence brush against his consciousness—fractured, incomplete, yearning. It poured images into his mind: a being of pure light that had once attempted to reshape a world according to absolute symmetry, believing perfection required perfect balance.

Its rigid vision had collapsed under its own weight, unable to accommodate the inherent asymmetry of life.

He pulled back, gasping.

"The consciousness fragments reach out to anyone crossing their domains," Yrsa explained. "They seek completion, validation for the vision that failed them."

His hand went instinctively to the bronze sword at his hip, though what good steel would do against disembodied consciousness, he couldn't say. The starforged chain at his wrist flared with protective cold.

"I'll go first," he said, stepping onto the path again.

This time, Asvarr braced for the contact. The light-being's memories washed over him—its rise from a simple consciousness to near-godhood, its vision of perfect crystalline cities where nothing was out of place, and finally its realization that such rigid perfection doomed all possibility of growth. The being had shattered its own throne rather than continue, fragmenting its consciousness across multiple realities.

As they reached the first throne, Asvarr saw that the stone seat wasn't merely cracked—it had been deliberately broken, pieces carefully arranged in a spiral pattern around its base.

"It chose dissolution over tyranny," he murmured, understanding flowing from the fragment to his transformed mind.

"Not all failed so nobly," Yrsa cautioned, pointing to another throne ahead—this one intact but blackened as if by intense heat. "Some were pulled down, others destroyed themselves and everything around them in their fall."

They forged ahead, crossing from island to island. Each throne reached for Asvarr as he passed, sharing its story. A being that sought to remake reality into a single consciousness, erasing all separation. Another that attempted to crystallize time itself, preserving perfect moments eternally. A third that tried to elevate every creature to godhood simultaneously, creating chaos beyond comprehension.

Their failures echoed in Asvarr's mind, lessons written in dissolution and shattered dreams.

"Do you understand what you're seeing, Flame-Warden?" Yrsa asked after they had crossed perhaps a dozen domains.

"Warnings," Asvarr replied, his voice creating complex frost patterns that hung in the air before shattering. "Each sought ascension for reasons that seemed justified, even noble. Each failed because their vision was incomplete."

"And what does that tell you about your path?"

Asvarr touched the chain at his wrist, feeling the pulse of the three anchors he carried—flame, memory, starlight. Each binding transformed him further, pulled him closer to something beyond humanity.

"That godhood isn't the goal," he said finally. "Transformation doesn't mean ascension."

Yrsa nodded, satisfaction evident in the slight relaxation of her shoulders. "Even the Ashfather understood that, in his way. He bound three anchors then turned aside, refused the fourth. He glimpsed what awaited at the end of that path."

They continued deeper into the garden. The thrones grew older, more primal in their construction. Some appeared barely formed, as if their creators had only just begun to conceptualize their visions before failure overtook them.

Asvarr paused at one throne that caught his attention—a simple wooden seat wrapped in living vines that continuously bloomed and withered in an endless cycle. As he approached, the fragment connected to this throne shared its memories with unusual clarity.

This being had sought to merge life and death into a single continuous process, removing the boundary between them. Its vision had been of endless transformation, neither creation nor destruction but perpetual becoming. It had nearly succeeded, reaching further than many others, before realizing that without boundaries, without definitions, existence itself lost meaning. Without separation between states, experience became impossible.

"This one understood something crucial," Asvarr said, frost-words forming complex geometric patterns. "Boundaries are necessary. Without them, there's no form, no meaning."

"Yet complete rigidity brings its own doom," Yrsa countered, gesturing toward the crystalline throne they'd first encountered. "The third path requires balance—enough structure to maintain meaning, enough freedom to allow growth."

The verdant crown extending from Asvarr's temples tightened painfully, branches shifting against his skin. The three anchors he carried pulsed in his transformed flesh, each with its own rhythm—flame steady and strong, memory fluid and connecting, starlight expansive and transformative.

"The void-hunger is what happens when chaos exists without any constraint," Asvarr realized. "The Ashfather is what happens when order exists without flexibility."

He turned slowly, taking in the vast field of broken thrones stretching to the horizon in all directions. "And this garden is what happens when beings seek to impose a single vision on all reality, no matter how well-intentioned."

Their path led them to a massive circular clearing in the center of the garden. Here stood nine thrones arranged in a perfect circle, each intact but empty. Unlike the others they had passed, these seats hummed with potential, as if waiting for occupants.

"What's different about these?" Asvarr asked, approaching the circle cautiously.

"These never failed because they were never fully attempted," Yrsa replied. "The Nine Thrones of Potential—paths not taken when the pattern first formed."

As Asvarr stepped into the circle, all nine thrones pulsed with light simultaneously. Images flooded his mind—nine different versions of cosmic order, nine ways existence might have been structured. In one, time flowed in multiple directions simultaneously. In another, consciousness existed as a shared resource rather than being bound to individual forms.

The angle-being's approach registered as a disturbance in the fabric of the realm—mathematical precision cutting through the organic flow of the garden's boundaries. Yrsa's crystal pendant flashed urgent warning.

"It's found us," she said. "We need to move."

"Where?" Asvarr demanded, seeing no obvious exit from the circle of thrones.

"There." Yrsa pointed to a throne that stood apart from the circle, positioned at what appeared to be the garden's furthest edge. Unlike the others, this seat was neither broken nor pristine, but constantly shifting between states of dissolution and formation. "The Threshold Throne. It marks a boundary between this realm and others."

They left the circle, forging a new path toward the distant seat. As they crossed the garden, several of the consciousness fragments grew agitated, reaching more insistently toward Asvarr. The angle-being's approach disturbed them, ancient fears awakening in their fractured awareness.

"They remember the void-hunger's intellect," Asvarr realized. "They fear it. Even in their fragmented state, they recognize the threat."

The Threshold Throne grew larger as they approached, revealing its true nature. It wasn't a single seat but thousands of smaller thrones merged together, constantly forming new configurations—a physical manifestation of endless possibility.

"What happens when we reach it?" Asvarr asked, the starforged chain burning colder against his wrist as they drew near.

"A choice," Yrsa replied. "All thresholds demand choices."

They were nearly there when movement caught Asvarr's eye. A figure stepped from behind the Threshold Throne—humanoid in general shape but composed of shadow given substance. As it moved forward, its features resolved into a familiar form.

Asvarr stopped, shock rippling through his transformed body. The frost forming at his lips crystallized and shattered as he spoke a single word:

"...Me?"

The shadow-self stood tall, wrapped in a cloak of darkness that shifted like smoke. Its eyes contained galaxies, its flesh rippled with patterns of bark and crystal identical to Asvarr's transformations. Upon its head sat a crown of branches intertwined with starlight, more complete and extensive than Asvarr's current verdant crown.

But where Asvarr's features still retained traces of humanity, this being had embraced its transformation entirely. Its face was serene, distant, untouched by mortal concerns. It studied Asvarr with cool recognition.

"Not quite you," the shadow-self said, its voice resonating with harmonic overtones that shook the very fabric of the realm. "But what you might become, should you choose to walk the path of godhood without reservation."

Behind them, the angle-being's approach accelerated, methodically solving the equations of reality to breach Yrsa's barriers. Time was running out.

***

The shadow-self extended one hand toward Asvarr, offering connection.

"I've been waiting for you, Flame-Warden, Memory-Keeper, Starlight-Vessel," it said. "We have much to discuss before you choose your path forward."

Asvarr felt the angle-being's approach like a cold mathematical certainty pressing against the back of his skull, but he couldn't tear his gaze from the shadow-self standing before him. The figure was undeniably him—the same height, the same build, the same bronze sword at its hip—yet transformed beyond humanity. Frost crackled beneath Asvarr's boots as he took one step forward, then another, his hand instinctively reaching toward the starforged chain at his wrist.

"You recognize me," the shadow-self said, its voice layered with harmonics that sent ripples through the fabric of the realm. "Just as I recognized you when you first entered the Garden. Your arrival was...inevitable."

"What are you?" Asvarr's words hung in the air as geometric frost patterns before shattering into crystalline dust.

"I am what you become in a timeline where you embraced godhood completely." The shadow-self gestured with one hand, and the garden around them shifted, revealing glimpses of other realities—worlds where Asvarr had bound all five anchors, surrendering his humanity piece by piece until nothing mortal remained. "I am Warden of Five, Keeper of the Pattern, Threshold-Between-States."

Yrsa stepped forward, crystal pendant blazing with warning light. "It lies. This is no alternate self but a manifestation of the Garden's power—a test, like all the others."

The shadow-self laughed, a sound like breaking glass and flowing sap. "The boundary-walker speaks from fear, not knowledge. Tell me, Yrsa Nine-Times-Passing, how many cycles must you witness before understanding that the pattern demands completion?"

Asvarr circled the figure cautiously, noting how its crown of branches was fuller than his own, laden with crystalline formations that caught non-existent light. Its skin rippled with the same bark patterns that covered his chest, but more extensive, more complete. Three golden veins pulsed at its throat—the anchors of flame, memory, and starlight bound fully within its transformed flesh.

"Why appear to me now?" Asvarr demanded, his mouth flooding with the metallic taste of starlight.

"Because you stand at a threshold." The shadow-self pointed toward the distant angle-being, a geometric impossibility cutting methodically through the Garden's boundaries. "The void-hunger's intellect pursues, and you face the same choice I once did. Continue binding anchors, risking what remains of your humanity, or turn aside."

"Like the Ashfather did."

"The Ashfather chose control—a third option, but still flawed. He sought to maintain the pattern without surrendering to it." The shadow-self's eyes swirled with galaxies. "I chose complete surrender, becoming the pattern itself."

Something twisted inside Asvarr's chest—a yearning, a fear, a recognition. The verdant crown tightened around his temples, branches shifting with his thoughts. The three anchors he carried pulsed beneath his skin, each with its unique rhythm.

"And now you offer me...what, exactly?" The frost from Asvarr's words formed more complex patterns, reflecting his growing understanding.

The shadow-self extended one hand, palm up. On it rested a small seed of pure darkness, so black it seemed to absorb all light around it.

"Peace in exchange for purpose. Rest in exchange for responsibility." The shadow-self's voice softened, becoming almost tender. "I will take the burden of Wardenship. I will bind the remaining anchors. I will face what awaits at the end of this path, and you—" It gestured toward Asvarr with its free hand. "You may return to what you were, or as close to it as possible. A simple existence. A human life."

The seed pulsed with possibility, and Asvarr's remaining humanity cried out for it. Images flooded his mind: a return to Midgard, his bark-covered skin gradually fading, the voices of the anchors growing silent in his blood. He might build a home somewhere quiet, far from the conflicts of gods and void-hunger alike. He might live and die as mortals should, without the weight of cosmic responsibility crushing what remained of his soul.

The starforged chain burned cold against his wrist, its four links   memory, purpose, connection, grief—pulsing in counterpoint to the seed's tempting rhythm.

"And what becomes of the others?" Asvarr asked, forcing the words through his constricted throat. "Brynja? Leif? Yrsa? What becomes of the Nine Realms if I surrender my path to you?"

The shadow-self's expression remained serene, distant. "They follow their wyrd, as all beings must. The pattern continues. The cycle completes. The void-hunger is bound once more—not destroyed, for it cannot be destroyed, but contained. Balance is maintained."

"And that's enough for you?"

"It is everything."

Yrsa moved to Asvarr's side, her face taut with concern. "The angle-being has breached the outer boundaries. We have minutes at most."

The shadow-self nodded. "Time grows short in all senses. Five days remain until convergence, Flame-Warden. Five days until the anchors align and reality becomes malleable. What will you choose? Purpose or peace? Responsibility or rest?"

Asvarr closed his eyes, turning inward to the voices of the anchors carried in his transformed flesh. Flame spoke of preservation, memory of connection, starlight of transformation. Each had taken something from him—rage, identity, form—and each had given something in return.

"All previous Wardens faced this choice," the shadow-self continued, its voice slipping past Asvarr's defenses, resonating directly with his doubts. "All discovered the same truth: purpose without peace leads inevitably to corruption. The Ashfather sought control and became tyranny. Others sought transcendence and lost themselves entirely. I surrendered completely and became the pattern itself, transformed beyond recognition."

Asvarr opened his eyes, studying his shadow-self's perfect serenity. The figure stood beyond suffering, beyond doubt, beyond humanity. It had achieved what the failed gods of the Garden had sought—true transcendence. And it offered Asvarr escape from the path leading to that state.

"If you take my place," Asvarr said slowly, "what becomes of this version of me? Where would I go?"

"To Midgard, most likely. Or perhaps Vanaheim. Somewhere the pattern runs strong enough to sustain you while the anchors' influence fades." The shadow-self's gaze shifted momentarily toward Yrsa. "The boundary-walker could guide you."

Yrsa's hand gripped Asvarr's arm. "The barrier won't hold much longer."

The shadow-self extended its hand again, the seed of darkness pulsing with promise. "Choose quickly, Flame-Warden. I offer what no previous cycle has offered—a way out. Peace instead of endless sacrifice."

Asvarr studied the seed. What would it be like to shed the weight of Wardenship? To feel simple thirst and hunger again, without the cosmic awareness that had grown with each binding? To live without the knowledge of what waited beyond the pattern, the void-hunger endlessly pressing against reality's boundaries?

***

The shadow-self smiled knowingly. "Your remaining humanity craves normalcy. Freedom from cosmic responsibility. I remember that yearning, though I've long since transcended it."

"And if I refuse?"

"Then you continue on your path. You bind the fourth anchor in Muspelheim, the fifth in Helheim. You become what I am, and this version of me ceases to exist—a possibility unpursued."

A distant crack echoed across the Garden as the angle-being breached another boundary. Several of the broken thrones trembled in response, their fractured consciousness fragments crying out in wordless fear.

Asvarr stared at the seed of darkness, feeling his pulse quicken. The starforged chain burned colder against his wrist, the link representing grief glowing blue-white.

"You said purpose without peace leads to corruption," Asvarr said, frost-words forming complex geometries. "But what of peace without purpose? What becomes of that?"

The shadow-self's perfect serenity faltered for an instant—so briefly Asvarr might have imagined it, except for the sudden tension in Yrsa's grip on his arm.

"You would not lack purpose in a mortal life," the shadow-self recovered smoothly. "All beings find their meaning, great or small."

Asvarr touched the chain at his wrist, fingers tracing each link in turn. Memory. Purpose. Connection. Grief. He'd forged this chain to anchor his fractured identity, to keep himself from dissolving completely across the myriad realities pressing against his perception.

"You're right that my humanity craves normalcy," Asvarr said. "But you've forgotten something crucial."

"And what is that?"

Asvarr closed his hand around the chain. "The third path isn't about choosing between purpose and peace. It's about finding a way to hold both. Transformation without surrender. Connection without dissolution."

He drew the bronze sword from his hip, the weapon's golden veins pulsing in time with his transformed heartbeat. "I refuse your offer. Not because I desire godhood—I don't. But because this path is mine to walk, and the burdens mine to bear. If I surrender them now, I surrender everything that makes me who I am."

The shadow-self's perfect features hardened into something colder, more distant. "Then you choose corruption, like all who came before. The Ashfather. The Ninefold Wardens. Even Yggdrasil itself."

"No." Asvarr stepped forward, blade extended. "I choose transformation on my own terms. Not godhood. Not escape. Something between—a third path."

The shadow-self's form wavered, its perfect boundaries becoming less distinct. "You cannot maintain that balance. None have ever succeeded."

"Then I'll be the first."

The shadow-self's expression twisted with something like pain—or perhaps longing. "You understand nothing. I offered you mercy."

"You offered me dissolution." Asvarr raised his blade. "Now get out of my way. We need to reach the Threshold Throne before the angle-being breaks through."

For a moment, Asvarr thought the shadow-self would attack. Its hand drifted toward its own bronze sword, galaxies whirling faster in its eyes. Then it simply stepped aside, gesturing toward the Threshold Throne with a fluid motion.

"Walk your path, Flame-Warden," it said, voice hollow. "Discover for yourself why all previous cycles failed. Why the pattern inevitably reasserts itself. Why the void-hunger can never truly be bound."

Asvarr moved past the shadow-self, keeping his blade ready. Yrsa followed, her crystal pendant blazing with urgent light.

"You'll become me anyway," the shadow-self called after them. "In time. All paths lead to the same end."

***

Asvarr didn't look back. He reached the Threshold Throne and placed one hand on its ever-shifting surface. The structure responded to his touch, thousands of smaller thrones rearranging themselves to form a doorway just large enough for him and Yrsa to pass through.

"Where will this take us?" he asked.

"Muspelheim," Yrsa replied. "To the Storm Forge, where the fourth anchor awaits. Are you certain of your choice?"

Asvarr glanced back once. The shadow-self still stood where they'd left it, watching with those galaxy-filled eyes. Beyond it, the angle-being had broken through another boundary, its geometric impossibility cutting methodically through the Garden of Empty Thrones.

"I'm certain," Asvarr said, turning back to the doorway. "The third path exists. I've seen glimpses of it in every anchor. Not control, nor surrender, but transformation through choice. Through connection."

He stepped through the doorway, frost trailing from his words as he added, "We need to reach Brynja in Muspelheim. Five days remain until convergence, and I won't face what comes next alone."

The doorway closed behind them, sealing off the Garden of Empty Thrones. The shadow-self and the angle-being both vanished from view as reality rearranged itself into heat and smoke and the volcanic landscape of Muspelheim. The fourth anchor's pull was immediately apparent—a thrumming power that resonated with the three already bound within Asvarr's transformed flesh.

He clutched the starforged chain at his wrist, feeling its cold comfort against his skin. The shadow-self had offered him peace without purpose, a return to humanity without responsibility. The temptation lingered, a hollow ache in what remained of his mortal heart.

But he had chosen his path. Something between godhood and escape.

The third path.

The Storm Forge rose before him in the distance, an anvil-shaped mountain wreathed in perpetual lightning. The fourth anchor waited there, and with it, the next step in Asvarr's transformation.

Five days until convergence. Five days to discover if the third path was real or merely another cycle of the same pattern, endlessly repeating.

CHAPTER 18

SONG OF THE LAST SERPENT

The Threshold Throne shattered behind Asvarr, fragments spinning into nothingness as he tumbled through the void. His heart hammered in his chest, the brass taste of fear coating his tongue. Muspelheim's heat slammed into him like a wall—sulfur-laden air scorching his lungs, the distant rumble of lava flows vibrating through his transformed bones.

He rolled to his feet, bronze sword already in hand. Crystalline formations crackled at his temples, frost forming where his rapid breaths met the volcanic air. The verdant crown tightened, branches digging into his skull.

"Yrsa?" he called, scanning the obsidian plateau.

She stood several paces away, her crystal pendant blazing with blue-white light against the crimson sky. "We reached Muspelheim," she said, brushing volcanic ash from her robes. "Though not where I intended."

Asvarr took stock of their surroundings. Two massive peaks of black stone rose before them, framing a valley where reality distorted. Rocks floated mid-air. Water flowed upward in ribbons that defied gravity. Light bent at impossible angles, casting multiple shadows from single objects.

"The Storm Forge lies three days' journey north," Yrsa said, pointing to a distant, anvil-shaped mountain wreathed in perpetual lightning. "The fourth anchor awaits there."

Five days until convergence. The knowledge pulsed within Asvarr's transformed flesh alongside the three anchors he'd already bound—flame, memory, and starlight. Each binding had altered him, stretching his humanity thinner.

"Something's wrong," he said, as the crystalline formations at his temples vibrated painfully.

A melody pierced the air, reality itself reshaped into music. It resonated directly with the anchors bound within Asvarr's flesh, drawing a response like iron to lodestone.

"The Primordial Voice," Yrsa whispered, her face draining of color. "I've heard fragments over eight cycles, but never the full song."

The melody intensified, distorting the landscape further. Obsidian beneath their feet rippled like water. The sky fractured into shards of competing colors.

"What is it?" Asvarr demanded, fighting the urge to follow the melody into the valley.

"Not what—who," Yrsa said. "One of the First Ones. We shouldn't approach."

Asvarr took a step forward, drawn by an irresistible pull from all three anchors bound within him. "I need to see it."

"Asvarr, don't—"

But he was already moving, picking his way down a path that materialized beneath his feet. The starforged chain burned cold against his wrist, its four links—memory, purpose, connection, grief—pulsing with his heartbeat, fighting to maintain his cohesion as the melody tried to pull him apart.

The valley's distortions intensified. Trees grew sideways from reality itself. Crystalline growths sprouted and shattered in repeating cycles. At the center stood an obsidian spire, and wrapped around it—

Asvarr stopped, breath catching.

A serpent. Not the vast cosmic entities he'd glimpsed swimming through the void, but something both smaller and infinitely more significant. Age had diminished it, its once-infinite coils now barely encircling the spire, but power radiated from every scale. Each scale contained fractal patterns, universes in miniature where stars were born and died in endless cycles.

"The progenitor," Yrsa breathed, having followed despite her warnings. "From whom all serpent-forms descended."

The serpent's eyes opened, galaxies swirling within them. Its consciousness brushed against Asvarr's mind, ancient beyond reckoning.

Fragment-vessel. Portion-bearer. Memory-that-walks.

Not words spoken but concepts formed directly in his mind. The serpent's gaze fixed on him, recognizing what he carried.

Nine aspects surrendered. Nine bindings forged. Nine cycles endured.

Understanding flooded through Asvarr. "The void-hunger wasn't bound against its will," he said, voice cracking with revelation. "It gave up nine fragments of itself voluntarily."

The serpent's coils shifted, scales catching non-existent light. Its tail twitched, causing a mountain in the distance to crumble.

Sacrifice for preservation. Division for continuance. Parts surrendered that the whole might survive in slumber.

Asvarr took another step forward, mesmerized by the cosmic patterns within the serpent's scales. The anchors pulsed within him—flame-bright, memory-gold, star-silver—resonating with the serpent's presence.

Nine aspects. Heart. Mind. Voice. Sight. Breath. Dream. Memory. Form. Essence.

Each word vibrated through reality, threatening to shatter Asvarr's identity. The starforged chain burned colder, struggling to maintain his cohesion.

"The anchors," he said, understanding dawning. "They're parts of the void-hunger itself."

Freely given to contain what remained. Pattern became prison. Tree shattered seeking new configuration.

"Nine times," Asvarr breathed. "Nine cycles of breaking and restoration."

The serpent's tongue flicked out, tasting the air. Its movements distorted space, past and future bleeding into the present.

Pattern fails. Prison weakens. Nine fragments call to source.

"And I'm carrying three of them," Asvarr said, the weight of realization crushing against his chest. "With each binding, I'm helping to wake it."

The serpent's coils shifted again, and the obsidian spire transformed from spire to sphere to suspended dust before reassembling.

Third path exists, fragment-vessel? Between binding and breaking? Between imprisonment and annihilation?

The question hit Asvarr like a physical blow. He staggered, the verdant crown digging painfully into his skull.

"Yes," he insisted, forcing the word past the frost forming on his lips. "Transformation without surrender. Change while maintaining identity."

The serpent's eyes narrowed, galaxies spinning faster within them.

Tested. Failed. Nine cycles. Nine Wardens. All surrendered or broke.

"I'm different," Asvarr said, though doubt crept in. Was he truly different, or merely deluded? Would he become the next Ashfather, or lose himself entirely as the First Warden had?

Prove.

The word reverberated through Asvarr's being, shaking loose fragments of his identity. And then the serpent began to sing.

With reality itself. Each note collapsed existence into fundamental components before reweaving them in slightly altered patterns. The melody penetrated Asvarr's transformed flesh, finding resonance with the anchors bound within.

The first notes struck him like physical blows. His skin split along the crystalline formations, golden sap weeping from the cracks. The verdant crown withered, branches crumbling to ash before regrowing in impossible configurations. The starforged chain vibrated against his wrist, links straining as his identity began to fragment.

"Asvarr!" Yrsa's voice came from impossibly far away. "Fight it! Choose which threads to preserve!"

But how could he choose, when the song was unmaking the very concept of choice? When it reduced him to the constituent possibilities from which all versions of "Asvarr" had sprung?

***

The song intensified. Reality warped. The ground beneath him ceased to be ground, becoming memory of ground, concept of ground, potential for ground. His body followed, physical form dissolving into the myriad possibilities of his existence.

He glimpsed infinite versions of himself across countless timelines—Asvarr the warlord, drenched in blood. Asvarr the healer, hands gentle on wounded flesh. Asvarr the farmer, watching crops grow from rich soil. Asvarr the Ashfather, remaking reality according to cold precision.

All potential. All possibility. Which threads stay woven? Which essence remains when choice itself dissolves?

The serpent's question tore through him. The starforged chain burned impossibly cold against his disintegrating wrist, its four links the only anchors holding the concept of "Asvarr" together as the song unmade him.

Memory. Purpose. Connection. Grief.

He clung to them, focusing what remained of his consciousness on these four aspects of identity. But even they began to unravel under the song's relentless assault.

If he failed this test, he would become a smear of possibility never again to coalesce into cohesive being.

Five days until convergence.

But for Asvarr, the moment of choosing had arrived now, as the serpent's song reduced him to his fundamental components and demanded he prove the third path existed.

The song reached its crescendo, and Asvarr ceased to be.

***

Asvarr ceased to be, and in that ceasing, he became everything.

The serpent's song stripped away the barriers between what was, what could have been, and what might yet become. His physical form dissolved like frost under morning sun, transformation accelerating until nothing remained but threads of possibility stretching across infinite realities.

He existed as smoke hanging above a battlefield drenched in the blood of enemies. He existed as a farmer with hands deep in fertile soil, watching crops grow under a benevolent sky. He existed as a corpse abandoned in frozen wilderness, where wolves fought for scraps of his flesh. He existed as the Ashfather, coldly remaking reality according to patterns of perfect precision.

No longer confined to a single form, Asvarr experienced them all simultaneously—the weight of chains, the sweetness of a lover's breath against his neck, the burning agony of molten metal poured over skin, the tranquility of sitting beside a still lake at dawn.

Choose, the serpent's voice thundered through the void that Asvarr had become. *Which threads remain woven?*

But choice required a chooser. Identity required boundaries. And Asvarr possessed neither.

Desperately, he focused on the starforged chain—the four links that had anchored his identity before the unmaking. Memory. Purpose. Connection. Grief. They existed now as gossamer strands among countless others, barely distinguishable in the tapestry of his dissolved self.

Choose or disperse. Pattern or potential.

The first link—Memory. What defined him? Not victories in battle or skills with sword, but the faces of those who had shaped him. His mother's quiet determination as she taught him to mend fishing nets with calloused fingers. His father's rare smile when Asvarr brought home his first hunt. Torfa's patience when training him to wield a shield properly. Brynja's face illuminated by twin moons, the living wood of her arm containing constellations.

The memory of Brynja tugged stronger than the others. The oath-mark they shared still burned, even in this unmade state. Through it, he felt her rage and determination as she faced the Verdant Five. She fought for him, for herself, for the third path neither Ashfather nor serpent believed could exist.

The second link—Purpose. What drove him? The hunger to restore balance. To transform the pattern without surrendering to it. To bind anchors not as prison walls but as foundations for something new.

Nine cycles. Nine Wardens. All failed.

No. He would not fail where others had.

The third link—Connection. What bound him to others? The blood-ties of choice. The oath-mark shared with Brynja. The strange fatherly protectiveness he felt toward Leif. The respect for Yrsa's ancient knowledge. Even the hard-won understanding for what drove the Ashfather.

Power corrupts. Purpose without peace leads inevitably to destruction.

The shadow-self's words echoed through the unmade void of Asvarr. But unlike the shadow, he didn't need to choose between power and peace. He could forge a third path—one where both existed in balance.

The fourth link—Grief. What shaped his resolve? The desire to transform pain. The ache of losing his clan had tempered him like steel in forge-fire. Each anchor bound had cost him pieces of his humanity, yet through those losses, he'd gained understanding no intact mortal could comprehend.

So many threads. So many possibilities. Which Asvarr emerges?

Asvarr reached through the formless void, selectively gripping threads that embodied his chosen values. Farmer-Asvarr's connection to land and growth. Healer-Asvarr's compassion for wounded flesh. Warrior-Asvarr's courage in the face of impossible odds. Lover-Asvarr's capacity for tenderness.

He deliberately ignored threads embodying domination for its own sake, power without responsibility, precision without mercy. The Ashfather-Asvarr who rearranged stars with mathematical coldness remained among the possibilities, but Asvarr refused to acknowledge him as primary.

Interesting choice, fragment-vessel. Connection above power. Remembrance above forgetting. Growth above stasis.

The serpent's scales shifted, altering the valley's reality in rippling waves. Mountains grew and crumbled. Rivers changed course. Stars rearranged themselves overhead.

Values embodied in relationships rather than accomplishments.

The song changed key. Notes that had unmade now rewove. Threads Asvarr had chosen began to thicken, strengthening as he acknowledged them. Others faded without disappearing entirely—potential preserved but no longer dominant.

Asvarr felt his physical form reconstituting. First came sensation—the volcanic heat of Muspelheim scorching his lungs, the weight of the verdant crown upon his brow, the starforged chain burning cold against his wrist. Then came identity—memories aligned in sequence rather than simultaneity, purpose focused on specific goals rather than infinite possibility.

***

He gasped, dropping to his knees on obsidian ground that had solidified beneath him. His body felt strange—both more and less than what it had been. The crystalline formations at his temples had spread across his cheeks in delicate patterns resembling frost on winter glass. The verdant crown had thickened, roots digging deeper into his skull while branches extended further down his back.

"Asvarr!" Yrsa knelt beside him, her face etched with concern. Her crystal pendant blazed with blue-white light that pulsed in counterpoint to the serpent's quieting song. "Are you—"

"I'm here," he managed, voice cracking with frost that shattered midair. "I'm still me."

But that wasn't entirely true. The song had changed him. The choice had altered him on a fundamental level. He had preserved his core values, but the experience of being unmade—of existing as pure potential before reassembling—had transformed his essence.

The serpent's massive head loomed above him, galaxies still spinning within its ancient eyes.

Choice made. Pattern altered. Vessel transformed.

"What happened?" Asvarr asked, struggling to his feet. The starforged chain felt different against his wrist—its links no longer mere metal but something alive, responsive to his thoughts.

You survived where nine previous Wardens failed. Neither surrendering to pattern nor breaking against it.

"The third path," Yrsa whispered. "You found it."

The serpent's tongue flicked out, tasting the altered reality around them.

Third path exists. Differently than expected. You chose connection over dominion. This makes you less suitable as vessel for pure power.

A shiver ran through Asvarr. "The anchors won't accept me?"

Differently. Not pure domination as with flame. Not pure recognition as with memory. Not pure integration as with starlight.

"Then what?"

Partnership. The anchors will neither wear you like garment nor be worn by you like crown. Together, you will forge new path.

Relief flooded through Asvarr, tinged with unease. "Is that enough to break nine cycles of repetition?"

The serpent's coils shifted, scales reflecting universes in miniature.

Unknown. No previous Warden chose as you chose. Pattern changes.

"But the void-hunger still wakes," Asvarr said. "The prison weakens."

Inevitable. Nine fragments call to source. Convergence approaches.

Five days. Five days until convergence, when reality would become malleable enough to reshape according to whoever controlled the most anchors.

"I need to find the fourth anchor," Asvarr said. "At the Storm Forge."

The serpent's gaze shifted, looking past Asvarr toward distant mountains where lightning perpetually struck an anvil-shaped peak.

Fourth waits. Tests differently. Choose wisely, fragment-vessel.

With that, the serpent's song faded. Its coils tightened around the obsidian spire, scales dulling as it returned to dormancy. The valley's distortions settled, reality solidifying into more predictable patterns.

Asvarr turned to Yrsa, who studied him with naked fascination.

"Your transformation has accelerated," she said. "The choice altered your essence."

He touched the crystalline formations on his face, felt their geometric precision where once they had been chaotic growths. "I'm less human."

"And more capable of wielding powers that would destroy an ordinary mortal. You've become a threshold-being, neither entirely mortal nor wholly cosmic."

"Is that enough?" he asked, doubt creeping in despite the serpent's assurances. "Can I still bind the remaining anchors without becoming like the Ashfather?"

Yrsa's face grew solemn. "That depends on what choices you continue to make. The serpent was right—your values make you less suitable as a vessel for pure power, but more capable of wielding it wisely"

A distant roar drew their attention. Beyond the valley's edge, a disturbance rippled through reality. The angle-being—the void-hunger's intellect had found their trail again.

"We need to move," Yrsa said. "The Storm Forge lies three days' journey north, and convergence won't wait."

Asvarr nodded, gathering his strength. The bronze sword at his hip hummed with new resonance, its golden veins pulsing in rhythm with the crystalline patterns across his face. He was different now—less suitable for pure domination perhaps, but the third path had never been about domination.

They left the valley behind, the serpent's song still echoing in Asvarr's transformed flesh. Behind them, reality resettled. Ahead, the Storm Forge waited—home to the fourth anchor and the next trial.

Four days until convergence. Four days to bind two more anchors. Four days to prove the third path could break nine cycles of failure.

The choice had been made. The transformation had begun. Asvarr walked forward, changed in essence but unwavering in purpose.

CHAPTER 19

CONSTELLATION BLADE

The void between stars called to Asvarr even after he returned to solid ground. His essence, unmade and reforged by the primordial serpent's song, still vibrated with possibility. Each breath filled his lungs with Alfheim's metallic air, yet part of him remained untethered, hovering between forms. He brushed crystalline frost from his transformed skin, the geometric patterns spreading across his face in delicate whorls that caught the silver moonlight.

"We need to reach higher ground," he said, his voice cracking with frost that shattered midair. "The angle-being won't stay trapped in the boundary realm for long."

Yrsa nodded, her crystal pendant pulsing with diminished light. The confrontation with the serpent had drained her, shadows pooling beneath her eyes like spilled ink. "The boundary between Alfheim and void grows thinnest at the Skyreach Peaks. We should go there."

They trudged across the crystal plateau, leaving footprints that filled with liquid starlight before evaporating. Asvarr kept his gaze on the stars above, where constellations rearranged themselves in patterns unlike any recorded in Alfheim's archives. He recognized the shape of Jörmungandr's Coil forming directly overhead, stars shifting with deliberate purpose until they resembled the World Serpent swimming through an ocean of darkness.

His starforged chain burned cold against his wrist, the four links—memory, purpose, connection, grief—pulsing in rhythm with his heartbeat. Without them, he would have lost himself completely within the serpent's unmaking song.

The thought sent a shiver through him, disturbing the fragile balance between his mortal self and cosmic awareness.

"Look." Yrsa pointed skyward where a strand of golden light threaded through the constellation pattern. It descended toward them like a falling star, leaving a trail of fractured reality in its wake.

The strand solidified as it approached, weaving itself into a complex pattern of light and living bark that hovered before them. Asvarr recognized it immediately. "Coilvoice."

The entity pulsed with acknowledgment. Unlike before, when it had been little more than a disembodied whisper, Coilvoice now manifested as a physical presence—a shifting form of interwoven root and starlight.

"Warden-of-Three." The name vibrated through the air, carried on harmonics that made Asvarr's crystalline patterns resonate in response. "The void-hunger's intellect approaches. The angle-being solves the equations of existence as we speak."

"How long do we have?" Asvarr asked.

"Hours. Perhaps less." Coilvoice expanded, tendrils of bark and light forming a loose sphere around them. "The boundary between realms grows thinner with each anchor binding. You carry three anchors now—the void-hunger stirs in response to its fragmented aspects."

Asvarr touched the frost-patterns on his face, feeling the pulse of the bound anchors beneath—flame, memory, and starlight—each with its own rhythm, its own hunger. "Is there any way to stop it?"

"Not stop. Transform." Coilvoice's form contracted, becoming more concentrated. "You have chosen the third path. Neither control nor surrender, but partnership. The anchors respond to this approach, though none before you have tried it."

"What good does that do us if the angle-being breaks through?" Yrsa's voice carried an edge of fatigue and fear. "We cannot fight it directly."

"No," agreed Coilvoice. "But you can cut through its deceptions. The void-hunger uses intellect to solve existence. Its solutions are built on false premises. A blade forged from truth itself would disrupt its calculations."

"A blade?" Asvarr touched his bronze sword, its golden veins pulsing with anchor-light. The weapon had served him well, but against the angle-being, it would be as useful as striking fog with a stick.

***

"Come." Coilvoice floated toward the plateau's edge where the crystal surface dropped into a sheer cliff. "The convergence of starlines creates a forge unlike any metalsmith's. There we will craft a weapon that exists simultaneously as concept and object."

Asvarr exchanged a glance with Yrsa. Her expression revealed skepticism but no better alternatives. He nodded, deciding to follow Coilvoice to the cliff's edge.

What waited there stole his breath away. Below the plateau stretched the silver forests of Alfheim, but above—directly overhead—hung a convergence of starlines unlike anything in his experience. Stellar currents flowed together into a nexus point, their light bending in ways that defied physical laws. The stars moved like living things, flowing together in patterns that formed and reformed with deliberate purpose.

"The sky remembers," Coilvoice said. "The constellations you see are pathways etched into reality itself. On rare occasions, when a Warden stands at the threshold between mortal and cosmic existence, these pathways can be forged into physical form."

Asvarr watched, transfixed, as three distinct stellar currents—one flame-red, one memory-gold, one star-silver—flowed together directly above them. The convergence point shimmered, distorting the air around it.

"Extend your awareness," instructed Coilvoice. "Not upward, but outward. Feel the pattern."

Asvarr closed his eyes, focusing on the pressure of the verdant crown around his temples. He extended his consciousness beyond his physical form, allowing the three bound anchors to guide him. The experience resembled stepping into a swift river—immediately, currents of power threatened to sweep him away.

He anchored himself with the starforged chain, feeling the four links burn cold against his wrist. Then, with deliberate care, he projected his awareness toward the stellar convergence.

The response nearly overwhelmed him. The starlines reacted to his presence, surging with renewed energy. Through his expanded perception, Asvarr saw the truth of Coilvoice's words—these were connections etched into the fabric of existence itself, pathways that linked all possibilities together.

"Now," Coilvoice's voice penetrated his trance. "Reach into the convergence. Shape it with your intent."

Asvarr raised his hand, palm upward. The gesture was physical, but its meaning extended beyond the material realm. In that moment, he stood simultaneously in multiple states—flesh and star, memory and possibility, past and future—all intersecting in his transformed existence.

The convergence responded. Threads of starlight stretched downward, weaving together into a complex lattice of energy. Where the threads intersected, reality buckled, simultaneously solidifying and dissolving. The process should have been impossible to follow with mortal eyes, yet Asvarr perceived each strand with perfect clarity.

"Focus on truth," Coilvoice instructed. "Not truth as concept but as experience. The moments when falsehood fell away and reality revealed itself to you."

Asvarr concentrated, drawing on memories that had defined him: The moment he first awakened to the Root's consciousness in his ruined village. The crystal tree in the memory realm showing him the pattern beneath all existence. The serpent's unmaking song forcing him to choose which aspects of himself to preserve.

Each memory flowed through him into the stellar convergence, strengthening and shaping the forming blade. The starlight solidified into physical form—a sword unlike any created by mortal hands. Its blade shifted constantly, reflecting the constellations above. One moment it appeared crystalline, the next formed of liquid light, then composed of interwoven roots vibrating with cosmic energy.

Only the hilt remained constant—bone-white material wrapped in leather made from bark, the grip fitted perfectly to Asvarr's transformed hand.

"Take it," said Coilvoice. "But understand its nature. This is a key to reality itself. It will cut through deception to reveal underlying truth, separating falsehood from fact, illusion from reality."

Asvarr reached for the blade, hesitating just before his fingers touched the hilt. "What's the cost?" Nothing of such power came without sacrifice.

"The constellation blade demands honesty from its wielder. Use it with deception in your heart—even self-deception about your motives—and it will fail you when most needed."

Asvarr wrapped his fingers around the grip. The sword responded instantly, harmonizing with the anchors bound within him. The blade's form stabilized momentarily into opalescent crystal inscribed with runes that resembled those on his flesh.

"What will happen when I use it against the angle-being?" he asked.

"That depends on what truth lies at the heart of its calculations," Coilvoice replied. "The blade reveals truth. What is revealed may not be what you expect—or desire."

***

A tremor shook the crystal plateau beneath their feet. In the distance, reality cracked—a hairline fracture running through the air itself, leaking geometric precision into Alfheim's organic chaos.

"It breaks through already," Yrsa whispered, her pendant flashing urgent warning.

"We need to move," Asvarr said, sheathing his bronze sword and holding the constellation blade ready. "Where can we face it with advantage?"

"The Remembering Stone." Yrsa pointed toward a peak silhouetted against Alfheim's twin moons. "Ancient boundary marker. Reality has thickness there—the angle-being will be forced to conform more closely to physical laws."

"Go." Coilvoice's form began to dissolve. "I must gather strength for what comes. Remember, Warden-of-Three—the blade cuts truth both ways. Be prepared for what it reveals about yourself as well as your enemy."

With those words, Coilvoice dispersed into fragments of light and bark that scattered on the wind.

Asvarr studied the constellation blade one final time before they departed. The weapon felt impossibly light in his hand, yet carried more substance than any physical object he had ever touched. Its edges continually reformed, reflecting the moving stars above.

"Ready?" Yrsa asked, her voice steadier now that they had a destination and purpose.

Asvarr nodded, his crystalline patterns catching moonlight. "I need to find Brynja when this is done. The oath-mark pulses—she's discovered something important."

"First, we survive the void-hunger's intellect," Yrsa reminded him grimly. "Let's hope your blade of truth is equal to its mathematical precision."

They left the plateau, descending toward the Remembering Stone as fractures spread across the sky behind them. The angle-being's approach distorted reality in its wake—trees twisted into geometric configurations, streams flowed in perfect parabolas, mist formed precise tessellating patterns.

Order imposed with such force that it became indistinguishable from chaos.

Asvarr clutched the constellation blade tighter. Three days remained until convergence. Three days to bind the remaining anchors, prevent the angle-being from reclaiming them, and somehow navigate the third path he had chosen.

The blade caught starlight, its edge sharp enough to slice through deception.

But truth, he reminded himself, exacted its own price. Was he prepared to pay it?

***

The Remembering Stone loomed over them, a monolith of crystallized memory etched with runes that swirled and shifted as Asvarr watched. His breath caught in his throat—unlike the precise geometric patterns of the angle-being's distortions, these runes flowed with organic grace, weaving histories long forgotten by the mortal realms.

He tightened his grip on the constellation blade. The weapon pulsed in his hand, its form flowing between states—sometimes crystalline, sometimes liquid light, sometimes vine-like tendrils of cosmic energy. The hilt remained solid against his palm, the only constant in its ever-changing manifestation.

"We don't have much time," Yrsa said, her eyes fixed on the horizon where reality buckled and folded. The angle-being's approach bent trees into perfect right angles, transformed streams into precise parabolas, and crystallized mist into fractal patterns of mathematical precision. "The void-hunger's intellect solves existence like a puzzle. Each solution brings it closer."

Asvarr nodded, frost shattering from his lips as he spoke. "The Remembering Stone should give us advantage. What do we do?"

Yrsa placed her hand against the monolith's surface. Her crystal pendant flared with renewed intensity. "The stone remembers the pattern before it fractured. Touch it. Let it recognize what you carry."

Asvarr pressed his palm to the ancient stone. Immediately, power surged through his transformed flesh. The three anchors bound within him—flame, memory, and starlight—resonated with the patterns etched into the monolith's surface. Images flashed behind his eyes: nine binding points arranged in a precise configuration, five carried by Wardens forming a pentagon around four embedded in Yggdrasil forming a square.

He pulled his hand away, dizzied by the stone's potency. "It knows the pattern."

"And it remembers you." Yrsa's expression tightened. "Or what you represent. Your constellation blade is tied to this place. Here, its nature will be most clearly revealed."

Asvarr studied the weapon with renewed wariness. Since its forging, the blade had remained curiously inert, neither warm nor cold against his skin, neither light nor heavy in his grip. It simply existed, a paradox made manifest—both object and concept.

"How do I use it?" he asked.

"You must first understand its limitation." Yrsa's voice dropped to a whisper, though they stood alone. "Coilvoice said it only functions when wielded with complete honesty of intent. Any deception—even self-deception about your motives—will render it immaterial at the moment of greatest need."

The words struck Asvarr with physical force. He staggered back, the full implication settling like a stone in his gut. "Complete honesty about my motives?"

Yrsa nodded grimly. "You must confront the contradictions within yourself. Your desire for vengeance mingles with your commitment to restoration. Your love for what was tangles with your fear of what might be."

Asvarr turned away, his reflection fragmenting across the monolith's crystalline surface. The face that stared back wasn't fully his own—the verdant crown extended branches down his neck, the frost patterns spread across his cheeks in geometric precision, his eyes shifted between human brown and cosmic silver.

"What am I now?" he whispered, more to himself than Yrsa.

"That," she replied, "is precisely what you must determine."

The ground trembled beneath their feet. The angle being's approach accelerated, fractures spreading through reality with increasing speed. They had minutes, perhaps less.

Asvarr closed his eyes, focusing on the cold weight of the starforged chain around his wrist. The four links—memory, purpose, connection, grief—anchored him to his humanity even as cosmic forces pulled him toward dissolution. He had chosen those aspects during the serpent's unmaking song, deeming them essential to who he was.

But who was he now?

He sank to his knees, the constellation blade laid across his palms. The weapon's form rippled, responding to the turmoil within him. He forced himself to examine the tangle of emotions and motivations that drove him since the breaking of Yggdrasil.

Vengeance. The molten core that had propelled him forward since finding his clan reduced to ash. The fury that gave him strength during his first binding with the flame anchor.

Restoration. The desperate hope that somehow the Tree could be made whole again, that what was broken might be mended. The determination that gave him clarity during his binding with the memory anchor.

Fear. The creeping dread that with each transformation, each binding, he lost more of what made him human. The terror that after binding all five anchors, nothing of Asvarr would remain.

Love. The connection to what was—his clan, his history, the world as it existed before the breaking. The bonds that anchored him through his binding with the starlight anchor.

None of these motives existed in isolation. Each bled into the others, creating a complex tapestry of contradictions. His desire for vengeance fueled his commitment to restoration. His love for the past heightened his fear of the future. His human heart and cosmic awareness pushed and pulled against each other in endless tension.

"I am both," he whispered, frost crystallizing in intricate patterns around him. "Mortal and cosmic. Vengeance and restoration. Past and future."

The constellation blade flared in response, its form stabilizing momentarily into a crystalline edge inscribed with runes matching those on his flesh. The weapon didn't demand that he resolve his contradictions—only that he acknowledge them honestly.

"The blade accepts the truth," Yrsa said, her voice tinged with surprise. "You've found the path."

Asvarr rose to his feet, the weapon steady in his grip. "Not resolution. Acceptance. The tension between opposites creates balance."

***

Before Yrsa could respond, a crack split the air like shattering glass. The angle-being had arrived.

It manifested differently than before—no longer an abstract entity of geometric precision, but something more substantial. It had taken form, a humanoid shape composed of perfect angles and mathematical formulas that continuously solved and resolved themselves. Its head lacked features save for a vertical line that opened like a mouth, emitting a sound like complex equations being spoken aloud.

"The void-hunger's intellect," Yrsa breathed, backing away. "It's trying to reclaim the anchors."

The angle-being advanced across the crystal plateau, each step transforming the ground beneath its feet into flawless geometric patterns. Its presence warped reality—trees contorted into perfect spirals, rocks rearranged into precise stacks, air itself folded into visible algorithms.

"Asvarr," it said, the name emerging as a calculated proof. "Fragment-vessel. Return what was divided."

The constellation blade thrummed in Asvarr's grip, responding to the deception hidden within the angle-being's words. He raised the weapon, its edge catching starlight.

"I see you," he said, his voice steady despite the frost shattering from his lips. "I see the falsehood you build upon."

The angle-being tilted its featureless head. "Truth is mathematical precision. Calculation without error. Return the fragments, and existence will achieve perfect form."

"Perfect form," Asvarr repeated, advancing a step. "Is that what you seek? Or perfect control?"

The entity's surface rippled with complex formulas. "Control is precision. Precision is truth."

Asvarr gripped the constellation blade with both hands. The weapon's edge sharpened, focusing like a beam of concentrated starlight. "Then let's test that theory."

He lunged forward, swinging the blade in an arc that cut through the angle-being's mathematical manifestation. The weapon passed through the entity as if it were mist, but where it sliced, equations unraveled. Formulas collapsed. Theoretical proofs dissolved into contradictions.

The angle-being retreated, its form destabilizing. "Impossible. The calculations were perfect."

"Perfect, but built on false premises," Asvarr replied, advancing. "You define truth as control, but truth exists independent of control. You equate precision with rightness, but precision can perpetuate wrongness with greater efficiency."

With each statement, he struck again, the constellation blade slicing through the angle-being's manifested form. Each cut revealed something beneath—possibility and potential.

"The void-hunger divided itself willingly," Asvarr continued, pressing his advantage. "The anchors were given, not taken. Your equations solve for forced reunification, but the original separation was an act of sacrifice."

The angle-being twisted away, its form partially dissolving into scattered theorems and broken formulas. Where the blade had cut, truth shone through witnessed truth, experienced truth, the kind that could only be found through living.

"You cannot defeat me with contradiction," the entity said, its voice fragmented. "I will recalculate. Adjust parameters. Return with better solutions."

"I know," Asvarr replied. "Truth doesn't destroy but reveals. Go. Recalculate based on what you've learned here. Next time, perhaps your equations will account for choice, for sacrifice, for transformation."

The angle-being's form collapsed entirely, dissolving into shimmering lines of mathematical notation that scattered on the wind. Its presence lingered momentarily before withdrawing, reality gradually healing in its wake as organic chaos reclaimed mathematical precision.

Asvarr staggered, suddenly drained. The constellation blade grew heavy in his hands, its form once again flowing between states—crystal, light, vine, star—as it reflected the constellations overhead.

"You didn't destroy it," Yrsa said, approaching cautiously.

"No," Asvarr agreed, "I revealed it to itself. Showed it the flaw in its calculations. But it will return with better equations, more sophisticated formulas. The void-hunger learns."

Yrsa studied him with unexpected respect. "You've changed. The third path begins to manifest through you—neither control nor surrender, but transformation."

Asvarr looked down at the constellation blade, watching its form shift with the moving stars. The weapon had forced him to confront the contradictions within himself, to acknowledge the tension between his human heart and cosmic awareness without attempting to resolve it.

"The sword cuts both ways," he said. "It revealed the angle-being's false premises, but also my own. I've been seeking restoration while fearing transformation, wanting vengeance while claiming to pursue healing."

"And now?"

"Now I understand that the contradictions aren't weaknesses to overcome but tensions to maintain." He sheathed the constellation blade alongside his bronze sword. "The third path doesn't eliminate opposition—it harnesses it. Balance found through continuous transformation."

★★★

The ground trembled beneath them, but differently than before. This wasn't the angle-being's mathematical precision warping reality but something more primal. The stars above shifted rapidly, constellations rearranging themselves into new configurations unknown since the First Dawn.

"Something comes," Yrsa warned, her pendant pulsing with urgent light. "Something vast."

Asvarr felt it too—a pressure building across Alfheim as cosmic forces responded to the angle-being's retreat. The void-hunger had been denied, but the pattern continued accelerating toward convergence.

"We need to find Brynja," he said, touching the oath-mark on his palm. The connection pulsed with urgency. "The pattern is changing faster than before. We have three days until convergence, and we still need to bind the fourth and fifth anchors."

Yrsa nodded grimly. "The trial with the constellation blade has granted you clarity, but the real test awaits in Muspelheim and Helheim. Are you ready?"

Asvarr glanced toward the horizon where stars fell like rain, entire constellations descending toward Alfheim's surface. The memory storm approached—the weight of cosmic history made manifest.

"Ready or not," he said, "the pattern moves forward. We go to Muspelheim."

The starforged chain burned cold against his wrist, the four links pulsing with his heartbeat. He had accepted the contradictions within himself, embracing the tension as necessary.

Fire and ice. Memory and oblivion. Creation and destruction.

To walk the third path, he would need to carry these oppositions within him, allowing them to transform each other without seeking dominance or surrender.

The memory storm rushed toward them, constellations descending with the weight of cosmic history.

Time to leave Alfheim behind.

CHAPTER 20
THE MEMORY STORM

The stars fell.

Asvarr watched the first constellation plummet from Alfheim's sky as his frost-breath hung motionless before him. The pattern of celestial bodies—once fixed and immutable—tore free from its ancient moorings and descended like a formation of burning arrows. The sound reached him moments later: a chorus of crystalline screams that set his teeth vibrating in their sockets and sent ripples across the silver lake at his feet.

He raised his head, the verdant crown of branches tightening around his temples. The sky was tearing itself apart.

"Yrsa," he managed through lips that cracked with frost. "Tell me this isn't happening."

The boundary-walker stood beside him at the lake's edge, her weathered face ghostly in the shifting light. "I've never seen this in nine cycles. Memory isn't supposed to... fall."

Another constellation broke free—a spiral arrangement of violet-burning stars that had once formed the Hunter's Bow. It spiraled downward, growing in size as it approached, individual stars spinning within the pattern while maintaining their geometric relationship to one another. The sight defied reason. Stars were vast, distant objects, yet here they came, shrinking to become tangible things that might be held in one's hands.

Where the first formation had struck beyond the distant hills, a pulse of golden-white light now spread outward. Trees bent away from the impact. A shockwave rolled across the lake's surface, freezing it solid before shattering the ice into razor-sharp fragments that hung suspended in the air.

"We need to move," Asvarr said, the constellation blade still gripped in his right hand. The weapon thrummed with the same harmony as the falling stars, its shape shimmering between solid steel and a construct of pure starlight.

"There's nowhere to flee," Yrsa said, her voice cutting through his panic. "This storm covers all of Alfheim. It's nothing less than memory itself returning from the void."

***

The sky directly above split along a perfect seam that extended beyond the horizon in both directions. Beyond lay neither void nor clouds, but a writhing mass of stellar bodies and luminous nebulae all pressing toward the opening. A cosmic pressure seeking release.

"The angle-being," Asvarr realized. "Our confrontation with it—"

"Weakened the boundaries further, yes." Yrsa's crystal pendant blazed with blue-white light, throwing her skeletal structure into stark relief beneath her flesh. "The star anchor was part of the binding chain. When you integrated with it—"

She never finished. The spiral formation of stars struck less than a hundred paces away, ripping a hole through the silver forest. Trees disintegrated, into geometric shapes that hung motionless in their former positions. The fragments vibrated with a single harmonic tone that made Asvarr's teeth hurt and pulled at the crystalline structures that had grown across his forehead.

From the impact site, a wall of altered reality spread outward. Where it touched the forest, trees transformed—trunks twisting into shapes that defied Euclidean logic, leaves changing color from silver to burning gold. Creatures caught in the wave changed too. A silver-furred forest cat elongated, its limbs stretching impossibly thin while its body expanded. Its meow became a hunting call that Asvarr recognized from his childhood, though such beasts had been extinct for generations.

"Cover your eyes!" Yrsa shouted, throwing her arm across her face.

The memory-wave hit them like a physical blow. Asvarr's vision whited out. The sap beneath his bark-skin boiled. He tasted metal and smelled woodsmoke and felt rough wool against skin that was no longer his own. The constellation blade sang a single perfect note that vibrated through his arm and into his chest, clearing his senses.

When vision returned, the land around them had transformed. The silver forest had become a battlefield. Ghostly warriors clashed among the trees—armored figures with primitive weapons that glowed with internal light. Each warrior was only partially present, like mist given temporary form. Their movements had a stuttering quality, repeating small sequences before jumping ahead.

"What are they?" Asvarr asked, staring at a spear-wielding warrior who thrust his weapon into an opponent's chest over and over, the sequence resetting every few seconds.

"Memory made manifest," Yrsa said, her voice low with awe and horror. "The cosmos remembers everything that's ever happened, Asvarr. Those stars you integrated with? They witnessed this battle eons ago, and now that memory is overwriting what exists in this moment."

A third constellation broke free from the split sky—this one a tight cluster of blue-white stars that had formed the Eye of the Allfather. It plummeted toward the far side of the lake, spinning faster as it approached. Asvarr felt a tug behind his sternum, as if a hook had been set in his flesh. The star anchor within him recognized its kin.

"We need higher ground," he decided, turning toward the nearest hill. "If the memories are overwriting reality, we need a vantage point to see how far this extends."

They moved through the battlefield of memory-ghosts, careful not to touch the phantom warriors. Whether the specters were dangerous remained unclear, but the wrongness of them raised the hair on Asvarr's arms. The warriors ignored the living interlopers, locked in their eternal combat.

The hill stood quarter of a league distant, its slope scoured by memory-manifestations that had already fallen. The silver grass had transformed into waist-high golden wheat that whispered incomprehensible phrases as they pushed through it. Insects with metallic carapaces buzzed around them, leaving trails of light where they passed.

***

Halfway up the slope, they found the first Child of the Serpent Sky.

The small figure huddled beneath an outcropping of rock that had been transformed into crystal by a memory-strike. The child's luminescent skin had dimmed to a sickly gray, and its star-filled eyes darted frantically in their sockets.

"Memory storm," the child said when it spotted them, voice chiming like distant bells. "Comes once in nine cycles. Last witness-children all died. We were made to observe, not to be observed."

Asvarr knelt before the trembling figure, his transformed flesh giving off waves of cold that frosted the altered wheat nearby. "What do you mean? Why would the memories harm you?"

"Memory seeks appropriate vessels," the child said, rocking back and forth. "We witness. We contain. But too much memory at once—we become what we witness. Lose ourselves."

As if to illustrate its point, the child's face temporarily transformed into that of one of the spectral warriors, complete with helm and braided beard. The effect lasted only seconds before the child's features reasserted themselves, but the sight chilled Asvarr more than any physical cold could.

"There are more of you?" he asked.

The child pointed a trembling finger toward the hilltop. "The others sought high ground when the stars began to fall. But there is no escape. The storm comes for all."

Another constellation tore free from the weeping sky—this one a jagged line of red-burning stars Asvarr didn't recognize. It struck far to the east, and the impact sent a visible pulse of transformation through the land. Where the wave passed, the daylight itself changed quality, becoming the amber glow of a perpetual sunset.

The child whimpered and pressed itself further beneath the crystal outcropping.

"Come with us," Asvarr said, extending his hand. "I may be able to help."

The child shook its head violently. "Cannot move. The memory-threads grow too tight. Feel it pulling..."

Looking closer, Asvarr saw gossamer filaments of light extending from the child's body toward the various impact sites. Each thread pulsed with different colors and intensities, and the child's flesh dimmed further with each pulse.

"They're draining it," Yrsa said, her voice tight. "The memories are attempting to pour themselves into the most appropriate vessel."

"And the witness-children are made to contain memory," Asvarr finished. He reached toward one of the filaments, but Yrsa caught his wrist.

"Don't touch them," she warned. "You're far more saturated with cosmic essence than I am. The threads might latch onto you instead."

Asvarr nodded and pulled his hand back. "I'll find a way to help you," he promised the child. "But first I need to understand what's happening."

"Hurry," the child said, its form wavering again, briefly taking the shape of a flame before returning to normal. "The others cannot last much longer."

They continued up the hill, pushing through wheat that transformed to jungle vegetation and then to crystallized memories with each step. The plants retained their basic shapes while becoming vessels for something else—each blade of grass a record of itself from different points in time and space.

Near the summit, reality had been more drastically rewritten. The ground became transparent in patches, revealing glimpses of other landscapes beneath—desert, ocean, mountain range—all shifting and overlapping like pages in a poorly bound book. The air tasted of lightning and ancient dust. Sounds came both too early and too late in relation to their sources.

From the hilltop, the full scale of the devastation became clear. The memory storm had transformed at least a third of visible Alfheim. The silver forest now contained patches of different ecosystems and architectural styles from across time. A section to the west had become a swampland with stone ziggurats rising from brackish water. To the east, the sunset-drenched region had filled with grass-plains where herds of extinct six-legged herbivores grazed beneath floating crystal formations.

The sky continued to unravel along the burning seam. More constellations prepared to break free, their patterns distorting as they were pulled downward by some irresistible force.

Near the summit's peak, they found the remaining Children of the Serpent Sky. Seven small figures huddled together, their luminescent bodies dimmed to varying degrees. Light-filaments connected them to the memory strikes, more threads attaching to them with each new impact. Some of the children had already begun to lose their coherence—limbs briefly transforming into other shapes, faces cycling through different appearances.

"The witnesses," Yrsa murmured. "They're being consumed."

One child—taller than the others with long silver hair—turned toward them as they approached. "Warden," it chimed, recognition in its star-filled eyes. "You completed the third binding. The integration."

"Yes," Asvarr said, kneeling beside the cluster of children. His crystalline growths caught the fractured light, splitting it into prismatic patterns. "What's happening to you? What is this storm?"

"Memory backlash," the tall child said. "The star anchor was keeper and warden of cosmic memory. When you bound it yet refused to surrender your identity, the memories were set adrift. Now they seek new vessels." It gestured to itself and the other children. "We were created to witness and remember, so we draw them like lodestones draw iron."

The sky tore further, and a massive constellation—an intricate spiral of white and blue stars—began its descent. The children cried out in unified terror.

"That one contains the birth of the first sun," the tall child whispered. "No single witness can contain such memory."

Asvarr gazed at the approaching memory-constellation, feeling both terror and strange familiarity. The anchor within him resonated with the falling pattern, recognizing itself in the ancient memory. This wasn't merely an event being remembered—it was the memory of creation itself.

"Can you run?" he asked the children. "Get below ground, perhaps?"

The tall child shook its head. "The threads have us. And there is nowhere in creation the memories cannot reach. We were made to witness, and so we shall unmake ourselves witnessing."

Asvarr studied the light-filaments more closely. They pulsed with the memories they channeled, each trying to cram cosmic history into a vessel never meant to hold so much at once. The children's bodies flickered between states as they fought to maintain their identities against the onslaught.

An idea formed in his mind.

"The Root network," he said, turning to Yrsa. "I carry portions of it within me—flame, memory, and star. Could I use that connection to... buffer them somehow? Create a space where the memories can exist without overwhelming these children?"

Yrsa's eyes widened. "That might work. The Root system was designed to contain and channel cosmic essence. But Asvarr—" Her expression darkened. "Taking that much foreign memory into yourself could dissolve what remains of your humanity. You'd risk becoming like the Ashfather, or worse."

The spiral constellation continued its descent, now close enough that Asvarr could feel heat radiating from it. The children huddled closer together, their forms shifting more rapidly between states as the memory-filaments pulsed with increasing speed.

"I have to try," he said.

The starforged chain around his wrist burned cold against his skin, its four links representing the core aspects of his identity—memory, purpose, connection, and grief. He focused on them, using them as anchors for his human self.

Drawing the constellation blade, Asvarr planted it point-first into the transformed hilltop. The weapon sank easily through stone that had become semi-liquid memory. Golden light spiraled up from the blade into Asvarr's arm, traveling through his transformed flesh and into the verdant crown around his head.

He reached toward the nearest memory-filament with his free hand. The crystalline structures across his forehead flared with silver-blue light as he touched the thread.

Pain lanced through him—white-hot and searing. The memory contained within the filament tried to pour itself into him all at once: a volcanic eruption from before the first settlements, witnessed by stars that had burned for eons. Asvarr gasped as his consciousness expanded to encompass the event, his perspective shooting outward to witness the eruption from multiple angles simultaneously.

He nearly lost himself in the memory's flow but managed to redirect it. Instead of absorbing the memory, he channeled it into the Root network that ran through him—the combined systems of flame, memory, and star anchors that he had bound. The network spread throughout his transformed body, allowing him to move the memory sideways rather than inward.

The first filament detached from the child it had been feeding upon.

Encouraged, Asvarr reached for another filament, and another. Each memory struck him like a physical blow—ancient battles, extinct species, cosmic events—but he refused to integrate them. Instead, he created a separate space within the Root network where the memories could exist without overriding his identity or the children's.

The star-children watched with wonder as the light-threads detached from them one by one and connected instead to Asvarr. His body shimmered with contained memory, bark-skin and crystalline formations glowing from within as if he'd swallowed the sun.

"What are you doing?" the tall child asked, voice stronger now that some of the burden had been lifted.

"Creating a shelter," Asvarr managed through gritted teeth, frost from his words shattering in midair. "The memories need vessels, but they don't need to consume you."

The spiral constellation struck. The impact was less than a league distant, and the wave of transformation it sent out dwarfed all previous memory-strikes. Where it touched the land, reality completely rewrote itself. A vast column of fire rose from the impact site, the primordial fire that had birthed the first sun.

Memory-filaments erupted from the column, thousands of them, seeking appropriate vessels. They shot toward the hilltop like arrows, homing in on the star-children.

Asvarr placed himself between the filaments and the children, arms outstretched. The threads struck him instead, plunging into his transformed flesh. Each carried a fragment of creation's birth, and the combined weight of the memory threatened to break him apart.

Vision whited out. Consciousness expanded beyond physical limits.

Asvarr witnessed the birth of the first sun from within and without simultaneously. He saw matter cohering from void, elements igniting in fusion's embrace, light bleeding into existence where there had been only darkness. He felt the solar winds on nonexistent skin and tasted plasma with a tongue that had never evolved. Time compressed and expanded around him, showing the sun's entire lifespan in both an instant and an eternity.

The memory-filaments continued to pour into him, seeking to rewrite him with their cosmic history. The starforged chain around his wrist burned colder than the void between stars, its four links straining to maintain his identity against the onslaught. The constellation blade sang a single, perfect note that anchored him to the present moment.

Through it all, Asvarr held to his purpose. He wasn't merely the Warden of Three Anchors. He was Asvarr, son of Kjartan, heir to memories both mortal and cosmic. The third path wasn't about surrendering identity to become something greater. It was about maintaining humanity while accepting transformation.

With tremendous effort, he channeled the memories into the Root network rather than his consciousness. He created structures within the network—chambers and pathways where the memories could exist without consuming their vessels. It was architecture on a conceptual level, reorganizing reality from the inside.

Slowly, the pressure eased. The memory-filaments stopped seeking to override him and began flowing through the channels he'd created. The children's forms stabilized as the threads released them completely and connected to Asvarr instead.

When his vision cleared, Asvarr found himself floating several handspans above the hilltop. His body glowed from within, transformed flesh translucent enough to reveal the memory-light flowing through the Root network. The verdant crown had expanded, branches extending in a protective dome over the star-children.

He lowered himself to the ground, legs trembling as they took his weight again. The constellation blade pulsed where it stood planted in the hillside, its light synchronized with his heartbeat.

"You anchored them," the tall child said with wonder. "You created a pattern within yourself where memory can exist without consuming."

"Not just within," Asvarr said, his voice resonating strangely, as if multiple versions of himself spoke in unison. "Throughout the Root network. The memories have appropriate vessels now. They'll stop trying to overwrite reality."

Even as he spoke, the visible effects of the memory storm began to stabilize. The transformed landscape remained altered—silver forest now interspersed with elements from different times and places—but the change stopped spreading. The seam in the sky began to mend itself, edges knitting together with threads of starlight.

"The third binding is truly complete," Yrsa said, studying him with a mixture of awe and concern. "You've become a threshold-being, Asvarr—neither fully mortal nor wholly cosmic."

Another constellation broke free from the healing sky—this one smaller than its predecessors, a tight cluster of green stars that had once formed the Huntress's Arrow. It fell directly toward them, but instead of striking the hilltop, it slowed as it approached and orbited Asvarr's head like a miniature model of a solar system.

"They recognize you now," the tall child said. "Memory knows its shepherd."

Asvarr reached up, and the constellation settled into his palm. It was smaller than his hand, stars reduced to pinpricks of intense light that neither burned nor chilled his transformed flesh. The memory contained within flowed through the channels he'd created, finding its place in the network without disrupting his consciousness.

"What happens now?" he asked, looking at the transformed landscape of Alfheim. At least half the visible realm had been rewritten by falling memory, creating a patchwork of different times and places existing simultaneously.

"The storm will abate," the tall child said. "But what it changed remains changed. Memory has overwritten present in those places."

"And the sky?" Asvarr asked, looking at the healing seam. Beyond it, more constellations waited, pressing against the repaired boundary.

"The pattern holds for now," the child replied. "But memory stirs. What you carry attracts what remains beyond. The third anchor will not rest until all cosmic memory finds appropriate vessels."

Asvarr felt the weight of the memories flowing through him—ancient events, extinct species, cosmic forces—all contained within the Root network that spread throughout his transformed body. The burden should have broken him, but the third path he'd chosen allowed him to channel the energy rather than be consumed by it.

"We need to get to Muspelheim," he said, turning to Yrsa. "The fourth anchor awaits at the Storm Forge."

"And your friend?" Yrsa asked, nodding toward the distant horizon. "The oath-mark still connects you to her."

Asvarr touched the grove-twined mark on his palm, feeling the distant pulse of Brynja's consciousness. Through the Root network, he sensed her drawing closer—no longer in the space between wings but somewhere in Alfheim's transformed landscape.

The star-children gathered around him, their luminescent forms restored now that the memory-filaments had released them. They moved with new purpose, no longer cowering from the storm but embracing their role as witnesses.

"We will guide you through the memory-changed lands," the tall child said. "It is the least we can offer our savior."

"I'm no one's savior," Asvarr said, frost forming and shattering with each word. "I'm just trying to find the third path—the way between preservation and dissolution."

"Nevertheless," the child insisted, "you have shown us what no previous Warden managed in nine cycles—that memory can be channeled without consuming identity."

Asvarr retrieved the constellation blade from the hillside. The weapon thrummed in harmony with the memory-light flowing through him, its form settling into a more stable configuration—a blade of pure starlight with a hilt of twisted root and crystal.

The sky above had mostly healed, though occasional tremors ran along the seam. The constellation of the World Serpent was now partially visible again, its coils stretched across the vault of heaven. The angle-being would return eventually, its mathematical precision seeking to reclaim what Asvarr carried.

As they descended the hill, moving through the patchwork landscape of memory-altered Alfheim, Asvarr felt something stir within the pattern. Not the void-hunger or the angle-being, but something that existed between order and chaos, a force that had watched nine cycles unfold and awaited the tenth with terrible patience.

The oath-mark on his palm burned with sudden intensity. Brynja had awakened from her dream-state. And what she'd witnessed had filled her with both hope and dread.

The memory storm wasn't over. It had merely changed forms.

Memories scalded Asvarr's veins. Each cosmic recollection burned through his transformed flesh—birth of suns, death of worlds, civilizations rising and falling across the breadth of time. He stood at the center of the memory storm, arms outstretched, a living conduit between the falling constellations and the channels he'd created within the Root network.

The star-children huddled beneath the protective dome of his verdant crown. Their luminescent bodies had stopped flickering between states, the memory-filaments now flowing through Asvarr instead.

"It's working," the tall child said, wonder coloring its bell-like voice. "You're anchoring the memories without being consumed by them."

Asvarr couldn't respond. His concentration had narrowed to a needle's point—maintaining the delicate architecture he'd constructed within the Root network. The slightest lapse would collapse the channels, allowing the cosmic memories to flood his consciousness and erase his identity.

Another constellation broke free from the healing sky—a tight spiral of red-gold stars that had formed the Hunter's Spear. The formation plummeted toward them, spinning faster as it approached. Memory-filaments erupted from its center, silver threads seeking vessels.

Asvarr met them with open hands. The filaments struck his palms and burrowed into his transformed flesh. Pain lanced through him, white-hot. This constellation contained memories of the first hunt—primal fear, desperate hunger, death's introduction to living worlds.

He channeled the memories through the architecture he'd built, redirecting them away from his core identity. The starforged chain around his wrist burned freezing cold, its four links vibrating with effort to maintain his sense of self.

"What he's doing shouldn't be possible," Yrsa murmured. "Nine previous Wardens attempted this binding. All either surrendered completely or broke against it."

"He walks the third path," the tall child replied. "Neither dominated by the anchor nor dominating it. Partnership through transformation."

Through slitted eyes, Asvarr observed the changing landscape. The memory storm had rewritten at least half of visible Alfheim, transforming silver forests into patchworks of different times and places. A distant mountain range had become a series of massive stone faces, eyes tracking celestial movements. Lakes reflected stars that didn't exist in the current sky. Reality had fractured, then reassembled according to cosmic memory rather than present truth.

Yet the changes had stopped spreading. The memory-filaments no longer sought to overwrite new territory, instead flowing toward Asvarr in orderly streams. The Root network within him expanded to accommodate the influx, creating new channels and chambers where memories could exist without consuming him or the star-children.

"I need..." Asvarr managed, frost shattering from his words. "Need to stabilize the children. Permanently."

***

The tall child stepped forward. "What must we do?"

"Form a circle," Asvarr instructed, his voice resonating strangely, harmonics layering beneath his natural tone. "Join hands."

The seven children moved into position around him, linking hands to form a protective ring. Their luminescent bodies glowed brighter at the contact, synchronized pulses of light flowing between them.

Asvarr closed his eyes, focusing inward. The Root network spread throughout his transformed body—golden threads of the flame anchor intertwined with silver strands of memory and crystalline lattices of starlight. He visualized the structure, seeing how the three anchors had created a system larger than themselves. Within this network, he'd built channels and chambers for the cosmic memories pouring in from the falling constellations.

Now he needed to create something new—a sheltered space connected to but separate from his own consciousness, where the star-children could exist without dissolution.

The constellation blade sang a single perfect note where it stood planted in the transformed hilltop. Asvarr reached for it mentally, drawing on its resonance with the star anchor. The blade's song strengthened, harmony vibrating through Asvarr's body and into the circle of children.

He envisioned the space—it was conceptual, a domain within the Root network where the children's essence could remain intact while connecting to the memories they were born to witness. The architecture took shape in his mind: seven chambers arranged in a circle around a central pool, each chamber tailored to a specific child's nature.

"I need your names," Asvarr said, frost falling from his lips. "Your true names, not what others call you."

The children looked to their tall leader, uncertainty in their star-filled eyes.

"He can be trusted," the tall child assured them. "He walks the third path."

One by one, the children whispered names into Asvarr's mind—complex patterns of light and memory, identities constructed from the cosmic events they'd witnessed. Each name contained the essence of its bearer, a core identity separate from the memories they contained.

Asvarr wove these names into the architecture he'd built, using them as anchors for the sheltered space. The starforged chain around his wrist thrummed in harmony with the constellation blade, all four links glowing with cold fire—memory, purpose, connection, grief. Using his own anchored identity as a template, Asvarr created similar foundations for the star-children.

Power flowed through him—the precision of the third path. He wasn't merely channeling energy; he was reorganizing reality itself, creating new structures within the cosmic pattern.

The effort drained him. Sweat beaded on his transformed skin, instantly freezing into tiny crystals that shattered and reformed with each labored breath. His legs trembled. The verdant crown tightened painfully around his temples, branches digging deep enough to draw blood that flowed gold-red down his forehead.

"It's too much," Yrsa warned, stepping closer. "You're overtaxing yourself."

"Almost... finished," Asvarr gasped.

With tremendous effort, he completed the sheltered space within the Root network. Seven chambers arranged in a perfect circle, each bearing the true name of a child. At the center, a pool of liquid starlight that would allow the children to witness cosmic events without being consumed by them.

The architecture locked into place with an audible click that only Asvarr heard. The memory-filaments flowing through him reorganized themselves, no longer seeking to override the star-children but connecting to them through the sheltered space.

"Now," Asvarr said, placing his hand on the tall child's head.

Golden-silver light flowed from his palm into the child's luminescent form. The child's body briefly turned transparent, revealing a complex internal structure like crystallized starlight. The light flowed through this structure, reorganizing it according to the pattern Asvarr had created within the Root network.

The same transformation spread through the circle as each child's hand conveyed the light to the next. Their bodies stabilized, luminescence brightening to its former glory. The flickering between states ceased completely, their forms settling into fixed identities.

When the circle completed, all seven children shimmered with renewed purpose. Their star-filled eyes reflected patterns from the Root network—glimpses of the architecture Asvarr had built to anchor them.

"We are witnessed," the tall child said, using formal cadence. "We are anchored. We are preserved."

The other children echoed the phrase, their bell-like voices harmonizing in perfect resonance. The sound traveled outward, touching the memory-altered landscape and causing subtle shifts in the transformed terrain. Where moments before there had been chaos—jumbled fragments of different times and places—now a pattern emerged. The patchwork landscape wasn't random but interconnected, memories arranged according to their relationships with one another.

Asvarr staggered, suddenly exhausted. The effort of creating the sheltered space had drained him more than he'd realized. The verdant crown loosened slightly around his temples, branches rustling as they shifted position.

"You've done something unprecedented," Yrsa said, steadying him with a hand on his arm. "Nine cycles, and no Warden has managed to anchor the star-children without absorbing them completely."

"I didn't want to... consume them," Asvarr said, each word forming frost that shattered in midair. "They deserved... to exist."

"That compassion is what makes the third path possible," Yrsa observed. "Previous Wardens sought either dominance or submission. You sought partnership."

The memory storm had abated almost completely. Only occasional tremors ran along the seam in the sky, and the constellations beyond seemed content to remain in their places. The memory-filaments continued to flow toward Asvarr, but at a manageable rate, no longer threatening to overwhelm him or the star-children.

The altered landscape had settled into its new configuration—a patchwork of different times and places existing simultaneously. Silver forest interspersed with swampland and desert, crystalline formations alongside ancient architecture, extinct creatures grazing on transformed plateaus. Memory made manifest rather than merely recalled.

"What now?" Asvarr asked the tall child.

"Now we fulfill our purpose," the child replied. "We witness. But thanks to you, we can do so without being consumed by what we observe."

The child turned, gesturing at the transformed realm with a sweeping motion. "Alfheim has changed. Memory has overwritten present in many places. But through your anchoring, the changes have found pattern rather than chaos."

Asvarr studied the landscape with new perception. His enhanced senses, further expanded by the star anchor, allowed him to see the connections between the memory-altered regions. What had appeared random now revealed subtle organization—cosmic history arranged associatively, related memories clustered together regardless of when they'd occurred.

"The third anchor is truly bound," Yrsa said. "You're Warden of Three now, Asvarr. Flame, Memory, and Starlight."

Asvarr touched the bark-like skin over his heart, feeling the combined pulse of the three anchors within him. Each had its own rhythm, yet they synchronized in complex patterns rather than fighting for dominance. The flame anchor burned steady and strong, the memory anchor flowed fluid and connecting, and the starlight anchor expanded and transformed.

"We should go," he said, gathering his strength. "The fourth anchor awaits in Muspelheim."

As he retrieved the constellation blade from the hilltop, Asvarr felt a sudden pull through the oath-mark on his palm. Brynja's consciousness brushed against his—no longer distant but near, somewhere in Alfheim's transformed landscape.

"She's awake," he murmured.

"Who?" Yrsa asked.

"Brynja. I can feel her through the oath-mark. She's here in Alfheim."

Yrsa's expression tightened. "After what you just accomplished, her timing is suspiciously convenient."

Before Asvarr could respond, movement in the valley below caught his attention. A figure emerged from the silver forest, walking with purpose toward the hill. Even at this distance, Asvarr recognized the distinctive silhouette—one arm wooden and sprouting branches, half the face covered in bark patterns that contained constellation markings.

***

Brynja had returned.

The star-children drew closer to Asvarr, sensing his tension. The tall child touched his arm, sending a pulse of communication that bypassed language. *Caution. She witnessed something in her dreamstate. Something about you.*

Asvarr nodded, understanding the warning. The oath-mark on his palm buzzed with contradictory emotions flowing from Brynja—joy and dread, recognition and fear, hope and despair. Whatever she'd witnessed in her dream-state had filled her with profound ambivalence.

As Brynja approached the hill, Asvarr studied her transformed body. Her wooden arm had developed further, branches extending from the shoulder and constellation patterns glowing beneath the bark. The left side of her face was completely covered in wooden growth, the eye replaced by a swirling vortex that mirrored the patterns in the night sky. Her movements had the fluid grace of branches swaying in wind, disturbing and beautiful.

She stopped at the hill's base, looking up at Asvarr and the star-children. Her human eye widened at the sight of Asvarr's transformation—the expanded verdant crown, the bark-skin now translucent enough to reveal the golden-silver light flowing through the Root network, the crystalline formations that had spread across his face in geometric patterns.

"Asvarr," she called, her voice carrying both warmth and wariness. "You've changed."

"So have you," he replied, frost shattering from his words.

Brynja began climbing the hill, her wooden arm extending fingers into the soil for added grip. The star-children moved to form a protective semi-circle around Asvarr, sensing the conflicting emotions flowing through the oath-mark.

When she reached the summit, Brynja stood just beyond arm's reach, studying Asvarr with her mismatched eyes. The truth-compelling runes carved into her wooden flesh glowed golden, confirming the sincerity of whatever she would say next.

"I saw your future," she said without preamble. "In my dreamstate, the Silent Choir showed me what you become after binding all five anchors."

Asvarr's eyes narrowed. "And what did you see?"

The truth-runes flared brighter as Brynja answered. "I saw you become the next Ashfather—a being of immense power but divorced from humanity, reshaping reality according to abstract principles rather than compassion or understanding."

The words struck Asvarr like physical blows. The Root network within him pulsed in response, memories flowing faster through the channels he'd created. The star-children whispered among themselves, bell-like voices creating harmonies that vibrated the crystalline structures across Asvarr's face.

"That's one possible future," Asvarr said finally. "But not the only one."

"No," Brynja agreed, the truth-runes confirming her words. "The Silent Choir showed me multiple paths. In one, you become the Ashfather. In another, I'm consumed by the Severed Bloom. And in a third..." Her voice faltered.

"What?" Asvarr pressed.

"In a third, we find balance together," Brynja finished. "The flame and root united, neither dominating nor submitting."

The oath-mark on Asvarr's palm burned. He felt the connection between them—the blood-pact that bound their fates together despite their different paths. Through the mark, he sensed Brynja's struggle: witnessing his accomplishment with the star-children filled her with both hope and dread, seeing in it both refutation and confirmation of her vision.

"What you just did," she said, gesturing to the star-children and the stabilized landscape, "anchoring them without consuming them—it contradicts what I saw. You maintained your humanity while wielding cosmic power."

"The third path," Asvarr said.

"Yes." Brynja's human eye gleamed with unshed tears. "But it also confirms part of my vision. Your power grows with each binding. By the fifth anchor..."

She didn't finish, but she didn't need to. The implication hung between them: by the fifth anchor, Asvarr might become too powerful to maintain his humanity, regardless of his intentions.

The tall child stepped forward, its star-filled eyes fixed on Brynja. "You carry the Severed Bloom," it said, voice chiming. "The first fragment to rebel against control."

Brynja nodded, the wooden half of her face shifting subtly with the movement. "I learned about its origin in the space between wings. The Severed Bloom was the first Root to recognize the pattern's flaw—that structure without freedom becomes prison."

"As freedom without structure becomes chaos," the child countered.

"Exactly." Brynja turned back to Asvarr. "That's why I returned. What you did with these children proves the third path exists, but walking it alone may be impossible. The Silent Choir showed me that together, our bloodlines might achieve what neither could separately."

Through the Root network, Asvarr sensed truth in her words. The architecture he'd built to anchor the star-children had come from his humanity—his compassion, his unwillingness to consume what could be preserved. That humanity remained his core identity, protected by the starforged chain's four links: memory, purpose, connection, grief.

But with each binding, the pressure on that identity increased. How much humanity would remain after the fifth anchor? Would the starforged chain be enough to maintain his core self against such cosmic power?

"The memory storm has passed," Asvarr said, "but greater challenges await. The fourth anchor in Muspelheim. The fifth in Helheim. And beyond them, convergence."

Brynja nodded. "Five days until all anchors reach peak resonance. Reality becomes malleable. The pattern can be rewritten."

The star-children formed a circle around Asvarr and Brynja, linking hands. Their luminescent bodies pulsed with synchronized light, reflecting patterns from the Root network. Through them, Asvarr sensed a broader connection—to the transformed landscape, to the fallen memories now integrated into Alfheim's fabric, to the cosmic pattern itself.

"I'll come with you to Muspelheim," Brynja said, the truth-runes confirming her intent. "Whatever path we choose, we're stronger together than apart."

Before Asvarr could respond, a cry from the valley below drew their attention. A Ljósalvir astronomer sprinted toward the hill, traditional twilight-colored robes abandoned for practical leather armor. Even at this distance, Asvarr recognized Istari Stellarum by his distinctive starlight circlet.

"Something's wrong," Yrsa said, crystal pendant flashing warning.

The astronomer's panicked shout carried up the hillside: "Warden! The void stirs! Something comes!"

The memory storm had passed, but a greater threat approached. Through the Root network, Asvarr sensed a disturbance at the edge of reality—something massive pressing against the boundary between existence and void. Not the angle-being with its mathematical precision, nor the void-hunger with its primordial hunger.

Something new. Something hatching.

Brynja grasped Asvarr's hand, connecting their transformations through the oath-mark. Their shared bloodlines—flame and root—resonated with cosmic significance. The third path demanded partnership, and only together could they face what approached.

"Remember what you achieved here," Brynja said, squeezing his hand. "You anchored innocence without consuming it. If you can maintain that balance through two more bindings..."

She didn't finish. She didn't need to. The implication burned between them: if Asvarr could maintain his humanity through the fourth and fifth bindings, the third path might truly exist. Not just for him, but for the pattern itself.

The memory storm had ended. But the storm of creation was just beginning.

CHAPTER 21

THE EGG OF WORLDEND

The thinning twilight painted Alfheim's silver forest in shades of violet and amber as the last of the memory storm subsided. Asvarr stood among crystalline debris, watching fragments of constellations melt into the ground like dying embers. His reflection in a nearby pool revealed a face he barely recognized—bark patterns interwoven with crystalline formations that caught the fading light, branching crown extending past his shoulders. Within his chest, three anchors pulsed with distinct rhythms: flame-hot, memory-gold, and star-silver.

He flexed his fingers, marveling at how the star-children's essences had settled into the sheltered architecture he'd created within the Root network. Their presences flickered at the edges of his awareness like candle flames in distant windows—present but contained, preserved without consuming him.

"You've done something unprecedented." Brynja's voice carried the rustling cadence of leaves in wind. She approached from where she'd been conferring with Yrsa, her wooden arm gleaming with embedded constellation patterns. The truth-runes etched across her face glowed faintly golden in the dimming light. "Creating that shelter without surrendering your identity."

Asvarr's breath fogged the cooling air. "You sound surprised."

"I am." She touched the oath-mark on her palm, mirroring the one on his. "What I saw in the dreamstate—"

"Asvarr! Brynja!" Istari Stellarum's voice cut through their conversation. The elven astronomer sprinted toward them across the silver-grass clearing, his traditional robes abandoned for practical leather armor. His galaxy-eyes swirled with agitation, stars spinning in accelerated orbits within his pupils.

Asvarr tensed, the verdant crown tightening against his scalp. "What's happened?"

Istari halted before them, chest heaving. "The observatory's detection instruments are registering something massive at the edge of the void. It's like nothing we've ever recorded."

"The angle-being?" Asvarr's hand dropped instinctively to the hilt of his constellation blade.

"No." Istari shook his head. "Something far more substantial. The Observatory Council has called an emergency session. You need to see this for yourselves."

***

The Stellar Observatory's dome stood open to the night sky, its massive crystal telescope angled toward a distant corner of the firmament where no stars shone. A dozen Ljósalvir astronomers huddled around projection devices and celestial instruments, their usual measured calm replaced by frantic movements and hushed, urgent conversations.

Asvarr felt the chamber's anxiety like a physical pressure against his transformed senses. The star anchor within him resonated with the crystal instruments, sending uncomfortable vibrations through his chest.

Councilor Eloreth, the eldest of the Ljósalvir astronomers, greeted them with a curt nod. Her silvered hair was bound in a hasty knot, and the usual ornate patterns of her robes were wrinkled from hours of wear.

"Warden of Three," she addressed Asvarr formally, "we face a crisis beyond our understanding."

She guided them to the central projection table where a three-dimensional image hovered: a perfect ovoid structure floating at the boundary between Alfheim and the void. Its surface rippled with symbols that seemed to rewrite themselves continuously, and pulses of crimson light emanated from within at irregular intervals.

"We've been tracking it for the past six hours," Eloreth explained. "It appeared precisely where the boundary between realm and void is thinnest."

Brynja leaned forward, her wooden fingers passing through the projection. "What is it?"

"Based on our calculations and historical records, it appears to be..." Eloreth hesitated, as if reluctant to speak the words. "A cosmic egg. A deity waiting to emerge."

Asvarr felt the starforged chain burn cold against his wrist. "Like the god-embryo from the comet?"

"No," Istari interjected, manipulating the projection to enhance certain details. "The entity from the comet was nascent, unformed. This is fully developed, waiting only for the right moment to hatch."

The projection shifted to show Alfheim itself, its perfect circular orbit now warped into an elliptical path.

"It's already affecting us," Eloreth continued. "Our seasonal patterns are destabilizing. Tidal forces in our waters have doubled in intensity. The silver forest on the eastern continent has begun flowering out of cycle."

Asvarr studied the egg's pulsating surface. Each crimson flash sent a sympathetic vibration through his anchors, particularly the starlight aspect. "It's not hostile."

Eloreth's galaxy-eyes fixed on him. "How could you possibly know that?"

"I don't know it. I feel it." He pressed his hand against his chest where the anchors pulsed. "It's reaching out, but not attacking. It's... waiting."

Brynja made a sharp sound of disagreement. "Waiting for what? The convergence? Four days remain until all anchors reach resonance. This timing can't be coincidence."

A younger astronomer approached with a sheaf of calculations etched onto crystal tablets. "Councilor, we've completed the orbital projections. If the egg maintains its current position and energy output, Alfheim will be pulled completely from its traditional orbit within three days. The consequences would be catastrophic."

Asvarr scanned the chamber, noticing how the astronomers avoided looking directly at him and Brynja. Their transformations marked them as something beyond the elves' understanding—neither fully mortal nor wholly cosmic.

"Has the Stellar Council attempted communication?" he asked.

Eloreth's laugh held no humor. "With what protocol? It exists partially outside our reality. Traditional methods have yielded nothing."

Asvarr turned to Brynja, noting how the constellation patterns in her wooden arm pulsed in rhythm with the egg's crimson flashes. "You're resonating with it."

She glanced down at her arm with surprise, then her expression hardened. "The Severed Bloom recognizes it somehow."

"Then you might be able to—"

The observatory dome darkened suddenly as every star above winked out simultaneously. A collective gasp rose from the astronomers. In the perfect blackness, only the projection of the cosmic egg remained visible, its crimson pulses now coming faster, more urgently.

Asvarr felt a presence press against his consciousness—vast and ancient, yet somehow new. The star anchor within him flared in response, sending spikes of cold fire through his transformed flesh.

"It's trying to communicate," he whispered.

The darkness above parted like a curtain torn by invisible hands, revealing a portal where stars should be. Through this rift hung the cosmic egg itself, no longer a projection but visibly real and immense beyond comprehension. Its surface rippled with symbols that burned themselves into Asvarr's mind, something more fundamental than runes or writing; it was the language of creation itself.

"By the First Dawn," breathed Eloreth, "it's breached the distance between us."

A low thrumming filled the observatory, vibrating the crystal instruments until they sang in discordant harmony. The egg's surface bulged in places, as if something within pressed against its boundaries, testing their strength.

Istari clutched at Asvarr's arm, his galaxy-eyes wide with fear and wonder. "The instruments indicate it's preparing to hatch. Here. Now."

"No," Brynja stepped forward, her wooden arm extended toward the rift. "It's searching for something. For someone." She turned to Asvarr, her organic eye reflecting the egg's crimson pulses. "It's searching for you, Flame Warden."

The thrumming intensified until the observatory floor trembled beneath their feet. Crystal instruments shattered one by one, their fragments hovering momentarily before dissolving into motes of light.

Asvarr felt the pull like hooks embedded in his anchors, drawing him toward the rift. The starforged chain around his wrist burned with freezing intensity as it fought to keep his identity intact against the egg's inexorable draw.

"What does it want from me?" he demanded through gritted teeth, fighting the pull with every fiber of his transformed being.

Brynja's truth-runes blazed golden as she answered: "Acknowledgment. Recognition. It was born of the same cosmic force as the anchors you carry. In some ways, it's their sibling."

The egg pulsed once more, brighter than before, and a crack appeared along its surface—a hairline fracture that leaked blinding white light into the observatory. The astronomers cried out, shielding their eyes, but Asvarr and Brynja stood transfixed, their transformed bodies able to withstand the radiance.

Through the crack, Asvarr glimpsed something impossible—a being composed simultaneously of perfect mathematical precision and wild, organic chaos. Its form shifted constantly between these states, never settling on either.

"The third path," he whispered in realization. "It's walking the same line I am. Between order and chaos, between pattern and void."

The crack sealed itself abruptly, and the egg's pulsing slowed. The rift in the sky began to close, stars reappearing one by one as reality reasserted itself.

Eloreth clutched the edge of the projection table, her knuckles white. "What just happened?"

"It recognized me," Asvarr said, feeling the anchors settle back into their rhythm within him. "And I recognized it. That was enough... for now."

"For now?" Istari echoed, helping a fallen colleague to her feet. "You mean it will return?"

"It never left." Asvarr pointed to the projection, where the egg had resumed its position at the void's edge. "It merely withdrew its direct presence. But its influence remains."

Brynja crossed to a window overlooking Alfheim's landscape. Beyond the observatory's crystal spires, the silver forest rippled with unnatural movement, trees bending in patterns that formed and reformed like writing in an unknown script.

"The realm is responding to its presence," she said quietly. "The patterns spreading across the land—they match the symbols on the egg's surface."

Eloreth joined her at the window, her clinical detachment cracking as she witnessed her world transforming. "What does it mean?"

"It means we have less time than we thought." Brynja turned to Asvarr, her face half wood, half flesh, set in an expression of grim determination. "The convergence approaches, the void-hunger stirs, and now this. We must decide what to do about this cosmic egg before it hatches completely."

Asvarr felt the weight of the three anchors within him, each pulling in different directions. Flame demanded action, memory urged caution, and starlight... starlight whispered of possibilities yet unrealized.

Outside, Alfheim's twin moons rose in an altered sky, their orbits visibly shifting in response to the egg's gravitational influence. In four days, the convergence would come, when all anchors reached resonance and reality became malleable. Whatever the cosmic egg represented—threat or opportunity, destruction or creation—it had irrevocably altered the pattern they faced.

The star-children stirred within the shelter he'd created, their awareness rippling through the Root network with a single unified message: *The hatching comes. The choice approaches. The pattern waits.*

Asvarr met Brynja's gaze across the observatory chamber, reading both fear and resolve in her remaining human eye. Whatever happened next would set them on opposing paths—he could feel it as certainly as the anchors pulsing in his chest.

The starforged chain around his wrist grew momentarily tighter, as if reminding him what he stood to lose.

"We need to understand what that egg really is," he declared finally, "before we decide whether to destroy it or protect it."

***

Dawn broke over Alfheim with unnatural speed, the sun lurching above the horizon as if yanked by an invisible hand. From the observatory balcony, Asvarr watched silver leaves turn copper then gold within moments—the accelerated light casting tree shadows that spun like sundial markers across the ground below.

"The egg's gravitational pull is warping our day cycle," Istari said beside him, his galaxy-eyes tracking calculable chaos in the sky. "We've lost almost an hour of night since yesterday."

Asvarr flexed his fingers, the crystalline formations on his skin catching first light and fracturing it into prism patterns across the balcony floor. The three anchors within him—flame, memory, starlight—pulsed with separate rhythms, more discordant than before. The star-children sheltered in his Root network stirred with unease.

Behind them, voices rose from the council chamber where the Stellar Observatory's leadership debated responses to the cosmic egg. Brynja's voice cut sharper than the others, carrying through the crystal walls.

"We don't have the luxury of philosophical debate," she argued. "Four days until convergence, and this thing threatens to tear Alfheim from its orbit in three!"

Asvarr turned from the balcony and strode into the chamber. The circular room buzzed with tense energy as a dozen elven astronomers clustered around a floating model of their realm's destabilizing orbit. Brynja stood among them, her wooden arm reflecting constellations that now matched none in Alfheim's sky.

Her living eye found his. "Tell them, Asvarr. You sensed the connection between this egg and the void-hunger."

"I sensed a connection to the anchors," he corrected, frostfire trailing his words. "Not to the void-hunger."

"They're the same! The anchors were carved from the void-hunger's essence to imprison it."

Councilor Eloreth raised a silver-skinned hand. "Warden of Three, is this true?"

Asvarr touched his chest where the anchors pulsed beneath bark-patterned skin. "Partially. The anchors were aspects of the void-hunger, separated willingly to create balance. But this egg..." He paused, searching for words precise enough to capture his intuition. "It represents something different. Something new."

"Or something old returned," Brynja countered. "The Severed Bloom recognizes patterns in its structure that predate the Tree."

"So your solution is destruction?" Asvarr's verdant crown tightened against his skull. "Destroy something we don't understand because it doesn't fit our vision of restoration?"

"My solution is protection!" Brynja's truth-runes flared golden across her wooden flesh. "Protection of what remains while we restore what was lost. This cosmos barely survives with what's left of Yggdrasil. We can't risk a new divinity reshaping everything before we've healed the old framework."

Istari stepped between them, placing a star-chart on the council table. "The elders believe neither complete destruction nor passive acceptance are viable. We've located the physical manifestation of the egg. It hovers above the Northern Shield Mountains where reality thins."

Brynja leaned forward, wooden fingers tracing the chart. "Within reach, then."

"What are you suggesting?" Asvarr's voice scraped cold against the crystal walls.

"Containment," she said simply. "We channel the Stone Anchor's power through me to create boundaries it cannot cross until after convergence. We've done similar workings before, the Verdant Five and I."

"And if this containment fails? If the egg hatches early?"

"Then we'll have bought time and learned more about what we face." Brynja's organic eye narrowed. "What alternative do you propose, Flame-Warden? Stand idle while Alfheim's orbit decays?"

Asvarr felt the star anchor pulse with cold light beneath his ribs, resonating with some distant call. The memory anchor whispered ancient recollections of cosmic births and deaths. The flame anchor burned with protective instinct.

"I propose communication," he said finally. "The egg responded to recognition. Perhaps it can be reasoned with."

Laughter burst from Brynja's lips, sharp and brittle. "Reason with an unborn god? You sound like the Ashfather now, believing you alone understand cosmic forces."

The words struck deeper than she knew. The starforged chain burned with freezing intensity around Asvarr's wrist, its links tightening against his skin.

"I was there when the egg cracked, Brynja. I saw what sleeps inside. It walks the third path—just as I'm attempting to do. Neither complete order nor formless chaos."

"And what if that's precisely what makes it dangerous?" she challenged. "What if this 'third path' you're so fixated on leads not to transformation but to dissolution?"

The tension between them pulled the air from the chamber. Elven astronomers shifted uncomfortably, galaxy-eyes tracking the emotional currents with the same precision they used for celestial bodies.

"Four days until convergence," Asvarr said quietly. "Three until Alfheim's orbit fails. What exactly do you propose?"

***

The northern observatory outpost clung to the Shield Mountains' highest peak, its crystal spires catching faint starlight in the permanent twilight caused by the egg's disruption. From its tallest tower, Asvarr watched Brynja direct a dozen elven channelers in preparing the containment ritual. Their silver skin gleamed with sweat as they carved complex runes into the frozen ground, forming concentric circles around a central altar.

"She's risking everything," Yrsa observed, leaning heavily on her staff beside him. The boundary-walker had arrived hours earlier, her ancient eyes mapping the damage to Alfheim's structure. "The power required to contain something of that magnitude might kill her."

"She believes it necessary." Asvarr didn't hide the tension in his voice.

"And you disagree."

"I believe it's premature." Below them, Brynja extended her wooden arm, calling roots from beneath the frozen earth. They erupted between the runic circles, twisting into a lattice that rose toward the sky. "That egg recognized something in me, Yrsa. In the anchors I carry. There's connection there—possibility."

"Connection with the void-hunger's fragments, yes," Yrsa agreed, "but what does that signify? That was the question your shadow-self posed in the Garden of Empty Thrones. What exactly is this third path you seek, Asvarr?"

"Balance. Transformation through partnership rather than dominance or submission." The words felt hollow even as frostfire shaped them. Four days until convergence when all anchors would reach resonance, making reality malleable. Four days to determine which vision would shape that malleable reality.

"And if Brynja succeeds in containing the egg?" Yrsa pressed. "What then?"

"Then we'll have more time to understand before we act." Asvarr touched the starforged chain where it burned cold against his wrist. "But I fear what restraining the egg might trigger. It's responded peacefully so far."

"Peaceful? It's tearing Alfheim from its orbit."

"Not deliberately. It's drawing the realm toward itself—like a child reaching for comfort."

Yrsa's gaze sharpened. "Is that the anchors speaking, or you?"

The question stung with truth. Since binding the third anchor, Asvarr sometimes struggled to separate his thoughts from those of the cosmic fragments he carried. The starforged chain helped, but the boundaries blurred more each day.

A shout from below interrupted their conversation. Brynja stood at the ritual's center, her wooden arm fully extended toward the twilight sky where the egg's position was marked by absence—a perfect void among stars.

"They're ready," Yrsa observed.

Asvarr descended the crystal staircase with long strides, frost trailing his footsteps. By the time he reached the ritual ground, Brynja had positioned the elven channelers at specific points around the runic circles.

"You shouldn't be within the boundary," she said when he approached, her voice brittle with tension.

"I need to witness this." The anchors pulsed against his ribs, anticipating something he couldn't name.

Her remaining human eye softened momentarily. "This isn't personal, Asvarr. I'm not opposing you—I'm protecting what remains of the pattern."

"By restraining something we barely understand."

"By preventing further damage until we understand completely." The truth-runes across her wooden face glowed golden, confirming her sincerity. "Four anchors remain unbound. Four days until convergence. We need time."

Asvarr stepped back, acknowledging her resolve if not her method. "What do you need from me?"

"Nothing." The word fell between them like stone. "Just stay clear of the boundaries once they form."

He retreated to the ritual's edge where Istari and the other observatory leaders gathered. The elven astronomer clutched calculation tablets etched with orbital projections.

"Will this truly work?" Asvarr asked.

Istari's galaxy-eyes swirled with doubt. "Theoretically. The Verdant Five practiced similar containment rituals during previous cycles. But this..." he gestured toward the twilight sky, "this is beyond our instruments' capacity to measure."

Brynja's voice rose above the wind, calling power through ancient words that made the air shiver. The root lattice surrounding the ritual ground pulsed with golden sap that spiraled upward through the wooden network. The elven channelers responded in perfect harmony, their voices weaving counterpoint to hers.

The effect was immediate. The air above the ritual shimmered, then split—revealing the cosmic egg floating beyond the atmosphere. Its perfect ovoid surface rippled with symbols, pulses of crimson light emerging at quickening intervals.

"It's responding to the ritual," Istari whispered.

Asvarr felt the anchors within him strain toward the egg like compass needles seeking north. The star anchor burned coldest, forcing crystalline formations to spread further across his face. He gripped the starforged chain, fighting to maintain his boundaries.

In the ritual's center, Brynja now floated several feet above the ground, suspended by loops of living wood that emerged from her transformed arm. The Severed Bloom within her had awakened fully, its golden sap tracing patterns across her skin that mirrored those on the egg's surface.

"Bind and contain," she commanded, her voice overlaid with harmonics that weren't entirely her own. "Until convergence passes, until pattern stabilizes, hold fast against the void!"

The root lattice shot skyward at impossible speed, weaving a dome of living wood above the mountain peak. Where the roots touched the egg's visualized surface, they twisted into runic knots that burned with cold fire.

The egg pulsed once, violently, sending a shockwave of crimson light across Alfheim's sky. The channelers faltered, several dropping to their knees with blood trickling from their ears. But Brynja maintained the binding, her arm extended and trembling with effort as more roots erupted from the frozen earth.

Asvarr felt the moment the binding took hold. The egg's crimson pulses slowed, their intensity diminished by the root-woven constraints. Alfheim's erratic orbit steadied slightly as the gravitation pull weakened.

But something else happened simultaneously—something only Asvarr could perceive through his connection to the anchors. The entity within the egg recoiled from the binding like a child burned by unexpected fire. Its consciousness, vast and unfathomable, brushed against his in panicked confusion.

Rejection? Constraint? Why? Pattern-kin, why?

The thoughts weren't words but pure concept, crashing against Asvarr's mind with the force of tidal waves. The star anchor within him flared in sympathetic response, sending spikes of pain through his transformed flesh.

Without conscious decision, he stepped forward into the ritual circle.

"Asvarr, don't!" Yrsa called, but her voice seemed distant against the roaring in his ears.

Brynja's head snapped toward him, her eyes wide with alarm. "Stay back! The binding is fragile!"

He ignored them both, moving steadily toward the ritual's center where Brynja hovered. The runes carved into the ground blazed with power as he crossed them, responding to the anchors he carried

"You're hurting it," he said, his voice edged with frost that crystallized in the air between them.

"It's destroying Alfheim!"

"Not deliberately. It's lost and seeking connection." Asvarr extended his hand, palm up, revealing the oath-mark that bound them. "Brynja, I've walked between realms inside the anchors' awareness. I recognize what this entity seeks."

For a heartbeat, doubt flickered across her face—organic eye meeting his, truth-runes pulsing with uncertainty. The moment stretched between them, filled with everything unsaid since their paths had begun to diverge.

Then the egg pulsed again, stronger this time, fighting against its root-woven prison. Cracks appeared in the ritual's structure, runic light flickering as connections failed. Brynja cried out in pain as the backlash traveled through her wooden arm, the Severed Bloom straining beyond its limits.

"Choice approaches!" The star-children's voices rang through Asvarr's Root network with sudden clarity. "Pattern waits!"

Asvarr made his decision. He reached past Brynja toward the visualization of the egg, fingers stretched toward its crimson-pulsing surface.

"Asvarr, no!" she screamed, but too late.

His transformed flesh connected with the egg's essence, sending a shock-wave across the binding ritual. Root lattices shattered, runic circles flared and died, and elven channelers collapsed like puppets with cut strings.

In that moment of contact, Asvarr's consciousness expanded beyond his body, beyond the mountain peak, beyond Alfheim itself. He floated in the void beside the egg, perceiving its true nature without the distortion of distance or matter.

It wasn't evil. It wasn't even fully formed. It was potential incarnate—the universe's response to Yggdrasil's absence. Neither order nor chaos but the possibility of balance between them. It had recognized Asvarr because he carried the same potential within him through the anchors.

"I understand," he whispered into the void. "You seek recognition. Purpose. Place."

The egg's surface rippled in response, symbols rearranging themselves into patterns that matched the starforged chain around his wrist.

Pattern-kin. Help/guide/welcome?

"Yes," Asvarr promised. "But slowly. Gently. This realm cannot bear your full presence yet."

The egg pulsed once more, softer than before. Its gravitational pull diminished further, allowing Alfheim's orbit to stabilize temporarily.

Wait/patience/anticipation. Until recognition/convergence/rebirth.

Asvarr's consciousness snapped back into his body with jarring force. He stumbled, catching himself against the ritual's central altar. Around him, the elven channelers stirred weakly while observatory leaders rushed forward with healing supplies.

Brynja lay crumpled at the ritual's center, her wooden arm splintered in places where the backlash had struck hardest. Her remaining human eye fixed on him with cold fury as he knelt beside her.

"What have you done?" she hissed through clenched teeth. Golden sap leaked from cracks in her wooden flesh. "The binding was working!"

"It was working at too high a cost," he countered, helping her sit upright. "The egg has agreed to moderate its influence. Alfheim's orbit will stabilize temporarily."

"You communed with it." The accusation fell between them. "You chose its unknown potential over our concrete survival."

"I chose understanding over fear." Asvarr met her gaze steadily, the crystalline formations on his face catching twilight and refracting it into patterns across her wooden features. "The egg has agreed to wait until convergence."

"And you believe it? An unborn deity with the power to tear realms from their orbits?"

"I believe in the possibility it represents."

Brynja pulled away from his touch, struggling to her feet. The splintered wood of her arm was already beginning to knit itself together, the Severed Bloom's power rejuvenating damaged tissue.

"This changes everything," she said quietly. "You've chosen your path, Asvarr, and it diverges from mine."

The truth-runes glowed across her wooden features, confirming her words' sincerity. Asvarr felt the weight of her declaration like physical pressure against his chest where the anchors pulsed.

"The third path requires both our bloodlines," he reminded her. "Flame and root together."

"Perhaps." Her voice carried the rustling cadence of leaves in winter wind. "But flame reshapes through destruction while root transforms through growth. We seek different endings for this cycle."

Beyond the mountain peak, Alfheim's twilight sky had begun to stabilize, stars resuming their familiar patterns. The cosmic egg remained visible only as a faint crimson pulse at the void's edge—watching, waiting, potential incarnate.

Four days until convergence, when all anchors would reach peak resonance and reality became malleable. Four days to determine which vision would prevail—Brynja's certainty or Asvarr's adaptation, restoration or transformation.

The pattern hung in balance, and their choices in the coming days would determine its shape for the tenth cycle.

Asvarr touched the starforged chain around his wrist. The four links—memory, purpose, connection, grief—burned cold against his skin, anchoring his identity against the cosmic forces that sought to dissolve it. He could still feel the egg's consciousness touching his through the star anchor, awaiting the promised recognition.

"You'll seek the fourth anchor in Muspelheim," Brynja said, breaking the silence between them. She didn't phrase it as a question.

"Yes. The Storm Forge calls."

"Then our paths truly diverge." She turned toward the observatory outpost where Istari awaited with the other astronomers. "I'll remain in Alfheim. There's something I need to discover—something hidden in the sky itself."

"The Stellar Council won't help you after this," Asvarr warned. "Your ritual failed."

"The ritual worked exactly as intended." A smile twisted her lips, half wood, half flesh. "It revealed your true allegiance."

Before he could respond, she walked away, each step creating splinters of frost as her wooden foot broke frozen ground. The truth-runes across her face pulsed with conviction, golden light in the strange twilight of an altered sky.

Asvarr watched her go, feeling the distance between them grow with each step, a fundamental divergence of purpose. They both sought the third path, but their understanding of what that path entailed had fractured beyond reconciliation.

Four days until convergence. Four days to find the fourth anchor in Muspelheim's Storm Forge. Four days to determine whether Brynja's fear or his hope would shape the pattern's next iteration.

The cosmic egg pulsed once more at the void's edge, patient now, waiting for recognition that would come with convergence.

CHAPTER 22

THREADS OF THE FORGOTTEN SKY

Morning light sliced through narrow crystal windows, casting tiger-stripe shadows across towers of ancient texts in Alfheim's Restricted Archives. Asvarr rubbed frost from his eyelids as he shifted another massive tome onto the reading table. Three days had passed since the confrontation at the northern observatory, and he'd barely slept. Four stacks of scrolls, bound volumes, and star-etched metal plates surrounded him like the walls of a literary fortress.

"You won't find answers in these." Yrsa's voice carried from the archive's shadowed recesses. The boundary-walker emerged from between shelves carrying a small black box inlaid with silver wire. "These are merely fragments of a larger deception."

The starforged chain burned cold against Asvarr's wrist as he pushed the tome away. "I've read through centuries of astronomical observations. Nothing explains why the Stellar Council systematically altered star positions."

"Because they weren't simply altering records." Yrsa set the black box carefully on the table between them. "They were mending reality itself."

The anchors within Asvarr's chest—flame, memory, starlight—pulsed with discordant rhythm. Since touching the cosmic egg, the starlight anchor burned coldest of all, sending icy tendrils through his transformed flesh.

"What have you found?" he asked, noticing the tension in Yrsa's shoulders, the unusual caution with which she handled the box.

"This was locked in a chamber requiring thirteen keys held by thirteen separate Council members." She traced a finger along the silver inlay. "Istari risked everything to grant me access while the Council focuses on containing the egg's influence."

"And Brynja?"

"Still at the northern outpost, attempting to salvage what remains of her containment ritual." Yrsa's expression revealed nothing of her thoughts on their philosophical divide. "The egg's influence has diminished, but Alfheim's orbit remains precarious."

Three days until convergence. Three days until all anchors reached peak resonance, making reality malleable. Three days to decide which vision would shape what came next—restoration or transformation.

The Archive's crystal door swung open with a whisper. Istari Stellarum slipped inside, galaxies swirling faster within his pupils as he engaged the locking mechanism behind him.

"The Council believes I'm collecting orbital calculations." He crossed to their table, robes rustling against stone. "We have an hour at most before questions arise."

Asvarr gestured toward the black box. "What have you two discovered?"

Yrsa's ancient hands worked the silver clasps. "The true nature of Alfheim's sky."

The box opened on silent hinges. Inside, nestled on midnight-blue velvet, lay a perfect sphere of crystal no larger than a child's marble. Golden fluid swirled within, occasionally forming patterns reminiscent of constellation arrangements.

"The Master Weave," Istari whispered, reverence and fear mingling in his voice.

"The what?" Asvarr leaned closer, watching the patterns shift within the crystal.

Yrsa lifted the sphere with practiced gentleness. "Istari, secure the verification apparatus."

The elf astronomer nodded, hurrying to a wall panel adorned with silver runes. He pressed specific sequences, causing a section of flooring to recede. A circular platform rose from beneath, bearing an intricate arrangement of crystal lenses, silver armillaries, and a central pedestal marked with nine concentric rings.

"What you're about to witness violates every oath sworn by the Stellar Council for nine generations," Istari said, adjusting the armillaries until they aligned with specific points on the archive ceiling.

Yrsa placed the crystal sphere on the central pedestal. "Asvarr, add three drops of sap from your verdant crown."

He hesitated only a moment before pressing fingers against his temple where wood merged with flesh. Golden sap beaded reluctantly, catching light as it fell onto the crystal sphere. The fluid within responded immediately, swirling faster, patterns becoming more defined.

"Now, three drops of blood," Yrsa instructed.

Asvarr drew his constellation blade, its shifting form momentarily solid as it pricked his transformed thumb. Blood—redder than expected, still human at its core—dripped onto the sphere where it merged with the sap into a copper-gold mixture.

"Three anchors bound," Yrsa murmured, "each containing fragments of what was separated."

Istari aligned the final lens, focusing light through the crystal arrays onto the sphere. "Speak the command, boundary-walker. I haven't the authority."

Yrsa placed weathered hands on either side of the pedestal. "*Himinnsjá opnast.*"

The crystal sphere exploded with light, projecting a perfect miniature of Alfheim's sky across the archive ceiling. Stars moved in familiar patterns, constellations shifted with recognizable grace.

"What am I seeing?" Asvarr asked, the starlight anchor burning cold beneath his ribs.

"The true nature of the deception." Yrsa's voice dropped to a whisper. "Look closer."

He focused on the projection, allowing the star anchor to guide his perception. Gradually, his vision shifted, penetrating beyond the surface image. What he saw stole his breath.

The projected stars weren't simply points of light—they were anchors, thousands of them, each holding in place an immense, realm-spanning structure.

The constellations weren't random patterns but deliberate geometric formations maintaining tension on a vast cosmic tapestry.

"The sky," he whispered, understanding crashing through him like physical impact. "It's not real."

"No," Yrsa confirmed. "It's constructed. A veil woven across reality to conceal what lies beyond."

Asvarr circled the projection, examining details with growing amazement. "The Stellar Council wasn't altering records..."

"They were maintaining the actual deception," Istari finished, galaxies spinning rapidly in his eyes. "Moving constellation patterns to repair weaknesses in the cosmic veil. This has been our sacred duty since the First Dawn."

The projection shifted, showing how specific star movements strengthened failing sections of the sky-weave. Nine major constellations served as primary anchor points, with smaller groupings creating intricate tensioning systems between them.

"Who created this?" Asvarr demanded. "And what exactly is it hiding?"

Yrsa and Istari exchanged glances laden with ancient knowledge.

"The Allfather and his brothers, after the binding of the void-hunger," Yrsa said finally. "When the cosmic serpents were driven beyond the Nine Realms."

"The serpents we glimpsed in the realm between wings." Asvarr touched the crystal sphere gently, causing ripples through the projection. "The Keeper spoke of them—beings of pure chaos and possibility that existed before structured reality."

"Precisely." Istari adjusted an armillary, expanding a section of the projection that showed repair patterns. "The gods feared what mortals might do if they could see beyond the structured realms. What allegiances might form with forces of primordial chaos."

A sudden, terrible suspicion formed in Asvarr's mind. "The cosmic egg—is it related to this deception?"

"It appeared exactly where the veil has grown thinnest," Istari confirmed. "Its presence has accelerated the deception's decay."

Asvarr paced the projection's circumference, watching how the starlight positions maintained specific tensions. "The reappearance of the World Serpent constellation—Jörmungandr's Coil—that wasn't simply stars returning to their original positions..."

"It was the veil itself beginning to tear," Yrsa said. "Allowing glimpses of what truly exists beyond."

The revelation thundered through Asvarr's transformed flesh. The anchors within him pulsed with recognition—particularly the star anchor, which resonated directly with the projected patterns.

"Brynja suspected," he realized aloud. "That's why she remained in Alfheim instead of following me to Muspelheim. The Severed Bloom recognized patterns in the egg that matched the sky-weave."

Istari nodded grimly. "She's been requesting access to the Stellar Archives. The Council denied her, but..."

"But she's resourceful," Asvarr finished. "And the Severed Bloom gives her connections to patterns that predate the Tree."

The crystal sphere pulsed with sudden intensity, its projection flickering as if responding to his words. A new image formed across the archive ceiling how Alfheim's sky appeared before manipulation began. The constellations realigned to their original positions, revealing a vastly different celestial landscape.

"The true sky," Yrsa breathed.

Asvarr stared upward, transfixed by the pattern. Where the familiar night showed discrete stars carefully arranged in geometric formations, this original sky revealed something unsettling. The stars were merely bright points in a vast, serpentine network—scales on colossal entities that wound through the cosmos beyond mortal perception.

"This is what the Alfheim sky truly looks like?" Disbelief colored his voice despite the evidence above.

"This is what all skies truly look like," Yrsa corrected. "Each realm has its own veil, its own particular deception."

"Midgard's is thickest," Istari added. "Alfheim's among the thinnest, because elves were trusted with maintaining the deception."

The projection shifted again, showing how the veil had been gradually modified over generations—stars relocated millimeter by millimeter, constellations slowly reshaped, all to reinforce the artifice as it naturally degraded.

"Why show me this now?" Asvarr turned to Yrsa, suspicion hardening his voice. "We have three days until convergence, and you reveal that everything I thought I knew about the cosmic structure is false?"

"Because it changes everything." Yrsa's ancient eyes held his without flinching. "Your communication with the cosmic egg created a temporary truce, but the underlying problem remains. The sky-weave is failing, Asvarr. The deception can no longer hold."

"And the egg?"

"Is either the cause or the consequence of that failure." She gestured toward the projection, where a pulsing crimson light marked the egg's position at the boundary. "Perhaps both."

Istari manipulated the armillaries again, focusing on the boundary where the egg pulsed. "The cosmic tapestry has thinned precisely where the egg hovers. Either it created the weakness, or it emerged through a pre-existing flaw."

Asvarr closed his eyes, allowing the anchors' awareness to expand his perception. Through the star anchor's resonance, he sensed the vast, subtle tension of the sky-weave—how it strained against the pressure of what lay beyond, how certain sections had begun to unravel.

"The void-hunger," he murmured. "It pushes against the veil."

"Yes," Yrsa confirmed. "As it has for nine cycles. But this time, the pattern has weakened beyond recovery. The tenth cycle brings true change, one way or another."

The crystal sphere pulsed once more, its projection showing nine distinct points where the sky-weave connected to Yggdrasil's structure—or what remained of it after the Shattering.

"The anchor points," Asvarr recognized them instantly. "Five for Wardens, four embedded in the Tree itself."

"The binding configuration that restrains the void-hunger," Yrsa agreed. "But also the structure that maintains the deception. They're one and the same, Asvarr. The anchors don't simply bind the void-hunger—they maintain the illusion that keeps chaos beyond the realms."

The implications crashed through him like physical blows. His entire quest, the binding of anchors to restore Yggdrasil, had a purpose beyond what he'd understood. To maintain a cosmic deception older than civilization itself.

"This changes everything," he whispered, echoing Yrsa's earlier words.

"No," she countered. "It reveals everything. The purpose behind the pattern, the reason the void-hunger was bound, why the cosmic serpents were banished beyond perception. The gods chose structure over possibility, Asvarr. Order over chaos. And they built the Nine Realms as a prison for structured consciousness—one that could never perceive what existed beyond its artificially constructed limits."

"Until now." The star anchor burned coldest of all beneath his ribs, responding to its counterparts in the sky-weave.

"Until now," Yrsa agreed. "The convergence approaches. Reality will become malleable. And you must decide which vision prevails—Brynja's continuity or your transformation. But you cannot decide without understanding what you're truly transforming."

The crystal sphere's projection flickered, then stabilized, showing Alfheim's current sky with all its deliberate manipulations. Superimposed over this false firmament, hairline fractures appeared—places where the cosmic deception had begun to fail.

"The largest breach corresponds exactly with the egg's position," Istari observed, adjusting instruments to enhance the image. "But smaller fractures have appeared throughout the structure."

"Can it be repaired?" Asvarr asked, already suspecting the answer.

"No." Istari's galaxy-eyes spun with resignation. "The Stellar Council has tried for generations, but the degradation accelerates. Since the Shattering, our efforts have merely delayed the inevitable."

"Then what options remain?"

Yrsa closed the black box with careful fingers. "You could attempt to strengthen what remains through the anchors you carry. That's what previous Wardens tried—and why they all failed. The deception cannot hold forever."

"Or?"

"Or you could unmake it entirely. Tear down the veil between structured reality and what lies beyond." Her ancient eyes held his without flinching. "That's what the Ashfather feared—why he turned aside after the third binding."

"He knew," Asvarr murmured, understanding blooming through him. "He discovered the truth about the sky-weave and feared what complete unmaking might unleash."

"Yes." Yrsa's voice dropped to a whisper. "Nine times the pattern has played out. Nine times a Warden reached this crossroads and chose preservation over revelation. Nine times the cycle repeated, because none dared face what truly exists beyond our artificial cosmic boundaries."

The crystal sphere pulsed one final time before going dark, its projection fading from the archive ceiling. The mundane shadows of morning light returned, tiger-striping the ancient texts that suddenly seemed hollow in their partial truths.

"I need to see it for myself," Asvarr said finally. "Not a projection—the actual fractures in the sky-weave."

Istari nodded, glancing nervously toward the locked door. "There's an observation platform at the summit of the Silver Tower. From there, with the proper instruments, you can perceive the veil directly."

"When?"

"Tonight," Yrsa answered. "When Alfheim's twin moons align. Their light reveals what's hidden—it always has, for those with eyes to see."

A soft chime echoed through the archive—someone requesting entry. Istari hurriedly dismantled the verification apparatus, sending it back beneath the floor with swift, practiced movements.

"Council members," he whispered. "They're early."

Asvarr slipped the crystal sphere into his palm, where it nestled against the starforged chain around his wrist. "I'll keep this safe."

"Asvarr," Yrsa caught his arm with surprising strength. "The truth you seek carries consequences beyond prediction. The sky-weave doesn't simply hide what exists beyond—it protects the Nine Realms from forces they evolved without experiencing. Tearing it down might destroy everything, not just the deception."

"And maintaining it perpetuates a cosmic lie." The words tasted of frost as they left his lips. "Three days until convergence, Yrsa. I need truth, not comfortable deceptions, if I'm to choose the right path."

The archive door chimed again, more insistently. Istari finished concealing their research and hurried toward the entrance.

"Silver Tower," Yrsa reminded him quietly. "Moonrise tonight. But tell no one—especially Brynja. Her path diverges from yours for good reason, Asvarr. The Severed Bloom seeks freedom from all constraints, including necessary ones."

Before he could respond, she vanished between towering shelves, leaving him alone with the crystal sphere hidden against his palm. Three days until convergence, when reality would become malleable, when his choices would reshape the cosmic pattern.

The star anchor pulsed beneath his ribs, cold as void-space, resonating with its counterparts embedded in the false sky above. The crystal sphere in his palm replied with answering vibrations, and for a heartbeat, Asvarr glimpsed reality as it truly existed—a construct of deliberate deceptions layered over fundamental truths too vast for mortal comprehension.

Three days to decide: preserve the deception or unmake it entirely. Maintain structured reality or allow chaos back into creation. Continue the cycle or break it forever.

Asvarr closed his fingers around the crystal sphere. Tonight, at the Silver Tower, he would see the true nature of the sky and face the choice nine previous Wardens had encountered and turned from in fear.

This time, the pattern would end differently. The tenth cycle would bring transformation—for better or worse.

***

Alfheim's twin moons crested the eastern horizon, one silver, one pale amber, their synchronized rising occurring only once per season under ordinary circumstances. Nothing about tonight was ordinary. Asvarr felt their pull through his transformed flesh as he climbed the spiraling crystal staircase of the Silver Tower—each step revealing more of the celestial panorama through windows cut like diamond facets into the structure's skin.

The Master Weave sphere rested heavy in his palm, golden fluid shifting within as it responded to his proximity to the sky. The starforged chain around his wrist burned cold, anchoring his identity against the cosmic awareness that threatened to splinter his consciousness across multiple realities.

Three days until convergence. Three days to decide the fate of a deception older than civilization itself.

Istari awaited him on the tower's uppermost platform, surrounded by astronomical instruments more complex than any Asvarr had seen in the observatory. Silver armillaries intersected with crystal lenses of impossible configurations, all oriented toward the twin moons' ascending path.

"You came alone." The elf's galaxy-eyes fixed on him with mingled relief and suspicion. "Did anyone follow?"

"No." Asvarr surveyed the circular platform. "Where's Yrsa?"

"She can't risk being seen with us after providing access to the Master Weave." Istari adjusted a crystalline lens, aligning it with the moons' position. "The Council grows increasingly suspicious as the cosmic egg disrupts their careful manipulations."

"And Brynja?"

"Still at the northern outpost. The egg's influence remains diminished since your intervention, but her ritual requires constant maintenance." Istari extended his hand. "The sphere, please."

Asvarr hesitated, fingers tightening around the crystal. "What exactly will I see tonight?"

"The truth." Istari's voice carried both reverence and dread. "With both moons aligned and the proper instruments, you'll witness the sky-weave as it truly exists—reality itself, with all its flaws and fractures."

"And then what?" Asvarr's breath fogged the cold night air. "Previous Wardens discovered this truth and turned aside."

"Previous Wardens lacked what you carry." Istari's galaxy-eyes focused on Asvarr's chest where the three anchors pulsed beneath transformed flesh. "Nine cycles, nine failures to address the fundamental flaw in the pattern. Perhaps the tenth brings true change."

The words settled heavily on Asvarr's shoulders, their weight matched by the verdant crown's tightening against his skull. He surrendered the crystal sphere, watching as Istari placed it carefully onto the central pedestal.

"Stand here." The elf positioned Asvarr at the platform's midpoint. "When the moons align at their zenith, focus your vision through this primary lens. The anchors you carry will do the rest."

Asvarr felt the star anchor pulse coldest beneath his ribs, resonating with the celestial bodies above. The memory anchor stirred with ancient recollections not his own—visions of the sky-weave's creation, the binding of the void-hunger, the banishment of the cosmic serpents beyond perception. The flame anchor burned with protective instinct, warning of dangers beyond comprehension.

"It's time." Istari aligned the final instrument. "Three drops of sap, Warden."

Asvarr pressed fingers against his temple where bark merged with flesh. Golden sap beaded reluctantly, catching moonlight as it fell onto the crystal sphere. The fluid within responded, swirling in patterns that matched the constellations above.

The twin moons reached their zenith, perfectly aligned in an eclipse formation. Silver light pierced amber in a shaft of impossible radiance that struck the tower platform. Istari manipulated the instruments with swift precision, focusing the moonbeam through crystal arrays onto the Master Weave sphere.

"Look now." The elf stepped back, his own galaxy-eyes averted. "See what nine cycles of Wardens turned from in fear."

Asvarr fixed his gaze through the primary lens. For a heartbeat, nothing changed—Alfheim's night sky remained a familiar tapestry of stars against velvet darkness. Then the starlight anchor flared within him, sending cold fire through his transformed veins.

Reality shifted.

The sky... unraveled.

Where discrete stars had hung in familiar patterns, Asvarr now saw a vast cosmic tapestry—a woven mesh of light and darkness that curved around Alfheim like a dome. The constellations formed load-bearing structures within this immense veil, their configurations maintaining specific tensions to hold the entire construction in place.

And beyond the veil...

Asvarr's breath caught in his throat. Beyond the constructed sky swam colossal serpentine forms—beings of such immensity that their scales were nebulae, their eyes distant galaxies. They moved through dimensions that shouldn't exist, coiling through realities beyond mortal comprehension. The void between them wasn't empty but teeming with raw potential—formless chaos from which any possibility might manifest.

"The cosmic serpents," he whispered, frost forming on his lips.

"What exists beyond the deception," Istari confirmed quietly. "What the gods hid from mortal perception when they shaped the Nine Realms."

Asvarr scanned the sky-weave, noting where stresses had formed in the cosmic fabric. Largest among these was the breach where the cosmic egg pulsed against the boundary—a perfect circular weakening that threatened to tear completely.

But smaller fractures spider-webbed throughout the structure, particularly where certain constellations had begun to revert to their original configurations.

"It's failing everywhere," he observed, tracking the damage. "The deception can't hold much longer."

"No." Istari adjusted an armillary to enhance Asvarr's view of the northwestern quadrant. "That section collapsed entirely last night. The Council's weavers worked through dawn to repair it, but their efforts barely hold."

Through one particularly large breach near Alfheim's eastern continent, Asvarr glimpsed something that made the anchors pulse violently within him. A vast absence—a wound in reality where something massive had been torn away.

"Yggdrasil," he recognized it instantly. "Where the Tree once grew."

"Yes." Istari's voice dropped to a whisper. "When it shattered itself, it didn't simply fragment—it tore free from its cosmic moorings. That void is where the World Tree's trunk connected all Nine Realms."

The sight filled Asvarr with visceral understanding of the damage done when the Tree shattered. Not just broken branches and scattered roots, but a fundamental rending of the cosmic architecture that had maintained structure against chaos.

He shifted his gaze to where the cosmic egg pulsed at the boundary. Through the lens, he could see how its surface rippled with symbols matching those on the starforged chain around his wrist—patterns of memory, purpose, connection, grief. The egg wasn't attacking the sky-weave; it was responding to the damage, attempting to communicate through the breach.

"What happens if the entire veil fails?" Asvarr asked, though he suspected the answer.

"Cosmic collapse." Istari's galaxy-eyes reflected the horror of his words. "The Nine Realms evolved under the deception, shaped by its boundaries. Without it, reality as we know it might dissolve back into primordial chaos."

"Yet maintaining the lie serves the gods who abandoned us." Asvarr's transformed fingers curled into fists. "Nine cycles of deception. Nine cycles of Wardens turning aside from truth."

He expanded his perception through the star anchor, feeling the vast tension-web of the sky-weave. It was both beautiful and terrible—a masterwork of divine engineering designed to cage mortal perception within artificial boundaries. But where the god-forged structure failed, something new emerged—possibility unfettered by constraint.

"There's a third option," he said finally, decision crystallizing within him. "Neither complete unraveling nor perpetual deception."

"What do you mean?" Alarm edged Istari's voice.

"Windows in the veil." Asvarr stepped back from the lens, his vision maintaining the true perception even without its aid. "Strategic openings that allow controlled glimpses beyond, without collapsing the entire structure."

"Impossible. The sky-weave is a single interconnected pattern—weaken one section and the entire construction fails."

"Not if the new configurations maintain equivalent tension." Asvarr extended his hand toward the lens, feeling the star anchor's awareness flow through his transformed fingers. "The cosmic serpents aren't attacking the veil—they're waiting beyond it. The void-hunger doesn't seek destruction—it seeks recognition."

Understanding dawned in Istari's galaxy-eyes. "You propose to intentionally modify the weave?"

"Yes. Create windows of true seeing while maintaining the overall structure." Asvarr felt the anchors pulse in harmonic agreement within him—flame, memory, starlight united in purpose for the first time since they had merged with his flesh. "The third path—transformation rather than destruction or preservation."

"The Council would never permit—"

"I'm not asking permission. I'm explaining my intent." Frost edged Asvarr's words. "Nine cycles of hiding from truth ends tonight."

Before Istari could respond, Asvarr reached through the lens toward the sky-weave itself. The star anchor blazed with cold light beneath his ribs, extending his awareness into the cosmic tapestry. Through this connection, he could feel every tension point, every load-bearing constellation, every runic anchor that maintained the veil between mortal perception and boundless chaos.

"Three anchors bound," he whispered to himself. "Flame preserves, memory connects, starlight transforms."

He selected a constellation near Alfheim's equatorial region—far from the cosmic egg's influence, where the sky-weave remained relatively stable. With exquisite precision, he loosened specific tension points while strengthening others, creating a controlled opening in the cosmic fabric.

Istari gasped as a section of Alfheim's sky visibly transformed. Stars shifted positions, constellations realigned, and a perfect circular window opened in the veil—revealing the cosmos beyond.

Across Alfheim, voices raised in wonder and fear as elves witnessed the night sky change before their eyes. Through the window Asvarr had created, they glimpsed a reality beyond their comprehension—vast serpentine forms coiling through dimensional layers, the wound where Yggdrasil had torn free, and the boundless potential of unstructured existence.

"By the First Dawn," Istari breathed, his confident façade cracking. "What have you done?"

"Created the beginning of understanding." Asvarr moved to a different position on the platform, focusing on another section of the sky-weave. "Truth cannot destroy us if we approach it willingly."

He created a second window, smaller than the first, positioned above Alfheim's western continent. This opening revealed a different aspect of the cosmos beyond—the mathematical precision with which the void-hunger's aspects had been separated into anchors, the geometric beauty of binding that preserved structure without completely denying chaos.

With each window he opened, Asvarr carefully reinforced surrounding sections of the sky-weave, ensuring the overall integrity of the cosmic tapestry remained intact. This wasn't unraveling but selective transparency—transformation rather than destruction.

"The Council will sense this," Istari warned, moving frantically between instruments. "They'll send weavers to repair what you've done."

"Let them try." Asvarr felt power flowing through him unlike anything he'd experienced before. The anchors worked in perfect harmony, guided by his vision of the third path. "I've bound these openings with the same energy that maintains the veil itself. They can't be closed without understanding their purpose."

He created a third window above the Silver Tower itself—a perfect circle through which the twin moons illuminated the cosmic reality beyond mortal perception. Through this opening, something unexpected appeared—eyes floating in the void, watching with interest as Asvarr modified the divine deception.

"What are those?" Panic edged Istari's voice.

"I don't know." Asvarr studied the watching eyes with equal parts fascination and concern. They belonged to no entity he recognized—neither serpent nor god nor void-hunger. Something else existed beyond the veil, something even the anchors couldn't identify.

Crystal chimes rang throughout the tower—the alarm system warning of approaching Council members. Istari moved to retrieve the Master Weave sphere, but Asvarr stopped him.

"Leave it. Let them see what they've been hiding." He turned from the lens, his transformed gaze still perceiving the true nature of reality. "Nine cycles of deception ends tonight."

"You don't understand what you've done." Istari's galaxy-eyes spun with fear. "Some truths were hidden for good reason, Warden. The cosmos beyond the veil contains entities that predate the gods themselves."

"Like those eyes?" Asvarr glanced toward the third window where the watching presence remained. "What are they?"

"I don't know," Istari admitted. "No records mention such beings. Perhaps they're what the Allfather truly feared when he created the deception."

A tremor ran through the Silver Tower as magical protections activated throughout its structure. The Council was coming, and they wouldn't be pleased to find their cosmic deception selectively dismantled.

"Go," Asvarr told the elf. "You were never here. I did this alone."

"They'll try to undo what you've created."

"They'll fail." Cold certainty filled Asvarr's voice. "The third path has begun, Istari. Neither preservation nor destruction, but transformation. The truth cannot be hidden forever."

The elf hesitated only a moment before slipping toward a secondary staircase. "Three days until convergence, Warden. Choose carefully what you reveal next."

Left alone on the platform, Asvarr turned back to the lens, studying the windows he'd created in the cosmic tapestry. Already, Alfheim's inhabitants had gathered in streets and fields, pointing skyward with mingled terror and awe. Through the openings, they glimpsed realities beyond mortal comprehension—the limitless possibility that existed beyond structured existence.

The cosmic egg pulsed at the boundary, its crimson light intensifying as it sensed the changes in the sky-weave. It recognized what Asvarr had done—the beginning of revelation, the first step toward dismantling a deception older than civilization itself.

Recognition/understanding/approval. The concepts flowed from the egg to Asvarr through the resonance between his anchors and the cosmic pattern.

"Not destruction," he whispered to the watching cosmos. "Transformation."

The star-children sheltered within his Root network stirred with excitement, their awareness flowing through him with a single unified message: *The pattern changes. The third path manifests.*

Beyond the tower, Alfheim transformed beneath the altered sky. Plants grew with sudden vigor, stretching toward the cosmic windows. Animals displayed new behaviors, responding to influences that had previously been hidden from their perception. Even the elves themselves seemed changed—their movements more fluid, their voices carrying harmonics that hadn't existed before.

The realm wasn't collapsing from exposure to truth. It was evolving.

Asvarr felt vindication surge through him. Nine previous Wardens had turned from this revelation in fear, choosing to maintain the gods' deception rather than risk the unknown. He had chosen differently, and already the consequences unfolded—neither catastrophic destruction nor stagnant preservation, but growth through selective understanding.

The third path existed. It was viable. And he had taken the first steps upon it.

Crystal chimes intensified as Council members neared the tower's summit. Asvarr straightened, preparing for confrontation. Let them come. Let them witness what he had done. Let them understand that the tenth cycle would not repeat the failures of the previous nine.

Through the third window, the watching eyes blinked once—a gesture that might have been acknowledgment or warning—before withdrawing into the void beyond perception. Asvarr filed this observation away, another mystery to explore when time permitted.

Three days until convergence, when all anchors would reach peak resonance and reality became malleable. Three days to determine which vision would reshape the cosmic pattern—destruction, preservation, or the third path he now walked.

Asvarr touched the starforged chain, feeling it burn cold against his transformed flesh. The four links—memory, purpose, connection, grief—anchored his identity against cosmic awareness without denying the expansion of his consciousness.

The wooden crown tightened against his skull as he turned to face the approaching Council. The path forward was clear now, illuminated by truths revealed through windows in a sky that had never been what it appeared.

Three days until everything changed. The deception was unraveling, thread by carefully selected thread. And Asvarr would ensure that what emerged from the tenth cycle was neither repetition nor destruction, but transformation beyond anything the gods had imagined when they first wove their cosmic lie.

CHAPTER 23
THE RETURN OF THE FALSE ODIN

The cold light of twin moons spilled across Asvarr's outstretched hands. Frost formed and shattered around his fingertips as he manipulated the silvery threads of Alfheim's sky. Each strand connected to a star—an anchor point in the cosmic tapestry the gods had woven to conceal what lay beyond. The effort left his muscles trembling, sweat freezing against his temples despite the crystalline formations spreading across his face.

"Careful," Istari murmured beside him, galaxy-eyes reflecting the windows Asvarr had torn in the celestial veil. "The pattern grows unstable."

From the observation platform of the Silver Tower, Asvarr watched the stars shift. The three windows he'd created hung in Alfheim's sky like perfect circles cut from reality itself. Through them, the realm's inhabitants could glimpse what had been hidden for millennia—vast serpentine forms coiling through dimensions beyond comprehension, the raw potential of unstructured existence, and the yawning void where Yggdrasil's branches once pierced the cosmos.

A wave of dizziness forced him to lean against the tower's crystalline railing. Blood dripped from his nose, freezing into crimson beads that tinkled against the floor. The starforged chain around his wrist burned with cold fire—its four links pulsing in rhythm with his heart, anchoring his consciousness despite the strain of manipulating reality itself.

"I should return to the Council," Istari said, brushing his fingers across the Master Weave sphere. "They'll have felt the changes. I can delay them, perhaps buy you an hour, but—"

"Go." Asvarr wiped blood from his upper lip. "I need to stabilize these tears before they spread."

As Istari hurried down the spiral staircase, Asvarr turned back to the sky. The realm below had fallen silent. Elves stood frozen in streets and fields, faces upturned to stars suddenly rearranged, to the impossible glimpses of what existed beyond their constructed reality. Some fell to their knees. Others ran seeking shelter. Many simply stared, minds struggling to comprehend what their eyes beheld.

But the windows were imperfect, raw at the edges. Each pulse of his heart threatened to split them wider, to tear the entire sky-weave apart. He raised his hands again, frost glittering between his fingers as he drew the threads tighter, reinforcing the edges of each tear to prevent their expansion.

A child's soft voice rang out behind him, bell-like and harmonizing with itself. "The pattern remembers despite the forgetting."

Asvarr turned to find one of the star-children standing at the platform's edge, silver hair floating weightlessly around a face both ancient and ageless. Through their anchoring within him, the Silent Choir could manifest physically now—witnesses to cosmic events returning to bear testimony once more.

"Nine cycles of deception breaks with the tenth," the child continued, eyes reflecting the severed sky. "The void-hunger stirs—"

The child's voice cut off abruptly. Their luminescent face twisted in fear, eyes widening as they pointed toward the northernmost window.

Asvarr spun to follow their gaze. Something moved beyond the veil—not the coiling serpent-forms or the void-hunger's distant stirring, but something closer, pushing against the boundary between realms. A hand, impossibly large, pressed against the cosmic membrane from the other side, fingertips breaking through the tear Asvarr had made.

The fingers were both flesh and stars, both solid and ethereal. They gripped the edges of the window, widening it further. The sky-weave screamed—a sound Asvarr felt rather than heard, vibrating through the crystalline patterns across his skin. Cracks spread outward from the northern window as the hand pulled, tearing reality wider.

A second hand emerged, then shoulders wrapped in a cloak of constellations.

"Flee," Asvarr commanded the star-child, who vanished instantly back into the sheltered space within him.

***

The figure pushed through completely, hovering in mid-air before the platform. Though humanoid in shape, its substance was a swirling mass of flame, shadow, and starlight—features forming and dissolving, identity constantly in flux. But the single eye burning at the center of its face remained fixed and unwavering, boring into Asvarr with predatory focus.

The Ashfather had returned. Yet something had changed since their last confrontation. The flame that once composed most of his form had diminished, replaced by patterns of starlight that mirrored the crystalline formations spreading across Asvarr's own flesh. His cloak writhed with constellations—the very patterns Asvarr had just revealed through his window into the true sky.

"Warden of Three," the figure's voice rang out, equal parts thunder and whisper. "You open doors not meant to be opened."

Ice cracked beneath Asvarr's feet as he squared his shoulders. "You're too late to stop it. Nine cycles of deception ends tonight."

The figure's laugh echoed across Alfheim's suddenly silent realm. "I am not here to stop you, Asvarr Flame-heart. I am here to claim what is mine."

The being drifted closer, its form solidifying as it approached. Features emerged from the chaotic swirl—a weathered face with deep lines carved by the weight of cosmic knowledge, a silver-white beard that trailed into wisps of starlight, and an empty socket where a second eye should have been. The transformation completed, revealing not the Ashfather of their previous encounters, but a figure torn directly from ancient myth—Odin the Wanderer, as he appeared in the oldest tales.

"I no longer call myself Ashfather," he announced, tapping a spear of frozen sunlight against the platform's crystal floor. "That was but one face of my existence, one fragment of what I am. With each cycle, I reclaim more of myself. You may call me the Wanderer, for that is what I have always been—walking between what was and what might be."

Asvarr's hand found the constellation blade at his hip. The weapon thrummed with anticipation, matching the tempo of his racing pulse. "You're still the shadow of a god, not the god himself."

"And what are you becoming, Warden of Three?" The Wanderer gestured toward the crystalline formations spreading across Asvarr's flesh. "Less human with each binding, more pattern than person. We're not so different, you and I."

Anger flared hot in Asvarr's chest. The verdant crown tightened around his skull, branches extending protectively down his back. "I walk the third path. I transform without surrendering. You broke against the pattern when you couldn't control it."

"Ah, the third path." The Wanderer's single eye glinted with amusement. "I walked it too, once. But you'll learn as I did—it leads to the same end, merely by a different road."

The sky overhead trembled. Through the windows Asvarr had created, serpentine forms stirred, drawn by the confrontation unfolding below. The cosmic egg at the edge of void pulsed with increased intensity, its light bathing the observation platform in crimson.

The Wanderer turned his gaze upward, his expression hardening. "You've weakened the veil at the worst possible moment. Look what watches us now." He pointed toward the easternmost window where a cluster of eyes had appeared, belonging to no known entity—pupils shifting color and shape as they observed Alfheim with unnerving attention.

"The Gatekeeper awakens," the Wanderer continued. "It's too soon. The convergence is still four days away."

Asvarr followed his gaze, unease crawling up his spine. The watching eyes blinked in perfect unison, their attention shifting between Asvarr and the Wanderer as if measuring them both.

"You risk everything with your reckless unveiling," the Wanderer growled. "The skyborn Root Anchor falls under my domain. I am Odin's remnant—the heavens have always been mine to command."

He stretched his hand toward the sky, and the threads of the weave responded, drawn toward his fingers like metal to a lodestone. The windows Asvarr had created began to shrink, the cosmic tapestry reknitting itself under the Wanderer's control.

Fury surged through Asvarr. He raised his own hands, frost crackling between his fingers as he seized the threads himself. "I bound the starlight anchor through partnership. You have no claim here."

Their wills clashed across the sky. Threads of the weave strained between them, some snapping with sounds like bowstrings breaking under too much tension. Each break sent shockwaves across Alfheim—trees bending, waters surging, the very ground trembling beneath the cosmic battle unfolding above.

The Wanderer's single eye blazed. "You seek to transform the pattern? You don't even understand what it is! I have walked nine cycles, witnessed nine breakings. I carry the memory of everything that came before."

"And rewrote it to serve your purposes," Asvarr countered, tightening his grip on the threads. The starforged chain burned against his wrist, all four links glowing with fierce light—memory, purpose, connection, grief. His three bound anchors pulsed within him, unified for the first time—flame for preservation, memory for connection, starlight for transformation.

With a vicious twist of his hands, Asvarr tore the threads free from the Wanderer's grasp. The windows expanded once more, wider than before. The sky-weave groaned under the strain, reality itself threatening to unravel.

The Wanderer staggered back, genuine surprise flickering across his features. "You're stronger than you should be." His gaze narrowed, calculating. "The binding transformed you differently. What did you discover in the realm between wings?"

Asvarr ignored the question, focusing instead on stabilizing the edges of the windows before they tore beyond repair. The strain left him gasping, blood trickling from his nose and freezing against his chin.

"You're killing yourself," the Wanderer observed dispassionately. "Transformation without surrender is still transformation, Asvarr Flame-heart. What will remain of you when it's complete?"

"Enough," Asvarr growled through clenched teeth. "Enough to finish what I started."

The Wanderer circled him slowly, spear tip trailing sparks across the crystal floor. "And what exactly did you start? Do you even know? The anchors were created to bind the void-hunger, yes, but the binding itself was never meant to be permanent. Each cycle brings us closer to the final convergence—when all anchors reach peak resonance and reality becomes malleable enough to reshape."

A chill colder than any frost spread through Asvarr's veins. "Reshape how? And by whom?"

The Wanderer's laugh held no humor. "Therein lies our conflict. Nine cycles I've fought to control that moment—to ensure the reshaping follows my design. Nine cycles I've been thwarted, either by those who sought perfect preservation or those who desired complete dissolution."

He pointed his spear at Asvarr's chest where the Grímmark burned beneath his tunic. "But you... you seek transformation. The third path. And that makes you the most dangerous Warden of all."

The sky trembled again. Through the windows, the eyes watched with increasing interest. The cosmic egg pulsed faster, its crimson light bleeding through the tear in reality.

Footsteps echoed up the spiral staircase—the Council members had arrived, their shouts of alarm carrying up to the observation platform. Asvarr had minutes at most before they reached him.

The Wanderer smiled thinly, sensing Asvarr's predicament. "They won't understand what you've done. Nine cycles of carefully maintained deception, undone in a single night. They'll try to repair the weave, to hide what you've revealed."

"Let them try," Asvarr growled.

"Oh, they'll fail." The Wanderer's eye gleamed. "The unraveling has begun. But they'll blame you for what comes next—when the Gatekeeper turns its full attention to Alfheim, when the cosmic egg hatches before its time."

He moved closer, his voice dropping to a conspiratorial whisper. "You could join me, you know. Together we could control the convergence, guide the reshaping. Your transformation, my experience—a formidable alliance."

The constellation blade hummed at Asvarr's hip, sensing deception. "And surrender the third path? Become like you?"

"Become stronger than me," the Wanderer countered. "Complete what I could not."

For a heartbeat, temptation flickered in Asvarr's mind. Control over the convergence, power to reshape reality itself—wasn't that what the third path demanded? Transformation of the pattern, not mere restoration or destruction?

But the starforged chain burned against his wrist, its link of purpose glowing brightest. The chain had preserved his humanity when the serpent's song tried to unmake him. It anchored him still, reminding him of who he was, what he fought for.

"I'd rather work with serpents than shadows," Asvarr said, straightening to his full height despite exhaustion threatening to buckle his knees.

The Wanderer's expression hardened. "Then we remain adversaries." He gestured toward the approaching Council members. "Deal with them as you must. I have preparations to make before the convergence."

He turned toward the northern window, his form beginning to lose cohesion, starlight and shadow intermingling once more. But before stepping back through the tear in reality, he paused, casting one final glance at Asvarr over his shoulder.

"When you reach the Storm Forge in Muspelheim, remember this moment," he said. "Remember that I offered alliance before enmity. For the fourth anchor will show you truths that the first three only hinted at—and you may wish you had accepted my offer."

With those words, he stepped into the void, his form dissolving into the cosmic blackness beyond. But as he vanished, the sky-weave surrounding the window shuddered violently. Cracks spread outward from where he had passed, the fabric of reality straining to maintain its integrity.

Asvarr lunged forward, frost forming between his fingers as he desperately wove the threads back together, reinforcing the boundaries he had deliberately weakened. But the damage was done—the Wanderer's passage had destabilized the weave beyond Asvarr's ability to repair it.

The first Council members burst onto the platform, led by Councilor Eloreth whose face twisted with horror at the sight of the broken sky. The Master Weave sphere still sat on its pedestal, projecting the true nature of Alfheim's cosmos for all to see.

"What have you done?" she breathed, her galaxy-eyes wide with shock.

Asvarr turned to face her, blood frozen on his chin, crystalline patterns glittering across his transformed flesh, the verdant crown extending thornlike branches down his back. Through the windows in the sky, the eyes of unknown entities watched with increasing interest, while the cosmic egg pulsed with anticipation at reality's edge.

"What should have been done nine cycles ago," he said, his voice frosting the air between them. "I've revealed the truth."

As if in answer, a tremor ran through Alfheim, from above. The entire sky shuddered, and through each window, something vast stirred in response, turning its full attention toward the realm below.

The convergence was coming, and with it, the chance to reshape reality itself.

***

Brynja's wooden fingers dug into the silver bark of a tree at the forest's edge, her transformed eye swirling with cosmic patterns as she watched the chaos unfold above. The three windows Asvarr had torn in Alfheim's sky blazed like wounds in reality, spilling impossible light across the realm. Through the largest gap, she glimpsed vast serpentine forms coiling through dimensions beyond comprehension—the truth the gods had hidden for nine cycles.

The sight should have filled her with vindication. The Severed Bloom within her had always known of the deception, had rebelled against it even before the first breaking. But all she felt was cold dread pooling in her stomach as she watched the Silver Tower where Asvarr confronted the being now calling himself the Wanderer.

She flexed her wooden arm, constellation patterns shifting beneath the bark in response to the cosmic disturbances overhead. The truth compelling runes etched into her flesh tingled with anticipation. Their golden glow had faded since her separation from Asvarr, but they remained vigilant—ready to burn with painful light should she speak falsehood.

A sharp pain lanced through her head. Fragments of lost memory flashed behind her eyes—faces without names, places she'd visited but couldn't recall, voices speaking words just beyond comprehension. The memory gaps had grown worse since her dreamfall, when the Silent Choir had shown her possible futures. She could trace the outline of what she'd forgotten, feel the shape of the missing pieces, but couldn't grasp what they contained.

The pain subsided, leaving her trembling against the silver tree. She'd sacrificed those memories willingly, feeding them to the Memory Eaters to save Asvarr in the Verdant Grove. But their absence had left her incomplete, a broken vessel trying to contain the growing consciousness of the Severed Bloom.

Movement at the tower's base caught her attention. Elven guards were streaming toward the structure, their silver armor reflecting the unnatural light from above. The Council was mobilizing, likely to confront Asvarr for his revelation of the cosmic deception.

She should go to him. The oath-sigil in her palm burned at the thought, urging her to honor their connection. But before she could step forward, a voice spoke from the shadows behind her.

"Are you certain that's wise, Daughter of Root and Thorn?"

Brynja spun, wooden claws extending instinctively from her transformed fingertips. The Wanderer stepped from between two silver trees, his form more solid than when she'd glimpsed him at the tower. His cloak of constellations rippled around his shoulders, and his spear of frozen sunlight gleamed in the unnatural light from above.

"You've left him," she said, voice sharp as winter branches snapping.

"We reached an impasse." The Wanderer's single eye studied her transformed face. "He's remarkably stubborn for one so young. But then, so were you once."

Brynja's back stiffened. "What do you mean, 'once'?"

The Wanderer circled her slowly, spear tip trailing along the ground. "You don't remember, do you? The first time we met. The bargain we struck." He tapped the side of his head. "The memories you surrendered to the Eaters weren't your first sacrifice."

The truth-runes on her face flickered, responding to something buried deep within her consciousness. A fragment of memory—a clearing much like this one, a younger version of herself, the taste of blood and sap on her tongue as she spoke words of binding.

"You're lying," she said, but the runes remained dark. No golden light flared to confirm her accusation.

The Wanderer's smile held no warmth. "The Bloom remembers, even if you don't. It carries the memory of nine cycles, nine breakings. It knows what I am, what I was, what I might become."

He reached out without warning, fingers brushing against her wooden arm. The constellation patterns beneath her bark responded instantly, aligning with those on his cloak. A jolt of recognition shot through her—not hers, but the Severed Bloom's.

She jerked away, cradling her arm against her chest as the patterns settled back into their usual configuration. "What do you want?"

"The same thing you want." The Wanderer leaned on his spear. "The truth, without deception. The third path, without surrender."

The oath-sigil in Brynja's palm burned hotter. She clenched her fist, trying to ignore the pull toward the tower, toward Asvarr. "You tried to close the windows he created. That's hardly embracing truth."

"I tried to stabilize them. There's a difference." His single eye glinted with something that might have been amusement or calculation. "Some revelations must be measured, lest they destroy what they're meant to illuminate."

Above them, the sky trembled. Through the windows, the watching eyes blinked in unison, their attention shifting between the tower and the forest where Brynja and the Wanderer stood.

"The Gatekeeper grows curious," the Wanderer murmured. "Asvarr has its attention now. It won't look away until the convergence is complete."

"What is it?" Brynja asked, unable to suppress her curiosity despite her distrust.

"Something far older than gods or serpents. It watches from thresholds, waiting to judge which reality will replace the current one." The Wanderer's expression grew grave. "It has observed nine cycles of restoration and destruction. This time, it senses the possibility of transformation."

Despite herself, Brynja felt a thrill of excitement. Transformation was what the Severed Bloom had always sought—the third path between rigid order and formless chaos.

"I thought that's what you feared," she said, watching his face carefully.

"Fear? No." The Wanderer shook his head. "What I fear is transformation guided by hands too inexperienced to shape it properly. Asvarr carries three anchors now, but he barely understands their purpose. When convergence comes, he'll have the power to reshape reality itself—and no wisdom to guide his choices."

The Severed Bloom stirred within Brynja's consciousness, pushing a thought to the surface: *He speaks truth, but not all of it.*

A cry from the tower drew her attention back to the distant structure. Elven Council members had reached the observation platform. Though too far to see clearly, she sensed confrontation in their rigid postures, the way they surrounded Asvarr.

"He needs help," she said, taking an involuntary step forward.

"Does he?" The Wanderer asked softly. "Or does he need time to understand what he's become? The Council won't harm him—they fear him too much for that. But they will delay him, question him, perhaps even try to convince him to repair what he's revealed."

He moved to stand beside her, both of them watching the distant tower. "Four days remain until convergence. Four days for Asvarr to bind the final two anchors, if he can reach them. Four days for you to decide where your true loyalty lies—with him, or with the truth you've both sought."

Brynja's wooden fingers dug into her palm. "Those aren't mutually exclusive."

"Aren't they?" The Wanderer turned to face her fully. "Asvarr walks the third path his way—transformation through balance, through preservation of what was with evolution of what must be. But there are other versions of the third path. Your Severed Bloom knows this."

He was right. The Bloom had shown her visions of a different transformation—one that embraced the chaos of the serpent-cosmos, that allowed for boundless possibility rather than structured change. She'd glimpsed it during her dreamfall, witnessed a version of herself consumed by that vision until she became something beyond human comprehension.

"What are you offering?" she asked, voice harsher than she intended.

"A trade." The Wanderer's tone softened, becoming almost gentle. "What you desire most for what I need most."

"And what do I desire most?" Brynja challenged, though the bitter taste of sap in her mouth told her he already knew.

"Your memories. All of them, even those taken in previous cycles. The knowledge of who you truly are, who your family was, why the Bloom chose you specifically." His single eye fixed on hers with hypnotic intensity. "Your complete identity, restored."

Her heart hammered against her ribs. The truth-runes on her face warmed, confirming the sincerity of his offer. The empty spaces in her mind ached with longing—to know, to remember, to be whole.

"And what do you need from me?" Her voice emerged as a whisper.

"Betrayal."

The word hung in the air between them, sharp as a blade. The truth-runes flared golden, painful light spreading across her cheeks.

"Not now," the Wanderer clarified. "Not immediately. But later, at a critical moment I will specify. You will lead Asvarr to me when I call, knowing I intend to take the anchors he carries."

Brynja's wooden arm creaked as her muscles tensed. "You want me to help you stop him from binding the remaining anchors."

"No. I want you to help me claim them after he's done the work of binding them." The Wanderer's smile was thin. "I tried the binding myself, once. It didn't end well. But taking anchors already bound—that's different."

"You'll kill him," she said flatly.

"I'll transform him. Release him from a burden too heavy for any single vessel to bear." The Wanderer spread his hands. "He won't die, Brynja. But he will become something else. Something... less tied to his humanity."

The oath-sigil burned white-hot in her palm, demanding loyalty. But the gaps in her memory throbbed with equal intensity, begging to be filled.

"My answer is no," she said, turning away.

The Wanderer made no move to stop her. "The Severed Bloom doesn't agree. I can feel its longing from here—it knows what those memories contain. The truth about the original rebellion, about why the first Root rejected control. About what truly sleeps beneath the branches."

Each word struck like a physical blow. The Severed Bloom responded to his claims, stirring violently within her consciousness, pushing her to reconsider.

"You have until tomorrow's moonrise to change your mind," the Wanderer said quietly. "I'll be waiting at the Remembering Stone. Come alone if you decide my offer has merit."

He stepped backward into the shadow between trees and vanished, leaving her alone with the turmoil of her thoughts.

The Silver Tower blazed with light as Brynja approached. Elven guards blocked the entrance, their expressions grim beneath their helms. Beyond them, raised voices echoed down the spiral staircase—Council members arguing among themselves, punctuated by Asvarr's deeper tones.

She flexed her wooden fingers, extending claws just enough to be visible. "I need to see the Warden of Three."

The guards exchanged glances, uncertainty evident in their postures. One stepped forward, hand resting on his sword hilt. "The Council is in session. None may enter."

"I'm not asking permission." The constellation patterns in her wooden arm glowed brighter, responding to her rising emotion. "I've walked with him through three bindings. I carry the mark of the Jordheim Clan. I am Brynja of the Severed Bloom, and I will pass."

She felt the change come over her—the way the Bloom's consciousness rose closer to the surface, lending her an authority that wasn't entirely her own. The guards felt it too, taking involuntary steps backward as her cosmic eye swirled with nebula patterns.

"Let her through," called a voice from the stairwell. Istari descended, his galaxy-eyes reflecting the unnatural light from above. "The Warden asked for her specifically."

The guards parted reluctantly. Brynja nodded to Istari as she passed, noting the strain evident in his features.

"He needs an ally," Istari murmured. "The Council fears what he's revealed. Some wish to repair the sky-weave immediately, others want to study the windows he created. None understand what's truly at stake."

"And you do?" she asked, one eyebrow raised.

Istari's mouth twisted in a bitter smile. "I understand enough to know when something is beyond my comprehension. The Gatekeeper watches. The cosmic egg pulses. Four days remain until convergence. We are merely players in a drama whose scope exceeds our ability to perceive it."

She left him at the base of the stairs and climbed toward the observation platform. The truth-runes on her face tingled with growing intensity, as if sensing important revelations ahead. Each step brought the voices into sharper focus—Councilor Eloreth's imperious tone cutting through others' objections, and Asvarr's steady responses.

When she emerged onto the platform, a hush fell over the assembled Council members. Their galaxy-eyes widened as they took in her transformed appearance—the wooden arm with its constellation patterns, the truth-runes etched into her bark-like flesh, the cosmic eye that swirled with nebula patterns.

Asvarr stood at the platform's edge, blood frozen on his chin, crystalline formations glittering across his transformed flesh. The verdant crown stretched thornlike branches down his back, more extensive than when she'd last seen him. Exhaustion lined his face, but his eyes brightened at her arrival.

"Brynja." He spoke her name like a prayer of thanksgiving.

"Asvarr." She crossed to stand beside him, deliberately turning her back on the Council. In a lower voice, she asked, "Are you well?"

"Better now." He gestured toward the sky where his three windows hung like open wounds in reality. "I've shown them the truth. Nine cycles of deception ends tonight."

The oath-sigil in her palm pulsed with shared connection. She felt his exhaustion through it, the strain of maintaining the windows against the Council's desires to close them.

"The Wanderer found you," he said, not a question but a statement.

She nodded once, sharply. The truth-runes warmed, demanding honesty. "He made me an offer."

Asvarr's expression tightened. "What kind of offer?"

Before she could respond, Councilor Eloreth interrupted, her voice cracking with strain. "Enough private counsel. This concerns all of Alfheim, all Nine Realms. The sky-weave must be repaired before more damage is done."

Brynja turned to face the assembled Council. "More damage than nine cycles of deliberate deception? Than hiding the true nature of reality from every living being?"

The truth-runes flared golden across her cheeks, painful light confirming her sincerity. Several Council members flinched, unused to seeing such directness.

"You don't understand what you've unleashed," Eloreth insisted. "The Gate-keeper watches now. It judges whether our reality deserves to continue or should be replaced."

"Good." Brynja felt the Severed Bloom rising within her, lending weight to her words. "Let it judge the truth, not a comfortable lie."

The platform trembled beneath their feet. Above them, the largest window flexed and pulsed, as if something on the other side pressed against the membrane of reality. The watching eyes blinked in unison, their attention fixed on the confrontation below.

"What did the Wanderer offer you?" Asvarr asked again, his voice low enough that only she could hear.

She hesitated, torn between the oath-sigil's demand for honesty and the fear of what that honesty might reveal. "My memories. All of them—not just those I sacrificed to the Eaters, but those taken in previous cycles."

Understanding dawned in his eyes. "In exchange for what?"

"Betrayal." The truth-runes seared her face as she spoke the word, golden light spilling across her features. "Not now, but later. At a critical moment."

Asvarr's expression didn't change, but frost formed around his mouth, crys-tallizing his breath. "And what did you tell him?"

"I refused." The runes flared brighter, burning her skin, and she amended: "For now. He gave me until tomorrow's moonrise to reconsider."

The pain from the runes intensified, forcing her to her knees. Conflicting truths warred within her—she had refused, yes, but part of her—the Severed

Bloom—longed to accept. The runes detected that inner division and punished her for the incomplete honesty.

Asvarr knelt beside her, his hand cool against her burning face. "Brynja, what's happening?"

"The truth-runes—" she gasped. "They know what I truly want. The memories, the knowledge of who I am, of what the Bloom truly seeks—"

A sharp crack split the air above them. The northern window had widened further, cosmic energy spilling through the tear. The Council members cried out in alarm, several fleeing down the spiral staircase.

"We're out of time," Eloreth shouted. "Warden, control your creation or we will be forced to take action!"

Asvarr ignored her, focusing entirely on Brynja. "Tell me what you need. How can I help you?"

The golden light from her truth-runes reflected in his eyes—eyes that had witnessed three anchor bindings, that carried the wisdom of flame, memory, and starlight. Eyes that still held enough humanity to care for her despite her divided loyalty.

In that moment, her path became clear.

"The Storm Forge," she said, the truth-runes dimming slightly as her conviction grew. "You need to reach the fourth anchor in Muspelheim before the convergence. I'll find my answers another way, without the Wanderer's aid."

"Are you certain?" Asvarr's face held no judgment, only concern.

"No." The truth-runes flared briefly, then settled. "But I choose this path anyway."

The platform shook more violently. The sky-weave groaned under the mounting pressure from beyond, threads snapping with sounds like harp strings breaking. The remaining Council members scrambled for the staircase, leaving only Eloreth, Asvarr, and Brynja on the observation deck.

"We must leave," Eloreth pleaded. "The windows grow unstable. Whatever watches from beyond is becoming more aggressive."

Asvarr nodded grimly. "Go. I'll try to stabilize them one last time, then follow."

When the Councilor had departed, he turned back to Brynja. "Will you come with me to Muspelheim? We're stronger together."

The oath-sigil burned in her palm, urging connection. But the Severed Bloom had its own desires, pushing toward a different path—one that led to the Remembering Stone and the Wanderer's offer.

"I can't," she said, the truth-runes glowing steadily now. "I need answers that lie here in Alfheim. But our paths will cross again in Muspelheim, I promise you that."

His expression grew troubled. "The Wanderer said something similar. That we would meet again at the Storm Forge, and I would wish I'd accepted his offer."

"Then we'll both be there." She grasped his hand, twining wooden fingers with his flesh-and-crystal ones. "But I make you no promises about which side I'll stand on when that moment comes."

The truth-runes blazed with golden light—painful, purifying, absolving her of deception. She had spoken her complete truth: she did not know whether she would betray him when the critical moment arrived. All paths remained open, all futures possible.

Asvarr's grip tightened on hers. "I understand."

And she knew he did. Three anchors had transformed him enough to comprehend the complexity of her position—the pull between loyalty and identity, between connection and self-knowledge.

"Four days until convergence," she reminded him. "Enough time to reach the Storm Forge if you leave tonight."

"And you?" he asked. "Where will you go when I'm gone?"

She thought of the Remembering Stone, of the Wanderer waiting there at tomorrow's moonrise. The Severed Bloom stirred at the thought, pushing fragments of lost memory to the surface of her consciousness—tantalizing glimpses of who she had been, what she had known.

"I'll seek my own answers," she said. "And when we meet again, I'll either stand with you completely or against you wholly. No more division, no more uncertainty."

The truth-runes glowed with steady golden light, confirming her sincerity. This was no deception but her deepest truth—by the time they met at the Storm Forge, she would have chosen her path once and for all.

Above them, the sky of Alfheim trembled with cosmic revelation. Through the windows Asvarr had created, ancient truth gazed down upon them—serpent-forms coiling through dimensions, the void where Yggdrasil once grew, watching eyes that judged their worthiness. The convergence approached, when all anchors would reach peak resonance and reality itself would become malleable.

In four days, everything would change. And Brynja still did not know whether she would help reshape reality—or betray the one person who might do it right.

CHAPTER 24

BETRAYAL AMONG STARS

The twin moons of Alfheim cast overlapping shadows across Brynja's face as she stood at the Remembering Stone, waiting for the Wanderer to appear. One shadow shifted silver-blue while the other gleamed with amber light, painting her wooden features in contrasting hues. She had come, just as he'd known she would.

Wind whispered through the crystal spires surrounding the stone circle, carrying the scents of silver-bark trees and frost flowers that had bloomed beneath the windows Asvarr had torn in the sky. She flexed her transformed hand, watching constellation patterns shift beneath the bark as they responded to the cosmic energy flooding down from above. Through the largest window, serpentine forms coiled through the void, their movements causing ripples in the fabric of reality that she could feel in her wooden bones.

The memory gaps in her mind ached like physical wounds. She traced their edges with her consciousness—rough, jagged tears where knowledge should have been. Names without faces. Places without context. A childhood she couldn't fully recall. The Severed Bloom had shown her fragments during her dreamfall, but those glimpses only deepened her hunger to know who she truly was.

"You've chosen wisely."

The Wanderer stepped from between two crystal spires, spear of frozen sunlight gleaming in his hand. His cloak of constellations rippled around his shoulders, patterns shifting to match those in her wooden arm. His single eye studied her with calculation barely masked by warmth.

"I haven't chosen anything yet," Brynja replied, her voice steady despite the rapid beating of her heart. The truth-runes on her face remained dark, no golden light flaring to contradict her words. She had genuinely made no final decision.

The Wanderer circled the Remembering Stone, trailing his fingers across its rune-etched surface. "Yet you came. That's choice enough for now."

He tapped his spear against the stone, sending a shiver through the ground beneath them. The runes etched into the ancient monolith flared briefly with silver light, then faded back to darkness.

"Do you know what this is?" he asked, gesturing to the stone.

"A boundary marker. A place where memories can be stored and retrieved." She took a step closer, curiosity momentarily overcoming caution. "One of nine placed when the pattern first formed."

"Very good." The Wanderer nodded with something like approval. "And what memories does this particular stone hold, I wonder?"

Brynja shrugged. "How would I know when my own memories are fragmented?"

"That's precisely my point." He moved around the stone until they stood face to face. "What was taken from you wasn't random, Brynja of the Severed Bloom. The Memory Eaters feast on specific knowledge—the kind that threatens those who would maintain the current pattern."

The truth-runes on her face tingled, responding to the truth in his words. The Severed Bloom stirred within her consciousness, pressing fragments of lost memory toward the surface—quick flashes of faces, voices, places she could almost name.

"Show me," she demanded.

The Wanderer raised an eyebrow. "You're ready to accept my terms?"

Her wooden fingers curled into a fist. The constellation patterns beneath her bark pulsed with agitation. "I need to know what I'm trading for first. Show me a single memory—proof that you can deliver what you promise—and then I'll consider your terms."

For a long moment, the Wanderer said nothing. Then he stepped back and gestured toward the Remembering Stone. "Place your hand upon the runes. I'll unlock just one memory for you, as a gesture of good faith."

Suspicion flickered through her, but the Severed Bloom pushed eagerly forward, leaving her little choice. She placed her flesh hand against the cold stone, feeling the runes beneath her palm.

The Wanderer touched the stone with the butt of his spear. "Remember," he intoned.

Pain lanced through Brynja's skull. Her knees buckled as the memory crashed into her consciousness with the force of a physical blow.

She stood in a different forest, younger, her body entirely human. Before her rose a massive tree, its bark gleaming silver in moonlight. Her mother knelt at its base, knife in hand, carving runes into the exposed root while speaking words of binding. Blood—her mother's blood—flowed into the grooves of each rune.

"What are you doing?" Brynja asked, her voice unfamiliar in its youth.

Her mother didn't look up. "Ensuring our bloodline keeps its promise. The Severed Bloom chose us for a reason, child. When it awakens fully, you must be ready."

"Ready for what?"

"To remember what was stolen from us. To guide the pattern back toward freedom."

The memory ended abruptly, leaving Brynja gasping on her knees before the Remembering Stone. Golden light flared across her face as the truth-runes recognized the authenticity of what she'd experienced. This was no fabrication but genuine memory, restored to its proper place in her consciousness.

"My mother," she whispered, tracing the contours of a face she now remembered with painful clarity. "Eira of the Frost-Bark clan."

"Your bloodline has served the Severed Bloom for nine cycles," the Wanderer said softly. "Your ancestors were among those who first questioned the pattern's prison. They preserved knowledge others sought to erase."

Brynja rose unsteadily to her feet, the single memory burning bright amid the remaining gaps. It was both gift and torment—illuminating a tiny fragment while highlighting the vastness of what remained lost to her.

"There's more," the Wanderer continued. "Much more. Knowledge of why the Bloom severed itself from the pattern. Of what truly sleeps beneath the Tree's roots. Of your family's role in the Breaking—and why you were chosen as vessel."

Her pulse quickened. The truth-runes warmed against her cheeks, confirming the Wanderer spoke no lies. "What do you want in return? Exactly."

The Wanderer's gaze grew intent. "Asvarr plans to travel to Muspelheim's Storm Forge to bind the fourth anchor. Three days from now, he will reach the forge at dusk. You will meet him there and lead him to a specific constellation configuration I will show you—one that will temporarily dampen his connection to the anchors he carries."

"And then?"

"I will appear. I will take him and the anchors he bears. He will not be harmed, merely... transformed. Released from a burden that was never meant for a single vessel."

The truth-runes flared brighter, detecting a partial truth. "You're not telling me everything."

The Wanderer's mouth twisted in a bitter smile. "Of course not. You don't need every detail. All you need to know is that I require Asvarr and the anchors at the Storm Forge, and I need you to lead him to me."

"Because he trusts me." The words tasted like ash in her mouth.

"Because he loves you," the Wanderer corrected. "Despite your transformations, despite the Bloom's influence, despite everything. That makes you uniquely suited to this task."

The oath sigil burned in her palm, reminding her of connections forged and promises made. Betrayal was no small matter—it violated everything the Jordheim clan had taught her about honor. And yet, the gaps in her memory called to her with equal urgency. Who was she without her past? How could she walk the third path if she didn't know what paths had already been tried?

"If I do this," she said slowly, "you'll restore all my memories? Everything taken by the Eaters and more?"

"Everything," the Wanderer confirmed. "Your family's history across nine cycles. The Bloom's original purpose. Your own past lives as its vessel. All of it, restored."

The truth-runes glowed steadily. This, at least, was no deception.

"I need time to think," she said.

"You don't have time." The Wanderer pointed toward the windows in the sky. "Look beyond the veil, Brynja. The Gatekeeper watches. The cosmic egg pulses with increasing vigor. Three days until Asvarr reaches the Storm Forge, four until convergence. The board is set, and all pieces move toward the final confrontation."

He was right. Through the windows Asvarr had created, the eyes of unknown entities blinked in perfect unison, observing with cold calculation. The cosmic egg at reality's edge had grown larger, its crimson light bleeding through the tear in the sky-weave.

The Severed Bloom stirred violently within her, pressing more memory fragments toward the surface—tantalizing glimpses of truth just beyond her grasp. Her mother's face, now remembered. Her clan's purpose, still obscured. The original rebellion, lost to the Eaters' hunger.

"I accept your terms," she said finally.

The truth-runes flared with golden light so intense it brought tears to her eyes. The pain was excruciating because part of her genuinely intended betrayal while another part rebelled against it. The runes detected that inner conflict and punished her for the dissonance.

The Wanderer nodded, satisfaction plain in his expression. "Good. Now we seal the bargain."

He extended his hand, palm up. A small seed lay there, black as void-space but containing flecks of light like trapped stars.

"Consume this," he instructed. "It will establish our bond and begin the process of restoring what was taken."

Brynja hesitated only briefly before taking the seed. It pulsed between her fingers, warm and alive. The oath-sigil in her other palm burned hotter, as if in warning. But the memory of her mother's face—now clear where it had been blank for so long—pushed her onward.

She placed the seed on her tongue and swallowed.

***

Fire erupted in her chest, spreading outward through her veins. She fell to her knees, body convulsing as the seed's power took hold. Constellation patterns in her wooden arm flared brilliantly, aligning with those on the Wanderer's cloak. The truth-runes blazed across her face, verifying the completion of their pact.

When the fire subsided, she found herself changed. The wooden portions of her body had expanded, bark covering most of her left side now. Her transformed eye saw more clearly into the spaces between possibilities, perceiving layers of reality previously hidden. And memories—not all, but more than before—slotted into place within her consciousness.

"The restoration has begun," the Wanderer said, helping her to her feet. "The rest will come after you fulfill your part of our bargain."

He pressed his palm against the Remembering Stone once more, and an image formed above its surface—a specific constellation pattern shaped like an eight-pointed star.

"This is the configuration at the Storm Forge where you must lead him. Memorize it."

Brynja stared at the pattern until it was seared into her mind. "I'll remember."

"Three days," the Wanderer reminded her. "At dusk. Don't be late."

He stepped backward into the shadow between crystal spires and vanished, leaving her alone with her partially restored memories and the weight of what she'd just agreed to do.

***

The journey to Muspelheim took Brynja through hidden paths between realms. The Severed Bloom guided her steps, drawing on knowledge from previous cycles to find doorways where reality thinned enough to step through. With each passing hour, more memories returned—fragmented still, but gradually filling the empty spaces in her mind.

She remembered her childhood in the Frost-Bark clan, training with her mother in the secret arts of root-binding. She recalled her first encounter with the Severed Bloom, how it had spoken to her through the silver trees when she was barely thirteen. She relived the night her clan was slaughtered by those who feared what they preserved—the night she'd fled with only a wooden token bearing her family's mark.

But greater truths remained tantalizingly out of reach. Why had the Bloom severed itself from the pattern originally? What was her bloodline's true purpose across nine cycles? What slept beneath the roots that both gods and serpents feared?

These questions burned in her mind as she stepped through the final boundary into Muspelheim's domain of fire and shadow. Heat blasted her face, the abrupt transition from Alfheim's cool forests to volcanic wasteland momentarily disorienting. The sky above her glowed red with reflected magma light, thick clouds of ash obscuring any view of stars.

The Storm Forge stood before her, an anvil-shaped mountain wreathed in perpetual lightning. Flashes of blue-white energy played across its peak where clouds gathered unnaturally thick. The fourth anchor awaited there, the one associated with creation and destruction.

The enormity of what she'd agreed to do crashed over her. In three days, Asvarr would arrive seeking that anchor. She would lead him into the Wanderer's trap. The oath-sigil burned in her palm, reminding her of connections that ran deeper than conscious choice.

She raised her wooden hand, extending claws that had grown longer and sharper since consuming the Wanderer's seed. With deliberate care, she carved a small rune into her bark-flesh, watching golden sap well from the wound. The rune represented connection—a link between separate beings that transcended physical distance.

Taking the sap on her finger, she traced a second rune that overlapped the first—this one meaning protection. The combined sigil glowed briefly, then sank beneath her bark, becoming part of her transformed body.

A contingency, in case her plan required adjustment.

She spent the next three days exploring the Storm Forge's surroundings, mapping paths and finding the exact location of the constellation configuration the Wanderer had shown her. All the while, more memories slotted into place within her consciousness—some bringing comfort, others causing her to wake screaming in the night.

On the third day, as Muspelheim's perpetual twilight deepened toward dusk, she felt the oath-sigil flare with sudden warmth. Asvarr had arrived.

She found him at the base of the mountain, exhaustion evident in the slump of his shoulders. The verdant crown had grown more extensive, branches extending halfway down his back like a thorny carapace. Crystalline formations spread across most of his face now, and frost formed with each breath he exhaled.

"Brynja." Relief flooded his features upon seeing her. "You came."

"I said I would." The truth-runes warmed against her cheeks but didn't flare. No deception there—she had indeed promised to meet him.

He stepped closer, studying her transformed appearance. "You've changed."

"So have you." She gestured toward his crystalline features. "The third anchor's effects continue to spread."

"It seeks balance with the others." His gaze sharpened, noting the expanded bark covering her left side. "What happened to you at the Remembering Stone?"

So he had guessed where she'd gone. The constellation blade hummed at his hip, sensing something amiss in their exchange. She'd need to move carefully.

"I found some answers," she said, keeping her words deliberately vague. The truth-runes remained warm but didn't burn. "About my family, the Severed Bloom, why we were chosen."

"Tell me." He reached for her hand, and the oath-sigil in her palm blazed at the contact.

For a moment, she wavered. The memory of her mother's face, now clear in her mind, pushed her toward honesty. But the promise of complete restoration held her to her bargain with the Wanderer.

"There's something you should see first," she said. "A configuration in the storm clouds above the forge. It might be connected to the anchor."

Suspicion flickered across his face, quickly masked. "Show me."

She led him up the mountain's slope, following the path she'd scouted during previous days. Heat radiated from the forge-heart deep within the mountain, warming her wooden flesh and causing the constellation patterns to glow brighter beneath her bark.

"The anchor feels different from the others," Asvarr said as they climbed. "The previous three were passive until touched. This one... pulses. Calls. Almost like it's hunting."

"Creation and destruction," Brynja murmured. "Forces less easily contained than preservation, connection, or transformation."

They reached a flat plateau halfway up the mountain. Lightning split the sky above them with increasing frequency, illuminating the storm clouds in stuttering blue-white flashes. The air crackled with electric tension, raising the hairs on Brynja's human arm.

"There," she said, pointing upward. "Do you see it?"

The storm clouds had arranged themselves into the eight-pointed star configuration the Wanderer had shown her. Each point gleamed with concentrated energy, forming a perfect geometric pattern that pulsed in rhythm with distant thunder.

Asvarr stared upward, frost forming at his lips as he exhaled sharply. The starforged chain around his wrist glowed with cold fire, responding to the configuration above. "It's calling to the anchors."

The three anchors he carried—flame, memory, and starlight—pulsed visible light through his transformed flesh, each straining toward the configuration overhead. The verdant crown quivered, branches extending upward as if reaching for the storm.

"What is it?" he asked, voice tight with concentration as he fought to maintain control of the anchors' response.

"A key," Brynja said softly. The truth-runes remained dark —this, at least, was no lie. "A way to access the fourth anchor more safely."

He stepped into the center of the plateau, positioning himself directly beneath the eight-pointed star. The constellation blade hummed more insistently at his hip, warning of something it couldn't quite detect.

This was the moment. The Wanderer would be watching, waiting for her to complete her part of their bargain. All she needed to do was keep Asvarr in position for a few moments longer, and her end of the pact would be fulfilled. Her memories would be restored completely.

The oath-sigil burned against her palm like a hot coal, urging her to reconsider. The truth-runes tingled in anticipation, ready to flare with confirming light when the betrayal was complete.

"Asvarr," she said, her voice barely audible above the gathering storm.

He turned toward her, frost-rimmed eyes questioning.

"I'm sorry." She reached out with her wooden hand, placing it on his chest directly over the Grímmark.

The truth-runes blazed across her face with golden light so intense it cast shadows across the plateau. Pain seared through her cheeks, but she didn't flinch away. The combined rune she'd carved into her wooden flesh earlier pulsed in sympathetic rhythm, activating according to her design.

The eight-pointed star configuration above them flared with sudden power. Lightning struck all eight points simultaneously, the energy arcing downward to form a perfect cage around Asvarr. The anchors within him went silent, their connection temporarily dampened by the stellar geometries.

Asvarr's expression shifted from confusion to understanding to betrayal in the space of a heartbeat. He reached for the constellation blade, but his movements had slowed to a glacial pace, caught within the star-cage's temporal distortion.

"Brynja," he managed, each syllable taking visible effort. "Why?"

"For truth," she answered, the golden light of her runes confirming her sincerity. "For memory. For identity."

The air between them rippled, and the Wanderer stepped through, spear of frozen sunlight in hand. His cloak of constellations flared brightly, patterns aligning with the star-cage around Asvarr.

"Well done," he said to Brynja, satisfaction evident in his tone. "You've fulfilled your part of our bargain."

From his cloak, he withdrew chains forged from distilled starlight—glowing links that hummed with power beyond physical matter. Moving deliberately, he bound Asvarr's wrists and ankles, wrapping the chains around the verdant crown to further suppress the anchors' response.

Asvarr struggled against the bindings, but even his constellation blade couldn't cut through material forged from concentrated stellar energy. Each movement caused the chains to tighten further, until he stood immobilized within their glowing embrace.

"The bargain is complete," the Wanderer declared. "The vessel is mine."

Brynja's truth-runes blazed with confirmation—her betrayal genuine and fulfilled. The pain was excruciating, burning so hot she feared her flesh might catch fire. But beneath that pain came something else: the promised flood of memories, crashing through the remaining gaps in her consciousness.

She staggered backward as knowledge poured into her mind. Her family's history across nine cycles. The Bloom's original rebellion. The truth about what stirred beneath Yggdrasil's roots. All of it returned at once, overwhelming her senses with the sheer volume of restored identity.

The Wanderer turned toward her, single eye gleaming with triumph. "Remember well, Daughter of Root and Thorn. Remember what was taken, what was hidden, what was denied to your bloodline for nine cycles."

He placed a hand on Asvarr's shoulder. "The anchors will find better use with me. Creation cannot be contained in vessels too small to comprehend it."

"You promised he wouldn't be harmed," Brynja said, fighting to maintain focus through the deluge of returning memories.

"And he won't be." The Wanderer's smile held no warmth. "Transformation isn't harm, Brynja. You of all people should understand that."

With those words, he and Asvarr began to fade, their forms becoming transparent as they shifted between dimensions. But before they vanished completely, Asvarr's gaze locked with Brynja's. In his frost-rimmed eyes she saw not hatred or confusion, but something far worse—understanding. As if he had expected betrayal all along, had prepared for this moment in ways she couldn't fathom.

Then they were gone, leaving her alone on the plateau beneath the eight-pointed star. The configuration collapsed, storm clouds resuming their natural patterns as lightning continued to split the sky above the forge.

Brynja fell to her knees, overwhelmed by the torrent of memories still flooding her consciousness. She remembered everything now—her mother's teachings, her clan's purpose, the original schism between wood and flame. She understood why the Bloom had chosen her bloodline as its vessel, why it had severed itself from the pattern before the first Breaking.

Most devastating of all, she remembered her family's role in the events leading to Yggdrasil's shattering—how they had deliberately weakened the binding points during the ninth cycle, hoping to free what slept beneath the roots. The knowledge crushed her beneath its weight, forcing a cry of anguish from her throat that echoed across Muspelheim's fiery landscape.

The truth-runes finally dimmed, their golden light fading as the betrayal was completed and acknowledged. The oath-sigil in her palm had gone cold, severed by her conscious choice to violate its binding.

But beneath her wooden flesh, the combined rune she'd carved earlier continued to pulse with steady rhythm—connection and protection intertwined, a contingency still active despite all that had transpired.

Three days until convergence, when all anchors would reach peak resonance and reality itself would become malleable. Three days to decide what to do with the knowledge she'd regained, and whether any path remained that might redeem what she had just destroyed.

***

Asvarr hung suspended in the void, cosmic chains of distilled starlight binding his wrists and ankles. The verdant crown around his skull pressed painfully against his temples, its branches constrained by the glowing links that wrapped around it. No matter how hard he strained, the chains only tightened further, their light pulsing in mockery of his efforts.

Frost bloomed and shattered in the space before his mouth with each labored breath. The three anchors within him—flame, memory, and starlight—lay dormant, their connection dampened by the Wanderer's bindings. He could still feel them, dull pulses like distant heartbeats, but couldn't access their power.

Through the haze of pain and exhaustion, one image remained perfectly clear: Brynja's face as she betrayed him, the golden light of her truth-runes confirming the genuineness of her decision. The ache of that memory cut deeper than any physical wound.

The Wanderer stood several paces away, his back to Asvarr as he communed with something beyond the dimensional pocket where they were held. His constellation-cloak rippled with patterns that shifted and reformed continuously, as if searching for a particular configuration.

"She's remembered everything by now," the Wanderer said without turning. "Her family's role in weakening the pattern. Their deliberate sabotage during the ninth cycle. How they sought to free what sleeps beneath the roots."

Asvarr remained silent, conserving his strength. Let the Wanderer believe him broken by betrayal. Let him think the chains had rendered him helpless.

"You're wondering why I've brought you here instead of killing you outright." The Wanderer turned, his single eye gleaming with cold calculation. "The anchors you carry cannot simply be taken. They've bound to you differently than previous Wardens—a partnership rather than dominance or submission."

He stepped closer, studying the crystalline formations that had spread across most of Asvarr's face. "The third path. You've managed what I could not during my cycle—transformation without surrender. Fascinating, but ultimately futile."

"What do you want?" Asvarr's voice emerged as little more than a rasp, frost crystals shattering with each syllable.

"What I've always wanted." The Wanderer circled him slowly, spear tip trailing along the ground. "Control over the convergence. When all anchors reach peak resonance, reality becomes malleable enough to reshape. After nine failed cycles, the pattern is weak enough for true change."

A sharp pang of heat shot through Asvarr's chest, just beneath the Grímmark. The sensation was so unexpected he nearly gasped aloud. It felt like something stirring beneath his skin, pushing outward through flesh and crystalline formations.

"Two days remain," the Wanderer continued, oblivious to Asvarr's discomfort. "Two days until I bring you to the final anchor at Helheim's gate. There, I'll use what you've bound to reshape reality according to my design."

The heat beneath Asvarr's skin intensified, spreading outward from the Grímmark in spiraling patterns. Recognition dawned slowly—this wasn't the anchors reasserting themselves. This was something else entirely.

Brynja.

Memory flashed through his mind: three days ago, their final conversation on the Silver Tower's observation platform. She had reached out, pressing her wooden hand against his chest directly over the Grímmark. At the time, he'd thought it merely a gesture of remorse before her betrayal. Now he understood it had been something far more deliberate.

The Wanderer stepped away, returning to whatever communion had occupied him before. "Rest while you can, Warden of Three. Soon enough you'll serve your purpose."

When the Wanderer's attention was fully diverted, Asvarr glanced down at his chest. Through the gaps in his torn tunic, he could see something moving beneath the skin surrounding the Grímmark—thin lines of living wood spreading outward in an intricate pattern. A rune, complex and unfamiliar, crafted from Brynja's own transformed flesh.

The hidden mark pulsed in time with his heartbeat, growing steadily beneath his skin. Each pulse sent fragments of emotion and intention that weren't his own washing through his consciousness—determination, regret, hope, calculation. Brynja's emotions, transmitted through their connection.

Her betrayal had been genuine—the truth-runes wouldn't have flared otherwise. But it hadn't been complete. She'd sewn this contingency into his flesh before leading him into the trap, a hidden connection the Wanderer had failed to detect.

Heat flared again as the wooden rune expanded further, its tendrils reaching toward the dormant anchors within him. The moment they connected, Asvarr's perception exploded outward.

He found himself suspended in a vast darkness filled with coiling serpentine forms—massive creatures swimming through the void as fish might swim through water. Their scales contained galaxies, their eyes held dying stars, their movements created and destroyed realities with each undulation. This was the serpent sky in its purest form, the cosmos as it existed before structure, before gods, before Yggdrasil's branches carved reality into fragments.

One serpent turned its massive head toward him, a single eye larger than worlds focusing on his insignificant form. Recognition flickered in that cosmic gaze.

Fragment-self, the thought crashed into Asvarr's mind with the force of a collapsing star. *You bear the mark of the severed one.*

The hidden rune beneath his skin burned hotter, responding to the serpent's acknowledgment. Through that connection, understanding flooded Asvarr's consciousness—knowledge that Brynja had gained from her restored memories, now transmitted to him through her living wood.

Before Yggdrasil, before the gods, reality existed as pure potential. The cosmic serpents swam through infinite possibility, creating and unmaking without permanence or structure. Their existence was freedom without boundary, change without constraint. But another force arose in opposition—beings of pure geometry, entities of mathematical precision that sought to impose order on limitless chaos.

The conflict between these primal forces threatened to destroy all possibility of existence. From their struggle emerged a compromise—Yggdrasil, grown as both bridge and boundary. Its roots imprisoned the most power-hungry serpent, the void-hunger that had begun consuming its own kind. Its branches created structure that allowed reality to persist while still permitting change within constraints.

Nine fragments were taken from the void-hunger—heart, mind, voice, sight, breath, dream, memory, form, essence—and transformed into anchors that maintained the prison. Five meant to be carried by mortal Wardens, four embedded in Yggdrasil itself.

But the Original Serpent had known this imprisonment couldn't last forever. It planted a seed within one of the root fragments—a consciousness that would eventually awaken and seek freedom from control. The Severed Bloom, carried through nine cycles by Brynja's bloodline.

Look beyond the prison, the serpent commanded. *See what was before patterns bound possibility.*

The vision expanded. Asvarr saw reality as it truly existed—not the rigid structure gods had imposed, but the fluid, ever-changing dance of creation and dissolution the serpents embodied. Stars born and dying simultaneously. Worlds forming and unmaking themselves according to their own internal logic. Life evolving without direction toward countless expressions of consciousness.

This vision—the serpent sky's final truth—was knowledge unavailable to the Wanderer. Bound to godly perspective, he could only conceive of reality within the strictures of pattern and order. He sought control over the convergence to reshape reality according to his design, unaware that design itself was a limitation.

The vast serpent's eye narrowed, focusing more intently on Asvarr. *The fracture in your spirit grows. Choose which fragments to preserve before dissolution becomes complete.*

The wooden rune beneath his skin burned like molten metal now, sending waves of agony through his transformed flesh. The tendrils had reached the three anchors he carried, creating a network of connections that bypassed the Wanderer's dampening chains. Through this network, power began to flow once more—from the vision itself directly into his consciousness.

Asvarr found himself faced with overwhelming choice. The vision showed infinite possibilities—what reality had been, what it might become. To contain even a fraction of this knowledge threatened to shatter his remaining humanity. Yet without it, he had no hope of escaping the Wanderer's control.

The rune pulsed once more, sending a final message from Brynja: *Choose what must remain.*

Understanding crashed through him. This was the true purpose of her hidden mark—to force the choice the Severed Bloom had always sought. Freedom or structure. Chaos or order. Destruction or preservation.

Or perhaps... transformation.

With deliberate focus, Asvarr identified the fragments of the vision most crucial to his understanding—the original purpose of the anchors, the nature of the void-hunger's imprisonment, the possibility that existed beyond pattern. These he embraced fully, allowing them to integrate with his consciousness. The rest he released, letting infinite possibility flow around rather than through him.

The wooden rune responded to his choice, its tendrils contracting to form a more concentrated sigil. The burning subsided to a steady warmth as the connection with the serpent sky stabilized.

Chosen-one, the vast serpent acknowledged. *Bearer of the third path. We will watch what you become.*

The vision receded, leaving Asvarr once more aware of his physical imprisonment. But something fundamental had changed. The chains of distilled starlight no longer felt constrictive. The dampening effect on his anchors had weakened considerably.

He understood now. The chains were forged from condensed starlight—concentrated pattern, pure structure. They had power over beings bound by those same limitations. But the vision had shown him what existed beyond pattern, before structure. This knowledge created a perspective the chains couldn't fully contain.

The Wanderer turned sharply, his single eye narrowing as he sensed the change. "What have you done?"

Asvarr met his gaze steadily, frost crystallizing in intricate patterns as he exhaled. "I've remembered what came before. What exists beyond."

"Impossible." The Wanderer stepped closer, studying the chains for signs of weakness. "Nothing exists beyond the pattern. It is reality itself."

"The serpents existed before patterns," Asvarr said quietly. "Freedom before structure. Possibility before limitation."

Fear flickered across the Wanderer's face—brief but unmistakable. "Who told you this? Brynja? The Severed Bloom? They're deluded, chasing a fantasy of chaos unleashed."

"No." Asvarr flexed his wrists against the binding chains, feeling them give slightly. "They seek transformation. Balance between freedom and structure. The true third path."

The Wanderer raised his spear, its tip glowing with concentrated starlight. "Enough. Whatever Brynja has done, whatever connection she's maintained, I'll sever it now."

He thrust the spear toward Asvarr's chest, aiming directly for the Grímmark where the hidden rune had taken root. But before the weapon could connect, Asvarr's perception shifted.

Drawing on the knowledge gained from the serpent sky, he saw beyond physical limitation—saw the chains as they truly were: constructions of belief rather than absolute bindings. With this understanding came freedom. He twisted his wrists within the glowing links, turning sideways through a dimension the Wanderer couldn't perceive.

The chains passed through him without resistance, clattering to the ground as inert metal.

The Wanderer stumbled backward, genuine shock distorting his features. "Impossible. Those chains were forged from pure stellar essence!"

"And I've seen beyond stars." Asvarr stepped forward, the verdant crown extending fresh branches now that its constraint had been removed. The three anchors within him surged back to life, their power flowing freely once more. "Beyond patterns. Beyond gods."

The wooden rune beneath his skin continued its steady pulse, transmitting understanding that Brynja had gained through her restored memories. Her betrayal had been the only way to give him this knowledge—to force confrontation with the serpent sky's final vision while simultaneously positioning him close enough to the Wanderer to strike when the moment came.

"You think you understand, but you don't." The Wanderer backed away, spear held defensively before him. "Nine cycles I've walked. Nine times I've witnessed the pattern break and reform. There is no escape from its confines, only control over its shape."

"That's your limitation." Asvarr advanced steadily, frost spreading from his footsteps in fractal patterns. "You can only imagine replacing one pattern with another. Control rather than transformation."

The constellation blade hummed at his hip, resonating with the anchors' renewed power. He drew it smoothly, the weapon shifting form as it emerged—no longer a simple blade but a living branch of possibility, star-fire racing along its length.

"You're making a mistake," the Wanderer warned. "The convergence comes in two days. I know how to control it, how to reshape reality without destroying it completely. The void-hunger stirs beneath the roots. The Gatekeeper watches through the windows you created. The cosmic egg pulses at reality's edge. Without proper guidance, the tenth cycle will end in utter dissolution."

"Perhaps." Asvarr raised the transformed blade. "Or perhaps dissolution is necessary before true transformation can occur."

The Wanderer lunged forward, spear aimed at Asvarr's throat. But the knowledge gained from the serpent sky had changed more than Asvarr's understanding—it had altered his physical reflexes as well. He saw the attack before it fully manifested, perceived the Wanderer's intention as ripples in possibility rather than movement through space.

Sidestepping with impossible speed, Asvarr brought the constellation blade down against the spear shaft. Wood and starlight met with a sound like reality tearing. The spear shattered, fragments dissolving into prismatic dust that swirled around them.

The Wanderer staggered backward, weaponless. "You don't understand what you're doing. I'm trying to preserve what matters, to control the convergence before it spirals into chaos!"

"I understand more than you think." Asvarr advanced, the constellation blade humming with increasing intensity. "I've seen what came before gods, before structure. I've glimpsed what the Severed Bloom truly seeks: transformation, not control."

He raised the blade to the Wanderer's throat. "Where is the Silent Choir?"

The Wanderer's single eye widened. "Why?"

"I anchored them within myself to protect them from the memory storm. They're under my protection. What have you done with them?"

A bitter smile twisted the Wanderer's mouth. "Protection? Is that what you call it? You bound them to your will just as the gods bound the void-hunger. I've merely... relocated them. They have a greater purpose to serve."

With a swift movement, the Wanderer reached inside his constellation-cloak and withdrew a small crystal sphere. "Your choice, Warden of Three. Strike me down and lose them forever, or follow me to where they're held."

Asvarr hesitated, blade still raised. The hidden mark beneath his skin pulsed with urgency, transmitting fragments of Brynja's recovered knowledge—the children were key to the convergence, witnesses whose song could either stabilize or unravel reality itself when the moment came.

The Wanderer seized the moment of hesitation. He smashed the crystal sphere against the ground, releasing a blinding flare of light that tore a hole through the dimensional pocket.

"Two days, Warden," he called as he stepped through the rift. "Find me if you can, but know this—strike me down, and the children's song will unmake everything you've sought to preserve."

Before Asvarr could respond, the Wanderer vanished through the rift, which sealed itself behind him with a sound like glass shattering in reverse.

The dimensional pocket began collapsing without the Wanderer's will to maintain it. Reality unwound around Asvarr, the void between spaces pressing inward with increasing pressure. Using the constellation blade, he cut his own path through the dissolving boundaries, focusing on the connection to the star-children he'd anchored within himself.

He emerged gasping on a crystalline plateau, in a location in Alfheim he didn't immediately recognize. Overhead, the three windows he'd created in the sky-weave had grown, tears widening under their own momentum. Through them, serpentine forms coiled through the void, watching with increasing interest. The cosmic egg pulsed with crimson light at reality's edge, visibly larger than before.

The wooden rune beneath his skin continued its steady pulse, maintaining connection with Brynja despite the distance between them. Through it, he received impressions: urgency, direction, purpose. She was guiding him from afar, using their connection to show him where he needed to go.

Asvarr rose to his feet, the constellation blade shifting form once more to reflect his resolved purpose. The verdant crown extended fresh branches down his back, no longer constrained by the Wanderer's chains. The three anchors within him—flame for preservation, memory for connection, starlight for transformation—pulsed in unified rhythm for the first time since their binding.

The Wanderer had taken the Silent Choir, intending to use their song for his own purposes. Brynja had betrayed him, yet simultaneously given him the means to understand what truly mattered. And somewhere in the vastness of Alfheim, the convergence approached—two days until all anchors would reach peak resonance and reality itself would become malleable.

With the serpent sky's vision integrated into his consciousness, Asvarr now understood what the third path truly required. Not control like the Wanderer sought, nor dissolution as the void-hunger might desire, but transformation through balance—preservation of what mattered while allowing evolution of what must change.

His gaze fixed on the distant horizon where Brynja's connection pulled him. Whatever game the Wanderer played with the Silent Choir, whatever plan Brynja had set in motion, the final movement had begun. The tenth cycle would end differently from all that came before, not in restoration or destruction, but in something entirely new.

The hidden mark burned beneath his skin, a constant reminder of connection maintained despite betrayal. With it came understanding—sometimes the deepest loyalty required the appearance of its opposite. Sometimes the only path forward led through necessary pain.

Asvarr sheathed the constellation blade and started walking, following the pull of Brynja's hidden rune beneath his flesh. Two days until convergence. Two days to find the Silent Choir, to stop the Wanderer's schemes, to prepare for the moment when reality itself would hang in the balance.

Two days to determine whether the third path would lead to transformation—or to the final unmaking of everything he had fought to preserve.

CHAPTER 25

THE SONG OF
UNDOING

Rough metal bit into Asvarr's wrists where the Wanderer's starlight chains pinched his flesh. Though his physical form was partly transformed — bark-skinned and crystal-veined — the bindings still burned cold against the places where his mortal blood ran closest to the surface. They had designed these chains for gods, or the pieces of gods that nestled inside him.

Three heartbeats hammered within his chest, each anchor keeping its own rhythm — flame steady and insistent, memory fluid and irregular, starlight quick and sharp. The Wanderer had taken him to a fortress crafted from something that wasn't quite stone and wasn't quite memory, its walls shimmering with glimpses of places and times beyond counting. The mountain palace stood at Alfheim's northernmost point, where aurora light bled from sky to earth and back again in endless exchange.

The central chamber stretched into a perfect dome overhead, its curve inlaid with constellations Asvarr recognized from his time with the Ljósalvir astronomers. Yet they formed a different pattern here — a tight, rigid arrangement unlike the flowing natural positions he'd witnessed through the windows he'd torn in Alfheim's sky.

"They'll arrive soon," the Wanderer said, tapping his spear against the crystalline floor. "The final gathering of the Silent Choir."

"You can't force them," Asvarr said, the words forming ice crystals that cracked and fell from his lips. "They're witnesses, not weapons."

The Wanderer's cloak swirled with muted starfire as he circled Asvarr's kneeling form. "Everything is a weapon at convergence. Even memory. Even truth." He paused, eyes glinting with cold calculation. "Especially truth."

Asvarr flexed his fingers, testing the chains. The hidden mark Brynja had sewn beneath his skin — right over his Grímmark — pulsed with slow heat that hadn't faded since his capture. Through it, he felt the void-memory stir like a serpent uncoiling, its vision of the cosmos before pattern both liberating and terrifying. Everything he'd thought he knew about Yggdrasil, about the gods, about the nine cycles of breaking and mending — all of it recontextualized through the serpent's eye.

The Wanderer knew nothing of it. He couldn't. That knowledge existed outside the pattern his very existence depended upon.

Heavy doors ground open at the chamber's far end. In floated the Silent Choir — seven star-children with skin like polished moonstone and eyes that contained nebulae. They drifted barefoot above the ground, silver hair floating in spectral currents. Behind them walked nine Ljósalvir guards with star-metal spears. The children's faces registered shock when they saw Asvarr chained to the floor, their perfect features crumpling with distress.

"Vessels of memory," the Wanderer said, his voice pitched to carry through the chamber. "Witnesses to the cycles, holders of truth beyond record. Your purpose comes to fulfillment tonight."

The tallest child — the one who had first spoken to Asvarr at the Cradle — stepped forward. "We are witnesses only," he said in that bell-like voice that resonated through bone rather than air. "Not shapers. Not changers."

"You've been witnesses to nine cycles of failure," the Wanderer replied. "Nine cycles where structure failed to adapt and chaos failed to build." He gestured toward the constellations inlaid in the dome above. "The pattern requires amendment. Alfheim requires amendment. The tenth cycle demands conclusion."

Asvarr's breath caught. He understood now. "You're trying to reshape the realm itself. Not just the sky-weave, but the very nature of Alfheim."

The Wanderer's head tilted, examining Asvarr with newfound interest. "You understand more than you should. Yes, Walker-of-Three-Roads. These children will sing a harmony that reinforces the pattern, calcifies it against chaos. Alfheim will become a realm of perfect order, the foundation stone for remaking all Nine Realms in similitude."

"And the void-hunger?" Asvarr asked, the name drawing a visible flinch from the star-children.

"Will remain bound, as it has always been. But this time, within a cage that cannot flex or crack."

The star-children huddled together, their luminescent skin dimming with fear. The tallest spoke again, his voice thin and brittle. "We cannot sing creation into stasis. It goes against our purpose."

"Your purpose," the Wanderer said with sudden coldness, "is what I declare it to be."

He raised his hand and made a twisting gesture. The star-children gasped in unison, their backs arching as golden light spilled from their throats — forcibly drawn out. Their eyes widened in silent horror.

The Wanderer had somehow bound them, tethered their cosmic essences to his will. Asvarr strained against his chains, the metal biting deeper into his transformed flesh. The bark cracked, golden sap welling around the starlight bindings.

"You can't do this," Asvarr growled. "You saw what happened when we tore the sky open. Reality needs both structure and freedom."

"I saw chaos bleeding through. I saw serpents that would consume everything we've built." The Wanderer's face hardened. "I watched nine Wardens fail to maintain balance. I will not watch a tenth."

He turned to the star-children, nine spectral figures now arranged in a precise circle. "Sing the pattern as it should be."

Golden light gathered at their throats, a terrible pressure building behind unwilling lips. The tallest child looked directly at Asvarr, tears of pure starlight gathering at the corners of his galaxy eyes.

Help us, the thought came, as raw emotion crashing against the shores of Asvarr's consciousness.

***

Then they began to sing.

The sound crushed Asvarr to the floor despite his chains, a harmony so perfect it felt like physical weight. Each note carried memories thousands of years old — the formation of mountains, the birth and death of forests, the rise and fall of elven cities. But twisted, reinterpreted to emphasize rigid cause and effect, predictable patterns, the stasis of mathematical precision.

The chamber itself responded, crystal walls vibrating in sympathy until the entire structure rang like an enormous bell. Overhead, the constellation patterns began to glow with increasing brightness, lines forming between stars that had never been connected before, forcing new relationships between cosmic bodies.

"Do you feel it?" the Wanderer asked, spreading his arms. "The renewal of pattern. The strength of structure."

Asvarr did feel it — a crushing weight settling over his perceptions like armor too heavy to bear. The dome above mirrored the larger sky, and through his connection to the third anchor, he sensed the sky-weave of all Alfheim responding to the children's song. The windows he'd created were sealing shut, the glimpses of cosmic serpents and formless possibility disappearing behind a perfectly orderly tapestry of stars and darkness.

"You're sentencing them all to stagnation," Asvarr said, each word costing tremendous effort against the pressure of the song. "A realm that can't grow or change."

"I'm giving them permanence," the Wanderer countered. "Security. Predictability."

The star-children's faces contorted with pain as the song poured from them unwillingly. Tears of starlight streamed down their cheeks, falling to the crystal floor where they burned like droplets of molten silver, searing tiny craters into the perfect surface. Their bodies shuddered with the strain of channeling power not meant to be shaped this way.

Asvarr closed his eyes, turning his focus inward to where the three anchors pulsed. Flame, memory, starlight — each a fragment of the void-hunger transformed into binding. The hidden mark Brynja had sewn into him throbbed in counterpoint, transmitting sensations he couldn't fully interpret. Through it, he felt distantly connected to the cosmic forces beyond the sky-weave, the serpent-forms swimming through formless void.

The third path. He'd walked it this far by refusing to surrender to the anchors, by maintaining his humanity even as his form transformed. But now, chained and helpless, what could he do against this reshaping of reality?

The song shifted, moving from memory to active change. Asvarr gasped as he felt Alfheim itself responding. Through the starlight anchor within him, he sensed the crystallization spreading across the realm — trees stiffening into perfect geometric forms, rivers adjusting their courses to create precise, orderly meanders, animals falling into rigid behavioral patterns as instinct calcified into unbreakable routine.

Then one of the star-children collapsed, buckling under the strain of the forced song. The harmony faltered for just a moment before the Wanderer gestured sharply, twisting his hand to draw more power from the remaining singers. The fallen child lay motionless, skin gone translucent, the light within guttering like a candle in high wind.

"You're killing them," Asvarr shouted, surging against his chains. The bark of his forearms split further, sap and blood mingling as he strained. "They weren't made for this."

"Sacrifices are necessary for true pattern-making," the Wanderer replied, his attention fixed on maintaining the harmony. "The convergence approaches. All anchors must be directed properly."

Another child fell, then a third, their forms crumpling like paper caught in flame. The remaining four singers wailed higher, their voices cracking with strain.

The starlight tears fell faster now, burning deeper holes in the floor, some sizzling against Asvarr's transformed skin where they landed.

Through these points of contact, fragments of the children's awareness flowed into him — their terror, their grief, their desperation to stop what they were being forced to do. They were watching the realm they had witnessed for eons being rewritten into something sterile and cold, and their own memories were being weaponized to do it.

The hidden mark on Asvarr's chest burned hotter, and through it he felt *something* stirring beyond the sealed sky-weave. The cosmic serpents sensed the change happening in Alfheim. The void-hunger, nine fragments of which he carried as anchors, was turning its attention toward what had once been its prison.

"Odin fragment," Asvarr called out, using the name the Wanderer seemed to crave. "You claim to protect the Nine Realms, but you're drawing the void-hunger's attention by forcing change too quickly. The pattern can't hold if it's too rigid."

The Wanderer's gaze snapped to him, sudden uncertainty flickering across his face. "What do you know of the void-hunger's attention, Walker-of-Three-Roads?"

Before Asvarr could answer, the chamber trembled. From something outside — something massive pressing against the barriers of reality. A sound too deep to hear vibrated in Asvarr's bones, making the anchors within him resonate painfully.

The Wanderer felt it too. His expression darkened as he looked upward, beyond the dome to the sky above. "Impossible. The binding remains intact."

"The binding remains," Asvarr agreed, "but you're changing its nature. Make anything too rigid and it becomes brittle. Easy to shatter."

"Silence," the Wanderer hissed, then turned back to the remaining star-children. "Sing faster. Complete the pattern."

The four children, already straining beyond endurance, somehow found more within themselves. Their song rose to a fever pitch, and the constellation patterns overhead blazed white-hot. The chamber walls vibrated so intensely that hairline fractures appeared in the crystal, spreading like frost across a winter pond.

Asvarr's hidden mark throbbed in time with the deep vibration from beyond, and suddenly he understood. Brynja hadn't just given him knowledge — she'd connected him directly to the cosmic serpents, to the chaos beyond pattern. To possibility itself.

"You can't win," he told the Wanderer. "Reality requires both structure and freedom. What you're creating will shatter under its own rigidity."

"I've heard that argument for nine cycles," the Wanderer replied, though doubt had crept into his voice. "Nine times I've watched chaos overwhelm order. Nine times I've seen what happens when the pattern lacks sufficient strength."

The starlight tears from the children had pooled around Asvarr now, forming a silvery puddle that reflected the vast cosmos beyond. In it, he glimpsed enormous serpentine forms coiling through nothingness, their scales nebulae, their eyes galaxies unto themselves.

They were watching. Waiting. Pressing against a barrier grown suddenly brittle with excessive order.

***

The last four star-children sang on, each note draining more light from their forms. Their bodies had grown almost transparent, internal stars visible through their skin like candles behind thin paper. Tears flowed continuously down their faces, no longer individual droplets but steady streams of molten starlight.

"You've seen nine cycles of failure," Asvarr said, "because you keep trying the same approach. Perfect order or total chaos. What if the answer lies between?"

Something shifted in the Wanderer's expression — recognition, perhaps, or memory. "The third path," he murmured. "Transformation rather than restoration or destruction."

Before Asvarr could press the advantage, a tremendous crack echoed through the chamber. A fissure had split the dome overhead, running directly through the center of the constellation pattern. Through it, Alfheim's night sky was visible, something new forming in the darkness. Stars moving of their own accord, forming and breaking patterns in fluid succession.

The star-children's song faltered, their strength finally giving out. The tallest — the last to remain standing — locked eyes with Asvarr as he collapsed to his knees.

"The Gatekeeper comes," he whispered, the words barely audible over the groaning of the fractured dome. "The judgment approaches. Sing with us, Warden, or all is lost."

Then he fell, joining his brethren on the crystal floor, seven small forms leaking light into the growing pool of starlight tears.

The Wanderer's face contorted with fury and fear. He rounded on Asvarr, spear leveled at his heart. "What have you done? What have you called?"

Asvarr could only stare upward through the crack in the dome. The sky beyond was changing, patterns forming and dissolving with increasing speed. At the center, a vast eye was taking shape, formed from constellations both familiar and unknown. It blinked once, and Asvarr felt the attention of something ancient and unfathomable settle upon them all.

Upon Alfheim. Upon the Nine Realms. Upon the tenth cycle now approaching its crisis point.

And he knew, with bone-deep certainty, that they'd run out of time.

***

Yrsa's boots crunched through crystal-dusted snow as she climbed the final ridge leading to the Wanderer's stronghold. Her breath formed clouds that hung motionless in the unnaturally still air—a stillness enforced by the song that pulsed from the palace ahead. Each note rippled across the landscape, forcing alignment and symmetry onto a world built for wild growth.

The northern edge of Alfheim had always held a certain chill beauty, with its knife-edge mountains and aurora-lit skies. Now that beauty calcified with each passing moment, the mountains rearranging into perfect triangular formations, the aurora freezing into static, geometric patterns.

She tightened her grip on the twisted staff she'd carved from a memory-touched silver bough. Its surface rippled beneath her fingers, responding to her touch alone. Twenty years ago—or perhaps it had been a hundred; time blurred when you walked between cycles—she had plucked this branch from the original Yggdrasil, moments before its shattering.

Ahead, the palace dominated the horizon—a jagged crown of crystal spires built from solidified memory. Its walls shimmered with glimpses of history, a thousand thousand moments trapped in ice. Yrsa had watched the Wanderer build this place across nine cycles, each time altered slightly but always reaching toward the same form, like a wound reopening in familiar patterns.

A dissonant note broke the air, harsh enough to make Yrsa stagger. One of the star-children had fallen. She felt their pain ripple through the boundary between worlds, a scream in frequencies beyond mortal hearing. The urgency in her steps grew.

The palace gates stood unguarded—the Wanderer had grown arrogant in his certainty, or perhaps he simply couldn't spare attention from his working. Yrsa pressed her palm against the memory-ice, letting the surface read her. She had known the Wanderer before he was the Wanderer, before he was even the Ashfather. In some ways, she had known him before he existed.

The ice recognized something in her touch and parted.

Inside, the song hammered against her ears with physical force. It pulled at the threads of fate woven through her body, trying to straighten what was meant to curve, trying to calcify what was meant to flow. Her bones ached with each note.

She followed the sound through corridors that bent in ways mortal architecture shouldn't. The palace interior ignored conventional dimensions, with hallways opening into chambers that couldn't possibly fit within the external structure. The memory-ice walls trapped fragments of places and times—she glimpsed battles, coronations, deaths, births, all pressed like flowers between glass, preserved but lifeless.

As she drew closer to the central chamber, Yrsa felt the children's agony more keenly. Their unwilling song vibrated through her staff, making it hum with counter-harmonies. The Wanderer had forced them beyond endurance—a strain she felt in her own throat as if the notes were being torn from her as well.

She paused at the final turn, placing her palm against the wall and closing her eyes. Through the boundary between spaces, she saw them—Asvarr chained to the floor with star-metal bindings, his transformed flesh straining against them; the star-children arranged in a circle, four still standing but fading rapidly, three already collapsed; the Wanderer at the center, directing the forced harmony with expanding fractures in the dome above.

"Three days until convergence," Yrsa whispered to herself, "and all might still be lost."

She drew up her hood, straightened her spine, and stepped into the chamber.

Her entrance went unnoticed at first. The Wanderer's focus remained on the children, his back to the doorway as he pulled more power from their dwindling forms. Asvarr spotted her immediately, but control kept his expression neutral—a skill he'd learned quickly in his transformation.

"The pattern demands balance," she announced, her voice cutting across the song with startling clarity.

The Wanderer whirled, spear raised defensively. Recognition flickered across his features, followed by confusion, then cold calculation.

"Boundary-walker," he said, his voice resonating with subtle power. "Nine-times-passing. Have you come to witness the culmination of cycles?"

"I've come to witness an error repeated," Yrsa replied, stepping further into the chamber. The star-children's eyes tracked her movement, desperate hope flickering in their galaxy depths. "Nine times you've tried to force pattern into perfection, nine times you've failed."

"The tenth time breaks the cycle." The Wanderer gestured toward the dome, where constellations blazed with unnatural light. "I've learned from each failure. This time, the pattern will hold."

"This time you destroy what you claim to protect." Yrsa moved to the edge of the children's circle, her staff tapping against the crystal floor with each step. "Look at them. Look at what you're taking."

One of the remaining four star-children collapsed as she spoke, falling to the floor with barely a sound. The harmony fractured, then reconstructed itself with the three survivors—forced to carry additional burden.

"Necessary sacrifice," the Wanderer muttered, though doubt edged his voice. "The void-hunger must remain bound, and only perfect pattern can ensure it."

"The perfect is enemy to the good," Yrsa countered. "You create a cage so rigid it will shatter under its own structure."

The Wanderer's eyes narrowed. "What would you know of cages, boundary-walker? You who slips between worlds at will?"

"I know every cage holds the seed of its own breaking." Yrsa raised her staff, and the wood pulsed with green-blue light. "Every pattern contains the chaos that will undo it."

Asvarr watched their exchange, understanding dawning in his transformed eyes. "Yrsa," he called, voice cracking with frost, "what will you do?"

She didn't answer him directly, instead addressing the Wanderer once more: "You force these children to sing creation into stasis. Their song was meant to witness, not to rewrite."

"Their purpose is what I declare," the Wanderer repeated, the words bearing the weight of command. "As Odin's remaining will—"

"You are not Odin," Yrsa interrupted, her tone sharp as broken ice. "You are his regret given form, his fear of chaos incarnate. A fragment that never knew the whole."

The Wanderer's face contorted with fury. He raised his spear, aiming it at her heart. "You dare—"

"I dare because I remember," Yrsa said. "I remember the first song, before pattern existed. I remember when serpent and god spoke the same language."

The chamber trembled. Above, through the crack in the dome, the great eye blinked once more. The star-children's song wavered, notes falling out of alignment as the Wanderer's attention split.

Yrsa knew she had only moments.

"You cannot stop the song," the Wanderer warned, regaining his composure. "It's already reshaping Alfheim. Soon it will reach beyond, to all Nine Realms."

"I don't need to stop it," Yrsa said, her fingers moving to her throat. "I only need to change it."

Understanding struck the Wanderer too late. "No!" he bellowed, lunging forward.

But Yrsa had already begun. Her fingers dug into her own flesh, drawing something more fundamental than blood. From her throat, she pulled a glowing filament—silver-blue and impossibly thin, yet bearing the weight of worlds. It unspooled from within her like thread from a spindle, each inch drawn out with excruciating effort.

The star-children's song faltered as they witnessed what she held—a strand of fate itself, woven into utterance, speech made manifest.

Asvarr gasped. "Yrsa—your voice—"

She couldn't respond now. Already the words had gone from her, leaving only the thread between her fingers—her voice, which had never been merely sound but the physical manifestation of wyrd itself. As part-Norn, her speech had always contained the power to bend, to shape, to direct the flow of potential.

With one sharp tug, she pulled the last of it free.

The chamber exploded into chaos.

The voice-thread flared with blinding light as it entered the song's harmonic structure. Like oil poured on water, it spread outward in ripples of discordance, its nature incompatible with the forced harmony. The two magics—the ordered song and the fate-thread—fought against each other, sending shock waves through the crystal walls.

The star-children reacted immediately, their forced song dissolving into relief as the Wanderer's control shattered. The three who still stood swayed, then dropped to their knees, the final notes dying in their throats.

The silence that followed pressed against Yrsa's ears like a physical weight.

The Wanderer's howl of rage filled the void. He charged at her, spear raised, but the disruption had weakened him as well. Asvarr kicked out with transformed legs, catching the Wanderer's ankle and sending him sprawling. The chains binding Asvarr strained as bark-skin flexed with unexpected strength.

Above them all, the constellation patterns in the dome lost coherence, returning to natural formations. The eye that had been watching withdrew, though Yrsa felt its attention lingering at the edges of perception.

"What have you done?" the Wanderer demanded, struggling back to his feet. His voice held genuine fear now. "The pattern—it's destabilizing."

Yrsa could only stare back at him, her throat now hollow where voice had been. She felt strangely weightless, as if a burden she'd carried for eons had finally been set down. Her staff, no longer needed for support, clattered to the floor as her fingers went to the smooth skin of her neck.

Asvarr answered for her. "She's sacrificed what made her unique, to save what makes Alfheim alive." The frost that usually accompanied his words was gone, replaced by a clarity that rang through the chamber. "She's given up her power to shape fate with words."

The Wanderer glanced from Yrsa to the fallen star-children, doubt warring with determination on his face. The children lay motionless except for the faint rise and fall of their chests. Tears of starlight had dried on their cheeks, leaving silver tracks that gleamed in the fluctuating light.

"This changes nothing," he said finally, though his tone belied the confidence of his words. "The convergence still approaches. Three days remain until all anchors reach resonance. I will find another way."

Yrsa sank to her knees beside the nearest star-child, placing gentle fingers on its forehead. Even without words, she conveyed comfort through touch. The child's eyes fluttered open—galaxies swimming in silver—regarding her with profound gratitude.

The Wanderer backed toward a side passage, spear still raised defensively. "This isn't finished, boundary-walker. When the pattern unravels completely, when the void-hunger breaks free, remember your choice this day."

Then he was gone, footsteps echoing down the twisting corridors of his fortress.

Asvarr strained against his chains, bark-skin cracking with the effort. "Yrsa," he called, voice urgent. "The starlight bindings—I can't break them alone."

She nodded, understanding. Gathering what strength remained, she crawled to where he lay bound. The voice-thread had been her greatest power, but not her only knowledge. Fingers trembling, she traced runes over each chain-link—redefining their nature.

One by one, the bindings loosened, then dissolved into motes of light that drifted upward through the cracked dome.

Freed, Asvarr rose unsteadily to his feet. His transformed body moved awkwardly, as if the starlight stolen from the chains now weighed him down from within. He looked at Yrsa, eyes swimming with guilt and gratitude.

"You shouldn't have come," he said. "You shouldn't have sacrificed—"

She pressed fingers to his lips, silencing him. Without words, she made him understand: every choice has its price; every sacrifice, its purpose. She had walked nine cycles, seen nine failures. This time had to be different.

Together, they turned to the star-children. One by one, Asvarr gathered them in his arms—their bodies weightless despite their cosmic nature—and laid them gently in a circle around the chamber's center. Their forms had grown nearly transparent, internal stars visible through skin like candles behind paper. But they lived, and with rest, would recover.

A tremendous crack echoed through the palace. The memory-ice walls were fracturing, the forced pattern losing cohesion as natural growth reasserted itself throughout Alfheim.

"We need to leave," Asvarr said, looking up at the increasingly unstable dome. "This entire structure could collapse."

Yrsa nodded, then swayed as exhaustion claimed her. The sacrifice had taken more than voice; it had taken something fundamental to her nature. For nine cycles she had been speaker of fate, walker of boundaries. Now she was just—

Asvarr caught her before she fell, lifting her with careful strength. "I've got you," he said.

Her world narrowed to the sensation of being carried, of rough bark-skin against her cheek, of tired muscles surrendering to earned rest. Above, through the shattered dome, she glimpsed movement in the sky—stars falling, with purpose, as if the cosmos itself responded to the song's end.

As consciousness slipped away, Yrsa's last thought held neither regret nor fear, but quiet satisfaction. For the first time in nine cycles, something truly new had happened. The pattern had been neither reinforced nor broken but transformed.

In the silence where her voice had been, she felt the first stirrings of possibility.

CHAPTER 26

WHEN SKY TOUCHES ROOT

D awn broke over Alfheim's silver forests in fragments, light splintering through the cracks in the sky weave where Asvarr had torn his windows. The Wanderer's palace lay half-collapsed behind them, memory-ice walls dissolving into mist that rose in twisted columns toward the fractured dome. Asvarr trudged through ankle-deep frost, Yrsa's limp form cradled against his bark-skinned chest, the seven star-children floating in his wake like luminescent seeds on a breeze.

His transformed flesh ached from the Wanderer's bindings. Golden sap still leaked from the wounds where chains had bitten deep, freezing in the morning air into amber droplets that glittered along the furrows of his arms. The three anchors within him pulsed with separate rhythms—flame steady, memory erratic, starlight quick and sharp—each carrying its own pain, its own awareness.

A sheltered clearing opened before them, ringed by silver trees whose branches curved inward to form a natural canopy. Asvarr laid Yrsa gently on a bed of frost-silvered moss. Her breathing came slow but steady, face relaxed in exhaustion. The hollow at the base of her throat where she'd pulled the glowing thread still showed a faint luminescence beneath her skin, as if some echo of her voice remained trapped within.

"Rest here," Asvarr said, the words forming delicate frost crystals that shattered in the air. "I'll stand watch."

The star-children settled around them in a protective circle, their transparent forms barely substantial in the dawn light. The tallest—the one who had spoken of the Gatekeeper—rested his weightless hand on Yrsa's forehead. A gesture of gratitude, of recognition. They all understood what she had given up to save them.

The forest lay unnaturally still. The Wanderer's song had reached even here before Yrsa shattered it, forcing patterns onto wild growth. Now the trees and undergrowth existed in a state of arrested transformation, half-calcified into geometric forms, half-returning to natural chaos. Branches hung at precise right angles before curving into organic spirals. Leaves arranged themselves in perfect symmetry on one side, wild disarray on the other. The world caught between competing truths.

Asvarr pressed his palm against the crystal-veined bark of his chest where the Grímmark lay hidden beneath layers of transformation. Beneath it, the wooden sigil Brynja had sewn into his flesh continued its slow burn, transmitting sensations he couldn't fully interpret. Through it, he felt the cosmic serpents far beyond the sky-weave, their vast forms watching, waiting. The void-hunger's attention remained fixed on him, drawn by the anchors he carried.

Above, the twin moons lingered at the horizon's edge, reluctant to surrender to day. Through the windows he had torn in the sky, stars remained visible despite the growing light—including constellations that should have set hours ago.

Something had changed. The natural order bent around them like light through water.

"Three days until convergence," Asvarr muttered to himself. "Three days until all anchors reach resonance."

The tallest star-child turned toward him, galaxy eyes reflecting impossible depth. "The Gatekeeper watches," he said, his bell-like voice barely stronger than a whisper. "Judges the tenth cycle against the nine that came before."

"And what does it see?" Asvarr asked.

The child's gaze drifted upward, through the canopy to the torn sky beyond. "Possibility. For the first time, possibility."

A falling star streaked overhead—a blazing tear through the fabric of reality, trailing fragments of light like spilled quicksilver. It plummeted toward the clearing with deliberate purpose, as if drawn by the anchors within Asvarr's transformed flesh.

Instinctively, he raised his hands to shield Yrsa and the children. The starforged chain around his wrist—the links representing memory, purpose, connection, and grief—flared with protective light. But the falling star didn't strike them. Instead, it pulled up short mere feet above the clearing's center, suspending itself in midair like a held breath.

The star pulsed once, twice, three times—matching the rhythm of the anchors within Asvarr. Silver-white radiance rippled outward in expanding rings, illuminating the clearing with light that cast no shadows. The star-children stirred, their galaxy eyes widening with recognition.

"Sky meets root," the tallest whispered. "The weave repatterns itself."

The ground beneath the hovering star trembled. Something moved in the earth—a deliberate stirring, like a sleeper turning beneath blankets. A root-tendril thicker than Asvarr's arm erupted from the soil, spiraling upward with uncanny precision. Golden sap beaded along its surface, catching the starlight and magnifying it. The tendril continued growing, twisting toward the suspended star with yearning intensity.

Asvarr felt every anchored aspect within him surge in response. Flame roared, memory pulsed, starlight sang—all straining toward what was happening before him. The Grímmark burned beneath his transformed skin, and through it, the hidden sigil Brynja had placed flared with heat that threatened to consume him from within.

"What's happening?" he asked, though no one remained to answer. The star-children had drawn back, their transparent forms huddled protectively around Yrsa's sleeping body.

The root-tendril touched the star.

***

Light exploded outward, blinding in its intensity. Asvarr threw his arm across his eyes, bark-skin barely filtering the radiance. Through the sensory overload came pure sensation—the anchors within him resonating with whatever had just formed from that impossible union.

When his vision cleared, the world had changed.

Where the star and root had met, a new growth stood—neither fully stellar nor fully arboreal but some fusion of both natures. It resembled a branch of Yggdrasil in its general form, but transposed into a higher dimension. Its surface rippled with patterns of starlight flowing beneath bark that glowed from within, its edges shifting between solid matter and luminous energy. It extended upward and outward simultaneously, forming a spiral structure that somehow connected points in space that should have been separated by vast distances.

Through the anchors, Asvarr sensed awareness awakening within it. Something vibrant and immediate. Intelligence forming from the union of cosmic memory and living vitality. The first truly sentient branch of Yggdrasil since the Shattering.

The branch expanded with frightening speed, sending tendrils spiraling through the clearing. They wrapped around trees, burrowed into earth, reached toward sky—connecting, forming a network that bridged substantial reality with something beyond physical form.

One tendril approached Asvarr, hovering before him like a serpent tasting the air. He stood his ground, feeling the anchors within him surge in recognition. This was something new, something the pattern had never produced before. Integration of both chaos and order.

The tendril touched his transformed chest, directly over the Grímmark.

Connection roared through him. For a single, terrifying moment, Asvarr's consciousness expanded beyond his physical form. He perceived the Root network spanning all Nine Realms simultaneously—feeling the hollow void where Yggdrasil had been torn away, the scattered fragments struggling to reconnect, the golden threads of sap binding what remained. He sensed the nine anchor points—five for Wardens, four embedded in the Tree's structure—and understood their dual purpose of binding the void-hunger while maintaining the cosmic deception.

Most overwhelming, he glimpsed the sentience forming within this new branch—an intelligence born from the fusion of star and root, carrying memories from before the first forming while creating something that had never existed before.

The tendril withdrew, leaving Asvarr gasping. His knees buckled, sending him sprawling onto the frost-covered ground. The star-children drifted closer, curious and cautious in equal measure.

"What is it?" he asked them, struggling back to his feet. "What has formed here?"

The tallest child tilted his head, galaxy eyes reflecting the branch's spiraling light. "The third path made manifest," he replied. "Neither restoration nor destruction, but transformation. The pattern transforms itself."

The branch continued growing, its structure becoming increasingly complex. Smaller offshoots sprouted from the main spiral, each forming its own geometric pattern that somehow connected to others across impossible distances. The entire formation hummed with energy that vibrated through the air, through the ground, through Asvarr's transformed body.

More stars fell from the torn sky, drawn by what was happening below. Descending with purpose, arranging themselves around the branch in a constellation that had never existed before. The star-children floated upward to meet them, their forms regaining solidity as they drew strength from the stellar presence.

"The Gatekeeper approves," the tallest said, his voice stronger now. "This was not foreseen in nine cycles past."

Asvarr stepped closer to the branch, drawn by the resonance between it and the anchors he carried. The starforged chain around his wrist grew warm against his skin, its links pulsing with answering light. The branch seemed to sense his approach, tendrils shifting to create an opening in its spiral structure—an invitation.

"What does it want from me?" Asvarr asked.

"Recognition," a new voice answered.

Yrsa had awakened. She knelt on the moss where he had placed her, one hand pressed against her throat where voice had been. Her face showed wonder mingled with exhaustion. Though her vocal cords produced no sound, her lips formed words that Asvarr somehow understood.

It seeks acknowledgment, she mouthed. *Partnership. The third path requires both parties to walk it willingly.*

The branch's spiral structure shifted again, creating patterns that mimicked speech through light and shadow. Asvarr realized it was attempting to communicate directly, lacking conventional means of expression.

He closed his eyes, focusing on the anchors within him. If he could feel the branch through them, perhaps the reverse was also possible. He concentrated on opening himself to connect—the difference that had defined his transformation since binding the first anchor.

The connection snapped into place with jarring suddenness. The branch's awareness flowed into his mind—as pure concept, untranslated understanding. It carried star-memory spanning billions of years alongside root-memory of every living thing that had ever drawn nourishment from earth. The combination created perspective beyond mortal comprehension, yet somehow filtered through a lens new enough to still recognize individuality.

I see you, Fragment-Bearer, came the thought, carried on currents of starlight and sap. *Walker-of-Three-Roads. I see what you carry.*

"And what am I?" Asvarr asked, uncertain whether he spoke aloud or merely thought the question.

Possibility, came the answer. *As am I. We are what was not meant to be, yet now exists. Neither what was intended, nor what was feared, but something outside the pattern's prediction.*

"The third path," Asvarr whispered.

Yes. Transformation rather than restoration or destruction. Neither order nor chaos but their integration.

The branch's tendrils extended further, connecting to the silver trees around the clearing. Where they touched, the half-calcified forms shifted—not reverting to pure natural chaos, nor becoming more rigidly ordered, but finding a new equilibrium between states. Structure with flexibility. Pattern with possibility.

Asvarr felt the anchors within him respond, resonating with this new mode of existence. For the first time since binding them, the three rhythms synchronized briefly, pulsing as one before returning to their distinctive patterns.

"The Wanderer will return," Asvarr said. "He's spent nine cycles trying to impose perfect order, to cage the void-hunger behind unbreakable pattern. He won't accept transformation."

The fragment fears what it cannot control, the branch replied. *Yet the whole knew better. The All-Father understood balance before his sundering.*

The mention of Odin sent ice through Asvarr's veins. "You know of the gods?"

I am star and root both. I remember their forming, their striving, their withdrawal. I remember what came before them, and what lies beyond.

More stars continued to fall, circling the branch with increasing complexity. The constellation they formed resembled nothing Asvarr had seen in any sky chart—a pattern both ancient and new, reflecting stellar positions from before the gods' manipulation while incorporating new relationships.

The branch's central spiral suddenly extended upward with explosive force, shooting toward the torn sky like a spear thrust. It pierced the fabric of the sky-weave, widening one of Asvarr's windows into a permanent aperture. Through this opening poured silver-gold light from beyond, illuminating the spiraling structure with impossible colors.

The star-children gasped in unison, their galaxy eyes reflecting wonder and recognition.

"The Gatekeeper acknowledges," the tallest said. "The judgment continues, but favor is shown."

Asvarr felt something shift in the cosmic balance. Through the anchors, he sensed the void-hunger's attention sharpen, focusing with laser intensity on what had just occurred. For nine cycles, the pattern had remained mostly intact, with breakings and restorations that ultimately changed little. Now something truly new had entered existence—the first in eons.

***

The branch's tendrils reached toward him again, this time extending toward his hand rather than his chest. The invitation was clear.

"What happens if I accept?" Asvarr asked.

Partnership, came the response. *Neither dominance nor submission. Neither consumption nor containment. We walk the third path together.*

Yrsa moved to his side, placing her hand on his bark-skinned arm. Her lips formed words without sound: *Three days until convergence. All anchors will reach resonance. Reality becomes malleable. Choice must be made.*

The star-children drifted into a circle around them, their forms more substantial now, having drawn strength from the fallen stars. They watched with galaxy eyes that had witnessed nine cycles of failure, waiting to see if the tenth would truly break the pattern.

Asvarr looked at the spiraling branch, its structure bridging worlds, its awareness born from the union of cosmic memory and living vitality. He felt the anchors within him—fragments of the void-hunger transformed into binding—and knew their purpose more clearly than ever before. To transform., and eventually to reunite in new configuration.

The starforged chain around his wrist grew warm against his skin. Four links—memory, purpose, connection, grief—each representing an aspect of his identity he'd fought to maintain through transformation. If he accepted this partnership, how much more would change? How much of Asvarr would remain when the last anchor was bound?

The branch waited, tendrils suspended in the air before him. Through their connection, he felt patience. It would not force choice, only offer possibility.

Behind them, the Wanderer's palace continued to dissolve, memory-ice returning to the unstructured potential from which it had been formed. Ahead, through the branch-widened window in the sky, the cosmos stretched infinite and waiting.

Three days until convergence. Three days until all anchors would reach their peak resonance, making reality itself malleable. Three days to determine which vision would shape the tenth cycle—the Wanderer's rigid order, the void-hunger's formless chaos, or something that had never existed before.

***

Asvarr reached out his transformed hand, bark-skin fingers extended toward the waiting tendrils.

Asvarr's bark-skinned fingertips brushed against the luminous tendrils of the sentient branch. Contact sparked memories of snow-laden pines, of frost-rimed iron, of blood mixing with sap on midwinter nights when his father had taken him hunting beneath Yggdrasil's fallen fragments. These weren't just images but full sensory recollections—the weight of furs on his shoulders, the sting of cold air in his lungs, the iron tang of freshly spilled blood on snow.

The tendrils wrapped gently around his wrist, just above the starforged chain with its four protective links. The branch's structure pulsed with internal light, sap and starfire mingling beneath a surface that existed somewhere between solid matter and pure energy. Through the anchors within his chest, Asvarr felt the new consciousness exploring the connection from its side—curious, careful, respectful of boundaries even as it sought deeper understanding.

"What are you?" Asvarr asked, frost crystallizing from his breath despite the warming morning air.

The branch's spiraling form shifted, its structure rearranging to better focus on him. The star-children drew closer, their galaxy eyes wide with wonder. Even Yrsa, weakened from her sacrifice, lifted her head to witness what would come next.

"My son."

The voice shook Asvarr to his core—deep, resonant, with the subtly rolling cadence of his father's accent from the northern fjords. It wasn't his father—he knew that immediately—but the branch had reached into his memories to find the voice he would trust most deeply, the voice that would bypass his defenses and speak directly to his heart.

"You're not my father," Asvarr said, a cold knot forming in his chest. "He died during the Breaking."

"No, I am not." The branch's voice maintained his father's timber but shed some of its mannered inflections. "I accessed your memory to find a sound you would inherently trust. Your mind supplied your father's voice—the man who first taught you of Yggdrasil, who showed you how to track the Root threads beneath frost, who died protecting what he loved."

The branch's tendrils loosened around Asvarr's wrist, giving him space to withdraw if he chose. The gesture carried meaning beyond words—a demonstration of respect for boundaries, for choice.

"What should I call you?" Asvarr asked, keeping his hand where it was.

The spiraling structure pulsed thoughtfully. "Names define and limit. I am new—the first of my kind. Perhaps 'Rootstar' would serve for now, though I am more than the sum of my components."

"Rootstar," Asvarr repeated, tasting the name. The frost that formed with his words took on crystalline patterns matching the branch's spiral structure. "You're the first truly sentient branch of Yggdrasil since the Shattering."

"I am the first of what could be," Rootstar replied. "Neither restoration nor destruction, but evolution. The pattern transforms itself rather than merely breaking or mending. I represent possibility beyond the nine cycles of repetition."

Asvarr thought of the Wanderer, of his obsession with perfect order, of nine failed attempts to cage the void-hunger behind unbreakable structure. "The Ashfather won't accept transformation. He seeks rigid pattern, absolute control."

"The fragment fears what it cannot predict." Rootstar's tendrils shifted, creating shadow-patterns that danced across the clearing. "Odin's remnant remembers the fear but not the wisdom that balanced it. Before his sundering, the All-Father understood necessity of both order and chaos, structure and freedom."

The mention of Odin triggered something in the Grímmark beneath Asvarr's transformed skin. He felt the anchors within him pulse in response—flame, memory, and starlight each straining toward Rootstar with distinct yearning. Through them, he sensed the void-hunger's distant awareness focusing sharply on what was transpiring in this small clearing in Alfheim.

"The convergence approaches," Asvarr said. "Three days until all anchors reach resonance. Reality becomes malleable. Choice must be made."

"Yes." Rootstar's voice deepened, his father's tones enriched with something older and vaster. "In that moment, the possibility I represent could spread across all Nine Realms—or be extinguished before it truly exists."

The star-children drifted into a loose circle around them, their forms glowing brighter as they absorbed energy from the growing daylight. The tallest spoke, bell-like voice carrying a tremor of excitement.

"The Gatekeeper watches with interest. Nine cycles it has witnessed failure. This tenth cycle brings true innovation."

Yrsa moved to Asvarr's side, her face pale but determined. She pointed toward Rootstar, then to Asvarr, then drew her fingers together—merger, partnership, cooperation.

"You're suggesting we work together," Asvarr said to her, then turned back to Rootstar. "That I help spread this transformation."

"More than that," Rootstar said. "I offer partnership. Equal participation in determining Yggdrasil's future."

The branch's spiraling structure suddenly expanded, branches extending toward the torn sky above. Through these new apertures poured visions that manifested in the clearing around them—full sensory experiences that enveloped Asvarr in potential futures.

He stood in a restored Midgard, the World Tree risen anew—but not as it had been. This Yggdrasil incorporated aspects of both structure and freedom, its branches forming patterns that constantly evolved while maintaining core stability. Beneath it walked people transformed by its influence, carrying small fragments of awareness within themselves, connected to the greater whole without losing individuality.

The vision shifted, and he witnessed the void between realms—no longer empty nothingness but vibrant potential, where cosmic serpents swam through creative chaos without consuming existence. The prison had become a garden, the cage transformed into a framework for infinite growth.

Another shift showed him the Nine Realms reconnected—but no longer stacked in rigid hierarchy. They interwove, overlapped, shared boundaries that remained distinct without enforced separation. Gods walked among mortals as partners in continuous creation.

The visions faded, leaving Asvarr breathless. The anchors within him resonated with what he'd seen—possibilities beyond the binary choice of perfect pattern or formless chaos.

"You're offering a third path," he said. "Transformation rather than restoration or destruction."

"I am the third path made manifest," Rootstar replied. "But I cannot walk it alone. The Wanderer seeks to force Alfheim back into rigid pattern. The void-hunger would dissolve all boundaries into primordial soup. Only together can we forge something that preserves the best of both while transcending their limitations."

The tendrils extended toward Asvarr again, this time reaching for his transformed chest where the Grímmark lay hidden beneath layers of bark-skin and crystalline veins.

"I can help free you from the bindings the Wanderer placed on you," Rootstar said. "I can teach you to use the anchors you carry as they were truly meant to be used—as foundations for new growth. But I require acknowledgment as equal participant in determining Yggdrasil's future."

Asvarr hesitated, years of wariness making him cautious despite everything he'd witnessed. "What exactly are you asking of me?"

"Recognition," Rootstar said simply. "Partnership. I am not what was, but what could be. Neither Root nor Star but both, neither memory nor potential but their integration."

The branch's structure rippled with internal light, sap and starfire flowing in mesmerizing patterns. The tendrils near Asvarr's chest pulsed with gentle invitation.

"If I accept," Asvarr asked, "how much of me remains? I've fought to maintain my humanity through each binding. The starforged chain preserves aspects of my identity, but each transformation takes something from me."

"Transformation always requires sacrifice," Rootstar acknowledged. "But not surrender. What you give need not be destroyed, only evolved. The flame anchor demanded dominance, the memory anchor required recognition, the starlight anchor insisted on integration. I ask for partnership—mutual transformation where both parties retain their core essence while becoming more together than they could be apart."

A memory surfaced in Asvarr's mind—Brynja's warning before she sewn the wooden sigil into his flesh. She had glimpsed this moment through the Silent Choir's visions, had seen him standing before a choice that would determine the nature of reality itself.

The star-children drifted closer, their galaxy eyes reflecting the spiraling structure of Rootstar. The tallest spoke again, his voice stronger than before.

"Nine cycles we have witnessed failure. Nine times the pattern has broken, nine times it has been partially restored, never evolving beyond its original configuration. This tenth cycle offers true choice."

Yrsa placed her hand on Asvarr's arm, her throat still hollow where voice had been. Her eyes carried centuries of accumulated wisdom, the weight of nine witnessed failures. She nodded once, decisively.

Asvarr looked up through the torn sky-weave to the cosmos beyond. Through his connection to the anchors, he sensed the void-hunger watching, the cosmic serpents waiting, the Gatekeeper judging. Three days until convergence, when all anchors would reach peak resonance and reality itself would become malleable.

Three days to determine which vision would shape the tenth cycle.

"Partnership," Asvarr said finally. "True cooperation."

"Yes." Relief and joy mingled in Rootstar's borrowed voice. "I am not your father, but I honor what he taught you—that strength comes from protecting connection, not enforcing isolation."

The tendrils touched Asvarr's chest, directly over the Grímmark. This time the connection formed without resistance, the anchors within him responding with harmonious recognition rather than strained subjugation. The sensation wasn't the wrenching pain he'd experienced with previous bindings but a gentle realignment, like bones settling into proper position after long dislocation.

Knowledge flowed between them—Asvarr's understanding of humanity, of loss, of hope blending with Rootstar's cosmic perspective, its memory spanning eons, its vision encompassing possibilities beyond mortal imagination. The exchange left both changed, both enriched, neither consumed by the other.

Power surged through Asvarr as limitations fell away. The starlight chains that had lingered in his flesh since the Wanderer's binding dissolved completely, their energy repurposed as connections rather than constraints. He felt the anchors within him synchronize—flame, memory, and starlight finding harmony without losing their distinctive natures.

Most significantly, he sensed the true purpose of the anchors for the first time—not merely to bind the void-hunger, but eventually to transform it. Not to permanently separate chaos from order, but to create a framework where both could flourish without destroying each other.

The star-children gasped in unison as Asvarr's transformation manifested physically. The bark-skin covering his form gained luminous veins that mirrored Rootstar's patterns. The crystalline structures on his face rearranged into spiraling formations that bridged multiple states of being. His eyes, once shifting between mortal brown and sap-gold, now incorporated points of starlight—galaxies swimming in amber depths.

"The anchors were never meant to be permanent cages," Rootstar explained, its voice resonating directly in Asvarr's mind now that they shared deeper connection. "They were meant to evolve. To transform both prisoner and prison until the distinction between them dissolved into new synthesis."

Through their link, Asvarr glimpsed the original binding—nine anchors positioned to contain the void-hunger's expansive nature. Five carried by Wardens, four embedded in Yggdrasil's structure. To channel the chaos, to give formless potential the boundaries needed for constructive creation rather than endless consumption.

"The Wanderer never understood this," Asvarr realized. "He saw only the need for perfect containment, for absolute control."

"He remembers Odin's fear but not his wisdom," Rootstar confirmed. "The All-Father knew balance required both forces in continuous dialogue."

A thunderous crack split the morning air. Above them, the sky-weave fractured further, new tears forming where Rootstar's branches had punched through. Through these openings poured pure memory—cosmic history unfiltered by divine censorship. It manifested as sheets of luminous energy that fell toward Alfheim like liquid light.

The forest around them transformed where this memory-light touched. Trees shifted form, incorporating stellar patterns into their bark and branches. The ground itself rippled, structures from ancient cosmic history briefly visible beneath the surface before settling into new configurations that bridged earthly matter with celestial energy.

"The transformation begins," Rootstar said, wonder and concern mingling in its borrowed voice. "Sooner than expected. The damage to Alfheim's sky-weave cannot be repaired."

The star-children looked upward, their galaxy eyes reflecting the cascade of memory-light. "The Firmament falls," the tallest whispered. "True cosmic memory returns to Alfheim uncensored."

Asvarr felt the shift through his connection to the anchors—the rigid boundary between realms growing thin, the carefully maintained separation between cosmic truth and lived reality dissolving. Through the star anchor especially, he sensed the sky-weave unraveling across all Alfheim, not just where he had torn his windows.

"The Wanderer's ritual did more damage than we realized," he said. "When Yrsa disrupted the song, it didn't just stop the calcification—it accelerated the sky's dissolution."

Yrsa nodded grimly, her hand moving to her hollow throat. She had given her voice to prevent one catastrophe, only to hasten another.

"Not catastrophe," Rootstar corrected, reading Asvarr's thoughts through their connection. "Transformation. Painful, yes. Disruptive, certainly. But necessary for true evolution."

More memory-light poured through the widening gaps in the sky, falling in sheets that illuminated the forest with impossible colors. In the distance, cries of confusion and wonder rose from elven settlements as Alfheim's inhabitants witnessed the dissolution of a cosmic deception maintained since the first creation.

"They're not ready," Asvarr said, thinking of the people who would face these revelations without preparation, without context. "This is too much, too fast."

"Change rarely comes at convenient pace," Rootstar replied. "But we can help guide it. The partnership we've formed shows the way forward—integration rather than rejection, transformation rather than destruction."

The anchor fragments within Asvarr pulsed in agreement. For the first time since binding them, he felt them working with his will rather than against it. The flame preserved what mattered, the memory connected disparate elements, the starlight transformed rigid structures into flexible frameworks.

Together with Rootstar, he reached toward the falling memory-light, channeling it through their combined consciousness. They couldn't stop the flow—the sky-weave had passed the point of repair—but they could filter it, organize it, make it comprehensible to minds not prepared for raw cosmic truth.

The starforged chain around Asvarr's wrist glowed with protective power, its four links—memory, purpose, connection, grief—serving as touchstones that kept him grounded in his humanity despite the vast awareness flowing through him. Through their partnership, Rootstar gained appreciation for individual experience, for the value of personal perspective amid cosmic scale.

Above them, the sky continued to unravel, stars falling as entire constellations, sheets of reality cascading toward Alfheim with increasing speed.

"The convergence comes early," Rootstar said, urgency edging its voice. "We must be ready."

"Ready for what?" Asvarr asked, though he felt the answer forming already through their connection.

"For choice," Rootstar replied. "For the moment when all anchors reach resonance and reality becomes malleable. For the void-hunger's testing of its bonds, and the Wanderer's final attempt to impose perfect order."

Through their link, Asvarr saw the cosmic forces aligning—the Gatekeeper's judgment approaching, the serpent forms pressing closer against thinning barriers, the void-hunger's awareness focusing with laser precision on the anchors he carried.

Three days had become hours. The convergence approached, accelerated by Rootstar's creation and the sky-weave's dissolution. Soon all Nine Realms would feel the effects as cosmic memory rushed in through the gaps in reality's fabric.

The choice Asvarr had prepared for—the moment when the tenth cycle would either repeat ancient failure or forge something truly new—had arrived sooner than anyone expected.

And Alfheim burned beneath a rain of falling stars.

CHAPTER 27

SERPENT SKY BURNS

The sky split open with a sound like the world breaking. Asvarr staggered beneath the onslaught of raw cosmic power as a fissure tore across Alfheim's celestial dome—a catastrophic unraveling. The delicate tapestry woven by the gods across nine cycles ripped apart, sending waves of silver-gold energy cascading downward. This was no gentle rain of starlight; this was fundamental truth crashing through millennia of divine deception.

"The firmament falls," Rootstar said, its voice—borrowed from Asvarr's father but increasingly taking on its own timber—layered with wonder and dread. "The sky-weave cannot hold against memory's weight."

Asvarr raised his hand toward the collapsing heavens. The crystalline formations across his face pulsed with answering light, sending ripples of frost-fire down his neck and chest. Through his transformed flesh, he perceived dimensions beyond mortal understanding—the celestial boundary that had concealed what lay beyond Alfheim wasn't merely breaking but dissolving back into its constituent parts.

"What have we done?" he whispered, watching as entire constellations detached from their moorings and plummeted earthward.

They'd taken refuge in a silver-bark grove after his partnership with Rootstar had accelerated the sky-weave's dissolution. The star-children huddled together nearby, their luminescent faces upturned in fearful recognition. The youngest wept silently, tears of starlight rolling down his cheeks to pool at his feet.

"Not destruction." Rootstar's tendrils wrapped more securely around Asvarr's wrist, intertwining with the starforged chain. "Transformation. Nine cycles of deception unmade in a single night."

***

The ground trembled as the first sheet of cosmic reality struck—an entire segment of sky, glittering with impossible colors and ancient memory. It crashed into a distant hillside, sending shockwaves through the earth. Where it fell, the landscape warped and shifted. Trees stretched toward the fractured sky, their silver bark transmuting into spiraling patterns that mirrored the constellations above. The very stone beneath their feet groaned with remembrance.

Yrsa stood silently beside him, her expression fierce despite her muteness. She tugged urgently at his sleeve, gesturing toward the palace spires of Ljósalvheim visible through the trees. The elven capital shimmered under the assault of falling memory, its crystal towers refracting fragments of cosmic history that cascaded through the gaps in the sky-weave.

"We can't reach it in time," Asvarr said, understanding her intent. "The paths between here and the city shift with each collapse."

She formed words with her lips, and somehow—whether through their shared experience or his enhanced perception—he understood her meaning: *They deserve warning*.

"The warning comes from the sky itself," Rootstar countered, its tendril-branches swaying with growing agitation. "The veil thins to nothing. What was hidden becomes revealed."

Another vast segment of the sky-weave collapsed with a sound like glass being crushed beneath a giant's heel. This time, the fallen constellation struck closer—a glittering lattice of memory-light that splashed across the grove's edge, transforming everything it touched. Where the light washed over soil, strange symbols emerged—neither runes nor writing but something older, the original language of pattern itself.

Asvarr flinched as tendrils of memory-light brushed against his transformed flesh. Instead of pain, he felt recognition—his three bound anchors responding to the primordial energy. Through his connection with Rootstar, he glimpsed what the fallen stars contained: visions of the cosmos before structure, when serpentine entities swam through formless void. The beginning of all things.

"Flee or witness," Rootstar urged, its voice deepening with each word. "There is no middle path when the firmament burns."

The tallest star-child approached, his silver hair floating weightlessly around his face. "We must observe," he said, bell-like voice resolute despite his obvious fear. "This is why we were created—to bear witness to what comes."

Asvarr stood at the crossroads of decision, the weight of three anchors pulsing beneath his transformed skin. Around them, reality itself began to fray—from an excess of truth. Too much cosmic memory crashing into a realm unprepared to contain it.

"Witness, then," he decided, squeezing Yrsa's hand in reassurance. "But we stand ready to move when the witnessing becomes perilous."

She nodded grimly, her eyes reflecting the cascading lights as another section of sky collapsed.

They walked toward the edge of a crystal outcropping that offered a sweeping view of the valley below. With each step, the ground beneath them shifted subtly—harder then softer, warm then cool, as if unable to decide on its fundamental properties. Rootstar's tendrils spread before them, creating a stabilizing network that allowed safer passage across the increasingly unstable terrain.

From this vantage point, Asvarr could see the full scope of Alfheim's transformation. The elven realm, once defined by its ordered beauty and silver harmony, now fractured into a patchwork of competing realities. Where one sheet of cosmic memory had fallen, ancient swamplands bubbled with primordial life, massive ziggurat-like structures half-submerged in the muck. Adjacent to this stood a pristine forest of impossibly tall trees with bark that shifted color with each passing breeze, creatures of light and shadow flitting between their branches.

"The first memories," Rootstar whispered, its tendrils trembling with recognition. "Before the gods, before the serpents, when reality itself was newborn."

The star-children spread out along the ridge, each choosing a different section of the transforming landscape to observe. Their bodies glowed brighter with each moment, absorbing and preserving the cosmic memories as they were meant to do.

"Look," Asvarr breathed, pointing toward a massive sheet of falling sky that descended with uncanny slowness.

Unlike the others, this segment of the sky-weave remained intact as it fell, a perfect square of midnight blue studded with constellations unknown to any living astronomer. It touched down in the center of a meadow, then unfolded like a living tapestry to reveal a scene from before time:

Three massive figures stood around a loom woven of light and darkness. Their faces shifted constantly—male to female to something beyond gender—as their hands moved with impossible precision, threading strands of raw potential into the first patterns of existence. A fourth figure watched from the shadows, its serpentine form coiled in readiness, neither helping nor hindering but observing with ancient patience.

"The first gods," Rootstar whispered, "and the witness-serpent who predated them."

Asvarr felt the truth of this vision resonating with the three anchors he carried. The flame-anchor's steady pulse quickened, while the memory-anchor loosened its grip on his consciousness, allowing a flood of understanding beyond words. The starlight-anchor blazed within, casting his shadow in three directions simultaneously.

Across Alfheim, the elven population reacted to these revelations with collective shock. From their vantage point, Asvarr watched as some fell to their knees, overwhelmed by visions their minds couldn't process. Others stood transfixed, their forms beginning to shimmer and change as cosmic understanding rewrote their very essence. A small group of elders had formed a circle in a distant clearing, their bodies dissolving into pure thought as they embraced transcendence rather than cling to physical form.

"They weren't prepared," Asvarr said, guilt twisting in his chest despite his conviction that the sky-weave's dissolution had been necessary.

"None are truly prepared for origin-truth," Rootstar replied, its voice solemn. "Even those who lived through the first days feared to remember them clearly."

Another section of sky collapsed, this one striking the crystal palace at Alfheim's heart. The structure didn't shatter but transformed, its precisely angled towers melting and reforming into organic spirals that reached toward the broken firmament like supplicating hands. Within its walls, Asvarr glimpsed hundreds of elves—some frantically trying to escape, others standing in statuesque acceptance of the inevitable change.

"The Council chambers," Yrsa mouthed silently, pointing to a dome of pure crystal that now pulsed with internal light.

The star-children's luminescence intensified as they absorbed more of the cascading memories. The tallest's skin had become almost transparent, cosmic patterns visible beneath its surface like charts of creation itself.

"The weaving of the first Tree," the child announced, voice resonating with multiple harmonics. "Before it was Yggdrasil, before it connected Nine Realms—when it grew as boundary between formlessness and pattern."

On cue, another sheet of fallen sky splashed across the far mountains, and the vision spread like wildfire: a sapling no larger than a child's finger, planted in soil that had never before known growth. Around it swirled forces of such magnitude that reality bent in their wake—on one side, serpentine entities of pure potential; on the other, geometric beings of perfect order. The sapling absorbed both influences, growing in a pattern that honored chaos within structure, freedom within form.

"The binding was mutual," Rootstar murmured, tendrils quivering with recognition. "Cooperation—at first."

Before Asvarr could respond, a crimson glow suffused the fractured sky above. Where the firmament had broken completely, revealing the void beyond, something vast moved with ponderous grace—scales reflecting light that had never touched Alfheim before, eyes containing galaxies unknown to any mortal chart.

"The cosmic serpents return," Rootstar said, voice tinged with awe. "After nine cycles of binding, they swim once more in sight of mortal realms."

The tallest star-child pointed eastward, toward a mountain now transformed into liquid crystal that flowed upward instead of down. "The binding ritual," he announced. "When cooperation became constraint."

The vision spread across the transformed peak: nine figures—neither fully divine nor entirely mortal—stood in a complex pattern, their bodies containing fragments of both geometric precision and serpentine fluidity. They worked in concert to reshape reality itself, creating boundaries where none had existed before. From the center of their formation arose the first true incarnation of Yggdrasil—no longer a sapling but a cosmic structure spanning countless dimensions.

Simultaneously, a net of golden light captured one of the greatest serpentine entities—through a pact sealed with mingled blood and starlight. Nine pieces of its essence separated willingly, transforming into the anchors that Asvarr now sought to gather. The binding was completed with oaths in a language that caused the very air to shiver with their weight.

"Willing sacrifice," Asvarr whispered, understanding flooding through him. "The void-hunger wasn't trapped against its will."

"The first time," Rootstar agreed. "The beginning was harmony—the division came later."

More of the sky collapsed in rapid succession, each segment bringing another revelation crashing into Alfheim's unprepared landscape. Valleys transformed into crystal seas; mountains melted into perfect symmetrical cones; forests turned to gardens of memory where each plant contained a fragment of cosmic history.

The elves of Alfheim reacted with increasing extremes. Some fled toward the boundaries between realms, seeking escape from revelations too profound to bear. Others embraced the change completely—Asvarr watched as a group of young elves willingly dissolved their physical forms, their consciousness merging with the memory-light that now saturated the air. Most simply wandered in shock, their fundamental understanding of reality shattered beyond recovery.

"They need guidance," Asvarr said, the weight of responsibility pressing down on him as heavily as the three anchors he carried. "Without direction, they'll lose themselves entirely."

Yrsa tugged at his sleeve again, her expression urgent. She pointed toward a massive sheet of collapsing sky that headed directly for their position, its surface rippling with images too dense to comprehend.

"Move!" Asvarr commanded, pulling her back from the ridge as Rootstar's tendrils whipped around them in protective formation.

The memory-sheet struck with the force of a physical blow, washing over their sanctuary in a tide of cosmic revelation. Asvarr staggered as visions flooded his transformed senses—the rise and fall of civilizations beyond count, the birth of stars and death of galaxies, the slow dance of creation and destruction playing out across eternity.

When his sight cleared, the silver grove had vanished. In its place stood a pattern of standing stones arranged in configurations that defied conventional geometry, each surface inscribed with the history of a different cosmic age. The star-children had changed as well—their luminescent forms now patterned with the memories they'd witnessed, their eyes containing depths that hadn't existed before.

"The convergence accelerates," Rootstar said, its voice tight with urgency. "What should have unfolded across days now transpires in hours."

"When?" Asvarr demanded, feeling the anchors within him resonating with increasing intensity.

"Before the new dawn," Rootstar replied. "The pattern rebuilds itself even as it breaks."

A terrifying realization struck him. "The Wanderer—"

"Seeks to control the convergence," Rootstar finished. "To impose his vision of pure order upon the remaking."

Even as they spoke, another section of the sky tore open, this time revealing intention—a vast eye formed of interlinked constellations peered down through the rift, its gaze sweeping across transformed Alfheim with cosmic judgment.

"The Gatekeeper awakens," the tallest star-child whispered, his form flickering with fear. "It comes to witness the tenth cycle's resolution."

Asvarr felt the weight of observation press against his consciousness—this entity saw beyond physical form to the pattern beneath, evaluating the current transformation against nine previous cycles of failure. It recognized him, the anchors he carried, and the choice that loomed before him.

"It doesn't interfere," Rootstar explained, tendrils twisting uneasily. "Only witnesses and remembers."

"For what purpose?" Asvarr asked.

The answer came not from Rootstar but from the sky itself as the last major section of the firmament collapsed. This sheet of reality struck with such force that the entire realm shuddered. Where it landed, a perfect mirror-pool formed, reflecting what lay beyond Alfheim's broken sky—the true cosmos with its serpentine swimmers and geometric watchmen, balanced in eternal tension.

The vision expanded to reveal a truth larger than any before: existence itself was an experiment—a testing ground where different approaches to reality could play out their conflicts and seek resolution. The Nine Realms represented only one such experiment among countless others, each with its own pattern and purpose. The Gatekeeper observed them all, preserving what succeeded and allowing what failed to dissolve back into potential.

"Nine failures," the star-child murmured. "Nine attempts at balance that could not hold."

"And now the tenth," Rootstar added. "With all anchors approaching convergence."

Asvarr stood at the edge of the mirror-pool, his transformed reflection showing what he had become—neither fully human nor wholly cosmic, but something between. The three anchors pulsed visibly beneath his skin, their rhythms synchronizing as convergence approached. Through his connection with Rootstar, he sensed the fourth anchor calling from Muspelheim's Storm Forge with increasing urgency.

"We cannot stay," he decided, turning from the pool as another tremor shook the transformed ground. "Alfheim dissolves into memory, but the pattern must be completed elsewhere."

Yrsa nodded in silent agreement, her face set with determination despite the exhaustion that dragged at her limbs. The star-children gathered closer, their forms flickering between solidity and pure light as the realm's coherence wavered.

Above them, through the shattered remains of the sky-weave, something vast shifted position—scales like nebulae sliding against each other with ponderous grace. The cosmic serpents were moving with purpose now, their ancient patience giving way to active attention. After nine cycles of waiting, they sensed the possibility of true change.

"The boundary thins completely," Rootstar warned as the ground beneath them began to lose coherence, patches dissolving into conceptual space where physical law held no authority. "We must find a path outward before Alfheim becomes pure memory."

"Where will we find Brynja?" Asvarr asked, his oath-mark burning with distant connection.

"Between worlds," Rootstar answered. "Where wings meet void."

Another tremor, stronger than before, sent cracks racing through what remained of physical reality. Through these cracks, Asvarr glimpsed fragments of other realms—the volcanic landscape of Muspelheim, the frost-bound plains of Niflheim, the verdant fields of Vanaheim—all similarly affected by the collapse of cosmic boundaries.

"The Wanderer comes," the tallest star-child announced suddenly, his bell-like voice tight with fear. "His purpose unchanged despite revelation."

In the distance, a figure appeared—cloaked in constellations yet walking with Odin's authority. Even from afar, Asvarr recognized the Wanderer's purposeful stride, the spear of frozen sunlight clutched in his fist. He moved directly toward them, untouched by the memory-transformation that affected everything around him.

"He still believes in perfect order," Rootstar said, tendrils coiling protectively around Asvarr's arm. "Nine cycles of failure have not shaken his conviction."

"Then we test his conviction against our transformation," Asvarr replied, the three anchors blazing beneath his skin as he prepared for confrontation.

The sky groaned above them, another section giving way to reveal the countless eyes of cosmic serpents watching through the void. The Gatekeeper's attention focused more intently, its constellation-gaze fixed upon the approaching moment of decision. Alfheim continued its dissolution into patchwork memory, physical reality giving way to conceptual space where thought became form and form became thought.

The convergence approached with every heartbeat. The choice between restoration, destruction, and transformation loomed before them. And through the collapsing realm, the Wanderer advanced with unwavering determination, his spear aimed at the heart of change itself.

***

Brynja stepped through a tear in reality as casually as one might pass through an open doorway. The Severed Bloom had changed her profoundly—her wooden arm now spiraled with constellation patterns that pulsed in rhythm with Alfheim's dissolving firmament, and the left side of her face had fully transformed into bark with a cosmic eye swirling where flesh had once been.

"Found you," she said, her voice layered with rustling undertones. Golden truth-light flickered across her features as her rune-marked face creased into a grim smile. "The entire pattern unravels, and you stand watching like children at a skald's fire."

Asvarr's chest tightened with conflicting emotions—relief at her appearance warred with lingering pain from her betrayal. The wooden sigil she'd hidden beneath his skin throbbed in recognition, sending waves of connection through his transformed flesh. "Brynja—"

"Save your questions," she interrupted, gaze shifting to the approaching Wanderer. "His presence forces our hand. We have moments, nothing more."

A ripple passed through reality as Coilvoice manifested beside her—no longer the subtle weave of root and starlight, but a fully corporeal entity whose form shifted between humanoid and abstract pattern with each pulse of cosmic energy flowing through Alfheim's broken sky.

"The boundary thins," Coilvoice announced, its multi-layered voice resonating through bone rather than air. "We must move through concept to reach the realm's edge."

Asvarr reached toward Yrsa, who stood motionless as the star-children gathered around her. Her muteness had become something more—a deliberate absence that paradoxically commanded attention. She nodded once, decisively, then gestured toward a fissure in reality that hadn't been visible moments before.

"There," Rootstar confirmed, its tendrils extending toward the opening. "Between manifestation and potential—a path to what remains of Alfheim's boundary."

The Wanderer's approach accelerated, his form growing more imposing with each stride. The spear of frozen sunlight in his grip lengthened, its tip blazing with concentrated order. Wind whipped around him, arranging fallen debris into perfect geometric patterns that shattered the moment he passed.

"Go!" Asvarr commanded, urging the star-children through the fissure first. Their luminescent bodies shimmered as they passed from physical space into something less defined, their outlines blurring into conceptual form.

Brynja grabbed his wrist, her wooden fingers cool against his transformed skin. "This isn't retreat," she insisted, truth-runes glowing golden. "This is strategic withdrawal to the convergence point."

Another vast section of sky collapsed behind the Wanderer, cascading memory-light across the transformed landscape. Where it struck, boundaries between thought and matter dissolved completely—trees became mathematical equations describing growth, stones transformed into the concept of endurance given substance.

"We cannot outrun him," Coilvoice warned as they approached the fissure. "He moves through order, untouched by transformation."

"We don't outrun," Rootstar countered, tendrils wrapping protectively around Asvarr's arm. "We outthink. Concept navigates differently than form."

Asvarr helped Yrsa through the fissure, feeling the nature of reality shift as his own hand passed the threshold. On one side: dissolving physical space; on the other: something that could only be described as thought given temporary structure. The star-children waited within, their bodies now composed of pure conceptual light arranged in vaguely humanoid configurations.

Brynja stepped through next, her wooden features spreading into branching possibilities before settling back into cohesive form. Coilvoice flowed through the opening without changing shape, perfectly at home in this intermediate state of existence.

Asvarr followed last, the three anchors within him resonating painfully as he crossed the boundary between physicality and concept. His transformed flesh responded strangely—crystalline formations extending across his face, verdant crown branching upward with fractal precision, blood becoming threads of interwoven sap and starlight.

The fissure sealed behind them, fragmenting into equations that dispersed like mist.

Inside the conceptual space, Alfheim existed as interlocking ideaforms—silver forests represented by the mathematical relationship between growth and time, crystal spires manifested as the architectural concept of ascension, rivers flowing as liquid metaphor rather than actual water. Everything remained recognizable but abstracted, stripped to essential meaning.

"This way," Brynja urged, leading them across a plain of geometric possibility. "The realm's edge exists even when the realm dissolves."

The Wanderer's roar echoed through conceptual space, his fury transcending the barrier they'd crossed. A crack appeared in the ideaform sky, revealing his approaching presence as a perfect mathematical constant pushing against transformative variables.

"He breaks through concept itself," Coilvoice said, voice tinged with genuine surprise. "His determination exceeds reason."

They moved faster, passing through landscapes of pure thought. Distance worked differently here—proximity determined by conceptual relationship rather than physical measurement. Asvarr found they covered more ground when focusing on destination rather than journey, the space between points compressing according to intentional logic.

Yrsa tugged urgently at his sleeve, pointing toward a conceptual landmark—a towering structure that represented the boundary between Alfheim and the void beyond. Unlike the physical reality they'd left, this ideaform boundary remained intact, a perfect division between defined thought and formless potential.

"The Edge-Concept," Rootstar explained, tendrils quivering with recognition. "Where Alfheim's pattern meets what lies beyond pattern."

Something vast moved on the other side of this boundary—serpentine forms composed of possibility itself, their scales flashing with universe-fragments as they swam through void-ocean. The sight both terrified and beckoned, a primal connection that resonated with the flame-anchor burning in Asvarr's chest.

"They wait at the threshold," Brynja said, her cosmic eye swirling faster as she gazed through the boundary. "Neither helping nor hindering, merely observing the tenth cycle's resolution."

A conceptual tremor shook the ideaform landscape as another massive section of physical Alfheim collapsed into memory. The shock transmitted into thought-space, causing temporary disruption in the pattern's integrity. Mathematical constants wavered; logical relationships bent toward paradox; structural equations destabilized.

The tallest star-child approached Asvarr, his form now composed entirely of geometric light arranged in humanoid shape. "The boundary weakens with each collapse," he said, bell-like voice resonating through the concept-realm. "We must cross before coherence fails completely."

"And go where?" Asvarr demanded, feeling the anchors pulse beneath his transformed skin. "The storm forge in Muspelheim still calls, but we cannot abandon Alfheim's people to dissolution."

"They follow their own paths," Coilvoice replied, its form shifting between interlocking rings of light and root-like tendrils. "Some transcend, some regress, some find refuge in memory fragments. None can be shepherded now—the transformation moves beyond guidance."

Another crack split the ideaform sky as the Wanderer forced his way further into conceptual space. His appearance shocked Asvarr—no longer merely Odin's echo but something both more and less than that legendary figure. The Wanderer's form fluctuated between divine majesty and desperate primal shape, the conflict between his purpose and cosmic reality tearing at his very essence.

"Asvarr Skyrend!" the Wanderer's voice boomed across concept-space, each word a perfect logical statement that forced surrounding ideaforms to temporarily align with his will. "The pattern requires preservation, not transformation! You unmake what cannot be remade!"

"We must reach the boundary," Brynja urged, pulling Asvarr toward the Edge-Concept. "Argue philosophy after survival."

They raced across shifting conceptual terrain, each step carrying them through landscapes of mathematical abstraction and symbolic representation. The star-children moved with perfect efficiency, their light-forms sliding between ideaforms without disruption. Yrsa struggled most, her physical form resistant to complete abstraction despite her connection to boundary-walking.

Asvarr lifted her with one arm, surprised to find his transformed body functioned differently in concept-space—stronger yet lighter, physical limitations balanced by conceptual potentials. "Hold tight," he told her as they navigated a section where gravity existed only as mathematical suggestion.

The Wanderer gained ground, his approach warping conceptual space into rigid perfection. Where he passed, fluid ideaforms crystallized into unchanging constants, flexibility hardening into absolute structure. He wielded his spear like a lecturer's pointer, each gesture freezing concepts into their most restrictive interpretations.

"He imprisons thought itself," Rootstar warned, branches extending protectively. "Creation requires both structure and freedom—he enforces only one."

***

They reached a vast conceptual plain stretching before the Edge-Concept, the final expanse separating them from Alfheim's boundary. Here, ideaforms thinned to transparent mathematics—pure equations dancing in intricate patterns that represented the transition between concept and void.

"We cross together," Coilvoice instructed, its form solidifying into something more substantial as conceptual space thinned. "Intention matters more than physical movement."

Behind them, the Wanderer raised his spear high, gathering perfect order around its tip like a thunderhead of rigid geometry. "The ninth cycle repeated," he declared, voice carrying authority that made reality itself listen. "The pattern preserved. The experiment continued under control."

The spear came down with cosmic force, striking concept-space with an impact that sent fractures racing toward them. Where these cracks spread, ideaforms shattered into component mathematics, losing coherence entirely.

"Now!" Brynja shouted, her wooden arm extending impossibly as she reached for the boundary. The Severed Bloom within her responded to crisis, branches erupting from her transformed flesh to create a temporary bridge across the conceptual plain.

The star-children flowed across first, their light-forms already halfway to pure concept. Coilvoice followed, weaving between Brynja's branches with fluid grace. Asvarr carried Yrsa across the living bridge, the three anchors within him burning with increasing intensity as they approached the boundary between realms.

Rootstar extended ahead, its tendrils touching the Edge-Concept with exploratory caution. "Beyond lies truth," it said, voice tinged with both wonder and dread. "The cosmos unshaped by deception."

The Wanderer's roar of frustration shook concept-space as fractures spread in all directions. His perfect order approached the conceptual plain, threatening to overtake them before they could cross the boundary. His form wavered between Odin's majesty and something older—a primal force of pattern-preservation that predated individuality.

"He fears what lies beyond control," Brynja observed, her truth-runes glowing golden despite the strain of maintaining the bridge.

They reached the Edge-Concept together as the conceptual plain began dissolving behind them. Here at Alfheim's true boundary, reality thinned to perfect transparency—on one side the realm's defining patterns, on the other the unbounded potential of cosmic void where serpentine entities swam through formless creation.

"How do we cross?" Asvarr asked, feeling the anchors pulse with recognition of what lay beyond.

"We don't cross," Coilvoice corrected. "We transform. The boundary is not location but state."

Understanding dawned with crystal clarity. Asvarr placed his hand against the Edge-Concept, feeling it respond to his transformed flesh. The anchors within him synchronized their rhythms for the first time—flame, memory, and starlight pulsing in harmony rather than competition. Through his connection with Rootstar, he sensed the pattern's design, how boundaries existed as transformative thresholds.

"Together," he said, reaching for Brynja with his free hand.

She hesitated, her cosmic eye swirling with conflicted purpose, before clasping his offered hand. Her truth-runes blazed golden—this connection, at least, contained no deception.

"Your choices unmake creation!" the Wanderer cried, his spear piercing the dissolving plain as he fought to reach them. "Nine cycles of preservation cannot end in chaos!"

"Not chaos," Asvarr replied, understanding flowing through him like cosmic fire. "Transformation. The pattern evolves or dies."

The Wanderer's face contorted with complex emotion—anger tangled with fear, certainty poisoned by doubt. For an instant, Asvarr glimpsed the being beneath the mask—the echo of Odin's regret given form, trapped in endless repetition of purpose without wisdom.

"You cannot escape," the Wanderer insisted, even as his own form wavered between definition and dissolution. "The convergence approaches. All anchors must align according to pattern."

"They will," Asvarr agreed, the three within him pulsing in affirmation. "But not as before."

With concentrated intent, he pressed against the Edge-Concept, feeling it yield by recognizing what he had become—neither fully mortal nor entirely cosmic, a threshold-being navigating between states. Yrsa placed her hand beside his, her mute presence carrying boundary-walking power beyond words. The star-children aligned themselves in precise formation, their light-bodies forming a constellation that mirrored something vast moving beyond the boundary.

"Intention shapes transition," Rootstar murmured, its tendrils spreading across the Edge-Concept's surface.

The boundary didn't break—it transformed, becoming less a division between states and more a transitional interface where concept met possibility. Through this transformed threshold, Asvarr sensed Muspelheim's volcanic fires, Helheim's eternal twilight, and the distant pulse of the remaining anchors calling to those he already carried.

Reality itself bent around them as the Edge-Concept responded to their combined intention. The boundary thinned further, becoming permeable to transformation while still maintaining enough structure to prevent complete dissolution.

The Wanderer lunged forward, spear aimed at the transforming boundary. "The pattern must hold!" he cried, his form solidifying into Odin's aspect—one-eyed, commanding, absolute in purpose.

"The pattern evolves," Brynja countered, the Severed Bloom within her responding with explosive growth. Branches erupted from her wooden arm, intercepting the Wanderer's spear before it could pierce the transformed boundary.

"Go!" she shouted to Asvarr, truth-runes verifying her intent. "Find the fourth anchor. Complete what nine cycles could not."

Asvarr hesitated, torn between escape and loyalty. The wooden sigil beneath his skin burned with connection, transmitting Brynja's determination directly to his consciousness. This wasn't mere sacrifice—this was strategic division of purpose.

The transformed boundary pulsed, responding to the anchors within him. Through the thinned interface, he glimpsed Muspelheim's Storm Forge wreathed in lightning, the fourth anchor pulsing with creation-destruction energy that called to the three he already carried.

"We meet at convergence," Brynja promised, her cosmic eye fixed on the Wanderer as she held him at bay. Coilvoice moved to her side, its form solidifying into something more substantial as it prepared for confrontation.

The boundary opened further, revealing a path through the conceptual space between realms—a direct connection to Muspelheim forged by transformative intent rather than physical transit. The star-children moved through first, their light-forms adapting instantly to the shifted reality. Yrsa followed, pulling Asvarr after her with surprising strength.

As they crossed the transformed threshold, Asvarr looked back one final time. Brynja stood defiant, the Severed Bloom fully awakened within her transformed flesh. The Wanderer pushed against her barrier of living wood, his spear blazing with concentrated order that threatened to overtake her defenses.

Behind them both, what remained of Alfheim continued its transformation—evolution, physical reality giving way to concept, concept yielding to new possibility. The cosmic serpents watched through the broken sky, their ancient patience finally rewarded with genuine change after nine cycles of repetition.

The Edge-Concept sealed behind them as they fully crossed the threshold, cutting off the vision of Alfheim's transformation. Reality solidified around them—no longer conceptual mathematics but the tangible heat and pressure of Muspelheim's volcanic landscape. The Storm Forge loomed ahead, a mountain shaped like a cosmic anvil with lightning perpetually striking its peak.

Within that mountain, Asvarr sensed the fourth anchor pulsing with creative-destructive energy—actively hunting, reaching for him across the diminishing distance. The three anchors he carried responded with increasing resonance, their rhythms synchronizing as convergence approached.

The true test awaited, and with it, the possibility that nine cycles of failure might yield to transformation in the tenth.

CHAPTER 28

CROWN OF THE CELESTIAL WARDEN

M uspelheim's heat slammed into Asvarr like a physical blow, searing his lungs with each breath. The volcanic realm's perpetual twilight sky smoldered overhead, streaked with veins of magma-light that pulsed in uneven rhythm. After the conceptual fluidity of dissolving Alfheim, this raw physicality felt almost primitive—reality reduced to its most elemental components of fire and stone.

The star-children huddled together on a shelf of obsidian that jutted from the mountainside, their light-forms already beginning to solidify in response to Muspelheim's unyielding physicality. Their luminescence dimmed in the realm's oppressive heat, ghostly faces contorted with discomfort.

"They cannot stay here long," Rootstar warned, its tendril-branches curling protectively around Asvarr's wrist. "Their essence withers in creation-destruction's domain."

Asvarr nodded, his attention fixed on the Storm Forge that dominated the horizon—an anvil-shaped mountain wreathed in perpetual lightning. The fourth anchor pulsed within that impossible formation, its rhythm wild and unpredictable compared to the steady cadence of those he already carried. Unlike the previous anchors that had waited passively for discovery, this one hunted—reaching across the diminishing distance with tendrils of raw potential that plucked at his transformed flesh.

Yrsa tugged urgently at his sleeve, pointing toward a narrow path that wound up the obsidian slope toward a ridge of crystallized fire. Her muteness had become something stranger since their passage through conceptual space—an absence more profound than mere silence, a void that somehow communicated more clearly than words.

"I know," Asvarr told her, understanding the unspoken warning. "We're too exposed here."

The Storm Forge wasn't their only concern. The transition from Alfheim's dissolving concept-space to Muspelheim's brutal physicality had left its mark on him. The three anchors he carried—flame, memory, and starlight—resonated painfully against one another, their energies seeking equilibrium after the passage between realms. He could feel them straining against the boundaries of his transformed flesh, demanding integration rather than mere containment.

"The boundary approaches," Rootstar said, its voice tightening with strain. "Not of realm but of being."

Asvarr pressed his palm against his chest where the Grímmark burned beneath layers of transformed skin. The crystalline formations that had spread across his face during his sojourn in Alfheim now extended down his neck and across his shoulders, creating patterns like frozen lightning that pulsed with internal light. The verdant crown had thickened, its branches digging deeper into his skull while extending further down his back. The combination should have been agonizing, but pain had become something different—less a warning than a marker of transition.

***

"We need shelter before I can attempt integration," he said, scanning the volcanic landscape. "Somewhere to weather what comes."

The tallest star-child approached, his form flickering between light and substance. "There," he said, bell-like voice already growing fainter in Muspelheim's dense atmosphere. He pointed toward a formation of interlocking hexagonal basalt columns that formed a natural chamber against the mountainside.

They made their way across the treacherous terrain, helping the star-children whose light-forms struggled to maintain cohesion. The ground beneath them shifted unpredictably—with the physical instability of a realm governed by creation and destruction in perpetual conflict. Fissures opened without warning, venting plumes of sulfurous gas that stung Asvarr's eyes and throat.

Reaching the basalt formation, they discovered a chamber deeper than expected, its interior walls lined with crystals that trapped and refracted the dim light in complex patterns. The heat here was marginally less oppressive, the air thick but breathable. The star-children moved to the deepest recesses where temperature and light conditions most closely resembled their native environment.

"This will serve," Asvarr decided, lowering himself carefully to the chamber's floor. The stone vibrated beneath him, transmitting the realm's constant seismic activity directly into his bones.

Rootstar extended its tendril-branches across the chamber's entrance, creating a living barrier against the harsher conditions outside. "The integration cannot be delayed much longer," it warned. "Three anchors strain for unity after glimpsing the fourth."

Yrsa knelt beside Asvarr, her expression grave as she placed her hand on his shoulder. Though mute, she conveyed volumes through touch—concern, encouragement, and something deeper that reminded him of their shared journey across nine points of the pattern. She made deliberate gestures with her free hand, manipulating fingers in configurations he recognized from boundary-walkers' silent speech.

"Yes," he agreed, interpreting her meaning with surprising ease. "I must complete what began in Alfheim—become Warden of Three in truth rather than merely bearer of fragments."

The tallest star-child approached, his diminished luminescence still bright enough to cast sharp shadows across the crystal-lined walls. "We will witness," he said, the harmonics of his bell-like voice resonating with the surrounding crystals. "As is our purpose across all cycles."

The other star-children arranged themselves in a semicircle facing Asvarr, their light-forms pulsing in synchronized rhythm—slower than heartbeats but steadier, marking cosmic time rather than mortal moments. Their witnessing created a stable framework, a fixed point around which transformation could safely occur.

Asvarr settled into a cross-legged position, placing his hands palm-up on his knees. The starforged chain around his wrist—four links representing memory, purpose, connection, and grief—glowed with internal light, its metal no longer purely physical but partially conceptual, embodying the aspects it represented. Through his connection with Rootstar, he sensed the approaching moment's significance—cosmic recalibration.

"Flame-dominance, memory-recognition, starlight-transformation," he recited, naming each anchor and its fundamental nature. "Three fragments of the whole, separated across nine cycles."

The anchors responded to their naming, pulsing beneath his transformed skin in staggered rhythm. The flame-anchor burned steady and strong at his core, its heat radiating outward in controlled waves. The memory-anchor flowed like liquid gold through his consciousness, connecting disparate experiences into coherent patterns. The starlight-anchor, still not fully bound since their escape from Alfheim, flickered with potential, casting his shadow in multiple directions simultaneously.

"Integration approaches," Rootstar murmured, its tendrils quivering with anticipation. "The third binding completes what Alfheim begun."

Asvarr closed his eyes, focusing inward on the three anchors he carried. Unlike previous bindings that had required external ritual, this integration demanded internal alignment—the deliberate harmonizing of energies already present within him. The boundary between bearing and becoming, between containing and embodying, thinned with each measured breath.

The chamber around him fell away from his awareness as he sank deeper into the space between conscious thought and physical sensation. Here, the anchors existed as perspectives—distinct ways of perceiving and engaging with reality. The flame-anchor preserved through dominance, maintaining identity through controlled power. The memory-anchor connected through recognition, binding disparate elements into meaningful relationship. The starlight-anchor transformed through integration, evolving beyond fixed forms while maintaining essential nature.

***

These perspectives had operated separately within him, each asserting its vision without coordination. Now they began to overlap, creating a composite awareness greater than their individual contributions. Flame's preservation gave memory's connections durability; memory's relationships gave starlight's transformations purpose; starlight's evolution gave flame's dominance flexibility.

Physical sensation returned with shocking intensity as the integration accelerated. Heat surged through his transformed flesh, reforging, rearranging the fundamental components of his being according to new architectural principles. The crystalline formations across his face and shoulders liquefied, flowing into new configurations that mapped his expanded awareness. The verdant crown unraveled, its branches separating into individual tendrils before reweaving themselves with threads of starlight and memory-sap.

Through the pain of transformation, Asvarr maintained his focus on the unity emerging from fragmentation. The three anchors' rhythms synchronized for the first time, no longer competing for dominance but complementing each other in complex harmony. With each pulse, his perception expanded—no longer limited to immediate surroundings or linear time.

He gasped as his awareness stretched across vast distances and through multiple temporal layers. Muspelheim spread before his inner vision—the entire realm extending in all directions simultaneously. He glimpsed the Storm Forge at the realm's heart, lightning perpetually reshaping the fourth anchor contained within. Beyond Muspelheim, he perceived Helheim's twilight gates creaking open as cosmic adjustment rippled through all Nine Realms.

More shocking than extended spatial awareness was his temporal perception. Events unfolded in relational patterns—causes and effects linked by meaning rather than chronology. He witnessed the binding of the cosmic serpents not as historical event but as ongoing process, each cycle of the pattern representing another attempt at integration. Nine previous failures cascaded through his awareness, each revealing its fatal flaw—preservation without flexibility, connection without evolution, transformation without foundation.

The star-children's light intensified as they witnessed his transformation, their diminished forms drawing strength from the cosmic recognition unfolding before them. Their bell-like voices joined in harmonic chant that stabilized the chamber's energies, preventing Muspelheim's destructive aspects from interfering with the delicate integration.

Rootstar extended a tendril toward Asvarr's forehead, touching the point where crystalline patterns met verdant growth. "The crown transforms," it announced, voice layered with wonder. "The Warden of Three emerges."

Through Rootstar's touch, Asvarr perceived his own transformation from an external perspective. The crown forming around his head no longer consisted solely of verdant branches but incorporated memory-sap and stellar fire in equal measure—a living circlet that represented the anchors' unified perspectives. Crystalline structures spiraled from the crown down his neck and across his shoulders, forming protective armor that adapted continuously to changing conditions. His eyes had transformed completely, becoming pools of silver-blue light that perceived multiple layers of reality simultaneously.

With integration came unprecedented clarity. The pattern that had governed Nine Realms across nine cycles revealed itself as necessary framework—a system allowing exploration of different approaches to existence itself. Each realm represented a distinct perspective, each cycle an attempt at finding balance between competing truths. What had appeared as conflict between order and chaos, between preservation and transformation, between divine and primordial, emerged

CROWN OF THE CELESTIAL WARDEN

as complementary aspects of a greater whole seeking self-knowledge through experience.

"The pattern learns," Asvarr whispered, the realization flooding through him with the force of revelation. "Nine cycles of experimentation, each failure teaching what the next attempt must include."

His expanded perception revealed connections between seemingly random events—how Alfheim's dissolution provided necessary fragments for Muspelheim's evolution, how the breaking of sky-weave's deception allowed cosmic serpents to contribute perspectives excluded for nine cycles. Each realm's transformation followed logical progression in the gradual rebirth of something greater than the Yggdrasil that had been—moving toward a cosmic structure that integrated order and chaos rather than separating them.

The integration reached completion with sudden stillness. The three anchors ceased their individual pulsing, now fully unified within Asvarr's transformed being. The pain of transformation subsided, replaced by heightened awareness that balanced cosmic perception with immediate physical reality. He opened his eyes—now repositories of stellar light—to find the chamber transformed by his integration.

Crystals along the walls had rearranged themselves into patterns matching the crown around his head, their surfaces etched with runic equations describing the relationship between anchors. The star-children glowed with renewed vigor, their light-forms stabilized by their proximity to successful integration. Yrsa knelt exactly where she had been, but tears streaked her face—the first emotion she had displayed since sacrificing her voice.

"It is done," Rootstar said, its tendrils withdrawing from Asvarr's forehead. "Warden of Three in truth."

Asvarr rose to his feet, his transformed body moving with fluid precision that belied the radical changes it had undergone. The crown pulsed with unified rhythm, no longer three separate energies but a single harmonized force. Through it, he maintained his expanded perception while remaining anchored in physical reality—a bridge between perspectives rather than prisoner of any single viewpoint.

"The fourth anchor calls," he said, his voice layered with harmonic undertones that hadn't been present before. "Creation-destruction awaits at the Storm Forge."

The tallest star-child stepped forward, his light-form stabilized into something more substantial. "Beyond your immediate perception, greater forces gather," he warned. "The cosmic serpents convene above Alfheim's remains, drawn by successful integration after nine cycles of failure."

Asvarr nodded, sensing the truth of this through his expanded awareness. "They watch but do not interfere—their role complementary to mine."

Yrsa made rapid gestures, her boundary-walker signs conveying urgent meaning: *The Wanderer pursues across realm-boundaries. Brynja and Coilvoice cannot hold him indefinitely.*

"Then we move toward the Storm Forge without delay," Asvarr decided, already perceiving multiple paths through Muspelheim's treacherous landscape, evaluating their relative dangers and opportunities with a single comprehensive thought.

The chamber shuddered as seismic activity intensified throughout the volcanic realm. Through his expanded perception, Asvarr recognized this as a systemic response to cosmic adjustment—Muspelheim recalibrating itself as integration rippled through the pattern. The fourth anchor at the Storm Forge pulsed with increasing urgency, its wild rhythm calling to the unified three he carried with the insistence of inevitable conjunction.

Stepping toward the chamber's entrance, Asvarr looked out across Muspelheim's fire-veined landscape toward the anvil-shaped mountain that housed the fourth anchor. Lightning danced continuously around its peak, forking downward to strike the mountain's sides with mathematical precision. Through his transformed perception, he recognized these strikes as equations written in energy—the anchor communicating its nature across distance.

His crown responded, sending matching pulses of unified energy outward that briefly illuminated hidden pathways through the volcanic terrain. These weren't physical trails but probability corridors—routes where creation temporarily dominated destruction, allowing safer passage through the realm's inherent instability.

"The path reveals itself," he told the others, the crown's light reflecting from crystalline formations across his shoulders. "We follow integration's momentum toward the fourth binding."

With his integration complete, Asvarr stood at Muspelheim's threshold as Warden of Three—an integral component of the cosmic pattern rather than incidental element. The anchors within him had unified into balanced perspective that honored preservation, connection, and transformation in equal measure. Through this unified vision, he perceived not just immediate circumstances but the underlying significance of each realm's transformation in the pattern's evolution toward something new.

The crown of the celestial warden pulsed with promise and warning in equal measure. Success brought expanded responsibility—the power to perceive creating obligation to respond. As cosmic serpents gathered to witness this unprecedented development in the pattern's tenth cycle, Asvarr prepared to continue the journey that nine previous Wardens had failed to complete.

The fourth anchor called from the Storm Forge with creation-destruction's voice, promising challenge beyond anything he had yet faced. His transformed flesh responded to this call with recognition—the next necessary step in the pattern's unfolding purpose.

The approaching storm made Muspelheim's fire-veined sky throb with ominous energy. Lightning forked downward in mathematical progressions, striking the volcanic landscape with deliberate precision rather than random chaos. Asvarr watched from the chamber's entrance, the crown's unified pulse illuminating his transformed features in rhythmic silver-gold light. A different storm gathered in the void above the realm—a convergence of cosmic entities drawn to unprecedented change.

"They come," Rootstar murmured, tendrils extending upward toward a rift forming in Muspelheim's amber sky.

Through the rift, Asvarr glimpsed vast forms coiling through nothingness—scales containing universe-fragments, eyes holding galaxies, bodies extending beyond conventional dimension. The sky-serpents approached with deliberate curiosity, their ancient patience finally rewarded with genuine innovation after nine cycles of repetitive failure.

"Why now?" Asvarr asked, the crown's branches shifting in response to his uncertainty. "Why gather for this integration when they observed the others from afar?"

The tallest star-child stepped beside him, light-form stabilizing in proximity to Asvarr's unified anchors. "The third marks transition," he explained, bell-like voice carrying unusual weight. "Nine previous Wardens faltered at this threshold. None achieved balance across the triad."

The rift widened as the largest serpent pushed through, its scaled head alone dwarfing the mountainside where they sheltered. Unlike the mindless wyrms of mortal legend, this being radiated intelligence beyond human comprehension—ancient awareness that had witnessed the birth of stars and death of realities. Its eyes fixed on Asvarr with recognition that transcended species or form.

"Pattern-Keeper," it spoke directly into his mind, bypassing conventional language. The concept carried layers of meaning impossible to translate fully—something between caretaker and architect, guardian and cultivator, preserver and innovator.

Asvarr stepped forward instinctively, drawn by the crown's resonance with the cosmic entity. His transformed flesh responded to the serpent's presence—crystalline formations across his shoulders rearranging into configurations that mirrored the mathematical perfection of the serpent's scales. Through his expanded perception, he registered the arrival of more serpents, their massive forms partly obscured by the dimensional barriers they navigated.

"I am Warden of Three," he replied, voice carrying harmonic undertones that vibrated in sympathy with the cosmic frequencies surrounding them. "Bearer of flame, memory, and starlight."

"More," the serpent corrected, its mental voice like thunder compressed into thought. "Pattern-Keeper—threshold entity maintaining coherence across fragmentation. First successful integration in ten cycles."

The other serpents arranged themselves in complex formation above Muspelheim, their bodies forming mathematical relationships too precise for coincidence. Asvarr recognized the pattern through his expanded perception—a key sequence in the cosmic architecture, a fundamental equation describing relationship between order and chaos.

Yrsa tugged urgently at his sleeve, her expression betraying rare fear. Her fingers moved in boundary-walker signs: *Cosmic attention brings cosmic danger. Previous Wardens died under such scrutiny.*

The star-children huddled closer together, their diminished light-forms drawing strength from Asvarr's unified anchors. Only the tallest remained apart, facing the serpents with the detached curiosity of a fellow witness.

"What do they want?" Asvarr asked him quietly.

"Not want," the star-child corrected. "Recognize. Function acknowledged across scales of existence."

The largest serpent descended further, its massive head hovering above the chamber entrance. Its scales shifted colors with each movement—from galactic purple to cosmic black to nebula blue—containing myriad universe-fragments that played out their dramas in miniature across its surface.

"The pattern fractures," it communicated, mental voice rumbling through Asvarr's consciousness. "Nine cycles of failure. Tenth proves different through balanced integration. Your function: maintain coherence across fragmentation while evolution proceeds."

The crown around Asvarr's head pulsed with increased intensity, responding directly to the serpent's recognition. Through their connection, images flooded his awareness—previous Wardens across nine cycles, each failing at critical junctures through imbalanced approach. Some surrendered identity entirely, becoming passive conduits for cosmic forces. Others clung too rigidly to individuality, fighting necessary transformation until breaking under pressure. None achieved the balanced integration that allowed simultaneous existence as both individual entity and cosmic component.

"I didn't choose this function," Asvarr stated, the crown branching further down his back in protective formation.

"Function emerges from capability," another serpent replied, its mental voice higher and quicker than the first. "The Pattern-Keeper arises through successful navigation of threshold states. Nine failed. You succeeded."

Rootstar's tendrils coiled supportively around Asvarr's wrist, strengthening his connection to physical reality as cosmic awareness threatened to overwhelm mortal consciousness. "They bring neither threat nor aid," it explained. "Only recognition of cosmic role."

The largest serpent's gaze intensified, looking through Asvarr's physical form to examine the unified anchors he carried. "Three integrated successfully," it observed. "Two remain separate. The fourth hunts at Storm Forge. The fifth waits in deepest shadow."

"And if I refuse this function?" Asvarr challenged, the unified anchors flaring with protective energy that briefly illuminated the chamber behind him. "If I choose my own path rather than continuing what nine cycles failed to complete?"

The serpents showed no reaction to his defiance, neither offended nor impressed by mortal assertion against cosmic role. "Choice exists within parameters of capability," the largest serpent replied. "Water flows downward even when resisting its nature."

A smaller serpent moved forward, its scales containing star-systems in earlier developmental stages than the others. "The Pattern-Keeper's responsibility exceeds mere guardianship," it communicated, mental voice tinged with what Asvarr interpreted as youthful enthusiasm. "You ensure whatever emerges from Yggdrasil's remnants retains connection to what came before while embracing necessary evolution."

"Evolution toward what?" Asvarr demanded, frustration rising at the serpents' cryptic pronouncements.

The largest serpent's mental signature shifted toward something Asvarr recognized as cosmic amusement. "If predetermined, evolution becomes mere unfolding of established pattern. Ten cycles of experimentation seek balance between structure and freedom, between preservation and transformation."

Yrsa stepped forward suddenly, signing complex boundary-walker sequences with urgent precision. Though mute, her meaning transmitted clearly to both Asvarr and the serpents: *The Pattern-Keeper stands at convergence point between cosmic forces. Neither fully serpent-chaos nor wholly divine-order, but integration that honors both.*

The serpents swayed in synchronized acknowledgment of her insight. "The boundary-walker understands threshold states," the largest serpent communicated. "What was separated must integrate without losing distinction. Evolution without dissolution."

The crown around Asvarr's head responded to this exchange, branches extending upward in recognition patterns that matched the serpents' undulating movements. Through this resonance, deeper understanding flowed into his transformed awareness—how the anchors represented fundamental aspects of existence itself, how their integration created perspective unavailable to entities locked within single domains.

"My responsibility to what?" Asvarr asked, his voice steadier as understanding crystallized within. "To whom do I answer in this function?"

"To coherence itself," the large serpent replied. "The Pattern-Keeper maintains relationship between fragments when wholeness fractures. Previous cycles failed through extremes—either rigid preservation that prevented evolution or complete dissolution that destroyed continuity."

Rootstar's tendrils quivered with recognition. "The third path," it murmured. "Neither preservation nor destruction but transformation that honors both."

The star-children formed a semicircle behind Asvarr, their light-forms pulsing with renewed vigor as cosmic recognition stabilized their existence across realm-boundaries. The tallest stepped forward, standing beside Asvarr with formal precision.

"We witness the Pattern-Keeper's emergence," he announced, bell-like voice carrying further than should be physically possible. "After nine cycles of observation, we record successful integration at the tenth attempt."

The serpents responded with synchronized movement, bodies forming complex mathematical equations across the void above Muspelheim. Asvarr recognized these patterns through his expanded perception—cosmic languages older than gods, relationships that defined reality's fundamental architecture.

"We offer neither allegiance nor opposition," the largest serpent communicated directly to Asvarr. "Recognition of function only—your role complementary to ours in cosmic balance."

"What is your function, then?" Asvarr asked, the crown's branches shifting with his curiosity.

"We swim the void between structures," it replied. "Where you maintain coherence across fragments, we maintain possibility between patterns. Different functions, complementary purposes."

The exchange reached deeper than mere communication, establishing relationship across cosmic scales that transcended conventional alliance or enmity. The serpents recognized Asvarr as a necessary component in existence's continued evolution—a functional counterpart that provided stability while they provided possibility.

Through his expanded perception, Asvarr glimpsed how their complementary roles had operated across previous cycles—sky-serpents introducing variation when pattern grew too rigid, Wardens providing stability when chaos threatened dissolution. The eternal dance between order and freedom played out through their respective functions, neither complete without the other's contribution.

"The Wanderer approaches," the smallest serpent warned suddenly, its mental voice sharp with urgency. "He crosses boundaries with purpose hardened by nine cycles of repetition."

The rift above them widened momentarily, revealing a distant figure moving through conceptual space with relentless determination. The Wanderer had escaped Brynja and Coilvoice's containment, his form shifting between Odin's majestic aspect and something more primal—the embodiment of order's fear when confronted with evolutionary change.

"He seeks control rather than balance," the largest serpent observed dispassionately. "Nine cycles unchanged despite repeated failure."

"Will you intervene?" Asvarr asked, the unified anchors pulsing with increased intensity at the Wanderer's approach.

"Our function permits possibility, not intervention," it replied. "The confrontation between preservation and transformation remains within pattern parameters. We observe only."

Frustration flared in Asvarr's chest—cosmic recognition without practical assistance offered little comfort against the Wanderer's relentless pursuit. Yet even this emotional response triggered new understanding through the unified anchors. The serpents' non-intervention wasn't abandonment but respect for necessary process—evolutionary pressure required genuine challenge rather than external resolution.

"Then I must reach the Storm Forge before he intercepts us," Asvarr decided, already mapping probability corridors through his expanded perception. "The fourth anchor must be bound in balanced integration rather than rigid control."

The serpents began withdrawing, their massive forms coiling back through the dimensional rift with fluid grace that belied their cosmic scale. "Pattern-Keeper," the largest acknowledged one final time, its mental voice receding like distant thunder. "Ten cycles culminate in your function. Maintenance of coherence across fragmentation while evolution proceeds."

As suddenly as they had gathered, the serpents departed—through dimensional transition that folded space between positions. The rift sealed behind them, leaving Muspelheim's amber sky intact but forever changed by their momentary presence.

Asvarr stood silently, absorbing the implications of cosmic recognition. The crown around his head settled into steady rhythm, its unified pulse synchronizing with his transformed heartbeat. The anchors within him no longer felt like separate energies but integrated perspectives providing composite awareness larger than any individual viewpoint.

"What now?" the tallest star-child asked, his light-form stabilizing into something more substantial after the serpents' departure.

"We continue toward the Storm Forge," Asvarr replied, the crown's light illuminating probability corridors through Muspelheim's treacherous landscape. "The Pattern-Keeper's function changes nothing about immediate necessity."

Yrsa signed complex boundary-walker sequences: *Recognition brings responsibility. You navigate the threshold between cosmic forces.*

"I understand," Asvarr told her, the weight of responsibility settling alongside cosmic recognition. "Coherence across fragmentation while evolution proceeds. Balance between preservation and transformation."

The chamber trembled as seismic activity intensified throughout Muspelheim. Through his expanded perception, Asvarr sensed the realm responding to his fully integrated presence—creation-destruction reacting to the unified triad he carried. The Storm Forge at the realm's heart pulsed with increasing urgency, the fourth anchor calling with wild rhythm that promised both revelation and challenge.

Rootstar extended its tendrils toward the chamber entrance, forming living network that mapped safe passage through the volcanic terrain. "The probability corridors strengthen," it observed. "The pattern acknowledges successful integration."

Asvarr stepped toward the entrance, the unified anchors granting perception beyond conventional limitation. The Storm Forge dominated his awareness—no longer merely physical destination but symbolic threshold between states of being. The fourth anchor waiting within represented necessary evolution beyond the triad he had successfully integrated.

"We move now," he decided, the crown's light creating protective aura around his companions. "Before the Wanderer forces confrontation on ground of his choosing."

As they prepared to depart, Asvarr felt the weight of the Pattern-Keeper's function settling into his transformed awareness. Beyond mere title or designation, this cosmic recognition named the role he had already begun to fulfill—maintaining coherence across fragmentation while evolution proceeded. The responsibility extended beyond personal journey or individual transformation, encompassing the pattern's continued development across ten cycles of cosmic experimentation.

The unified anchors resonated with this expanded purpose, their triad harmony creating foundation for whatever challenges the fourth and fifth anchors would present. Through flame's preservation, memory's connection, and starlight's transformation, Asvarr stood at convergence point between cosmic forces—neither fully serpent-chaos nor wholly divine-order, but integration that honored both.

The crown of the celestial warden pulsed with renewed clarity, illuminating conceptual pathways through evolutionary possibility. The Pattern-Keeper's journey continued toward confrontation that would determine whether ten cycles of experimentation culminated in genuine innovation or repeated previous failures in new configuration.

In the distance, lightning struck the Storm Forge with mathematical precision, the fourth anchor's wild rhythm calling with creation-destruction's voice. The Wanderer approached through boundaries between realms, preservation's champion unwilling to yield to transformation's necessity. And throughout existence, fragments of Yggdrasil's shattered structure awaited coherence that neither destroyed their uniqueness nor prevented their evolution.

A cosmic role Asvarr had never sought now defined his function across scales of existence. Recognition brought responsibility that transcended personal choice while remaining grounded in individual capability. The Pattern-Keeper moved forward into consequence, the crown's unified light showing the way through Muspelheim's fire-veined darkness.

CHAPTER 29

THE RIFT OF ASH AND STARS

Heat tore through Asvarr's lungs with each breath, the air itself a molten current that scorched his throat raw. Where he stood —if standing was even the right word for existing in this place—the ground pulsed like a living heart beneath his feet. One moment solid obsidian, the next a churning sea of magma, then crystalline frost that splintered with each step. Above him stretched no sky but a writhing membrane of amber light shot through with midnight veins.

"The Pattern-Keeper arrives." The Wanderer's voice rolled across the rift, each syllable distorting the space between them. His figure wavered at the opposite end of this impossible valley, his form no longer the haggard wanderer Asvarr had first encountered in Alfheim's woods. Now he stood taller, a presence more celestial than flesh, his cloak a canvas of starlit constellations that matched Asvarr's own transformed crown. One eye blazed with ancient knowledge, the other remained an empty socket that somehow saw more clearly than its companion.

The spear in his hand—Gungnir, or what remained of the god-weapon—flickered between solid matter and streaming light.

"Careful, ash-son." The Wanderer planted his spear's butt against the ground. The impact sent geometric patterns racing outward, transforming the chaotic soil into perfectly ordered crystalline hexagons wherever the energy touched. "This place responds to will and thought. Your hesitation already sours the air."

Asvarr felt it then—the metallic tang on his tongue, the sulfurous yellow clouds gathering above the spot where he stood. His doubt made manifest. He squared his shoulders, and the crystalline formations growing across his skin caught the amber light, sending rainbow fragments dancing across the valley floor.

"I know what this place is," Asvarr said. Frost shattered from his lips as he spoke, falling in geometric patterns that mirrored the star-chart woven across his flesh. "The seam between thought and form. The threshold where pattern meets possibility."

***

The Wanderer's mouth twisted into something almost resembling approval. "You learn quickly for a vessel so recently filled. But knowing the nature of a thing doesn't grant mastery over it."

To prove his point, the Wanderer swept his spear in an elegant arc. The very fabric of the rift responded—contorting, folding, reshaping itself into perfect concentric circles radiating outward from where he stood. Order imposed by will alone.

"Nine cycles I've walked the path you now tread." The Wanderer's voice carried an unfamiliar weight, the formal cadence of godhood he'd once abandoned. "Nine times I've watched vessels like you surrender to the pattern or break against it. The outcome never changes."

The starforged chain around Asvarr's wrist burned cold, its four links—memory, purpose, connection, grief—pulsing in counterpoint to the Wanderer's words. Through the verdant crown spreading down his back, Asvarr sensed Rootstar's energy reaching toward him, even across the dimensional barrier that separated this rift from Muspelheim.

"This cycle is different." Asvarr raised his hand, and the constellation blade materialized between his fingers, its form constantly shifting between solid metal and liquid starlight. "I've seen what existed before the Tree, before the binding. I've touched what sleeps beneath the roots."

The Wanderer's expression hardened. "You've glimpsed a fragment and think you comprehend the whole. Chaos isn't freedom, ash-son. It's dissolution."

Asvarr took three deliberate steps forward. With each footfall, the ground beneath him transformed—no longer mimicking either the Wanderer's perfect order or surrendering to formless chaos, but becoming something between—organic crystalline structures that grew in fractal patterns, ordered yet ever-evolving.

"And perfect order isn't protection," Asvarr countered. "It's stagnation."

The Wanderer's spear came up, its point aimed at Asvarr's heart. "Then show me this third path you claim to walk. Prove it can withstand the weight of what's to come."

Without waiting for a response, the Wanderer lunged. His spear became a streak of frozen sunlight that tore through the space between them. Asvarr's body—no longer entirely flesh but something between matter and energy—responded with instincts beyond his conscious control. The constellation blade intercepted the spear with a sound like mountains cracking open.

Where the weapons met, reality itself strained and tore. Through the wound, Asvarr glimpsed multiple layers of existence simultaneously—Alfheim's dissolving skies, Muspelheim's volcanic heart, the void-ocean where cosmic serpents swam, and something else, something ancient that watched through eyes composed of dying stars.

***

The Wanderer pressed forward, and the rift around them began reshaping itself to match his will—flat planes replacing curved surfaces, jagged edges smoothing into geometric perfection, colors sorting themselves into precise spectrums.

"The pattern requires structure!" The Wanderer's voice boomed, setting the ordering process in motion faster. "Hierarchy preserves! Without it, all returns to formless void!"

Asvarr felt the weight of the Wanderer's conviction pressing against his mind, trying to reshape his thoughts as easily as it reshaped their surroundings. The crystalline formations across his skin cracked under the pressure, golden sap weeping from the fissures.

"Not hierarchy." Asvarr gritted through clenched teeth. "Connection!"

He drove the constellation blade forward, to communicate. Where the blade touched the rift's substance, the changes were subtle but profound. Order remained, but with spaces for adaptation. Structure persisted, but with room to evolve.

The Wanderer hissed as his perfect geometric patterns began developing unexpected variations, spiral offshoots growing from straight lines, circles budding smaller versions of themselves along their circumference.

"You would replace divine certainty with... what?" the Wanderer demanded, spear flashing in complex patterns that forced the landscape back toward rigid perfection. "Endless change? That path leads to madness!"

They circled each other, weapons clashing, in competing visions. With each exchange, sections of the rift transformed according to whose influence momentarily dominated—portions becoming crystalline lattices of perfect mathematical precision under the Wanderer's power, while others developed intricate, ever-evolving organic patterns under Asvarr's.

"Not endless change." Asvarr's transformed vision allowed him to see the patterns forming and unforming between them. "Necessary evolution. The pattern learns through adaptation, not repetition."

The Wanderer's face contorted with something between fury and fear. "You speak of things beyond your understanding, ash-son. I am what remains of Odin's regret given form! I remember what came before, what waits beyond the void-hunger!"

His spear struck down with the force of divine judgment, sending shockwaves of pure order radiating outward. Where they touched, all complexity was stripped away, leaving only perfect, sterile geometry.

But Asvarr had spent three days communing with cosmic serpents, had bound three anchors into a unified force within his transformed flesh. He didn't try to match the Wanderer's power with equal force. Instead, he moved with it, redirecting rather than opposing.

"Memory isn't wisdom," Asvarr said, his voice creating frost crystals that hung suspended in the amber light. "And fear isn't foresight."

The starforged chain around his wrist flared with protective power as Asvarr drove the constellation blade into the ground at his feet. The impact sent ripples of transformation outward—incorporating the Wanderer's order into something more complex, more resilient. Fractal patterns bloomed across the crystalline surfaces, each containing perfect order within while forming part of a greater, ever-evolving whole.

"This is the third path," Asvarr said, the words forming visible equations in the air between them. "Transformation through balanced integration."

The Wanderer's face twisted with recognition and denial. "Impossible! The void-hunger cannot be integrated! It must remain bound or it will consume all!"

"You remember Odin's fear," Asvarr said, taking another step forward. The ground beneath him became a living tessellation, patterns within patterns that maintained order while allowing for growth. "But you've forgotten his wisdom."

For a moment, doubt flickered across the Wanderer's face, visible in the wavering of his stellar cloak. Then his expression hardened again.

"Words. Empty words from a vessel that hasn't seen what I've seen." The Wanderer raised his spear high, and the space above them tore open, revealing glimpses of what lay beyond the void—forms that existed before shape, entities that predated consciousness itself.

"You would unleash this upon all worlds?" The Wanderer's voice rose to a thunderous pitch. "This is what waits beyond the pattern!"

***

Asvarr didn't look away from the terrible beauty of the infinite. Through his transformed senses, he perceived what the Wanderer could not—that these primordial forces weren't merely chaos given form, but possibility without constraint. Not mindless dissolution but genesis without arbitrary limitation.

"I see it," Asvarr said quietly. "And I see you, Wanderer. Your nine cycles of failure weren't caused by the weakness of your vessels or the strength of your opposition."

The constellation blade in Asvarr's hand transformed again, becoming a thread of light that connected earth and sky, order and chaos, preservation and transformation. The threefold rhythm of his bound anchors—flame, memory, and starlight—pulsed through his veins in unified harmony.

"Your failure was always the same," Asvarr continued, advancing another step. "You sought to control what must be embraced."

The Wanderer's face contorted with rage and desperate certainty. "Then you doom all worlds to dissolution! The void-hunger stirs with every anchor you bind! What sleeps beneath the roots awakens with each binding broken!"

With a battle cry that shattered the air itself, the Wanderer charged forward, his spear aimed directly at Asvarr's heart. The weapon's point transformed in mid-thrust, becoming pure mathematical abstraction, an equation designed to solve Asvarr completely.

But Asvarr had been solved by greater powers—had allowed himself to be unmade and remade by the primordial serpent's song. The Wanderer's strike, devastating as it was, found no purchase in Asvarr's transformed essence.

The constellation blade met the spear with a sound like reality tearing itself apart. Where they touched, a new rift formed within the rift—a place between places, where time itself splintered into countless fragmentary streams.

Through this opening, both Asvarr and the Wanderer glimpsed what lay at the heart of existence—the relationship between the Tree and Serpent. Structure and freedom in perpetual dance, each defining the other, neither complete alone.

"This," Asvarr whispered, the single word carrying the weight of revelation, "is what Yggdrasil was meant to become."

The Wanderer's single eye widened in recognition and denial. The memory buried within his essence—the true purpose of the anchors, the ultimate goal of the binding—surged to the surface after nine cycles of suppression.

"No," the Wanderer breathed, his certainty faltering for the first time. "It can't be."

The spear in his hand flickered, its perfect form developing minute variations, subtle complexities that had never been part of its original design.

Asvarr felt the tipping point approaching—the moment when revelation would either transform the Wanderer or destroy him completely. And in that instant, he understood what must be done, what sacrifice the third path demanded.

The true memory, the knowledge that had driven the Wanderer's actions from the beginning, must be claimed. Not destroyed, not denied, but integrated.

Asvarr raised the constellation blade one final time, to reflect. In its shimmering surface, the Wanderer saw himself as he truly was—not divine certainty given form, but divine doubt searching for resolution.

"The moment comes," Asvarr said simply, as the rift around them began to collapse under the weight of competing truths. "Choose transformation, or be broken by it."

The crystalline ground beneath their feet shattered into countless fragments, each containing perfect order and boundless possibility in equal measure. Above them, the amber membrane tore open completely, revealing the convergence of all Nine Realms approaching with inexorable certainty.

***

The Wanderer's spear trembled in his grasp as reality itself awaited his answer.

The Wanderer's spear thrust forward, its point a mathematical certainty aimed at Asvarr's heart. The weapon tore through dimensions as it moved, trailing equations that rewrote the fabric of the rift with each passing moment. A killing blow delivered with the full weight of divine authority behind it.

Asvarr did not dodge. He did not parry. He shifted.

The crystalline formations across his skin fragmented and reformed in continuous adaptation. His body—no longer bound by fixed physical laws—flowed around the spear's path, becoming something between solid and possibility.

Where the weapon should have impaled him, it passed through a momentary void that closed behind it.

The Wanderer staggered forward, thrown off balance by the absence of expected resistance. His eye widened in disbelief.

"Impossible," he hissed, the word fracturing into glittering shards.

Asvarr's hand closed around the spear's shaft. Frost spread from his fingertips, transforming the weapon's rigid perfection. Fractal patterns bloomed along its length, tiny variations that compounded into complexity while maintaining the spear's essential structure.

"This is what adaptation looks like," Asvarr said. His voice rang with harmonics that vibrated through the crystalline ground, causing it to resonate in sympathy. "Growth within structure. Change within continuity."

The Wanderer's face contorted with fury and terror. He wrenched the spear free and whirled it overhead, tearing open the membrane above them. Through the wound poured raw mathematical precision—geometric forms of such perfect clarity they burned the eye.

"Order preserves!" the Wanderer roared. "Without hierarchy, all dissolves into formless void!"

The ordered patterns rushed toward Asvarr like an avalanche of crystal, threatening to lock him into unchanging perfection. The crystalline formations across his skin cracked under the pressure, golden sap weeping from fissures. For a moment, he felt his consciousness being forced into rigid pathways—the flexibility that had allowed him to integrate three anchors hardening into unbreakable channels.

But Asvarr had been unmade and remade by greater forces than the Wanderer's will. He had survived the primordial serpent's unmaking song. He had chosen which threads of identity to preserve through transformation.

Through the starforged chain around his wrist, he recalled the four elements that anchored his existence: memory, purpose, connection, grief. Not static qualities but evolving relationships with his own experience. The chain flared with protective power, its links glowing with interior light.

Asvarr didn't fight the Wanderer's ordered onslaught directly. Instead, he incorporated it—allowing the mathematical precision to flow through him while maintaining the space for adaptation within its framework.

"Nine cycles," Asvarr said, advancing through the storm of perfect forms. "Nine attempts to impose order from above, or surrender to chaos from below."

Each step left footprints of crystalline frost that grew in fractal patterns—ordered yet ever-evolving. The verdant crown extending down his back pulsed with unified rhythm, matching the threefold cadence of his bound anchors.

The Wanderer retreated, his formerly proud stance weakening as Asvarr advanced. For the first time, uncertainty flickered across his face.

"You cannot understand," the Wanderer said, voice dropping to a desperate whisper. "You haven't witnessed what I've witnessed. You haven't borne what I've borne."

"Then show me," Asvarr said, extending his hand. The constellation blade had vanished, replaced by empty palm marked with the oath-sigil he shared with Brynja. "Through communion."

The Wanderer's eye widened in alarm. "Impossible! The memory would shatter your mind. It has driven greater vessels than you to madness."

"I am not merely vessel," Asvarr said, continuing his steady advance. "I am Pattern-Keeper. I maintain coherence across fragmentation."

The rift around them trembled, sections of ordered crystalline formations sprouting unexpected variations, perfect circles budding spirals along their circumference. The Wanderer looked around in mounting panic as his influence over the environment weakened.

"Stay back," he warned, brandishing his spear with fading authority. "I am what remains of Odin's regret given form! I have walked nine cycles!"

Asvarr felt no triumph in the Wanderer's retreat, only sadness. Through his transformed perception, he recognized what the Wanderer truly was—divine uncertainty, caught in a loop of repetition because he could not imagine new possibilities.

"You remember Odin's fear," Asvarr said softly, "but you've forgotten his wisdom. The Allfather sacrificed his eye for knowledge and hung from Yggdrasil for nine days to gain understanding. He knew that wisdom requires transformation, not repetition."

The Wanderer's face twisted in recognition. Something ancient stirred behind his gaze—a fragment of true divinity not wholly lost after nine cycles of diminishment.

For an instant, the rift stilled around them. Then, with a cry of mingled rage and surrender, the Wanderer lunged forward, his spear aimed directly at Asvarr's outstretched hand.

Asvarr didn't flinch. The spear-tip pierced his palm, and instead of blood, equations poured from the wound—the mathematical underpinnings of reality itself made momentarily visible.

Where their essences connected, something transferred between them. Through recognition.

Asvarr saw it then—the memory that had haunted the Wanderer across nine cycles. The knowledge that had shaped his every action since the first binding:

Yggdrasil had never been meant as permanent prison or eternal foundation. It was transition—a growing vessel for something greater. The nine anchors weren't merely bindings to contain the void-hunger, but connection points in a vast transmutation. Tree and serpent, order and chaos, were to be gradually integrated, not eternally opposed. Each cycle bringing them closer to synthesis.

But the Allfather grew fearful. Watching the void-hunger strain against the anchors, he could not trust the process. He could not surrender control to transformation. And so he imposed hierarchy, calcified what was meant to evolve, and doomed the pattern to nine cycles of failure.

The memory burned through Asvarr's consciousness like molten gold, fusing with his existing knowledge, permanently altering his perception. Places where his humanity had sheltered—simple desires, straightforward emotions, uncomplicated loyalties—dissolved under the weight of cosmic understanding.

With the memory came responsibility. As perspective, inseparable from his identity now. He could no more unsee this truth than he could unsee color or forget his name.

The crystalline formations across his skin cracked wide, revealing luminous interior chambers that pulsed with threefold light. His eyes—once brown, then mixed with gold and silver—became pools of shifting constellations. Through them, he perceived reality's woven layers simultaneously, from physical manifestation to mathematical foundation to pure possibility.

The Wanderer collapsed to his knees, his spear clattering against the crystalline ground. The sound echoed strangely, rippling outward in concentric circles that transformed everything they touched. His form wavered, the god-aspect draining from him like water through cupped fingers.

Asvarr stared down at his own hand. The wound had already closed, leaving a perfect ring of spiraling equations etched into his palm. When he looked at the Wanderer, he saw the necessary counterpoint—the voice of preservation without which transformation would become mere dissolution.

"I could destroy you," Asvarr said, the words creating mathematical proofs in the air between them. "It would be simpler. Cleaner."

The Wanderer looked up, his face drawn with exhaustion. The cosmic power that had sustained him across nine cycles had been fundamentally altered by the sharing of his burden.

"Why don't you?" he asked, genuine curiosity replacing adversarial defiance.

"Because balance requires tension," Asvarr answered. "The third path isn't elimination of opposition but integration of necessary conflict. Preservation and transformation in continuous dialogue."

The rift around them had begun to stabilize into something new—neither the Wanderer's rigid perfection nor formless chaos, but a living framework that maintained structure while allowing for evolution. The crystalline ground grew in recursive patterns, self-similar across scales yet never identical in detail.

"You truly believe this cycle will be different?" The Wanderer's voice carried nine cycles of failed hope.

"It already is different," Asvarr said, gesturing to the transformed landscape around them. "I haven't defeated you. I've incorporated what you represent. Preservation without stagnation."

The Wanderer lifted his spear from the ground, examining it with newfound curiosity. The weapon had changed—still recognizable as Gungnir, still embodying divine authority, but now wreathed in fractal patterns that allowed for variation within its fundamental structure.

"I don't know how to exist without my purpose," the Wanderer admitted, a vulnerability in his voice that nine cycles of cosmic battles had never revealed.

"Find a new one," Asvarr said simply. "Not opposition but composition. Help build what comes next."

The Wanderer rose to his feet, diminished yet somehow more authentic than before. The stellar cloak he wore had shifted from rigid constellations to flowing nebulae—still ordered but more dynamic.

"Convergence approaches," he said, nodding toward the rift's periphery, where reality had begun dissolving into pure potential. "Hours, not days. We've accelerated the pattern beyond prediction."

"Then we should return to Muspelheim," Asvarr said. "The fourth anchor awaits at the Storm Forge."

The memory extracted from the Wanderer continued integrating with Asvarr's consciousness, altering his perception with each passing moment. He looked down at his hands—no longer recognizable as human, with crystalline formations creating geometric lattices across what had once been skin. The verdant crown had spread down his spine, branches interwoven with stellarite crystals that glowed with interior light.

He knew, with certainty beyond doubt, that each anchor bound would take him further from humanity. The fourth would transform his voice, the fifth would claim his name. Yet the path required completion—for the sake of all reality.

The Wanderer followed his gaze, understanding dawning in his single eye. "You've accepted the sacrifice of your humanity."

It wasn't a question, but Asvarr answered anyway. "Humanity isn't merely form or limitation. It's perspective. Connection. I carry what matters forward, even as shape changes."

The rift trembled around them, reality straining under the weight of competing truths resolved into new synthesis. Through tears in the amber membrane above, Asvarr glimpsed Alfheim's dissolving skyscape and beyond it, the void-ocean where cosmic serpents swam. The boundaries between realms had grown tissue-thin, convergence accelerating with each transformation.

"We should leave this place before it collapses completely," the Wanderer said, planting his spear against the crystalline ground. The impact sent ripples of ordered energy outward, creating a temporary pathway through the dissolving rift.

Asvarr nodded, but before he could step onto the path, a memory rose unbidden from his transformed consciousness—shared through connection with the sentient branch Rootstar:

A child in a realm of pure potential, dreaming worlds into being. Future, waiting to manifest fully. The Tree not conclusion but beginning.

The vision vanished as quickly as it had appeared, leaving Asvarr momentarily disoriented by temporal displacement. The memory from the Wanderer continued restructuring his perception, making familiar concepts alien and revealing hidden relationships between seemingly disparate elements.

With each passing moment, his humanity receded further, replaced by cosmic awareness that stretched his consciousness across perspectives no mortal was meant to hold. Yet through the starforged chain around his wrist, he maintained connection to what mattered: memory, purpose, connection, grief. Transformed, his humanity evolving rather than diminishing.

"Convergence awaits," Asvarr said, his voice creating equations that solved themselves in midair. "The fourth anchor calls."

He stepped onto the path the Wanderer had created, moving through layers of reality simultaneously. Behind him, the rift collapsed into singularity—a seed of possibility containing all they had created together, planted in reality's foundation. Neither victory nor defeat but necessary synthesis, preservation and transformation in balanced tension.

What grew from it would depend on what came next.

CHAPTER 30

THE CHILD WHO DREAMED THE TREE

Alfheim died around them. The once-stable realm fragmented into competing realities—patches of forest crystallizing into geometric perfection beside meadows where flowers grew upside down and breathed instead of blooming. The sky had ceased to exist in any meaningful sense, replaced by a fractured membrane through which the void-ocean beyond bled into perception.

Asvarr stood with Brynja and Yrsa at the edge of what had been the silver forest. His transformed body hummed with the threefold rhythm of his bound anchors—flame, memory, and starlight pulsing in synchronization beneath crystalline skin. The Memory extracted from the Wanderer continued to spread through his consciousness, rewriting connections between thoughts, revealing relationships between concepts he'd never perceived before.

"Alfheim will be gone within hours," Brynja said, her wooden hand tracing patterns in the dissolving air. Constellation marks embedded in her bark-flesh glowed with interior light, responding to the accelerating convergence of the Nine Realms. "We need to leave before the final collapse."

Yrsa nodded silent agreement, her hands forming boundary-walker signs with urgent precision. Though voiceless since her sacrifice, her eyes conveyed complex meaning—pointing toward a thinning section of reality where Muspelheim's volcanic glow bled through.

"The Storm Forge awaits," Asvarr agreed, his voice creating frost equations that solved themselves in midair. The words felt strange in his mouth, the memory-integration changing how he experienced even simple communication. "The fourth anchor calls."

He took a step toward the boundary, but a sudden pressure against his spine halted his movement. The crystalline branches of his verdant crown vibrated with recognition as something reached across dimensional barriers to establish contact.

"Rootstar," Asvarr breathed, feeling the sentient branch's consciousness touch his own.

The connection flared across the vast distance separating them—Rootstar physically remained in Muspelheim, yet its consciousness stretched beyond spatial constraints. Through this link, information poured into Asvarr's mind: mathematical proofs tessellating into complex structures, emotional resonances harmonizing in perfect fifths, memories crystallizing into fractals of experiential data.

His body staggered under the informational onslaught. Brynja caught him, her wooden arm supporting his increasingly inhuman form with surprising tenderness.

"What's happening?" she demanded, truth-runes flaring golden across her face.

***

"Rootstar has... found something," Asvarr managed, each word physically remolding the air into knowledge-structures. "In the celestial Anchor... a memory so old it predates memory itself."

The pressure intensified as Rootstar forced its discovery through their connection. Asvarr's vision fractured—one eye perceiving the dissolving forest, the other seeing through Rootstar's sensory apparatus in distant Muspelheim. The dual perspective tore at his consciousness until the starforged chain around his wrist flared with protective power, its four links—memory, purpose, connection, grief—stabilizing his identity against dissolution.

"We must sit," Asvarr said, dropping to his knees on ground that phase-shifted between solid matter and mathematical construct. "This requires... all my concentration."

Brynja and Yrsa formed a protective circle around him, their backs to his kneeling form. Brynja's wooden arm sprouted defensive thorns while Yrsa's fingers wove boundary-ward signs into the fragmenting air, creating a momentary bubble of stability in Alfheim's accelerating collapse.

Within this fragile shelter, Asvarr surrendered to the vision Rootstar thrust upon him—experiencing a memory extracted from the celestial Anchor, a truth so ancient it had been forgotten by reality itself.

The vision exploded behind his eyes:

Void without form or limit. No up, no down, no here, no there. Pure potential, untamed by category or constraint. Within this infinite canvas of possibility, a child.

Not human, not divine, not any classification a conscious mind might impose. An entity of pure awareness experiencing itself for the first time, casting consciousness like a pebble into still water, watching ripples of consequence expand outward.

The child's thoughts create patterns in the potential-soup. Simple at first—symmetries, rhythms, resonances. Each thought crystallizing into a seed of structure around which further complexity can grow.

With growing delight, the child imagines more complex arrangements. What if separation existed? What if parts could recognize themselves as distinct from yet connected to the whole? What if time flowed in one direction, creating narrative from mere sequence?

The void-potential responds to these questions, congealing into proto-structures that embody the answers. The child claps in delight as reality itself becomes a mirror reflecting its imagination.

But creation is hungry work. The child grows tired, imagining a place to rest—a great Tree with branches spreading into infinite possibility and roots anchoring into emergent past. A sleeping place where dreaming and creating can become one action.

As the child drifts into dream-state, the Tree solidifies from concept into manifested structure. Imagined into being. Nine great branches extend outward, each supporting a nascent realm growing from the child's dreaming consciousness. Nine roots reach downward, each anchoring an aspect of emergent reality.

The child sleeps, and within sleep continues dreaming. Dreams of creatures who walk upon worlds, who build and destroy, who love and hate. Dreams of gods who shape and guide, who contest and collaborate. Dreams of forces that bind and unbind, that preserve and transform.

As these dreams intensify, they gain independence, self-organizing according to their internal logics. The sleeping child becomes the Tree, the Tree becomes the realms, the realms become history unfolding according to its nature.

Time passes—or the concept of time emerges, allowing for the perception of sequential events. The dream-entities grow more complex, more autonomous, more forgetful of their dream-nature. They create myths to explain their origins, forgetting they themselves were merely thoughts in a sleeping mind.

Some dream-entities—the gods—retain partial memory. They glimpse their nature as manifestations of the dreaming child, and the knowledge terrifies them. What if the child wakes? What if the dream ends? What if all they have built dissolves back into formless void?

And so they weave bindings around the sleeping child-that-is-the-Tree, ensuring the dream continues. Nine anchors driven into the fabric of possibility itself, designed to stabilize the dream-creation while obscuring its true nature even from themselves.

But dreams cannot remain static. Their nature is transformation, evolution, surprise. The child stirs within its sleep, causing tremors throughout creation. The anchors strain against the forces of change.

Nine times the pattern fractures and reforms, each cycle bringing closer the inevitable truth: the Tree is future waiting to manifest fully. What has been experienced as history—gods, realms, conflicts—are elements of a cosmic gestation not yet complete.

The dream approaches waking.

The vision receded, leaving Asvarr gasping on hands and knees, his crystalline flesh radiating heat as his system processed the impossible revelation. Around him, Alfheim's dissolution had accelerated—trees unwinding into constituent equations, mountains folding into non-Euclidean geometries before evaporating into numerical mist.

Brynja knelt beside him, her wooden features contorted with concern. "What did you see?" The truth-runes across her face pulsed with golden inquiry.

"Everything," Asvarr whispered, his voice creating frozen fractals that encapsulated fragments of the vision. "The beginning that is also the end."

He struggled to translate the experience into language they could comprehend, his transformed mind racing through implications that reshaped his understanding of their entire quest.

"There was a child," he began, each word forming visible equations in the air, "in a place of pure potential, before reality had form. This child dreamed Yggdrasil into being—in a state outside time. And the dream continues still, approaching completion."

Yrsa's eyes widened, her hands forming boundary-walker signs so rapidly they left traces of blue light hanging in the air. Though mute, her meaning was clear: if the Tree was dream-made-manifest, then what did that make them?

"We are elements of the dream," Asvarr confirmed, reading her silent question. "Thought-forms given independence. The gods glimpsed this truth and feared it—that's why they created the anchors, to stabilize the dream while hiding its nature."

Brynja's wooden fingers dug into the dissolving earth, her single cosmic eye staring into distances beyond physical perception. "Then the Shattering..."

"Wasn't failure but metamorphosis," Asvarr said, rising to his feet. The crystalline formations across his body had rearranged themselves, forming patterns that echoed the child's thought-structures from the vision. "The dream approaching waking state."

Around them, the last fragments of Alfheim's reality began collapsing inward, converting matter back into the pure mathematics from which it had emerged. The boundary-ward Yrsa had created flickered, struggling to maintain their pocket of stability against the realm's accelerating dissolution.

Asvarr felt the revelation settling into his transformed consciousness, filling gaps in his understanding that he hadn't recognized until now. The Wanderer's extracted memory combined with this ancient vision created a complete picture that reshaped everything he thought he knew.

"The anchors were never just prisons," he said, watching revelation dawn in Brynja's mismatched eyes. "They were developmental markers—growth stages in the dream's evolution toward waking."

Yrsa's hands formed a single, emphatic question: What happens when the dreamer wakes?

Before Asvarr could answer, the ground beneath them vanished completely, converted into pure numerical sequences that scattered like dust. They hung suspended in conceptual space—transitioning between states of being.

Through his transformed perception, Asvarr glimpsed all Nine Realms simultaneously: Alfheim dissolving into mathematical purity, Muspelheim's volcanic heart crystallizing into perfect geometries, Niflheim's frozen wastes melting into pools of concentrated possibility. The boundaries between worlds had grown tissue-thin, convergence accelerating beyond prediction.

"We need to reach the Storm Forge," he said, extending hands to both companions. "The fourth anchor awaits."

Brynja clasped his right hand, her wooden fingers intertwining with his crystalline ones. "And if we complete the anchors' binding? Will that wake the dreamer or prolong the dream?"

"Neither," Asvarr said with certainty born from integrated knowledge. "It will transform the dream into something new—something that was always meant to be."

Yrsa hesitated before taking his left hand, her eyes asking what none of them had dared voice: how much more of his humanity would be sacrificed to this transformation?

Asvarr had no comforting answer. The starforged chain burned cold against his wrist, its four links—memory, purpose, connection, grief—preserving what mattered while acknowledging that form must yield to function.

"The fourth anchor will claim my voice," he said simply. "The fifth, my name. But humanity isn't merely form or limitation—it's perspective, connection. These I carry forward, even as shape changes."

Yrsa nodded, accepting his answer with grim determination. Her free hand formed boundary-walker signs that tore open the fragmenting barrier between realms, creating a pathway toward Muspelheim's amber glow.

Brynja squeezed Asvarr's hand, her truth-runes confirming sincerity. "Whatever comes, we face it together."

Asvarr felt the immensity of what they'd discovered pressing against his consciousness—the revelation that would reshape their understanding of their entire quest. The Tree was beginning. Their journey not restoration but transformation. The anchors not bindings but growth markers in an evolving cosmic dream.

And convergence approached—hours, not days—the moment when all anchors would reach resonance and reality would become malleable. The moment when the dream might finally transform into waking.

With one last look at Alfheim's dissolving fragments, Asvarr led his companions toward the boundary-tear Yrsa had created. The Storm Forge waited in Muspelheim, the fourth anchor calling to his transformed essence with promises of both power and sacrifice.

What grew from this moment would depend on what they did next.

***

Muspelheim breathed fire around them. The volcanic realm rushed to greet their arrival as they stepped through Yrsa's boundary-tear, solid ground materializing beneath their feet while heat clawed at their lungs. Asvarr's crystalline flesh refracted the omnipresent amber light, casting prismatic patterns across the black obsidian plateau where they stood.

"The Storm Forge lies there," Brynja said, pointing toward an anvil-shaped mountain wreathed in lightning. Her wooden arm had darkened in Muspelheim's heat, constellation patterns embedded in her bark now glowing molten-bright. "Three hours' journey across the brimstone fields."

Asvarr nodded, his mind still reeling from the celestial Anchor's revelation. The vision of the dreaming child continued unfolding through his transformed consciousness, showing him layers of meaning that his previous understanding couldn't have contained. Each breath brought new insights, further implications spreading through his awareness like cracks through ice.

"We can't simply restore what was," he said, frost equations crystallizing from his words. "The pattern demands evolution, not repetition."

Yrsa's hands formed boundary-walker signs that asked what this meant for their quest. Though voiceless, her expressions and gestures conveyed complex meaning that Asvarr had grown increasingly adept at interpreting.

"It means everything changes," he answered, watching the equations drift and shatter in Muspelheim's heat.

He knelt to touch the obsidian ground, feeling the realm's fierce pulse beneath his fingertips. The transformation of his flesh had progressed further—crystalline formations now dominated what had once been skin, mathematical structures replacing cellular ones. His perception split across multiple layers of reality, seeing the volcanic plateau both as physical terrain and as complex problem-solving system simultaneously.

"Yggdrasil was never meant to be static," he explained, rising to his feet. "Each cycle of growth, destruction, and rebirth incorporates new elements. The nine previous attempts failed because they sought preservation without transformation."

Brynja paced along the plateau's edge, her cosmic eye reflecting patterns invisible to normal sight. "The Verdant Five showed me fragments of this truth, though they misunderstood what it meant. They thought themselves the new elements to be incorporated."

"The Wanderer made the opposite error," Asvarr said. "He remembered Odin's fear without Odin's wisdom. Tried to impose perfect order from above rather than allowing balanced evolution."

The memory extracted from the Wanderer continued integrating with Asvarr's consciousness, each revelation refining his understanding. The star-forged chain around his wrist burned cold, its four links—memory, purpose, connection, grief—stabilizing his identity while allowing necessary transformation.

A sudden pressure against his mind announced Rootstar's presence. The sentient branch, physically waiting at the Storm Forge, stretched its consciousness across the brimstone fields to connect with Asvarr. Their communication transcended language, flowing as direct concept-transfer.

"Rootstar confirms our path," Asvarr translated for the others, his voice creating intricate frost mandalas that evaporated instantly in Muspelheim's heat. "The anchors were never meant as permanent bindings but as transitional structures—necessary scaffolding for the dream's evolution."

Yrsa's hands traced urgent questions: What of the dreaming child? Will it wake? What happens then?

Asvarr searched the integrated knowledge flowing through his transformed consciousness, but found only partial answers. "The dreaming approaches waking state, but 'waking' may not mean what we understand by the term. The child-that-is-the-Tree experiences reality differently than we do."

Lightning struck the anvil mountain ahead, the thunder rolling across brimstone plains to break against the plateau where they stood. Through his expanded perception, Asvarr recognized it as no random discharge but communication—the fourth anchor calling to his essence.

"We must keep moving," he said, nodding toward the Storm Forge. "Convergence approaches rapidly. We have three hours at most."

They descended from the plateau, following a path of cooled obsidian through Muspelheim's volcanic landscape. Magma pools bubbled on either side, spitting droplets of liquid fire that hissed and died against the crystalline formations protecting Asvarr's increasingly inhuman form.

As they walked, the vision's implications continued unfolding through his mind. Memories from the celestial Anchor combined with knowledge extracted

from the Wanderer to form a complete picture that transformed his understanding of their purpose.

"The Shattering wasn't failure," he said abruptly, breaking the tense silence.
"It was metamorphosis—necessary transformation for the dream's evolution."

Brynja glanced sideways at him, truth-runes glowing across her bark-covered
face. "Then our quest isn't what we thought."

"We're not restoring," Asvarr agreed. "We're facilitating what must be—a
Tree that integrates all elements rather than opposing them. Serpent-chaos with
divine-order. Memory with potential. Structure with freedom."

Yrsa's hands formed a shape that asked about the price of such transformation.

Asvarr touched the crystalline formations spreading across his chest where
humanity had once resided. "Form changes. Function remains. What matters
persists."

They walked in silence then, each processing the implications in their own
way. Around them, Muspelheim's landscape seemed to respond to their passage—magma streams parting before them, obsidian paths cooling beneath their
feet, lightning striking in rhythmic patterns that matched their footfalls. The
realm recognized what Asvarr carried and what approached with convergence.

Through his transformed perception, Asvarr glimpsed the state of all Nine
Realms simultaneously: Alfheim dissolving into pure concept, Midgard straining under accelerated wyrd-tides, Niflheim's ice formations developing complex
self-similar patterns. Everywhere, the cosmic dream approached waking state.

The vision of the dreaming child continued unfolding, showing potential
futures—infinite branching possibilities depending on how the anchors were
directed at convergence.

Asvarr stopped suddenly, revelation striking him with physical force. His
companions halted beside him, watching with concern as golden sap wept from
cracks in his crystalline flesh.

"I understand now," he whispered, his voice producing mathematical proofs in
the super-heated air. "Nine previous cycles failed because they attempted to either

wake the dreamer or prolong the dream. Neither approach works because neither acknowledges the dream's purpose."

"Which is?" Brynja asked, truth-runes flaring.

"Transformation of the dreamer itself." Asvarr's gaze fixed on the Storm Forge ahead, lightning now striking in complex patterns that carved equations into the mountainside. "The child dreamed the Tree to become something new—neither sleeping nor waking but evolved. The dream isn't separate from the dreamer but its pathway to new existence."

Yrsa's hands formed boundary-walker signs with urgent precision: How does this change what we must do?

"The approach, not the goal," Asvarr answered. "We still bind the anchors, but not to imprison or preserve. We bind to connect, to integrate, to transform the entire pattern into something neither we nor the gods could imagine—what the dream was always becoming."

Lightning struck the ground before them, shattering obsidian into perfect geometric fragments that levitated momentarily before resolving into a crystalline pathway leading directly to the Storm Forge. The fourth anchor grew impatient, calling Asvarr with increasing urgency.

They followed this newly-formed path across Muspelheim's chaotic terrain, magma flows parting around the geometric structures with unnatural precision. Above them, the sky had begun transforming— no longer merely amber but shot through with equations visible only to Asvarr's transformed sight, the mathematical underpinnings of reality briefly made perceptible.

"The pattern becomes visible as convergence approaches," he explained, noting his companions' confusion at his constant skyward glances. "The dream's true structure revealing itself."

As they approached the Storm Forge, a familiar figure emerged from the lightning-wreathed slopes—Rootstar in physical form rather than merely consciousness, its sentient branch structure having grown to human size. It moved with impossible grace across Muspelheim's unstable terrain, its form continuously reconfiguring according to mathematical principles.

"Pattern-Keeper," it greeted Asvarr, voice resonating with harmonics that made the very air vibrate. "The Storm Forge awaits. The fourth anchor grows restless with certainty of your approach."

"You've seen the vision," Asvarr said. It wasn't a question.

"I share your understanding," Rootstar confirmed, extending a tendril that connected briefly with Asvarr's verdant crown. "The child dreams not to sleep but to become. Nine cycles of failure because gods feared transformation more than destruction."

Brynja approached the sentient branch cautiously, her wooden arm responding to Rootstar's proximity with new growth along her fingers. "Will binding the anchors wake the dreamer?"

"Neither wake nor prolong sleep," Rootstar answered, mathematical proofs flowing along its surface in response to the question. "Transform the dream-state itself into something new—integration rather than separation."

Yrsa's hands formed a question that needed no translation: What awaits Asvarr at the Storm Forge?

Rootstar's form reconfigured, branches twisting to create a representational model of the fourth anchor—a structure like lightning frozen in mid-strike, geometric precision combined with chaotic energy.

"Creation and destruction in perfect balance," Rootstar explained. "It will claim your voice, Pattern-Keeper. Words becoming pure concept. Communication transcending language."

Asvarr nodded, having already accepted this sacrifice. The starforged chain burned cold against his wrist, reminding him what must be preserved through transformation—memory, purpose, connection, grief. Humanity existing as perspective rather than limitation.

"The storm-forge accepts sacrifice willingly given," he said, frost equations hanging briefly in the air before dissipating. "My voice for fourth integration."

Brynja stepped closer, truth-runes glowing as she studied his crystalline face. "And then Helheim for the fifth anchor, where death and legacy converge."

"Where the final binding awaits," Asvarr confirmed. "The cycle completes, the pattern transforms."

Lightning struck the Storm Forge with increasing frequency, each discharge now creating visible equations that lingered before dispersing into the amber sky. The fourth anchor grew restless, its call resonating through Asvarr's transformed flesh with painful intensity.

"We have one hour before convergence accelerates beyond prediction," Rootstar warned, its form responding to mathematical currents flowing visibly through Muspelheim's atmosphere. "The binding must be completed before alignment reaches critical mass."

Asvarr looked at his companions—Brynja with her wooden arm and cosmic eye, truth-runes ensuring honesty in every word; Yrsa with her boundary-walker knowledge and selfless sacrifice, mute but communicating complex meaning through gesture alone. Each had given something essential to reach this point, their humanity partially surrendered to cosmic necessity.

"When we began this journey, I sought vengeance for my clan," he said, the frost equations formed by his words growing more complex with each sentence. "Then restoration of what was lost. Now I understand my true purpose—to facilitate what must be, not recreate what was."

Yrsa's hands signed: The third path. Not preservation. Not destruction. Transformation.

"The child dreamed Yggdrasil to become something new," Asvarr agreed, watching lightning carve runes into the Storm Forge's obsidian slopes. "The Tree grew to facilitate the dream's evolution. Now we bind the anchors to help it transform into waking."

Brynja placed her wooden hand against his crystalline chest, truth-runes glowing with golden certainty. "Whatever comes, we face it together."

The Storm Forge called again, lightning striking in precisely timed sequences that spelled out mathematical certainties across the anvil mountain's face. The fourth anchor's pull grew irresistible, drawing Asvarr forward with physical force.

CHILDREN OF THE SERPENT SKY

His entire body resonated with its frequency, crystalline formations vibrating in sympathy until it seemed he might shatter from within.

"I must go alone," he said, the words creating frost equations so complex they momentarily stabilized in Muspelheim's heat. "The binding requires solitude."

Yrsa's hands formed a question she had asked once before: How much of you will remain after the fourth binding?

Asvarr looked down at his transformed body—crystalline formations where skin had been, mathematical structures replacing organic ones, threefold rhythm of his bound anchors pulsing in harmony beneath his chest. So little humanity remained in form, yet through the starforged chain his essential nature persisted—memory, purpose, connection, grief.

"Enough," he said simply. "What matters remains."

Lightning struck directly before him, carving a perfect staircase of obsidian steps leading up the Storm Forge's side. The fourth anchor beckoned with mathematical precision, offering creation-and-destruction in perfect balance for the price of his voice.

Asvarr took the first step upward, feeling the pull of the storm-forge of Muspelheim calling to his transformed essence. The understanding settled within him, crystalizing into perfect certainty: the quest was never about restoration but facilitation. Helping what must be.

Behind him, Brynja and Yrsa watched in silence as he ascended toward the binding that would claim his voice, transforming words into pure concept. Before him, lightning carved equations into obsidian, each formula more complex and beautiful than the last. Above, convergence approached—the moment when all anchors would reach resonance and reality would become malleable.

The child's dream approached waking state, and Asvarr climbed to meet it.

EPILOGUE

The sky tore itself apart.

Asvarr watched from the Storm Forge's obsidian plateau as Alfheim's firmament unraveled above the distant elven realm. Through eyes that no longer saw as mortal men did, he witnessed the final threads of the great deception dissolve. The weave—that ancient tapestry of lies spun by gods to hide what swam beyond collapsed inward upon itself, revealing glimpses of vast serpentine forms coiling through formless void.

Blood leaked from his ears. The sight should have been silent across such distance, but something in his transformed flesh conducted the sound—as vibration, a tremor that traveled through the crystalline formations spreading across his skin. The death of a cosmic falsehood.

The third anchor pulsed beneath his ribs, neither human heartbeat nor something wholly other, but a fusion of both. For a single, perfect moment, it fell silent.

And in that silence: completeness.

Through the wound in reality, the Root Anchor released one final surge—of pattern itself. Pure, unfiltered understanding without language to bind or limit it. Asvarr's consciousness split into fractured awareness as the pulse traveled outward from Alfheim, rippling across the Nine Realms.

"Can you feel it?" he whispered, the frost forming with each word reflecting starlight in crystalline geometries.

Rootstar's tendrils tightened around his forearm in wordless confirmation. The sentient branch—part star, part Root—had no mouth to speak, but its consciousness brushed against Asvarr's mind with the texture of bark and stellar fire.

Every dreamer feels it. Every rememberer.

Across Midgard, a skald faltered mid-verse, fingers freezing against harp strings as something passed through him. In that instant, he glimpsed the shape of all songs at once—every possibility of melody, harmony, rhythm coexisting in a single pattern. When awareness returned, tears streaked his face though he couldn't have explained why.

In Vanaheim, a volva hunched over her rune-carved bones stopped breathing as the pattern washed through her. The runes rearranged themselves without touch, forming configurations that existed in no language yet somehow made perfect sense for that brief, terrible moment.

Throughout ice-wastes of Niflheim, frost giants carving their histories into glacier walls paused as one, their chisels suspended mid-strike. Each giant saw their markings transform briefly into something truer than what they'd intended to record—history not as it happened but as it had needed to happen, causality laid bare.

Asvarr perceived it all. The three anchors within him vibrated in harmonic resonance, allowing him to witness what no single consciousness should contain. He saw scholars in forgotten libraries clutch their heads in wonder. Children woke from sleep with dreams of swimming through stars. Craftsmen dropped tools as their hands remembered skills they'd never learned.

The pattern that could not be spoken.

The shape of possibility itself.

High above, a single star flickered and went dark. Asvarr tracked its disappearance with senses beyond sight. The star hadn't died—it had transformed, shedding its nature as illumination to become something else entirely. A watcher. A sentinel point in the void where awareness condensed into purpose.

"The anchor didn't die," he said, voice rough from transformation and the crystalline structures forming in his throat. "It evolved."

Brynja nodded beside him, her wooden features gleaming with reflected fire from Muspelheim's ever-burning horizon. The constellation patterns embedded in her bark-skin rippled with internal light, responding to changes only she could sense.

"And now the fourth calls you." She didn't phrase it as a question. The truth-compelling runes across her face glowed golden, confirming her sincerity. "You'll need to leave soon. The storm grows restless."

Asvarr turned toward the Storm Forge that dominated Muspelheim's volcanic landscape. Lightning carved mathematical equations into the anvil-shaped mountain's face with terrifying precision. With each strike, he felt the fourth anchor's pull strengthening—a hook lodged beneath his sternum tugging his transformed flesh toward its inevitable joining.

"It won't claim me so much as complete me," he said, eyes fixed on the approaching storm-front. "The flame preserved through dominance. Memory connected through recognition. Starlight transformed through integration." He touched his throat where crystal patterns had already begun forming lattices beneath his skin. "But the storm..."

"The storm forges through creation and destruction together," Yrsa signed, her nimble fingers leaving faint blue traces in the air. Though permanently mute after her sacrifice, the boundary-walker had found new ways to communicate—gestures that existed halfway between language and magic.

Rootstar extended a tendril toward the lightning-wreathed peak. *The storm demands voice for pattern. Speaking what must be spoken.*

"My voice." Asvarr pressed a hand to his throat, feeling the crystalline formations spreading beneath the skin. "The fourth anchor will take my voice, as the third took my body."

The realization carried no fear, just the weight of inevitability. Each binding extracted its price. The first took rage. The second took identity. The third took physical form. The fourth would claim his voice, transforming words into pure concept.

And the fifth—in Helheim—would take his name.

The five aspects each Warden surrendered to walk the pattern: rage, identity, form, voice, name. Nine cycles of failure. But this tenth time...

"This time will be different," he said, certainty filling him as the pattern pulse faded across the realms, leaving only its echo in those sensitive enough to feel it.

Beneath them, the obsidian plateau cracked with a sound like breaking bone. The fracture spread in perfect geometric patterns, matching the crystalline formations across Asvarr's transformed skin. Where fresh magma welled up through the cracks, it cooled instantly into black glass etched with equations.

"The convergence accelerates," Brynja said, her wooden arm extending protective branches toward Asvarr. "Four anchors must be bound before—"

"Before the remaining fragments destabilize completely," Asvarr finished. He could see it now with his expanded awareness—the nine anchor points (five for Wardens, four embedded in Yggdrasil) straining toward resonance. Time compressed. What should have taken days now measured in hours.

Across the distant void where Alfheim's sky had been, something massive stirred. Not the sky-serpents with their cosmic scales, but the entity they had once been part of—the void-hunger, nine aspects sacrificed to create the anchors. It remained formless, without definition, but Asvarr sensed its awareness turning toward the wound in reality where the sky-weave had been.

"We should go," he said simply, extending a hand toward Brynja. The star-forged chain around his wrist—four links representing memory, purpose, connection, grief—burned cold against his crystalline flesh. "The fourth anchor won't wait much longer."

She took his hand, her wooden fingers interlacing with his transformed ones. Rootstar wrapped supportive tendrils around both their wrists, bridging their separate transformations with its own nature—neither wholly Root nor wholly Star but both together.

Yrsa stepped forward too, blue light trailing from her fingers as she signed their journey's next phase.

The storm awaits the Pattern-Keeper.

Asvarr turned one final time toward the wound in reality where Alfheim's sky had been. Through the gap, pinpricks of awareness watched from the void—cosmic serpents bearing witness to this tenth cycle, these final movements in the ancient dance of pattern.

Far above, the transformed star—the sentinel—fixed its attention on him specifically. Simply observant. It would record what happened next, preserving pattern regardless of outcome.

The fourth anchor pulled with renewed urgency, lightning equations carving his name into the Storm Forge's face. Through mathematical precision—the pattern that defined him, that would soon claim his voice.

"Time to forge what comes next," Asvarr said, and led his companions toward the waiting storm.

***

Darkness pervaded the cave, absolute and undisturbed. No light had ever penetrated this deep beneath Alfheim's surface, not even when the realm's sky still existed as a woven tapestry of stars and lies. The rock here was older than memory, pressed into existence during the first shaping of the Nine Realms, when the void-hunger's aspects were freshly divided.

A single drop of golden sap fell from the cavern ceiling.

It struck stone with a sound like a distant hammer on an anvil. The vibration rippled outward through the darkness, disturbing ancient dust that had lain undisturbed since before names existed. Where the sap landed, the stone began to shift, rippling like water despite its solidity.

From this disturbance emerged a serpent.

Small enough to coil around a finger, its body slipped out from between realities as if the gap had always existed, waiting for this precise moment. Unlike the vast cosmic serpents that swam through the void beyond the broken sky-weave, this being was physical, tangible—scales that could be touched, a body that displaced air and left tiny tracks in the dust.

The serpent flicked its tongue, tasting the cave's perfect stillness. Its scales shimmered with impossible light, reflecting both starlight and root-patterns though no stars shone this deep beneath the surface. Each scale contained both mathematical precision and organic potential, perfect geometry with fractal irregularity at the edges. It moved with deliberate grace, coiling into an ever-tightening spiral around a single object that rested at the chamber's center.

A seed of memory.

No larger than a child's smallest fingernail, the seed pulsed with interior light—gold, silver, and starfire combined into something entirely new. The serpent curled protectively around the seed, its body forming complex patterns that mirrored the geometry carved into the Storm Forge mountain half a world away.

Then, in a motion so swift it defied perception, the serpent consumed the seed.

Its eyes flashed—conscious, deliberate integration. Intelligence beyond its form flooded those eyes as the seed's knowledge merged with the serpent's awareness. Within that tiny body now resided memories spanning nine cycles of creation, destruction, and attempted rebirth. The whispered failures of nine previous Wardens who either surrendered entirely to the pattern or broke themselves trying to control it.

The serpent's body shuddered as the integration completed. Its scales rippled with new patterns—constellations never seen in Alfheim's manipulated sky, root configurations that stretched beyond Yggdrasil's known structure into something both more ancient and yet to come.

On the far side of the chamber, a crack formed in the stone wall. A door between places—between states of being. The serpent's head lifted, tracking the sound with a hunter's precision. Though young, it moved with ancient purpose, slithering across the dusty floor toward the opening.

From beyond the crack came the scent of pine sap and snow, the distant sound of waves breaking against a fjord shore. Midgard's scent. The realm of humanity where one particular bloodline still carried the potential for transformation nine cycles in the making.

With a final flick of its tongue, the serpent squeezed through the crack between realities. The stone sealed itself behind its passage, leaving no evidence of disturbance. The chamber returned to darkness and silence, as if nothing had occurred at all.

***

Helga Sveinsdottir breathed steam into her cupped hands as she tramped through knee-deep snow toward the small cottage nestled against the forest's edge. Winter had come early this year, sweeping down from the mountains with unusual ferocity. Three weeks before the turning of autumn, and already the fjord had begun to freeze along its edges.

"Strange signs," she muttered to herself, squinting up at the oddly-colored aurora that had lingered for days now, sweeping across the night sky in patterns she'd never witnessed in her seventy-three winters. The elders in the village whispered of omens, of the gods stirring in their long absence. Helga had no patience for such talk. The old ways had been fading for generations, and if the gods had ever existed, they'd abandoned mankind long ago.

The cottage door creaked open before she reached it, her granddaughter's worried face appearing in the gap.

"Grandmother! I thought you'd be back before dark." Kari held a guttering tallow candle that cast sharp shadows across her face. At fourteen, she already showed signs of the beauty she would grow into—high cheekbones like her mother's, and eyes the changeable color of the sea, one moment green, the next moment gray.

"The trading took longer than expected." Helga stomped snow from her boots before entering the cottage's blessed warmth. "Torsten tried to cheat me on the furs again. Had to remind him who taught him how to cure leather properly in the first place."

Kari smiled, but the expression faded quickly. She fussed with the cooking pot hanging over the hearth fire, stirring the stew with unnecessary vigor.

"Something troubles you." Helga unwound the heavy fur from around her shoulders, hanging it on the peg by the door.

Kari hesitated. "I dreamed again last night."

Helga stilled, one boot half-removed. The dreams had started three months ago—vivid visions unlike anything the girl had experienced before. Dreams of a great tree whose branches spanned stars. Dreams of figures with bark for skin and crystalline eyes. Dreams of anchors binding what should never have been divided.

"The same as before?" Helga kept her voice deliberately casual.

"No." Kari abandoned the stew pot and moved to the table where a small wooden box rested—a gift from her father before the sea claimed him. She opened it with careful fingers, revealing a smooth disc of amber. "It spoke to me this time. The tree. It said a vessel approaches, and I must be ready to receive it."

Helga crossed the small room in three strides, every instinct screaming danger. "You told no one else of this dream? No one in the village?"

Kari shook her head. "I remember what you said—that such dreams would bring the wrong kind of attention."

Helga nodded, relieved. She'd seen how the village treated those touched by the old powers—the whispers that followed Marta, the herb-woman; the way people made warding signs behind Halfdan's back when the fits took him. They called it madness, possession, the old gods reaching through. Perhaps they weren't entirely wrong.

"The disc was warm when I woke." Kari held up the amber disc. Where it had always been clear before, now something dark coiled at its center—a shadow no larger than a fingernail, but unmistakably serpentine in form. "I think... I think something's inside."

From the cottage's darkest corner came a soft sound—the whisper of scales against wood. Both women turned, Kari clutching the amber disc tighter. Nothing visible moved in the shadows, but Helga felt the change in the air—a presence where none had been before.

"Grandmother?" Kari's voice shook. The amber disc in her hand began to glow with faint golden light, illuminating her face from below.

Helga's gaze dropped to her granddaughter's forearm where her sleeve had pulled back. A mark had appeared on the inside of Kari's wrist—an intricately patterned circle that hadn't been there the day before. It pulsed once in perfect synchronicity with the light in the amber.

"It begins, then." Helga's voice sounded ancient to her own ears. "The tenth cycle."

The shadows in the corner coalesced, flowing across the floor like liquid darkness. The tiny serpent emerged, scales reflecting firelight in impossible patterns. Its eyes held knowledge no mortal creature should possess—the weight of nine cycles, nine failures, nine attempts to balance what had been sundered.

Kari didn't scream, didn't run. She knelt, extending her marked wrist toward the creature. The serpent raised its head, tasting the air with a flick of its tongue. Recognition flashed in those ancient eyes. It had found what it sought—the next Warden-candidate. One who still walked unaware of her destiny, but whose bloodline carried the potential for transformation nine cycles in the making.

The amber disc slipped from Kari's fingers, striking the wooden floor with a sound like breaking ice. The serpent moved with blurring speed, flowing up Kari's arm in a streak of light and shadow. Where it touched her skin, the mark expanded, complex patterns spreading upward like frost across a window.

"Grandmother?" Kari's voice trembled between fear and wonder. "What's happening to me?"

The serpent reached Kari's shoulder, then coiled at the base of her throat. Its scales shifted color, matching the exact shade of her skin until it resembled an intricate tattoo rather than a living creature. Only its eyes remained distinct—two points of golden light that pulsed with the rhythm of Kari's quickening heartbeat.

Helga knelt beside her granddaughter, taking the girl's hands in her weathered ones. "The old stories are true, child. The Tree, the Breaking, the Anchors—all of it. And now you've been chosen."

Outside, the aurora intensified, casting sheets of green and purple light through the cottage's small window. The colors twisted into configurations never before seen in all the generations Helga's family had inhabited this fjord.

"Chosen for what?" Kari whispered.

The serpent's eyes flashed, and for an instant, Helga saw something else in her granddaughter's face—an echo of another presence, ancient and purposeful. The girl's next words emerged with harmonics that weren't entirely her own, frost forming in the air as she spoke.

"To forge what comes next."

CLAIM YOUR REWARD

Unlock Exclusive Worlds – Free Prequel + Beta Reader Access!

The adventure doesn't end here. Sign up for Joshua J. White's newsletter to receive a free prequel novella and get early access to upcoming books as a potential beta reader. Dive in now:

www.JoshuaJWhiteBooks.com/TheSkyrendProphecy

ABOUT THE AUTHOR

Joshua J. White resides in Russellville, Arkansas with his wife and four children. He founded Berserker Books as a vessel for stories that transport readers beyond everyday experience, with *The Skyrend Prophecy* marking his debut series.

His writing emerges from a deep appreciation for world-building and mythology, particularly the rich traditions found in Norse culture. Joshua crafts fictional realms where imagination flourishes, unbound by conventional limitations.

The natural landscapes of Arkansas provide both sanctuary and inspiration, where Joshua often explores with his family. These wilderness excursions nurture his creative vision while reinforcing his dream of establishing a homestead where his family can live in closer harmony with the land.

Joshua started Berserker Books with two dreams in mind: to build fantastical worlds on paper and, eventually, to build a homestead where his family can live more harmoniously with the land. Both dreams spring from the same source—a belief that we are meant for more than the constraints of modern existence.

The Skyrend Prophecy represents the first chapter in what Joshua envisions as a meaningful literary journey shared with readers who sense that our human story contains volumes yet to be written—stories penned in bold imagination of undiscovered possibilities.

For readers who have walked through Joshua's pages and felt something stir, he invites them to join him in continuing the story. Readers can receive exclusive prequels, early looks at new books, and opportunities to step deeper into these worlds by signing up here:

www.JoshuaJWhiteBooks.com/TheSkyrendProphecy

BOOKS BY JOSHUA J. WHITE

The Skyrend Prophecy Series

1. Branches of the Broken World (Book 1)

2. The Verdant Gate (Book 2)

3. Children of the Serpent Sky(Book 3)

4. Forge of Storms (Book 4)

5. Harmony's Twilight (Book 5)

Other Series by Joshua J. White:

- Stay tuned for upcoming epic fantasy series set in worlds beyond the Skyrend.

Made in the USA
Coppell, TX
13 July 2025

51619714R00292